The

CARTOGRAPHER

of

NO MAN'S LAND

The
CARTOGRAPHER
of
No Man's Land

A NOVEL

P. S. Duffy

PENGUIN
an imprint of Penguin Canada Books Inc.

Published by the Penguin Group
Penguin Canada Books Inc., 90 Eglinton Avenue East, Suite 700, Toronto, Ontario, Canada M4P 2Y3

Penguin Group (USA) Inc., 375 Hudson Street, New York, New York 10014, U.S.A.
Penguin Books Ltd, 80 Strand, London WC2R 0RL, England
Penguin Ireland, 25 St Stephen's Green, Dublin 2, Ireland (a division of Penguin Books Ltd)
Penguin Group (Australia), 707 Collins Street, Melbourne, Victoria 3008, Australia
(a division of Pearson Australia Group Pty Ltd)
Penguin Books India Pvt Ltd, 11 Community Centre, Panchsheel Park, New Delhi – 110 017, India
Penguin Group (NZ), 67 Apollo Drive, Rosedale, Auckland 0632, New Zealand
(a division of Pearson New Zealand Ltd)
Penguin Books (South Africa) (Pty) Ltd, 24 Sturdee Avenue, Rosebank, Johannesburg 2196, South Africa

Penguin Books Ltd, Registered Offices: 80 Strand, London WC2R 0RL, England

Published in Penguin paperback by Penguin Canada Books Inc., 2013
Simultaneously published in the United States by Liveright Publishing Corporation, a division of W.W. Norton.

1 2 3 4 5 6 7 8 9 10 (WEB)

Manufactured in Canada.

LIBRARY AND ARCHIVES CANADA CATALOGUING IN PUBLICATION

Duffy, P.S., author
The cartographer of no man's land / P.S. Duffy.

ISBN 978-0-14-318686-1 (pbk.)

I. Title.

PS3604.U45C37 2013   813'.6   C2013-904277-6

Visit the Penguin Canada website at **www.penguin.ca**

Special and corporate bulk purchase rates available; please see
www.penguin.ca/corporatesales or call 1-800-810-3104, ext. 2477.

For Joe

The

CARTOGRAPHER

of

NO MAN'S LAND

PROLOGUE

The boy had been laughing under the clouds on a flat gray sea as his father sang an old and funny song about all the fishes climbing upon the seaweed trees. But then the sun broke through in a banded stream that coursed across the water to their boat. His father stopped singing and stopped rowing and looked about. And the boy stopped swinging his legs beneath his seat and looked about as well. His hair ruffled in the breeze. All around them the sun revealed water dancing in a way not firmly lashed to the here and now. It mesmerized the senses, suffusing everything in its catchy-caught ripples upon the open water, so that there was nothing but the dance.

His father drew in the heavy oars, and the sound of their smooth, worn wood slipped into the boat. The light was golden against the floorboards. The spangled sea was so bright they could not tear their eyes from it—rippling, flickering, drawing them in. His father drew the boy toward him without taking his eyes off the silver sea. The boy turned between his father's long legs and rested a small hand on his father's knee. His father circled him with his arm and felt the boy's heart beat into his hand.

In all this world there was only the gently rocking boat and dancing water. All time—past, present and future—gathered and expanded and released. There were no boundaries, and there was no fear of being without them.

The boy wanted to reach out to catch the water's dance, but more than that he wanted to remain forever leaning lightly against the rough wool of his father's shirt, with his father's hand resting against his chest.

They stayed like that, the boy and his father, until a wide breeze blew over the boat, and his father said quietly, "We have witnessed God's beauty, had an encounter with the Divine." Or maybe that's only what he thought. What he may have said was nothing at all as the breeze freshened and a deep blue returned to the water, and the waves grew rougher and stopped shimmering. He took up the oars and shoved them through the wooden pins. The boy turned and hopped back up on his seat. His father pulled in long smooth strokes and sang once again of all the fishes in the sea climbing upon the seaweed trees.

ONE

February 1st, 1917
Western Front, France

ngus MacGrath unbuttoned his greatcoat and leaned back against the one tree left on the bank of a river he did not know. Not far downstream, a private, standing waist-deep in the river, squeezed a bar of soap between his hands. It shot upward, and four or five other soldiers lunged for it, splashing and falling over themselves. Their uniforms, boots, and rifles lay in a heap by a jagged row of blackened tree stumps. Under a weak early morning sun, bands of mist rose from the cold river, occasionally engulfing the soldiers so that they took on a dream-like quality of white arms and torsos appearing and disappearing.

Above the river on a low stone bridge sat the engine of the troop train where, a day into their journey, it had lurched to a stop, unable or unwilling to carry on. Sunk between endless flat fields, the tracks ran east-northeast toward the Front. Angus flipped open his old pocket compass for confirmation, for comfort, really, and slipped it back in his pocket. He figured they'd be on the march soon, the engine still on the bridge.

While repairs were attempted, the ranks milled about the train, grousing over the delay, but grateful for it all the same. And for the sudden break in the weather. Housed in drafty huts in a camp thick with mud near Le Havre, most of them hadn't bathed since they'd crossed the Channel and arrived on French soil five days earlier. Those in the river were taking up a challenge. "Baptism and bless me!" one shouted, wading in. "Sweet Jesus, it's freezing!" cried another, plunging in after him. In the train, the owl-faced ranking officer drank steadily from his flask.

Like Angus, the boys in the river and those cheering them on from the bridge were fresh recruits from battalions broken up after training in England to be bled into existing battalions. Most would join the 61st. But Angus had been singled out and reassigned to replace a dead lieutenant in the 17th Royal Nova Scotia Highlanders—a decision no more random than any he'd encountered since joining up. If there was one thing Angus, now Lieutenant MacGrath, had learned, it was that there was no predicting how things would turn out. Of all the predictions he might have made, himself as an officer in the infantry was not among them.

In the state of suspension between the world as he'd known it and the absolute unknown, Angus considered the interplay of light and mist, the hazy edges, blank spaces and mute eddies at the river's edge. Above him, the sky turned a gauzy gray, and a fine rain fell. He tipped his head back and closed his eyes.

Rain. It had been a constant in the collected bits and pieces of the past few months. It had slicked the deck of the ship that carried him to England and slanted in rushes off the tents in the camp where he'd held a rifle for the first time, adjusted to the heft and length and balance of it, and where, surprisingly, he'd found he was a good shot. And where, not surprisingly, he'd found a heady release in charging straw-filled burlap bags, bayonet plunging into their sodden bellies.

Rain and rage. Rain and regret. He'd been sent over with assurances in a letter from Major Gault to a Colonel Chisholm that he'd be a cartographer. In London. Behind the lines. But Gault was unknown to Chisholm, and there being no shortage of cartographers, Angus had been dispatched to the infantry, where shortages were never-ending. "The infantry?" A chasm of disbelief had opened up.

"You heard me," Chisholm's adjutant had snapped. "You can bloody well draw terrain maps on the field. Meantime, the infantry can use your other skills—the ones you'll get soon enough."

And get them he did, with the rest of the 183rd, in an onslaught of rain that left bedding heavy and damp, uniforms drenched, and the camp awash in mud. Good preparation for the Front, he was told.

Rain had dripped steadily into a bucket by the major's desk the day Angus was told he'd been promoted to lieutenant. "Your education is one thing," the major had sighed. "Not orthodox exactly, with time in divinity school, but nothing in this war is orthodox. This is a citizen army, and we—"

Can't be too choosey?

"What I mean to say is that combined with your age and maturity—and the fact that you've been a captain of, what was it, a cargo vessel? In the Maritimes?" He tapped his pen on the desk.

"Coastal trader. Nova Scotia, yes sir," Angus answered. Small schooner, crew of three, nothing grand, he might have added.

"Understand you were headed for cartography." The major coughed, put the pen down, picked it up again. "Look, you seem to have your head on straight. You're steady, well educated, and Sergeant Campbell thinks, as do I, that you'll be well placed as a first lieutenant."

Campbell? Campbell the bulldog had recommended *him*? That very morning he'd slapped up glossy photos on an easel, depicting in revolting detail just what a bayonet could and should do. Disemboweling men was quite another thing from ripping through straw targets. When he'd closed by saying the pictures were of *Allied* soldiers, he had men frothing for revenge. Head down, Angus had not joined in. Aww . . . squeamish? Campbell had mocked. Angus had known better than to reply. Squeamish was the least of it.

"Well?" the major asked impatiently. "First lieutenant. What have you to say to that?"

Angus had had little to say. Lieutenants were as expendable as the rank and file—more so. They dropped like flies, leading the charge. His education was hardly the preparation called for, but at thirty-four, age he did have. "Maturity" was a kind way of putting it. What did he think? He was astounded and afraid. How exactly did one grow into the hope of taking another man's life?

All that was left to say was, "I'll do my best to honor the regiment. Thank you, sir."

"Yes, yes, of course," the major said, turning back to his paperwork. But then looked Angus in the eye and said, "I'm sure you will, MacGrath."

Standing outside on the rickety steps, Angus wasn't so sure. He turned up the collar of his coat against the heavy mist. "Lieutenant MacGrath," he repeated softly. That night, the rain's steady drumming took on the beat of a cold rain on the *Lauralee*'s canvas. It called up the rush of her bow wave curling and falling back, the lull of it transformed to repetitive regret.

Three weeks after his promotion, on leave in London, the rain stopped and the skies suddenly cleared. All around him black umbrellas came down, were shaken and folded. People were smiling, and the puddles, shimmering on gray flagstone, took on the pale blue of the sky and caught the reds and blues and whites of the Union Jack in a child's hand. Without effort, Angus reproduced the image in a quick sketch in a pub, right down to the fragmented reflection. He wanted to memorialize blue sky in case he never saw it again, he'd said to the amusement of his fellow officers. The drawing was in charcoal.

Now, as the men hopped about in the cold and toweled off with an army blanket, Angus let that memory of color and reflected sky engulf him. Allowed himself the luxury of going further back—to the tall white house on the hill above the bay, and the low-roofed sheds behind it, to the sharp smell of turpentine, the twist of sable brushes in the dented tin can, the paint-splattered floorboards. And on down the hill to the stony beach where seaweed draped over itself in the low tide and where Hettie Ellen, hair coming loose in the wind, leaned against a boulder, watching Simon Peter skipping rocks with ease, one after another, three, four, five skips. And beyond them to the *Lauralee*, nodding at her mooring, bright work gleaming in the last, long rays of sunlight.

Idealized images, every one. Angus knew it. He dealt in such images, after all. Could paint them, could sell them. And had. Idealized or not, they flooded through him in all their tender beauty—fragile strands of memory which even the faint crump of distant artillery could not touch—until it did, and the memories spun out and away, replaced by the unadorned image of his father, slumped at his desk, unable to comprehend how Angus could have turned against him.

ANGUS WAS RIGHT about the train. And the march. He fell in with the rest of them and they marched fifteen miles to a railhead, arriving worn and hungry. Another troop train headed to the Front was expected, they were told, in less than an hour. Chunks of bread and fruitcake were passed out. A young soldier named Mueller fell over—with exhaustion, it was thought, or too much fruitcake. But he was burning up with fever.

The promised train arrived. A space was cleared in the aisle so Mueller could lie flat. Angus helped him drink from his canteen and called for a blanket to put under his head, then found a seat next to a young lance corporal who said not a word. The train clacked on. Angus reached for a cigarette and pulled out the picture of Ebbin. He'd shown it to just about everyone he'd met, an automatic gesture that along with the words "Ever seen this man?" led to nothing, until he'd begun to feel as tattered at the edges as the photograph. In London, he'd finally bought a leather sleeve to keep it in. "Your brother?" people would ask, studying it. "Brother-in-law," Angus would patiently explain. Angus, a head taller, with dark hair and darker eyes, bore no resemblance to the carefree, light-featured Ebbin, but "brother" might indeed have been as accurate. In the picture Angus stood, rope in hand, to the side of Ebbin on the deck of the *Lauralee*. A photographer named Klein from the States, dressed in a suit, tie askew, juggling cameras and tripod, had taken the picture and many more of Snag Harbor and the islands, hoping to turn them into picture postcards. Angus, just back from Yarmouth, was tying the boat up at Mader's when Ebbin strolled down the wharf. The photographer instantly wanted Ebbin in the picture. Only too willing, Ebbin had hopped aboard and slung Angus's duffel bag over his shoulder in the pose of a seaman home at last, though he was a bad sailor and prone to seasickness. Hence his grin and the wry smile on Angus's face. The photographer wanted more pictures and suggested a sail, with Ebbin at the helm. You come along, too, he'd said to Angus as an afterthought. Ebbin had laughed out loud. Suppose we buy you a drink instead, he suggested. It's the safer course, trust me. The photographer had readily agreed. There was a better photo, a portrait of Ebbin in uniform taken a year later, but it was this picture that Angus had chosen to bring with him.

He slipped it back in his pocket and conjured up Ebbin waving his arm in a wide arc on the gangway of the troop ship with an enthusiasm that had vanished from his letters the minute he'd hit the Front. Ebbin Hant, on the brink of promise.

"Off to save the world from the Hun," he'd said, chin up, at the crowded Hant family dinner in Chester one Sunday in 1915. "Signed up yesterday." He'd tousled the hair of the nearest young half-brother, but grew serious when he caught his father's eye. At the head of the table, Amos Hant adjusted his great bulk. Chatter died out. "Well, boy, you go ahead," Amos said slowly. Angus shot a look down the table at his own father, Duncan MacGrath, his boyish face grim.

Amos pounded the table with his ham-like fist. Plates jumped. Cider splashed. "Go ahead, by God! Blast them to Kingdom come!" He stood. "To Ebbin! Make us proud!" He raised his glass and looked round the table. "To Empire, God and King!" he bellowed.

Duncan spun a salt shaker in half-circles on the table. Hettie Ellen sat back as if she'd been shot. Everyone else, children included, raised their glasses. Stood up. "King and Country!" they said. "To Ebbin!" Ebbin cocked his head, then rose himself. "To Canada!" he said, and emptied his glass.

Angus reached for Hettie's hand, limp at her side, but she didn't return his squeeze and pulled away as war talk took over, as pot roast and vegetables were served up and plates passed hand to hand down the long table.

Elma Hant, at the opposite end of the table from Amos, excused herself to the kitchen. Angus found her leaning on the table, her raw-knuckled hands spread before her, head bowed. "Not to mind me," she said, pushing away and straightening as he entered. "I'll get over it." She was a big woman, broad and tall. She looked out the window, slowly folding a towel. "I may not be Ebbin's real mother, God rest her soul, but . . ."

"Ebbin can take care of himself," Angus said.

She heaved her shoulders. "I suppose . . . Done it well enough up in the Yukon, out West." She shook her head and met his eyes. "How's Hettie going to manage, is what I want to know—her brother off to war? Did he think of that? And Amos. What's to become of him if something happens? If you'd ever seen the care he took with them two as babies when he'd come to pick them up at night, scrubbing the dirt off his hands afore he touched them. Tying up their bonnet strings . . ."

Amos Hant's thick fingers fumbling with bonnet strings made Angus say, "The war will be over soon."

"They say by next Christmas, don't they?" She shot him a hopeful look. "Or was that what they said last year?"

"They did, but it'll be over soon."

"That's right. Long before the younger boys are of age." She recovered herself and said, "Now. What do you need?"

"Only a fork."

She wiped her nose and opened the cupboard drawer. "Well, that's one need I can fix up straight away. You never ask for much, Angus." She placed a fork in his palm and folded his fingers over it.

Late that night, back home in Snag Harbor, Angus watched Ebbin jump out of Zeb Morash's truck at the bottom of the hill road and saunter up to the house—a dark silhouette against the moonlit water until the black spruce closed in behind him. He tried to imagine Ebbin in uniform, but couldn't for the life of him see him succumbing to regimentation, yes sir, no sir, at the bottom of the heap.

An hour before, in the upstairs hallway, with Young Fred's head drooping on her shoulder, Hettie Ellen had begged Angus to change Ebbin's mind. He's already signed up, Angus told her. There's no changing that. She wanted him to try anyway. Thirteen years into their marriage, she remained as much Ebbin's sister as Angus's wife, a fact Angus accepted as part of the bargain, a price to be paid.

When Ebbin hopped up on the porch, Angus lifted the jug of rum at his feet, withdrew the cork with a satisfying *thup*, and handed it to him. Their glasses stood empty on the porch railing. "Off to save us from the Hun, eh?" Angus said.

Ebbin took a long swallow, wiped his mouth and grinned. "Someone's got to do it," he said. "I take it Hettie's in bed."

"You expect *her* to do it?"

Ebbin gave a quick laugh. He leaned back on the railing and said,

"She wouldn't talk to me after dinner. I'll catch her in the morning. She'll come around."

"Doubt it. Not this time. What the hell, anyway? Were you drunk?"

"Yeah, maybe. Me and the boys had a few." He lit a cigarette.

"Who was with you?"

"Virgil, George Mather. We'd have signed on anyway. No families of our own. Tough to justify *not* going. The Germans can't just stomp all over Europe and claim it for themselves, for Christ sake. England's at risk."

They talked about the course of the war and the boys they knew who were over there. Then Ebbin tipped his head back and waved the cigarette across the night sky. "This is the shape of things to come, the grand sweep. I want to be part of it." He paused and looked back at Angus. "Don't tell me your old man's got you against the war. He's gone pacifist, hasn't he?"

"*Gone* pacifist? Always has been. You know that."

"I always thought that for him 'pacifist' was just another word for 'anti-Empire.'"

"No. Maybe. Dangerous in this climate, either way." Angus lit his own cigarette. "As for me, I'm not against the war, just you in it."

"Yeah. I'd feel the same. I'll tell you something, though—when I signed up, I felt different. I felt . . ." He shook his head.

Proud, Angus thought. He felt proud. Ebbin had studied law, worked for his father at the forge, and rejected both. He'd considered stage acting, but saw no future in it. He'd disappear for months at a time—working horses out West, tramping around in the wilds of northern Quebec, the Yukon. Once spending a winter in Wyoming at the base of the Beartooth Mountains with a survey team. Trailing hints of a roughshod world, he'd return with money in his pocket and stories to tell, ones that made you laugh, and ones that made you wonder—fending off a maniacal Mountie who rode into their camp bareback and backwards; sipping water from a stream so pure it tasted of earth and sky and sugar. He had Hettie's fine features and restless nature, but unlike her had an endless store of self-confidence and an unforced, infectious optimism. Ebbin just needed to find the right opening and he'd do fine, everyone said. But Angus had seen the trace of lines around his eyes, the shadowed doubt. Now this sudden singularity of purpose. How often did that come around? Only in war perhaps. Or in love.

"Come with me, why don't you? We'll fight them like we did the pirates on Mountain Island," Ebbin said. "Seriously, how long are you going to drag up and down the coast on the *Lauralee* for the old man? When are you going to escape?"

"The *Lauralee is* my escape."

"Not for long, eh? A fella risks his life just stepping aboard."

"She's not that old." She was, of course.

"Yeah, she is. Rotting away, and you along with her. Railroads, motorized transport—that's the ticket to trade these days." Ebbin jabbed his cigarette at Angus. "Or so Hettie whispered to me like a sweet song yesterday." He raised his brows in theatric exaggeration.

"Railroads? She *said* that?"

"Something like that," Ebbin shrugged. "Thinking of the future, unlike you. Point is, coastal trade was supposed to be temporary. Remember? Yet there you are, still going, resenting every minute of it."

"Except when I'm out there," Angus countered.

"True enough," Ebbin agreed.

It was true. As much as Angus resented working for his father, sailing the *Lauralee* fed something deep, made him feel part of "the grand sweep"—not of history, but of the sun's first rays breaking over the curve of the earth, the currents below, the wind above, propelling him forward, and letting him know just how small a part of the grand sweep he was, but still—a *part* of it. Suspended, sustained in the territory beyond the points of the compass. And it was that he wanted to capture on canvas—more than capture, he wanted to let it flow through him and out and back again. God had given him talent, or maybe just the longing, but either way, not enough courage to trust it. He took another drag on his cigarette.

As if party to these thoughts, Ebbin said, "Maybe you should chuck it all, rent a garret and—"

Angus held up his hand. "Let old dreams die a good death, would you? For once?"

"Dreams never die a good death. Seabirds, seascapes. They're so easy for you."

"Too easy. Failures of imagination." He'd never studied art, had never been to a museum or gallery. What he did came naturally, easily, but he wanted more than sentiment. Wanted to get down what he felt, not just copy what he saw. Wanted to capture things beyond his knowing—a unification, closely rendered, expanding out. Yet only rarely did he risk it, and all too often it left him feeling a fool.

"Weir loves your pictures," Ebbin reminded him.

"Weir loves them because they sell. 'Illustrations,' he calls them, and rightly so. Sailors buy them for their mothers."

"And that's not enough for you—pictures that sell?"

"Sell for a song. And no."

"What about those ones you're afraid to show around? Why not take them to Weir?"

Angus flicked his cigarette into the yard.

Ebbin shook his head and sighed. "Always shortening sail when you could go with the full set. You make life hard. You know that, don't you?"

"Fair enough. And you make it all seem so easy."

"By choice! There's always a choice. Until you decide there isn't."

Angus folded his arms and cocked his head. "That's about the dumbest thing I've ever heard you say."

"Or the most profound," Ebbin countered with a grin.

Angus returned his smile. "Hand over that jug. I'm not near drunk enough for your platitudes."

They were next to each other now, facing the yard. After a moment Ebbin said, "I don't know what you're after exactly, but I know it's more. I wouldn't be talking this way, but with me heading off . . ."

A bat fluttered past. Angus said, "I wish you weren't. But I know what you're after, too."

"Yeah? Do you?"

"Sure I do."

Ebbin threw his arm up around Angus's shoulder. "Remember that day we met a hundred years ago? When you were afraid to go sledding?"

"I wasn't *afraid*. Jesus."

"Yeah, you were. Afraid of what your old man would say, anyway. Still are, as far as I can see."

Angus lifted the jug and took a long swallow. Golden was the memory of that overcast day on the snow-packed hillside so long ago. Angus's mother dead a year; his father holed up on dry land, the two of them at opposite ends of the long mahogany table, night after night in silence. And then the burst of the Hant family onto the scene. Hettie Ellen, a toothpick in thick woolens and scarves, on a sled behind Tom Pugsley that day. Her shrieks echoing down the steep run ricocheted against Angus's hesitation and longing. And Ebbin, whom he'd just met, waving his hand over his sled with a bow, saying, "She's yours. Just steer around them two boulders. Be the ride of your life." The dazzling smile, the gallant gesture—a perfect counterpoint to his father's newfound adherence to an angry, puritanical Old Testament God, sucking the life out of pleasure and the pleasure out of life, which in Ebbin's presence seemed so attainable, so utterly possible. Angus had put a cautious knee on the sled, had shot down the hill, and had the ride of his life.

Ebbin swung over the porch railing and dropped like a cat onto the yard. "Take the pictures to Weir and see what happens. For me. It's a long way to Tipperary, you know." He whipped out his harmonica and played the first notes.

"Longer still to France . . ." Angus said. "Oh, alright. I'll do it. Give Weir a good laugh."

"There's the spirit." The silver harmonica flashed, and the sweet notes of "Annie Laurie" drifted down the hill to where the maples, hiding among the spruce and silvered by the moon, stirred, their new leaves clinging. Ebbin gripped the porch railing and swung back up. "Home before you know it."

Angus, a little unsteady on his feet, handed him a glass. "Home before you know it," he agreed, and they clinked their empty glasses.

TEN MONTHS LATER, in March of 1916, shortly before the Battle of Saint Eloi Craters, where the Canadians had over 1,300 casualties, Ebbin's regular letters stopped. He was seen afterwards, that much the home folks heard from George Mather, back from the Front in a wheelchair—no one returned without wounds; signing up meant "duration." George claimed to have seen Ebbin in September after Courcelette, near Thiepval. Embedded as this information was in repeated number sets and words like "silver," "angel" and "whirlwind," it was hard to know what he saw. And after those first few days of incoherent ranting, George had gone nearly mute.

In the months between Ebbin's departure and his disappearance, Hettie Ellen drifted like a leaf in a current, as she had several times over the years. When he went missing, she seemed to spiral away from herself.

For Angus, Ebbin became a phantom limb, painfully there and not there. His unknown fate offered hope at first. But hope grew dimmer by the day. Letters to Ebbin's commanding officer went unanswered. Letters to higher-ups had been met with uncertainty. Ebbin was not yet officially declared missing in action. There was nothing to fill the space where Ebbin had been—no sign, no word, no body and no grave.

Was he in hospital without identification? Blown to bits? Maybe he'd wandered off with a concussion, unable to tell some poor peasant his name. Maybe in a prison camp, forbidden from writing. Maybe . . . Maybe . . . Angus lay awake at night next to Hettie, the two of them silently conjuring scenarios, his hand a cradle for hers under the quilts.

With Ebbin missing, thousands of casualties mounting and the war escalating, the tenuousness of Angus's own purpose grew pronounced. He had feverish dreams about his painting that startled him awake and filled him with regret. It was there in the milky white stone clattering in on the surf, in the streaked semicircles etched in a black mussel shell. There, too, in the sweep of clouds racing away from a chalice of blue sky. It was in fog seen through a lace curtain, in bloomers pinned to the line, sailing on the wind. It was in paint chipping off a lone bell buoy and in the dull clang of the bell itself on the slowly rising, slowly falling sea.

A fine hobby for your mother, his father said of his painting, *but a man works by brawn or brains, and you have plenty of both. Use them, would you? You've a life to live. Make it count.*

And so it was, with a family to support, Angus agreed to ply goods up and down the coast for his father—the once and great schooner fishing hero, a wealthy man by Snag Harbor standards, owner of fishing vessels and the timber to build them. A man who had given up a life at sea to raise his son and never let him forget it. A man for whom words about the sanctity of life and honor and obligation and money in the bank were sufficient expressions of love. And a man who had supported him, no questions asked, when Angus had needed him most, seeing to it a house was built for Hettie and the baby when, at nineteen, Angus stood before him in paint-splattered boots, pockets empty.

In charge of the *Lauralee*, Angus could grasp some essential part of himself. Now she was heavy in the water and her rigging groaned with fatigue. Refitting her was an exercise in futility. The days of hauling cabbages, potatoes, timber, salt and barrel staves in a sailing vessel were drawing to an end. Still, every now and then, as he brought her up to the edge of the wind, she'd take hold, and he'd feel the synchronized perfection of water pouring off her foredeck, running along the lee rail and back again to the sea. "Drive her, boy! She's singing now," Wallace would shout.

On a brilliant July morning, with Ebbin still missing and the Battle of the Somme raging, Angus and his father spread out the *Lauralee*'s mainsail in the yard behind the house. On his knees checking for weak seams, of which there were plenty, Angus said, "Stevens says it's new or nothing. He'll cut us a new set of sails on Hutt's Pond as soon as it freezes over." Duncan grunted to a stand. "Well," he said, "Randolph Stevens might be the best sailmaker around, but she's well beyond them. And she won't do with an auxiliary motor. The vibration would knock her timbers loose."

And knock the soul out of her, Angus thought. He placed the flat of his palm on the soft cotton canvas, bleached white by the sun, and remembered the deep cream color the sails had been to start, and how he and Wallace had taken pains to let the light winds of sunrise and sunset work the perfect curve into the main. He thought of how in a wild sea, the jib in tatters and the main halyard jammed, they couldn't get the mainsail down, and how a crack raced halfway up the mast before the wind blew out two seams. Thought about Stevens's perfect repair, and ran his hand along the length of it.

It was at this moment that his father chose to tell him that he'd been thinking of talking to Balfour.

"Balfour?" Angus looked up sharply. "Why? You're not trading on Hettie's friendship with Kitty, are you?"

Unfazed, his father replied: "Of course not. I'm trading on that summer she helped him out when his clerk dropped dead. Balfour's coming down from Halifax to check out property in Chester, and I aim to go over there and show him around. Talk a little business. I want you with me."

Angus sat back on his heels. It was the last thing he wanted to do. And the mere mention of Kitty and her father, the silver-haired Balfour, a Halifax financier, brought Angus back to the summer Hettie had spent in their big stone house on the Northwest Arm. Back to the lawns and gardens and Kitty's invitation to go out for a sail with her cousin Blanchard—"BB," he was called—on the sleek little thirty-two-foot Herreshoff sloop that Balfour had bought him. Reclining in the cockpit in pleated white trousers, passing a silver flask around, BB and his friends had let Angus rig the boat and sail it for them like a hired hand. All these years later, Angus still remembered how responsive the sloop was, how she'd cut through the chop like a knife, how she'd tempered his humiliation, and how it had returned full throttle when, rowing back to the Yacht Squadron after the sail, BB and his friends tossed Hettie's name around as if she belonged to them.

"Connections. That's how things are done," his father was saying. "Even Hettie understands that."

"Maybe you should take her on as a partner."

"You can joke all you want, but I'm serious here now. Balfour's heard about the pretty penny I'm turning up at Dawson's. He might want me to invest in a brickworks he's looking at in Bridgewater. Wants to merge it with one in the Valley. There's money to be made by the high rollers that make that happen. Mergers and whatnot. And Hugh Balfour is honest enough to avoid war-profiteering. A good man. The problem is, I don't pretend to understand this high-finance business, and I'm too old to learn. What I understand are things I can grab hold of—timber turned to boats, land you can plant your feet on. But I wouldn't mind some of the action. High time you came in off the water and helped me out. Expand your horizons."

"You're going to scrap the *Lauralee*."

"I didn't say that!"

Angus had hit a nerve, as he knew he would. It was a line of defense that had worked before to protect him from a life onshore under his father's thumb, working as a glorified clerk, a manager, checking up on properties and holdings and other men's work. And now even worse—high finance, high rollers, the money game—all that animated men like Balfour. His father, unlike them, lived almost as simply as he always had. The fortune he was building and the one he dreamed of was just another way of coming in off the Banks with a hold full of fish. A race to the finish. Angus may not have known a paper stock from a rolling stock, but he knew just how high the stakes were and what denying that legacy would do to the man he hated and admired and loved. And what capitulating might do to himself.

His father unrolled his tobacco pouch and slowly filled his pipe and lit it. Squinting off toward the bay, he said, "We'll haul her up, see the kind of repairs she needs, but we best face it. She's not worth a new set of sails. Coastal trade in a sailing vessel is over. No money in it. And I didn't raise you to be a common sailor."

Angus got to his feet. The world was closing in. "Maybe that's just what I am and what I want to be," he said. "Just because you gave up a life on the water doesn't mean—" He stopped. Too late. His father seized upon the opening with "And who'd I do that for? *You*. A motherless boy."

It had taken years for Angus to recognize the fiction of that response. After his mother's death, his father had in fact headed straight to the Banks, driven by his own demons, whatever they may have been, and driven back to shore by them as well, where like a drowning man he clung to his Bible and went from singing sea shanties to ruminations on fate and the hand of God. As time went on, every deal he made seemed to come out in his favor, which he began to see as part of God's plan as well, reward for a moral, upright life, the outcome of which, his legacy, might not outsmart death, but would give it a good run for the money.

His father jerked the sail and started pleating it into folds. "It took years for me to move up from catchie to captain. Years. I wasn't just handed a boat like you. You want to toss your life away, roving around at sea? My God. Look at Ebbin. Never settled down. Never got serious. And where'd he end up? At the bottom of a trench. No more senseless way to die."

"We don't know he's dead yet," Angus snapped. It was all he could do not to rip the sail from his father's hands and shove him against the wall of the barn.

"Only an idiot would believe otherwise. Accept it. And get your wife to do the same. Look at her. Barely eats, barely talks, wanders around like a boat adrift. Good thing I can spare Ida so she can see to you folks down here."

With utmost control, Angus replied, "We can do well enough on our own," though Ida's sturdy presence in their midst was a relief. He turned and started down the hill. "It's the uncertainty that's killing her," he said.

"Then give her some certainty," his father shouted after him. "Convince her. And get on with life."

A WEEK LATER, Angus took three of his oils to Weir's shop in Halifax—the one of the phalarope on the storm-tossed Lynch bell buoy, which loomed out from the lower left corner of the canvas, and the two others, nearly devoid of color—a line of huddled gulls facing the wind on the bleached bones of a gray whale, and a white-gray canvas, masts and hull emerging from fog in the faintest of lines. All three were rendered in oils of thick application, none of them quite capturing the suspended mystery, the tender, flawed visions he was after. Weir set them up and stood before them, brows furrowed. Gone was his heavy-lidded disdain, his feigned disinterest. He took the odd step forward and back. He smoothed his well-oiled hair. But in the end, he pronounced two of them colorless and strange, experimental without conviction, and all three, particularly the bird on the buoy, as impossible to sell. "Stick to real birds," he said. Angus picked up the paintings and left.

On the sail home, with Chebucto Head off the starboard quarter and Wallace pumping away at the bilge water, Angus tossed the pictures one by one over the side. The last of the three, the phalarope, one foot up, one on the bell buoy—almost in flight, still clinging to uncertain refuge—hovered in the following wind. Angus lunged for it just as it dropped into the wake and stared back at it long after it had disappeared from view, then swung the wheel, checked the compass, and set the boat on course.

He considered telling Hettie when he got home. In her starched white blouse and blue skirt she was suddenly talkative, fully there. But it wasn't the sort of thing he had the words for, and she was on about Balfour. How Duncan had brought him round for a visit while Angus was away. How he'd been pleased to sit around the kitchen table as if he were used to it, how he'd invited her to sit right down and filled her in on Kitty's life in New York, and included her when talk came round to brickyards and paper mills, "papering our way out of the 1913 depression," she added with a shy smile, quoting Balfour. Stocks and securities, a play on words, she had to explain to Angus. Through it all and on that note, Angus thought of the phalarope, floating on the waves, slipping under.

In August with yet another unsatisfactory response from the army in his pocket, Angus went over to Chester and entered the gloom of the forge where the furnace raged against the silhouette of Ebbin's father, Amos Hant, gripping the clamps and pounding away at the hot lead on the block. Amos stopped pounding when Angus spoke and went back to it when he finished, without looking up. Angus put his hand on Amos's massive shoulder and glanced away from the tears cutting tracks down his broad, soot-stained face.

Back in Snag Harbor he headed straight for the tavern, where talk was of a U-boat sighted by a Newfoundland schooner off Sambro Light, and where from an enlistment poster on the far wall, Lord Kitchener pointed his finger straight at Angus.

It was Andrew Rennick, dean of the Hill Theological School, pitching the plight of the boys over there from the pulpit at St. Andrew's— the honor of sacrifice, which *was* God's greater purpose, which *defined* Faith—who after the service suggested cartography and said he could put Angus in touch with a Major Gault, who would smooth the way. Rennick reminded him of the amendments Angus had made to official provincial charts over the years, correcting misplaced shoals, uncharted rocks, inaccurate depths. Angus could search the hospitals for Ebbin himself while making maps *in London*, the dean stressed— *behind the lines*—risking neither life nor limb.

Standing there in the church vestibule, Angus thought about Hettie and about Amos; about certainty and uncertainty, and about the mechanical precision and reproduction that was mapmaking. He knew about charting depths, not elevations. Knew nothing about surveying, but that would hardly be required. And surely he could learn how to turn a photograph into a flat-line map.

"Men risk their lives flying over enemy lines to get those photographs," Rennick said. "You could help save lives by transforming them into maps."

Perhaps, Angus thought, he'd been led to this point all along. After all, he was good at drawing "real" birds. *Accept who you are*, Rennick had told him years before, agreeing with Angus's decision to leave the seminary. Here was the opportunity to use his skill and do something that mattered.

Art with a purpose, his father called his chart work, something Angus reminded him of when, white hair wild, eyes wide, shaking with controlled rage, his father warned him about the immorality of serving as a cog in the engine of war, no matter how remote from the field, about putting his talent to evil purpose.

It was the first time Angus had heard him use the word "talent."

ON THE FLOOR beside him Mueller moaned, and Angus jerked back to the troop train, which was slowing to a stop at a Casualty Clearing Station. Flags snapped brightly above the Matron's tent as Angus and some others helped Mueller off the train, where he was collected by two oddly cheerful young women. Ambulance drivers. From Toronto, they told him. Behind them a group of privates, recovered from wounds and illness and cleared for duty, climbed aboard. One man was left on the platform. His shoulders were raised up awkwardly on his crutches, and he swung forward and back, his good leg barely sweeping the ground. His only leg, Angus saw on second glance. The soldier stretched his lips into a grin. "I get to go home now. Grand, ain't it?" Angus forced his own smile and nodded. "I'm a logger," the soldier said. Still grinning, he bobbed his head up and down.

The logger's cockeyed grin stayed with Angus as the train rocked on, as did the words "casualty clearing station." Casualties . . . 57,000 casualties on the opening day at the Somme, 24,000 Canadian casualties in two months of fighting in and around Courcelette. And "clearing"—sorting men out, fixing them up for another go at becoming a casualty. In his search for Ebbin, Angus had seen enough in the London hospitals to understand that burns, blindness, amputation, loss of speech, and mechanical contraptions to fill in missing parts of the face were but the order of the day. Ebbin's name would have been registered if he had been in hospital, Angus was told. Soldiers without tags rarely made it back to England, and if they did, their identities were almost always sorted out. But Angus had been taken to the nameless, and, upon seeing the drooling, slack-jawed faces, the vacant eyes and those for whom death would be a prayer answered, had thanked God Ebbin was not among them.

As guns, like thunder, boomed in the distance, the Brits on the train broke out in a rendition of "Marching to Pretoria." The Canadians took up the song and added a few bawdy verses. The Brits added a few of their own. Everyone got a good laugh out of it, even Angus.

What was truly laughable, he thought as the song ended and another began, was the idea that he could have found Ebbin from a safe distance behind the lines like some kind of armchair hero. Now he was on his way to inflict wounds and likely become a casualty himself. Yet to lose Ebbin was to lose a link to himself—and to Hettie. Ebbin was her other half. She used to hang on his every word. Angus thought of her as Ebbin's kid sister, for years, in fact, until she went away to school. And then came that summer she spent with Kitty—happy to wear Kitty's handoffs to dances, to sit on a terrace wall and sip champagne from a fluted glass beneath the hanging lanterns, seemingly oblivious to the effect she had on BB and his crowd.

On his increasingly frequent visits, Hettie and Angus had broken faith with Ebbin and discovered each other, tentatively at first and then with growing confidence that had culminated in a moment of passion behind the gazebo at the bottom of the Balfour lawns. An endless moment, out of time, that had ended nonetheless, and was followed by a fumbling, fruitless search for two pearl buttons in the shadowed grass and tears over the torn lace and streaks of green up the back of Kitty's best white linen. More confusion and regret followed. Ebbin, stunned and speechless at first, had found it in himself to forgive Angus, and not long afterwards, pronounced the marriage and baby to come a gift forever linking the three of them.

That Simon Peter was a gift was never questioned in the thirteen years since. Easy, imaginative, unspoiled, he was their golden boy— their only child. The flame of passion that brought him into the world had failed to rekindle. Angus remained tenderly protective of Hettie, wanted her happy, hoped for but expected little in return, and tried not to think how he'd cut her chances short. She said she had no regrets, claimed he'd rescued her from Kitty Balfour's silly crowd. But after the wedding, sitting beside her, her delicate gray-gloved hands lightly resting in her lap as the wagon jounced over the rutted road past the sheds and fishnets, the stacked lobster traps and sturdy wharfs of Snag Harbor, he doubted that.

Removed, remote, almost ethereal, Hettie was a mystery, drawing him in, keeping him at bay. Yet she could on occasion, like a tourist innocent to local custom, ask a question that cut through long-held assumptions to the heart of the matter, weaving disparate strands into a whole with stunning originality and pragmatism. It was she who suggested that Angus sell his bird and shore pictures on cargo runs, and that he make them consistent enough to be associated with the name A. A. MacGrath; she who had encouraged Duncan to help set up an insurance fund in Lunenburg, beneficial in the long run to widows and fishing consortiums alike, she pointed out. No wonder she'd been taken into Balfour's confidence. She'd shrugged it off as she did her looks.

She once told Angus that her favorite word was "and" because it meant something always came before and something always followed, which, like the infinity of numbers, was reassuring. Her practical visions of the future, countered as they were by her dreamy detach-ment from the physical world, and her fairly constant detachment from him, were perhaps her way of ensuring a future was possible.

But the past and future were nothing now. Only the grinding

present. Next to him the lance corporal leaned over his knees, hands folded in prayer. The train was pulling to a stop. Finding Ebbin was a fast-fading hope and the only hope Angus had. What lay ahead was not the training for war, nor war's ginned-up national pride. What lay ahead was the certainty of battle and his own uncertain place in it. Even as this thought shuddered through him, he held out hope that there was a larger purpose at work, that he was meant to be here, could do some good, and that Ebbin was just around the corner, in some trench, lying on a field, or hiding in a farmhouse, eating an apple and waiting for Angus to find him.

As the train came to a full stop and Angus angled around the lance corporal into the aisle, what came to him was his last glimpse of Simon Peter at the railway station in Chester—shoulders back, legs apart, hands stiff at his sides. But what stayed with him as he stepped off onto the platform and wove through the crowd of soldiers pushing ever onward was that last little wave—a child's wave. Stay alive, Angus told himself. Stay alive.

TWO

February 3rd, 1917
Snag Harbor, Nova Scotia

imon Peter MacGrath, quilts piled over him, lay wide awake, unable to move, thinking he might be dead. He blinked into the darkness, willing objects back to their familiar shapes.

The bureau persisted as a wharf; its drawers, ladder steps nailed to pilings. The floor, the mudscape of the harbor bottom. His boots, exposed rocks. In his dream, Snag Harbor and all of Mahone Bay had been sucked dry of water, every rock and belt of seaweed exposed. Boats lay forlorn on their sides, their crosstrees tipped into the muck; their keels, the fins of so many dead fish. The *Lauralee* hung at an angle from Mader's wharf, her bow line a hangman's noose. From the opposite shore, through the spruce marched a thin line of tunk-tunks, those miniature, menacing, empty-eyed deer that so often populated his dreams. Over the slick rocks they came, over the flattened sea-weed, over the fish, pathetically flipping their tails, gills slowly open-ing and closing, until they stood, silently rocking in formation, as if waiting for a signal. At the mouth of the bay, the sea had sucked back to a towering wall, blocking the sun, and poised to roar back in.

Simon slowly turned out of the bed and allowed his feet to flatten against the broad, painted floorboards until the cold penetrated the fog of his dream. There across the room was his cousin, Young Fred, a huddled shape, thick with sleep. On the desk under the window between their beds were Simon's schoolbooks, just as he'd left them, the lamp, a red-and-white speckled rock from Fundy, and the heavy magnifying glass with its silver handle and intricate scroll work—a loan from Mr. Heist. There, too, the jaunty, puffed-up puffin in his striped scarf, painted by his father on a small square of canvas just for him.

Simon draped the soft old top quilt around his shoulders and crept over to the desk. He hunched onto the chair, feet on the seat, knees pulled up to his chest and stared out the window. Through frosted panes, he made out the northeast field leading down to the finger of water and the little bridge over the causeway that separated the peninsula where they lived from the mainland. The white of the snow looked lit from within, so dark was the night. He could make out the spruce at the bottom of the hill and a hint of the harbor in the reach of blackness beyond. He had to take it on faith that the water was still in it. On the windowsill stood a lead soldier, a solitary sentry. Simon had taken it from the box weeks ago and had given the rest to Young Fred, who rarely played with them, preferring his "people," pilfered pencils of various lengths, some chewed, some not. At thirteen, toy soldiers were beneath Simon. Still, he was glad to have saved this one. Its colonial costume was masked by the darkness, but the musket stood straight up. His father, this very minute, would be holding the line, rifle in hand—the Krauts, cowering in their trenches, across from his watchful eye. There were thousands of soldiers at the Front, but at this moment, Simon could only imagine one.

An icy stillness held everything in suspension. When he was little and suffered night terrors, his mother would shush his screams with murmured incoherencies, her hair falling around him like a silk cocoon. Then she'd lie next to him, then fall asleep, oblivious to empty-eyed tunk-tunks and mastodons prowling and pawing in the dark corners of the room.

But when his father was home, he'd stride in, swing Simon up, and pace the floorboards, holding him tight until the world came back to itself, no matter how long it took. Then, together, waving stiff arms a few inches above the covers, they'd clear the area of whirligigs, his father's name for night terrors, and Simon would fall back to an easy sleep, his father's hand resting on his back. Sometimes his father was in need of comfort, but rarely, and only in the art shed, which no one could enter without permission.

Standing at the threshold once when he was small, Simon had been shocked to find his father, paintbrush clamped in his teeth, hunched over on the stool, head in his hands. Simon had summoned all his courage and whispered, "Whirligigs?" The silence in the room was so deep, his father's acknowledgment so profound, that Simon had been unable to breathe until, without looking up, his father had thrust his arm out, and together they thrashed away at the whirligigs on the canvas, their mighty efforts securing the notion that terrors, even of monstrous proportion, could be gotten through—though perhaps only in shared company.

But Simon had outgrown whirligigs, and now he was alone.

On the day his father left for England, Simon had sat on the bed, watching him pack. Ida Corkum, his grandfather's housekeeper since before Simon was born, had knit far too many socks, every pair in cream wool with a red and brown stripe at the top. His father plucked at them, rolling them into pairs and setting them back down. They were useless.

"Too short, aren't they," Simon said.

"Yep, but you can wear them in your boots and tuck the long hose over when it's freezing."

"But how do you keep your legs warm under a skirt?"

"Kilt, Simon. You know better. Ah, I see—making light of the uniform, eh?"

Simon smiled. "Yeah. But still, how do you?"

"A kilt is twice as thick as trousers and your legs harden from exposure, so you don't feel the cold any more than on your hands and face. Just ask old Athol McLaren—ever see him in trousers? Besides, I'll be indoors most of the time."

"So . . . you'll be in the army, but you won't be fighting the Germans?" Simon had asked this many times, the answer never quite resolving his simultaneous disappointment and relief.

His father rolled his eyes.

"I know. Cartography."

"Exactly. I'll be detached from my unit and assigned to cartography in London. But the maps I make will be used at the Front. So I'll be supporting the war."

Simon then asked the question he hadn't yet dared to ask. "Will Grandpa still be against the war with you in it?"

His father was quick to respond. "Of that I have no doubt. He has a right to his views. Just remember, moral certainty is a luxury of the very young and the very old."

"Define moral certainty." Simon had been trying this out instead of "What's that mean?" But it struck a tone he hadn't intended.

"Alright," his father said slowly. "Seeing the world in black and white. How's that?" He raked his hand through his hair and tossed three pairs of socks into the duffel bag. "Look, I know this won't be easy on you," he said.

He was right. There was no escaping his grandfather nor his anger over the war. He lived right up the hill, owned the land they lived on, the house they lived in—was in it as often as not, and knew everything that went on even when he wasn't. Lately, when his grandfather chastised Simon for some minor infraction, he was Captain Bligh to Simon's Fletcher Christian, secretly plotting a mutiny. The story of the H.M.S. *Bounty* was one he'd been told many times by his grandfather, who had no use for an officer defying his captain and setting him adrift, and by his father, who had a more sympathetic take on Mr. Christian. Simon sided with his father, but his grandfather made more of an event of the telling, filling it in with a good deal more drama and colorful detail.

His father was speaking again. "It's fine to be against war—admirable," he said. "But we've got to play the hand we're dealt. We're not pacifists, and neither is your grandfather, not in a formal sense anyway. I was raised to respect life, not take it, but it doesn't mean I'm going to stand by and . . ." He whipped the bag off the bed and jerked the drawstring tight. "I have to do what *I* feel is right." He stood staring at the bag with his hands on his hips. "I may not be cut out to be a soldier, but . . ."

Simon glanced up and took in his father's tall, lean frame, his strong profile and broad shoulders. "What d'you mean? You're captain of the *Lauralee*."

"That's right." His father smiled at him. "But she isn't a ship of the line, is she? I haven't exactly been sailing under Nelson." He sat down on the bed and put his hand on Simon's knee as if he was going to say more. There was a long white scar that sucked the flesh down between his thumb and forefinger. He'd sliced it open freeing a line in a storm, bound it up in a rag, and never batted an eye. Even now, his father never spoke about it. Wallace was the one who filled Simon in, as he always did. "A right fine skipper," Wallace and others who sailed with his father agreed. "*Right* fine. Knows these waters like the back of his hand. Can find his way through the thick of fog and black of night like his father before him," Putnam Pugsley always added.

Sitting on the bed next to his father, breathing in the same air, resting comfortably in the same easy silence they shared when out on the water, Simon began to think about how much more empty the house would be with his father overseas than it was when he was up the coast. He asked what would happen to the *Lauralee* with his father gone, and would Wallace take her out.

"Wallace is looking for other work. The *Lauralee* belongs to your grandfather, and he wants out of the coastal trade." His father ran his hand through his hair again as he always did. A thick wave of it tumbled forward.

"He'd never sell her . . . would he?" Simon whispered.

His father's gaze shifted to the window, where the predawn sky was filling in, slate gray. "Course not," he said after a moment. "Who'd buy her?" But his smile was strained.

"I won't let him. I'll see she's hauled up proper at Mader's 'til you get home."

"There's my boy. My boy of big heart, sound mind and strong body . . ."

Caught off guard by the familiar words spoken in so sad a tone, Simon felt tears well up. "Do you think Uncle Ebbin's alive?" he whispered. "Will you come home if you find him?"

His father stood abruptly. "Christ, Simon. Why do you think I enlisted? I'm going over there to do my part." He rifled through some papers and stuffed them in his bag. "I can't just walk away when I feel like it, and wouldn't want to if I could." He stopped himself. "Sorry, son," he said. "Sorry. Forgot who I was talking to." Then he patted Simon's head, which made Simon feel small and useless, so he chose that moment to say, "Since the *Lauralee* isn't going out, how about I go out on the Banks this summer? Carl Keddy, Martin Rafuse, Daryl Nauss and a bunch of others will be out there." *The Banks is where boys become men.* Daryl repeated this line from his old man at every opportunity.

His father's dark eyes grew darker. "Fishing the Banks is a rough life for a boy. Backbreaking. Dangerous. Those boys have no choice. Their families need the money. Don't romanticize it."

"I'm not. I just want to go."

His father nodded in appreciation. "Sure you do. Or think you do. But Banks fishing is not for you. You have other talents. You just haven't found them yet. Besides, summer's a long way off and right now, you're needed here at home." When Simon didn't reply, his father said, "C'mon now. Chin up. I'll write. You'll write me back, right? Keep me posted on what you're up to, and fill me in on Young Fred."

"Guess we're stuck with him forever," Simon said with exaggerated resignation.

"Maybe. I doubt Cousin Turley is coming back anytime soon. You don't mind, do you—sharing your room with him?"

"Nah. Every night he tells me he's ready to sleep in the spare room *all by himself*. At least he's not sleeping in my bed anymore." Simon managed a grin.

"That's right. It's hard not having a mother. We're all that boy has right now."

Turley, Young Fred's father, was a sometimes logger and a steady drinker. No one was sure when his wife died, but sometime afterwards, Turley brought the two-and-a-half-year-old Fred for an extended stay without mention of when he'd be back. Fred was now almost four. Why did everyone have to be lost? Simon wondered. His father cinched up his duffel bag. Both of them stared down at it. "Dad?" Simon said without looking up. "What if Uncle Ebbin is dead? What if—"

"No *what-ifs*. We'll find out. Not knowing is worse than knowing, even if it's the thing you fear most. And now," his father pulled out his watch, "time's running short. You'd better go get your grandfather. And, Simon? You mind what Ida says, your grandfather, too, when I'm gone. And your mother," he added.

Simon might have liked to mind his mother, but she hardly noticed if rules were broken. The rules weren't hers anyway.

HIS GRANDFATHER DID not come to say good-by at the train station in Chester. "Too hard on this old man. Too long a journey," he said when Simon went up to fetch him—though the train station at Chester was only sixteen miles away. When Simon pleaded with him, his grandfather just stared out at the harbor. It was a beautiful morning, sharp and crisp and perfect. "I've said my good-by. You'd better get on. Go on, boy. Go to the station."

"Dad's going to find Uncle Ebbin," Simon said, arms crossed.

His grandfather's pitying look ushered Simon out the door.

CAUGHT NOW IN the threads of dream and memory, Simon huddled deeper into the quilt and rested his head on his knees and thought about France and wondered how the constellations lined up over there.

There was a globe worthy of a university library on a stand in his grandfather's study. He and his grandfather used to navigate it together and, more often, the charts his grandfather would spread on the massive chart table. "Here," his grandfather would say, his calloused hand over Simon's, moving it along, "is the route Champlain took to the South Shore before it was called the South Shore and before it was Nova Scotia, before it was New Scotland. And here, settled on an island at the mouth of the St. Croix. A disaster. And here, John Cabot's route a hundred years before. Lowered baskets like a pail down a well and scooped up cod without so much as a hook. Bottom feeders, mind—so plentiful they must have been stacked one on top of the other to find their way into buckets dropped from a deck." The grand finale was always, "And here is Mahone Bay, most beautiful bay in the world, where God has granted us the privilege to live."

Now they shared something else—a passion for war reports. It was serious business. He and his grandfather devoured and analyzed every scrap of news from the Front, often at cross purposes, but always enjoying their time together. Simon relished being treated with respect—enough to ignore the occasional antiwar rant. And he secretly suspected that war news was his grandfather's way of keeping up with his father.

The previous afternoon, the paper brought news that the Canadians were massing forces in the Arras Sector at a ridge called Vimy, which no one had been able to wrest from the Germans. "The French failed to take that ridge twice in 1915 and racked up over a hundred fifty thousand casualties," his grandfather said, lowering the paper. "My sources tell me the western slope of it is an unending graveyard. Now the French insist the Brits should try it. So the Brits have enlisted the help of our boys. Arras—that's where your father is this very minute." He'd rattled the paper into its folds and slapped it against the desk. "War to end all wars, eh? My God, the simple-minded lunacy of it."

"Maybe," Simon said, "that's where the war will end."

THINKING BACK ON the news and on his dream, Simon reached for the lone soldier on the sill, encircled the cold lead in his fingers, and held it there until it warmed in his palm.

THREE

February 3rd, 1917
Arras Sector, France

ngus slipped. He'd been having a hard time keeping his footing. An odorous fog, lying low to the ground in wisps and patches, made it difficult to see the sergeant crouching just a few feet ahead, constantly leading him on as if sure of where he was going, then gesturing with a straight arm to stay down, stay down. The shallow communication trench had fallen in or been blown away, and they were on open ground. No sign of the 17th.

His breath grew short. He kept trying to remember the sergeant's name. Shell holes to the right and left—pools of stinking water, sulphurous yellow, phosphorous green, leaching up unexploded shells, empty gas canisters, rusted shrapnel, and bits of bodies. Under the chalky mud lay stick bones, blackened flesh no doubt clinging.

The moon slid out of the clouds for a moment, revealing an undulating, featureless landscape, cut through by massive belts of barbed wire. The two of them, he and the sergeant, were eerily alone. Where was all the nighttime activity—supplies coming up, working parties, troop replacements, trench repairs? Not a star in the sky, but they were angling north instead of east toward the Front Line, Angus was sure of it.

They were lost.

Angus was much taller than the sergeant, so it was no easy task crouching along behind him. Angus slipped again and his leg was sucked into what felt quicker than quicksand.

The sergeant sensed he'd stopped moving. "Lieutenant?" he whispered as he turned around.

The sergeant, on all fours, crawled back to Angus and set the pack down. Angus leaned back, and the sergeant heaved his leg straight up like a log. Mercifully, the boot was still attached. Slimed with muck, but still on tight.

Mercifully, too, the sergeant didn't whisper, "Don't worry, sir, you're not the first to fall off a trench mat." He'd simply pulled, then smiled. Kind eyes in an angular face. He looked much older than Angus. What was his name? What was his name? They knelt face-to-face for a moment, as if in prayer. Angus whispered his thanks. "Not at all, no worries," the sergeant whispered back, and then, slapping his thighs as if to say there then, that's done and off we go again, he unaccountably stood up and turned around, and on the crack of gunshot, fell back, knocking Angus flat and the wind right out of him.

Angus lay there sucking air, then cautiously lifted his head. Do not fall off this duckboard, he told himself. He slowly eased back. The sergeant lay between his legs, staring upward.

"Sergeant!" Angus hissed. The sergeant's head was angled back. How strange his face looked upside down—the cheekbones and chin sharper than before, the lips thinner, the eyes, oddly asymmetric, open to the sky. Angus brushed his fingers over a dark smudge on the forehead. But the smudge was a hole and the sergeant wasn't blinking. A warm trickle filled Angus's other hand from the back of the sergeant's head. Filled it to overflowing.

Angus ducked back down. A star shell lit the sky with a cascading trail of sparks, and everything took on its silver-white illumination. Heart in his throat, he dared to lift his head. The duckboard ended a few feet beyond, then a break, and some twenty yards out, great belts of barbed wire, and then . . . but the flare died out. He needed to get to that break.

Trembling, he stretched out over the sergeant, whose body answered with movement of its own. Angus imagined the two of them rolling off the side, sinking in, never heard from again. The duckboard listed to the left just as Angus reached an arm beyond the sergeant's boots. He elbowed his way to the end, rolled over the edge and into a ditch on top of a pile of sandbags. The forward trench! No sentries. No sign of life. Abandoned—long ago, from the look of it.

Keeping his head low, he lunged for the sergeant's boots as the torso slipped into a water-filled hole. There the sergeant lay, half in and half out. And there lay Angus, stretched out of the trench holding the man's boots with both hands. The boots rattled against the boards. He gripped them tighter, but they kept at it. It was his own hands shaking. All he could think of was helping the sergeant, the two of them somehow finding the 17th.

A sudden crack and a winging zip, and Angus was at the bottom of the trench, bent double—chest, neck, stomach, limbs clenched. The sandbags at the parapet were missing. Blown in. Blown away. No wonder the sniper had such a clear shot. Angus started crawling down the ditch, catching his knees on his greatcoat, crawling over—what— bodies? No, sandbags. Ripped open some of them, his hands sinking into their oozing contents.

Some ten yards along, the filled-in trench angled down. Protected by an intact parapet and timbered trench wall, he sat back and hung his head and stared at his hands. *Blood on the battlefields of France and Flanders shares kinship with the precious blood of our Lord whose sacrifice was made for us.* Dean Rennick's high-flung words circled back from the pulpit to the bottom of the trench, where Angus was beginning to understand something of blood sacrifice. *Sacrifice lifts us to our true humanity, our true calling; through it comes salvation,* Rennick had said.

Died in the bottom of a trench, no more senseless way to die, came his father's words.

Angus stared at the timbers in front of him, one atop another. In the hazy moonlight, the grain of the wood stood out in sharp relief. Oak, Angus thought. Against the noxious air he conjured up creosote on the town wharf and fragrant wood shavings curling under a boat in Mader's shed, and the tangle of oars, trap buoys, nets, linnet. And there was Simon Peter, clear as day, smiling at the shed door, sun framing his blond head, sunlight sparking the harbor beyond. Angus opened his eyes, and the grain of the timbers became narrow slots through which he might slip unnoticed and never look back.

When the trembling stopped, he risked his silhouette against the next German flare. Two boots on the rim of the shell hole were slowly sinking in, and with them, the sergeant disappeared.

"Wickham," Angus whispered into the night. "John Wickham."

"BAD NEWS ABOUT Wickham," the captain said when, in the wee hours, Angus finally made it to the 17th. "A good man. Fought as a private in the Boer War. Made it to sergeant." Tunic unbuttoned, legs wide apart beneath his kilt, dark eyes gloomy, he'd offered only a shrug to Angus's salute. He lined up two tin cups, then poured. Not a ration of rum, but Scotch. From a bottle. "A drink to Wickham," he said, and handed Angus a cup.

Angus took it with a shaking, mud-crusted hand and downed the contents.

"Another?" The captain's broad face had a yellow tinge in the glow of the lantern. "Thought so. Won this in a bet with an unlucky quartermaster. Step above the standard-issue rum, eh?" Angus threw the Scotch back. Its burn reassured him he was alive. He took the rag the captain offered and water from a spouted can to rinse his hands and face. Mud sloughed off, blood with it, onto the dirt floor.

"You were sent up from . . . the 183rd?"

"Yes sir."

"Well, you're with the 17th now. The Royal Nova Scotia High-landers, assuming you survive the next two weeks up here. Glad to see you're in the right tartan anyway. Got your papers?"

Angus reached into his greatcoat.

"And close that, would you?"

Angus looked dumbly at his coat. "The door," the captain sighed, taking the papers. "Bastard weather. We're either up to our knees in slime or freezing our balls off in snow. Out here where the world actually *is* flat and the drainage system was shelled to death two years ago, you're wet most of the time. Take a seat."

Angus shoved the corrugated door shut and sat down heavily beside the plank table that served as the captain's desk. A lantern radiated warmth. The smell of kerosene cut through the dirt and damp, and things were suddenly cozy, if a bit foggy under the low roof of the earth-and-timbered dugout.

The captain pushed aside a rusted tin of sardines, a pair of wire cutters and a little green book, open to a page with words underlined. The sardines and wire cutters held down a stack of disordered papers that got more disordered as Angus stared at them. His eyes slid to the book, facing him now. Homer. *The Odyssey?*

"You with me, MacGrath?"

Angus jumped. "Sir!"

"Try to stay awake," the captain said patiently. "And you can drop the 'sir' for now. It's Jim. James McCusker Conlon. There are times when I can only tolerate so much formality. This is one of them." He studied the papers in the light of the lantern. He was thick, broad-shouldered, as tall as Angus, and strong-looking, but soft-spoken in a way that made you pay attention. "So, how'd you come to be with us?" he was saying.

"Major Tucker's orders." Tucker had sent something more detailed to Major Rushford, but Angus hadn't met Rushford, only his adjunct, who had paired him with Wickham and sent him on up.

"So where's the rest of your boys?"

"Bled into the 61st, the ones I came up with. The rest are still on the other side of the channel."

"You might end up wishing you were with them. Did the major say why? Outside of our need for officers? Okay. Here it is. Says here you might be of use in intelligence-gathering. Now that," Conlon said, staring at Angus with weary eyes, "assumes intelligence on the part of the gatherer. Haven't seen action yet. Obviously."

"Not yet." Hadn't *seen* action. Had just had it drop in his lap.

"We like to worry Jerry with our raids. That's how we get intelligence. Take a few prisoners. Wreak a little havoc while we're at it." Conlon finished off his Scotch and reluctantly corked the bottle.

"Yes sir. Quite a reputation back of the line."

"Good fodder for the papers, anyway. Morale booster for the home-folks." Conlon's humility seemed genuine. "That's how we lost those last two lieutenants," he added. "One captured. One bled out in No Man's Land before we could bring him in. A colonel somewhere back of the line had the bright idea of conducting a raid in broad daylight to add an additional element of surprise. Raids keep the men on their game until the next big push. Maybe not in broad daylight, though. Maybe *that's* not a good idea." He shook his head and wagged the bottle by the neck. "This keeps *our* morale up, eh?" Then he flipped open the lid of a dented footlocker and placed the Scotch carefully back in it. "Sadly, we can't afford to dip into morale boosting too often. Nothing like a good whisky, Scotch or Irish." He put his feet on the locker, his hands behind his head and faced Angus. "Though I prefer Irish. So, which are you, MacGrath?"

"Sir?"

"Scotch? Irish? Farmer, fisherman? Tinker, tailor . . . man about town?"

"Sailor," Angus filled in. "Coastal trader, out of Snag Harbor, Nova Scotia."

"Quaint."

"Snag. Snag Harbor, not Snug."

"Alright, not so quaint. Might have heard of it. Down Lunenburg way?"

"Across the bay."

"My mother's got people there in Mahone Bay. Marriott's Cove, I think it is." Conlon picked up the letter again. "Says here you're a good leader. Unfortunately, good leaders lead, and then get killed because of it . . . Special talent in the art department." Conlon looked up quizzically. "You an artist?"

"An artist?"

"That's what it says. 'Special talent in the art department.' Okay, now I get it. They sent you up because what I need in this landlocked hell is a sailor who can paint. And here I thought you were just another warm body."

Angus stared into his palm for traces of Wickham's blood. He cleared his throat. "The C.O. saw some quick sketches I'd done from memory. I'm not an artist. I can draw," he mumbled.

Conlon waited.

"Maps," Angus said. "I've had experience drawing charts."

"And why at the Front instead of in London with the rest of the cartographers? Didn't make it?"

"Turns out they had plenty of men in cartography."

"No surprise there, eh? Cushy job back of the line. So they herded you over to the infantry."

"That's right."

Conlon seemed to be waiting for more, so Angus added, "I guess the major was referring to terrain maps. And uh, navigational skills, sailor, you know—good at night vision, estimating distances. Night raids maybe?" He'd turned into a babbling idiot.

"Uh-huh. And you're a good sailor? Because so far there's not much evidence you're a good navigator."

Got myself here, didn't I, Angus wanted to say. But before he could reply, Conlon smiled. "Forgive me. Like I said, it's been a long night. There's a crater out there. Vicar's Crater, it's called. Krauts and us eye each other across it day and night. Routine patrol and suddenly we're down four men. So, our reputation isn't all it's cracked up to be. But that's our job, guarding holes in the ground. Maybe could have used your night vision. So, now tell me. How'd you and Wickham get so far off track?"

The question was conversational, lacking urgency or blame. Yet Angus felt his throat constrict and his tongue grow thick. He said something about how there had been shelling, and in the smoke and confusion, Wickham beckoned him onto a different path, less traveled, safer, he said. Abandoned, it seemed. Even without checking his compass, Angus had a sense they were going in the wrong direction. But he had no idea how far off they were and didn't know exactly where the 17th was, anyway. When he finished, Angus wasn't sure he'd made sense of it in the telling or the remembering because the blood, bright red, still seemed to be on his hand as he looked at it.

"So Wickham, chosen to lead you up here, got spooked and then took off on a route of his own design, and then got killed because of it. Poor sap," Conlon said. "And you didn't think to question him about going off track, you being his superior officer. And a good navigator."

Angus hung his head. His eyes slid to the underlined words in the green book on Conlon's desk. *The Iliad*, not *The Odyssey*. Armies gathering now, "as when from gloomy clouds a whirlwind springs, that bears Jove's thunder on its dreadful wings, Wide o'er the blasted fields the tempest sweeps . . ." He could read no more. He might just sink into the chair with his boots forever planted on the earthen floor, armies of seabirds—gulls, terns, phalaropes, frigate birds—winging through his head. . . .

"Sorry, sir. After the shelling I . . ." He could still feel the ground shudder. "I failed you—him," he said in a miserable whisper.

"Alright," Conlon said, his voice kind. "I'll take your report later. Lieutenant Publicover will show you to quarters and cover for you at stand-to. Get some sleep. Apparently you need it." His bear-like shadow swept up the timbered walls as he stood. "That's *The Iliad*, by the way," he said. "We're not the first to gather beneath the cliffs of Troy. Some comfort in that. Maybe some of us will live to tell the tale . . . Ever read the opening lines?" Angus shook his head. "Might want to," Conlon said. He opened the door to a rush of cold air. "That ridge will be our making or our breaking."

Angus half-stood as he left, then thumped back down, the Scotch working its way through him, his limbs heavy. He glanced back at the book just as Lieutenant Publicover burst in. Before Angus could rise from his chair, Publicover introduced himself with a broad smile, snapped a salute and opened the door again.

Angus came to enough to state his name.

"Yep. Got it from the captain," Publicover said. "C'mon." Angus followed him with heavy steps to their dugout, smaller but otherwise not much different from the captain's. It was almost 4:30 in the morning, the hour of stand-to when the men lined up on the fire steps of the parapet, bayonets fixed, eyes forward and unblinking, as they did every dawn for possible attack and every evening as the sun set. Across No Man's Land, the Germans would be doing the same.

Why anyone would attack at dawn or sunset when everyone was fully prepared was a mystery. Yet that was precisely when frontal assaults took place. Back in training, Roddy Gordon, a great moose of a man with red whiskers from Antigonish, had concluded it was an elaborately staged play—curtain up at dusk, everyone in their places, second act at night, curtain call at dawn. Angus had liked Roddy. Wondered if he'd ever see him again.

Publicover showed Angus his bunk and started a rapid-fire

complaint about the losses the night before. They'd have had better luck, he said, if he'd been in on the raid. "Might have captured a few Krauts or had a few more kills. We're down a couple of officers—guess that's why you're here."

"Those two lieutenants," Angus said slowly. "Pals of yours?"

Publicover shrugged. "Barely knew their names." He pointed to the wall. "Here's your peg." He slung Angus's haversack on it. Then he grabbed a rifle off Angus's bunk. "This here's my friend, my Lee Enfield," he said, stroking the barrel. "Not as accurate as the Canadian Ross, maybe, but less likely to have the bolt fly into your forehead."

"You carry a rifle? An officer with a rifle?"

"I carry a revolver like any good officer. This is my souvenir. Got it off a dead private a year ago, back when you couldn't abandon the old Ross. See, the thing is—"

"Hold it. You've been here a year?"

"Joined in '15. Didn't get in it 'til '16. I'm still an 'original' though." Publicover's eyes glittered in the gloom.

He was Simon Peter grown up. Same sandy hair, same almond-shaped eyes, but his were brilliant blue. Taller. Older, of course, but not by much. Smattering of freckles, visible even in the dim light. "How old are you?" Angus asked. He didn't look a day over seventeen.

"Keep her oiled and in perfect condition," Publicover continued, cradling the rifle and turning it over slowly. "Mud fouls things pretty quick here. They're never *not* fouled. I hate that. I'd really like a knife, too, but haven't found the right one. I'm holding out for a good solid Bowie—not store-bought. One that's seen action and will see some more." He placed the Lee Enfield evenly on his bunk. "Twenty. I'm twenty."

"Really." Angus didn't believe it for a minute.

"Okay. Nineteen, which is almost twenty."

"So, been in it since you were seventeen."

"Yep. And still here. Even better." The boy-lieutenant smiled. "Get some sleep. I'll handle our end of stand-to. Captain's orders. Wake you later," he said as he left.

LATER CAME ALL too soon. Publicover was shaking him awake when a man's scream pierced the air. Sniper? Angus flashed a look at Publicover.

"It's in the trench! C'mon!" Publicover raced off, Angus right behind him.

Around a traverse they came upon four men and one more on the ground, tunic open, blood pouring over his collar. A sergeant was ranting at a dumbstruck private, "What the hell were you doing?" and, alternately, at a stretcher-bearer, on his knees, cutting away at the man's tunic, "What the hell are *you* doing? He's dead, I tell you!"

"Ricketts! What happened here?" Publicover demanded. The sergeant wheeled around.

"Seems Fallows here fired on Orland. By accident. He's a stiff, sir, Orland is."

The stretcher-bearer continued his ministrations. Angus bent to the wounded soldier. Publicover turned on the stricken Fallows. "Fallows?"

Fallows stammered out his explanation. "I, I . . . come back from a working party. Was cleaning my rifle and the safety—I don't know sir. It went off just as Orland came round the traverse."

"I saw it. Happened as he said, sir." Ricketts had composed himself.

Angus felt for a pulse and shook his head at Publicover. The stretcher-bearer continued cutting away at Orland's jacket and reached in his pack for dressings. "Stop now, soldier," Angus said. "It's over." But the man worked all the faster, splashing iodine on the wound, pressing bandages against it. More men gathered.

"Orland's got it," one of them said.

"How?" another asked.

"Fallows. Gun misfired."

The stretcher-bearer reached for more dressings. "That's enough!" Angus said. "He's dead. You'll not waste dressings on a dead man." The stretcher-bearer ignored him. Angus again felt for a pulse, for breath against his hand, but there was none. So much blood. The bullet must have struck the jugular.

"That's an order, soldier," Angus said.

"It's his brother, Orland's brother, sir," Ricketts said, indicating the stretcher-bearer, who was pressing yet another dressing against the wound. The other stretcher-bearer sat back on his haunches.

"You heard him. Stop. That was an order," Publicover said. He withdrew his revolver. "Soldier! Did you hear me?"

The stretcher-bearer kept right on. Publicover, arm down and taut, revolver in hand, pushed through to the kneeling figure. The men fell back as he slowly raised the gun to the man's head. Publicover's response was controlled and rehearsed. Even in the shadows, his eyes were blue ice. Angus grabbed the stretcher-bearer's wrist. The stretcher-bearer did not move. "Dead," Angus said. "No," the man whispered, "no," and pressed the bandage against the wound.

Angus tightened his hold, and with his right hand inches above the body made the sign of the cross. "I am the resurrection and the life," he said softly. "He that believeth in me, though he were dead, yet shall he live. In the midst of life we are in death." Slowly the stretcher-bearer raised his eyes. Tears filled them. Angus met his gaze. "And, here, in the midst of death, we are in life," he said.

Publicover cocked the gun. The stretcher-bearer, eyes fixed on Angus, gun pressed to his temple, slowly opened his fingers, releasing a streak of cotton gauze that unraveled across the body and into the mud. Then he sat back on his heels, head and bloodied hands hanging. Angus stood, and without missing a beat, Publicover said, "Sergeant, get these men to their breakfast, then report to Captain Conlon. Fallows, you'll come with us to report in now. You two," he said to the stretcher-bearers, "take Orland back." Orland's brother, sobbing outright now, and the other stretcher-bearer lifted the body onto the stretcher.

HOURS LATER IN their dugout, Publicover, hands on his hips, stood inches from Angus. "You a goddamn padre or a madman or both?" he demanded, nostrils flaring. "The men need to know an order from an officer is an order. I've a mind to report you to Conlon."

Angus countered that the boy had been stunned, that all he'd seen was his brother bleeding out.

"You're the one gave him the order!"

True enough.

"Better think about that, MacGrath. Think very carefully. There were five men there, not just one. You give an order, you damned well better mean it."

"The man was in shock," Angus replied. He could hardly believe this boy was right, but he knew he was.

"Not enough to ignore a cocked revolver."

"You'd have killed him?"

"The gun spoke to him and the others with or without your holy ministrations. Let me introduce you to the Front, Lieutenant. It's a place where men's lives depend on following orders, or hadn't you heard?"

Something scrabbled nearby. They both looked down. A plump rat with a sleek coat and a pink, lavender and yellow nose was continuing his inspection of Angus's haversack, drooping at an angle from its peg. Near the rat's hindquarters lay a box of pastels, a slot for every color. The pastels were scattered about in half-gnawed crumbs.

"Jesus. What the hell?" Publicover shot an incredulous look at Angus.

"Pastels," Angus replied calmly.

"*Pastels?* Jesus. Sweet, sweet Jesus. Pastels . . ." Publicover whistled a falling note. "You *are* a madman. And we thought they were sending us an officer."

"I've heard only madmen survive."

The rat waddled toward them. "Well, that may be true, but I'll tell you something," Publicover said slowly, folding his arms. "Ratty doesn't much care for your chalks."

Angus folded his arms as well. "Should have brought oils. Or maybe he'd prefer watercolors."

Publicover snorted out a laugh. The rat, streaked nose quivering, looked up and blinked. "And that," Publicover said, staring back at it, "might be the only made-up face we'll see for months."

Angus squatted down and picked through the chalk crumbs. Only the browns and blacks and a single gray remained intact.

THAT EVENING DURING stand-to, the sky crossed itself with streaks of lavender, yellow and rosy pink over the unhinged earth, over the coiled barbed wire, unexploded shells, rusting equipment left to rot in No Man's Land—a cratered landscape of ruin. Had his pastels survived, Angus would have been hard-pressed to put them to paper. For in that silken sky above and wounded earth below lay all one needed to know—a knowing so obvious, it hardly needed an artist to expand it into a larger truth.

FOUR

February 9th, 1917
Snag Harbor, Nova Scotia

A von Heist, schoolmaster for the combined sixth, seventh, and eighth grades, closed his book and removed his spectacles. He withdrew a perfectly folded, perfectly white handkerchief and rubbed each lens. He refolded the handkerchief, tucked it in his pocket and announced that lessons were over—that he now wished to speak to them about something else. Behind him the chalkboard was clean, the maps loosely rolled. Above the maps, framed portraits of King George and Queen Mary, poorly hung, tilted forward.

Mr. Heist surveyed the faces looking up at him. He rose from his desk and walked to the bank of windows lining the west wall. With his back to the class, he said, "Germany."

He rocked for a time on his short feet, hands clasped behind his back. Fat flakes of snow drifted past the windows. The class shifted in their seats. The clock ticked a notch closer to 3:00.

"Germany," Mr. Heist repeated. He unclasped his hands, tugged his black wool vest and turned to the class. "Germany is not one state, but many. We would do well to remember that."

Simon and Zenus Weagle exchanged puzzled glances.

"Germany, composed of many states, is now a country held hostage by the few."

Held hostage? Simon sat up.

"This morning, a fight broke out in the schoolyard. Ruffians and hooligans, you know who you are. But that is not important. What *is* important," Mr. Heist continued with brisk strides back to his desk, "is that during this exchange of fisticuffs there was a good deal of name-calling. *Kraut. Fritz. Hun.* Pejoratives spat out, friend against neighbor. Words said without a thought to their meaning."

Out came his pencil, rat-a-tat-tat on the desk. He lined it up just so and said, "I've decided to use this as an opportunity to inform and educate against the ignorance these words convey. A lesson in tolerance, if you will."

An ash-covered log in the woodstove plumped softly down to dying embers. The room was growing colder. Mr. Heist took no notice. "Do you know of Mr. Fritze from La Have?" he said. "No? I didn't think so. A loyal Canadian these many years, a Canadian of German extraction, he was not allowed to enlist. Volunteered and was *refused*. Barred because of his name—a name that evokes the worst sort of bigotry."

Tim Bethune leaned back in his seat and folded his arms.

"Many among us are of German lineage," Mr. Heist continued, "as am I. Some of us more recently than others."

"No kidding," Robbie McLaren sniggered at Tim.

"Many are descendants of Protestants who came here in the 1750s to farm and fish at the behest of the British. And why?" Mr. Heist paused. "Nora?"

Nora Church, usually quick with answers, hesitated. "Why are we descended?"

Mr. Heist closed his eyes in pain. "No, not why are we *descendants*. Why did the British invite people, largely from *German* states, to colonize these shores?"

"To make settlements against the Catholics, I mean, the French?"

"Precisely! On both counts. A settlement, a living fortress, if you will, of Protestants in Lunenburg against the French Catholic settlements and French forts. You see how life changes? We were against France in the eighteenth and nineteenth centuries. Now, at the dawn of the twentieth, we are lined up with her against Germany. Now, where were these German-speaking settlers from, one hundred and sixty years ago?"

Before they could answer, he loosened the strings holding the map of Europe in suspension. It crashed to the floor. Laughter rippled through the room. Simon winced. This was just the sort of thing that happened to Mr. Heist. A scholar among Philistines was how his grandfather described him. With his back to the class, Mr. Heist remained still until the laughter evaporated. "Simon," he said.

Simon, in charge of maps and chalkboard that day, stepped handily over the outthrust leg of Tim Bethune, collected the map and helped Mr. Heist reassemble it. When it was hung up again, Mr. Heist took up the pointer, whirled around and struck it against Germany. "Teacher's pet," Tim hissed as Simon resumed his seat. "Philistine," Simon retorted, pleased at the flummoxed look the word evoked.

"Another syllable, and we'll be here until darkness falls." Mr. Heist raised his brows. "Now, again, where did the German settlers come from?" When no one answered, he struck the map again. "Here. Bavaria, one of the southern states of Germany. From parts of Switzerland and eastern France as well, but it is the German states I'm focused on. Bavaria. Can we say that together?"

"Bah-vaaar-ee-ahh," the class repeated halfheartedly. It was 3:02. Across the hall, the primary grades were charging out of their classroom.

Daryl Nauss drew a question mark on a scrap of paper.

"And, up here, what do we have? Class?"

Maisie Morin raised her hand. "Prussia," she said with a flip of her curls.

"Precisely, Maisie. Thank you. Prussia, another German state. Now," again he clasped his hands behind his back, "make no mistake, the German people have a rich heritage of letters, music, science and philosophy. But the *Prussians* have all along stood for something else."

He was pacing now. His words came faster. His accent grew thicker. "Prrrussians are part of the old Junker aristocracy—arrogant, unlettered, with aspirations conceived of by the sword!" The pointer slapped the Prussian state on the map. "No less than Visigoths and Vandals before them, the Prussians are against freedom!" Another slap. "Against culture!" Another slap. "Against parl-i-a-mentary government!" A final slap. "And out of this primitive set of mind rose who? Who?" The pointer shot straight up above his balding head and nearly tipped King George sideways. Not missing a beat, Mr. Heist poked the other edge to straighten him. "Well?" he said. The whisper of laughter rippling through the class died a quick death.

"Bismarck?" little Otto Brink, in the second row, responded.

"Otto von Bismarck! *Precisely*! Thank you, Otto. Not to worry over your Christian name."

Little Otto sat up straighter. Mr. Heist carried on, his voice rising. "Bismarck, whose political genius led him to the highest levels of power. Under him, Germany was not *united*, as we see in our history book." He held the offending book aloft. The class was mesmerized. The book was wrong?

"Not united"—he slapped the book down, placed his fists on the desk and leaned toward the students, his voice falling to a stage whisper—"but *subdued*." He straightened up. "Subdued to his iron will! And after? And then? Then he set his sights on the rest of Europe, beginning with . . . ?"

"Alsace and Lorraine!" Simon Peter shouted. They had just covered the Franco-Prussian War.

"Yes! Very good! Took on the weak and corrupt French government in 1870 and won. How could he not? But the Junker Prussians weren't satisfied, were they? No! Of course not!" His voice rose again. "Intoxicated with success, they took their militaristic aspirations to the high seas, building up their navy to take over the world. Who and what stood in the way?"

"The British navy!" Danny Boer called out.

"The whole British Empire!" came another voice.

"George the Fifth!"

"The Canadian Expeditionary Force!" Zenus yelled. Then there was a rumbling of feet and the beat of hands on desks.

"Yes! Yes!" Avon Heist shouted back at them. He tore off his spectacles and, eyes shut, pinched the bridge of his nose, as if in gratitude for students so smart. Then he narrowed his eyes at them. "And the peace-loving peoples of Bavaria? The rest of Germany?" he said, waving his spectacles about. "What of them? Held hostage to these monstrous aims! Just as the Allies are protecting your freedoms, so too will they bring freedom to the peoples of Germany! The Kaiser will *fall* and the *Prussians* will be crushed! Not the German people, *the Prussians!*"

Snow was falling hard now. He slowed to the finish. "*Krrraut* and *Hun*, *Bosch* and *Frrritz*! I will not tolerate this intolerance. No, I will not. Fathers and brothers and uncles, some of them Zincks and Zwickers, Kaisers and Heislers, Nausses and Bremners, men of peaceable German heritage from all up and down this province, are this very minute fighting in the Canadian army. And a man named *Fritze*"—here he shook his head sadly—"was prevented from going with them." He let that sink in. "Ostracized!" he said, looking up. "A man as Canadian as you. As Canadian as me, now fifteen years a citizen!" He stretched up a little taller than he was and yanked his vest with two hands. "Class dismissed!"

The students, all twenty-three of them, remained seated for a fleeting second, then pounded out to the cloakroom, winding mufflers around their necks, strapping their books, pulling on hats and coats and bolting out the door. Simon Peter grabbed his jacket and looked back. Mr. Heist was again at the window.

A hard shove and Simon was knocked to the ground. "What're you going to do about it?" Tim whispered, jerking Simon close. "Eh? Cry to the Kraut?" He let loose a gob of spit into Simon's ear, laughed and pushed through the door past Zenus, who leaned his head in and told Simon to hurry up for God's sake, it was freezing out.

Simon scuffed through the snow down Queen Street next to Zenus and behind Maisie's group of chattering friends. "I'd like to beat that Tim Bethune to a pulp," he said, rubbing his ear.

"He's got four inches and forty pounds on you. He'll be in grade six for the rest of his life. Forget him," Zenus answered. "Wasn't that something, though, old Heistmeister ranting on about the Krauts and sounding just like them?"

"Yeah. He's not, though. He's Canadian, like us," Simon said. "That's the point." But Simon was still trying to sort it all out. Prussians, Bavarians. Parts of Germany holding other parts hostage. None of this had been said before. "You ever hear about that Mr. Fritze?"

"Nope. Making it up, I bet."

They had reached Hennigar's Dry Goods and Grocery. Maisie turned back to Simon and said she had to buy some thread for her mother to take to the Red Cross tea at Simon's house. "*You* can take it to her," she said, and led her group into the store.

Simon rolled his eyes. "How'd I get so lucky?"

"Forget her, too," Zenus said. "There's our girl." He pointed at the store window. The two of them fell silent as they always did at the face of Little Belgium, staring out at them from a war poster behind sacks of Beaver Flour and a pyramid of canned pears. Little Belgium—a soft-featured peasant girl with dark curls loosely framing her face and a gray cloak set back on her head. The cloak fell in folds around her shoulders, revealing a deep red dress topped with a hint of lace. In her shadowed eyes, something sad and weary; in the tilt of her head, something vulnerable and imploring. She was framed by a pale circle of gold. Above her the words HAVE YOU ANY WOMEN FOLK WORTH DEFENDING? You bet they did. Below her, nearly hidden by the tinned pears, pale blue script slanted up with the words, "Remember the women of Belgium."

How could they forget? How could *anyone* forget? Poor little Belgium, raped and pillaged, houses burned, women dragged through the streets by their hair, children murdered by the swords of the advancing German hordes, exacting revenge on common citizens. And for what? Because the teeny-tiny Belgian army had chosen to defend their teeny-tiny country. "Outrageous propaganda" his grandfather called it, but to Simon and Zenus, the girl in the window *was* Little Belgium, and she needed rescue.

"Just a couple more years . . ." Simon leaned forward, hands in his pockets, resting his forehead on the glass.

"Three, if the war's still on," Zenus said.

Simon jerked upright. "It will be. My grandfather's sure of it. Besides, in a year or two, we can fake our age."

"Right," Zenus agreed. "Say, how about that enlistment card? You've had it for a week."

The card was tucked away in Simon's copybook. "A week is seven days. I get one more day with it."

"Let's see it anyway. Whata ya figure, the gorilla is a Hun or a Prussian?" Zenus laughed and thrust his hand out.

Simon squatted down and unstrapped his books. "It's Prussian or *Bavarian.*"

"Yeah . . . so, our boys over there are supposed to go up and say, 'Howdy do. Could you tell me if you're Bavarian or Prussian so me and my chums know whether to blow your brains out?' A Kraut's a Kraut. Period."

It did seem strange how hot and bothered Mr. Heist was over it. Simon dug through his books for the enlistment card, carefully hiding the poems, composed by Mr. Heist himself and bound into a book with covers of dark green linen. He'd told Simon he could keep it as long as he wanted because maybe Simon had some poet in him.

"Damn it! Hurry up!" Zenus hissed. "Too late. Here they come."

The girls, leaning into one another, giggled their way out of the store. Maisie grabbed Simon's hand and dropped the thread in it in a grand gesture. Simon rolled his eyes again.

As he left the group, Zenus shouted, "Don't forget, my turn tomorrow! Have fun with the Red Cross ladies, ya stinking Prussian!"

Simon whipped a snowball at him. "Who ya calling a Prussian, ya blasted Kraut?"

ALONE ON THE short bridge over the causeway to the peninsula, he lingered, watching snow fall silently onto the islands—Snake, Saddle, and beyond them, out of sight, Mountain, Mark, Woody, Lynch, Quaker, Rafuse, Clay, Gooseberry, Oak, and so many more. And to the southwest, Big Tancook and Little Tancook. Barrels of sauerkraut put up by the islanders, lined up on the Tancook wharf and lowered into the hold of the *Lauralee* for transport to Halifax. *Kraut.* Of course! He'd never made the connection before.

He thought about poor Mr. Fritze left behind and about Mr. Heist, out on Owl's Head Point, two inlets over, all alone with no one to cook for him. Why didn't he live in town, people asked. But Simon knew. Mr. Heist liked to be out there in his cottage where he could play his violin and tend his garden and write his poems in peace and quiet—so quiet, he'd written in one verse, that you could hear the beating of bird wing and the soundless rise and fall of the tides.

The sky was growing dark and obscuring the islands. Drumlins, his father called them. Drumlins is what they were—oval hills rising up from the bay, not those dark outcroppings along the Maine coast, his father said, with their straggling trees clinging desperately to jagged rocks, but rounded mounds of islands, sloping down from the high windward side to a lee beach tail. Made by the glacier's retreat, perhaps. Who knew? It wasn't known. It wasn't important. The shape was what mattered. Rounded ovals, "the rounding of a woman's hip, the oval of a whaleback, the curve of the earth itself. Feast your eyes on them," his father told him. "No shape more pleasing to man." Nowhere else in all the world were drumlins so perfectly protected, thanks to the cliffs of Ironbound and Pearl Islands at the mouth of the bay. Beyond those last two, stretching out to the edge of wonder, was the rounded curve of the earth's blue orb.

Snow swirled and vanished in the black water. Nothing, his father said, is black and white. Simon turned in the late afternoon gloom up the hill toward the house, and the snow turned gray before his eyes.

THE WOMEN WERE crowding into the front hall, rubbing their hands and shaking snow off their boots. Gracious, when would the snow stop and wasn't it bitter out and didn't the fire smell good? Cold air clung to their wraps. Simon let it engulf him as he hung them on the wooden pegs. He helped his mother move the table closer to the hearth and pulled up a chair for old Mrs. Bethune, who said, as she always did, "I'll need a good stiff-backed chair that I don't sink into, Simon Peter, or I might never get up." He looked down at the top of her little gray head. If only she knew what a rotter her grandson was.

Young Fred wandered in, a couple of pencils in each fist, and found himself a spot under the parlor desk where, not surprisingly, his pencil people entered into a heated argument. Young Fred's pencil people talked a great deal more than he did. Their differences were rarely settled.

Simon pulled out a chair for Lady Bromley, who waved him off, saying she had things to dig out of her bag first. There was a good deal of talk about how Simon had grown, which he hadn't. The man of the house now, they said. He smiled and nodded, which was all the response they wanted, except for Delsie Walker, who took his hand and asked how his father was.

There was a sigh of relief when Ida bustled through the back door with apple squares to round out the crumbling shortbread his mother had made. "Your mother is many things, but a good cook isn't one of them," his Uncle Ebbin used to say as she set out failed bread, thin chowder or roast that stuck in your throat. She'd just shrug as if there were more important things in life than good cooking.

To Ida, there was nothing more important than good cooking, except maybe a clean floor. Nearly as old as his grandfather, the muscles in her short arms still jumped when she rolled out dough or kneaded bread. And lord help the bread if it didn't rise fast enough. She reminded Simon of a stout little kettle, bubbling over.

"Simon," Delsie was saying. "I have a new book for you. Came to me by way of Dr. McInnis in Halifax."

"Is it a novel?" asked Mrs. Bethune, suddenly animated. "I do like those. They can be stirring!"

"I'm so glad to hear you say that," Delsie said, patting her hand. "You must tell me what authors you like, and I'll try to get them in." The library was in her house.

Lady Bromley muttered darkly about current-day rubbish, but Delsie rifled through her yarn bag. "*First Voyage*, it's called. A boy who runs off on a ship to South America. Just your sort of adventure. Well, oh dear . . . looks like I forgot it. Stamped and everything."

Lady Bromley cleared her throat in disapproval—at the book or the delay in the proceedings or both—and asked for her shawl. Simon draped it around her shoulders. She slid her spectacles from the leather case on a black cord round her neck and gathered her papers.

"Lady B." was what Simon's father called her. She'd once been plain Hespera Church—something to remember when she was on her high horse, his grandfather liked to say. She'd fancied him in her youth, but her affections were not returned. Late in life, visiting relatives in England, she'd met and married Lord Edward Andrew Thurston Bromley—a man of title, a man of many promises, older than she, and thin as a rail. Back in Snag Harbor, he sat on the porch in summer, by the fire in winter, starting each day with a pint of beer and ending it the same way with nothing much going on in between. Undaunted by his lack of dash and property, Lady B. had assumed title enough for them both. And a bit of his British accent to boot.

The accent was in force as she suggested to Simon he might want to hear the first order of business. When he'd seen her the day before at the post office, she'd mentioned starting a local chapter of the Blue Cross, "Our Dumb Friends League," to support the horses in wartime. They'd had a nice talk about the help horses might need— stables to sleep in, blankets ("dreadful winter over there"), hay and oats, of course, and rubdowns after charging forth. She'd set her mail down and looked Simon square in the eye and said that he was as patriotic as the next boy and not to forget it. He liked hearing the word "patriotic" attached to himself.

It was not a word heard in the MacGrath house unless spat out in one of his grandfather's rants. Never mentioned by his mother, certainly. Even with his father in the Front Lines, she took neither inspiration nor comfort in words about love of country, duty or sacrifice. Once, when Simon pressed her for her opinion on the war, she shrugged and said, "What I think isn't important. I'm not the one in it. If I was, I'd be for it, as every man over there must be to survive. But since men I love are in it, I'm against it."

Across the table from Lady Bromley, his mother leaned for the bandage basket. Loose strands of her hair drifted down. She tucked them back with hazy indifference. Her slim ankles were crossed beneath her green wool skirt, her feet shod in shoes of a bright blue with short black heels and an openwork pattern of blue leather laces.

No one had laces like that, nor blue shoes. Not that color blue. His father had bought them for her in Yarmouth. Sky-blue shoes for a blue-sky summer day, he'd said with a rare carefree smile. She was so beautiful, it didn't matter, really, what her hair looked like or whether her shoes were right for winter. Her features were as fine as cut glass, but then, too, there was something slightly unraveled about her, some loose thread that Simon would very much have liked to have knotted up, but for which he was ready to defend her. In her world, clothes did not matter and time did not pass until she happened to glance at a clock. She could spend hours making fancy labels for jams, oblivious to the jam itself burning down to nothing on the stove.

Next to her, Ida, needles clacking, was turning out socks just like the ones she'd made for his father. Edith Andrews and Flora Zinck measured and snipped gauze and bandages, which Enid Rafuse and Delsie rolled to exacting Red Cross specifications. Maisie's mother sat back under the lamp sewing rolled hems on handkerchiefs. Mrs. Bethune was already asleep.

With many-chinned authority, Lady Bromley called the meeting to order, corrected Enid's minutes and approved his mother's treasurer's report. "Accurate, as always, Hettie, thank you."

His mother shrugged. "Numbers," she told Simon when he struggled over them, "are comforting. They never lie." She kept the books for Simon's grandfather. "You're a wonder," he'd say, shaking his head over a four-cent error she'd spotted or her offhand yet invariably accurate projection of net gains for the next quarter. "Been to the oracle, have you?" he'd ask. "Perhaps," she'd say with an air of secret amusement.

Lady Bromley smoothed out a letter. "This comes to us from a member of the Woman's Patriotic League of Toronto. She has a job for us. What she wants is sphagnum."

"*Sphagnum?*" Flora asked. The women stopped rolling. Ida stopped knitting.

"Yes, Flora, sphagnum moss. We can't collect it now, but come spring, we can and should."

"Why ever would they want them mosses?" Ida asked.

"Because," Lady Bromley read, "sphagnum *'can absorb twenty-five times its weight in liquid, more quickly than cotton, retains and distributes fluids better, and is more soothing.'* That's what the letter says."

"You mean peat moss," Ida broke in. "We're to put peat into dressings."

"Exactly, my dear Ida." Lady Bromley smiled with unmasked condescension. "Highlanders have used it to treat boils and wounds for centuries. Here, the president of the Royal College of Surgeons of England has a comment on what he calls the 'widespread persistence of sepsis.'" She ran a finger down the letter. "He says that last year they estimated that the minimum number of dressings needed would be thirty per man. And he says with the cost of cotton rising, sphagnum would be an excellent alternative."

"Thirty dressings per man?" Maisie's mother whispered.

Simon pictured a man with thirty wounds, patched together with sphagnum dressings.

"Thirty per man . . ." Enid Rafuse echoed.

"It's an *estimate*, a mathematical average," Lady Bromley said, looking to Hettie for confirmation.

"Did you hear about Rutherford Lynch over to Western Shore? Came back last week. Blinded by gas," Ida put in. "I wonder how poor George Mather's doing. Haven't seen him in months."

"Terrorizes his poor mother, I've heard. She's afraid to bring him to town," Flora said. "He poked my backside with one of his crutches at the post office last time I saw him."

"They say he's lost his mind since he's come back. He's a menace," Enid whispered. "He should be put away for his own sake . . . and his mother's."

"Ladies, please!" Lady Bromley broke in. "Let's not sink into discouraging talk. Our duty is to keep spirits lifted. Our boys depend on it. Now, here's where you come in, Simon. Organize some of your chums to gather moss from the bogs." She peered over her glasses. "How does that suit you?"

"Fine," Simon said. A manly way to do his bit.

"You're a stouthearted youngster, Simon. Maybe get your grandfather involved."

Glances were exchanged around the table. Lady Bromley sighed. "No, I suppose not. You'd think with his own son in it now. Well . . . Let's see, we're to clean and ship the moss to Halifax or Saint John. Obviously, we'll ship it to Halifax. Our own provincial Red Cross will be perfectly capable of making sphagnum dressings to spec. This is a great opportunity, a great war effort. Are we agreed?"

The women agreed.

"Except," Simon's mother said, retrieving a bandage that had unraveled across the table, "we shouldn't promise a set amount until we know what it takes to collect and clean it and how many men are around to help in the spring, with the fleet out."

Lady Bromley exhaled a long, loud breath. "Yes, yes. Thinking ahead. Good for you, Hettie. But you see, we're just trying to settle on a single effort, and I think we agree this is a good one."

Simon's mother brushed his back with a featherweight touch. "Get the tea ready, would you?" In the kitchen he rearranged his mother's random placement of cups on saucers—the rose cup on the rose saucer, the sweet-pea cup on the sweet-pea saucer—until they matched. The cups and the scalloped silver tray on which they sat had belonged to his grandmother Lauralee MacGrath, who'd come from Halifax, where ladies' teas had been the order of the day long before they'd been introduced for the war effort in Snag Harbor. Simon set the kettle to boil and put the comfort boxes he'd made on top of the basket of socks and gloves, wristlets, mufflers and sleeping caps knit by women too busy with chores and children to attend a ladies' tea.

He'd made four comfort boxes that month with money he'd earned at Mader's boatyard. He lifted the lid off one to admire the contents. Clean handkerchiefs! A chocolate bar to share with my chums! He waved the chocolate bar around, then rooted through the rest of the box. Look here now, pins to patch my uniform and string to tie my gloves to my belt. And a razor and soap to lather up with! A good razor was IMMEASURABLY APPRECIATED IN THE TRENCHES FOR THEIR SUPERIOR KEENNESS, the adverts in the *Halifax Chronicle* proclaimed. THE 85TH HIGHLANDERS OVERSEAS BATTALION, SONS OF ROBERT THE BRUCE, USE GILLETTE! THE LUSTY BEARDS OF SCOTTISH BLOOD GROW EVEN LUSTIER IN THE VIGOROUS LIFE OF ACTIVE SERVICE. The man with thirty wounds might need a nurse to open his box for him, but it would bring comfort and a clean shave. He'd know he wasn't forgotten.

Simon replaced the lid, pulled on his gloves, and leaped over the back steps. Snow was coming hard, a million flecks of ash against the slate sky. But on the ground, they fell flake on flake, each one glittering on top of the one beneath. He blew out a long breath, watched it hang in the air, then dashed into the path he'd dug to the sheds. He ran, then crouched, aware at every step of snipers nested behind the raspberry bushes, dug in on the slope to the west, watching his every move. Him without so much as a rifle. He had to make it to the shed. Now! Run for it! Fritz was spraying his machine guns at the trench. But wait! A Mills bomb in his jacket! One left. He pulled it out, released the pin, and tossed it into the raspberry bushes. BAM! Fifty Germans flung fifty feet in the air. Mad brutes! He didn't have time to watch. He was at the shed, bursting through, panting. He was a wonder! He was his father's son.

He collected the logs, carried them in, and dumped them in the bin by the kitchen stove. The wind moaned around the eaves. He considered the next installment of the story he was telling Young Fred at bedtime—a story loosely based on *Treasure Island* with himself as Jim Hawkins and Young Fred as a character he named "Finn Venable."

He gave a quick check to the goings-on in the parlor. Satisfied it was safe, he flipped open his copybook and withdrew the enlistment card.

The crouching ape in his German spike-tipped helmet leered up at him, clutching the fainting maiden in his brutish arm, her thin gown soaked and torn and twisted, one breast barely covered by her loosened hair, the other actually exposed. Simon focused on the breast, the faint nipple, the rounded curve. Behind the ape, a sinking navy ship, and beyond it, a town in flames. The ape's raging mouth exposed pointed fangs. In his free hand he carried a spiked club with the word "*Kultur*" dripping in blood on it. Culture—just as Mr. Heist had said. Culture and decency dragged into the mud by the Prussians. DESTROY THIS MAD BRUTE! arced over the ape's head in orange block letters. ENLIST! was printed at the bottom.

"Simon! Is that water boiling yet?" a distant voice called out.

The kettle! He threw his book on the table, grabbed a towel and lifted the kettle off the stove. His mother materialized by his side. She finished making the tea and ferried the pot, wrapped in the towel, into the parlor. He lifted the tray of cups and set it back down. The card. Where was it?

"My, what's this?" A gagging noise from Enid Rafuse. He rushed to the parlor where Delsie and Flora were slapping her on the back. Lady Bromley snatched up the card from her hand and adjusted her spectacles. Simon felt himself go warm, then cold. Young Fred came out from under the desk and stood by Lady Bromley. "Let me see! Let me see!" he cried, reaching up for the card.

"Good day, ladies!" Simon's grandfather called from the kitchen. He stamped the snow off his feet and strode in. "Sorry to interrupt. Snow's coming hard and the wind's kicked up. Might be a blizzard. I just saw Walter Zinck coming up the road to fetch some of you, and I've got Rooster chomping at the bit, ready to take the rest of you home . . ." He stopped short at the face-fanning and throat-clutching. "What's all this now? Has Enid taken a pale spell?"

"A bit of a shock, is all, from a recruitment card," Lady Bromley said.

"Recruitment card? Are you passing those out to the ladies here, Hespera? Figuring they'll join up?" His tone was light, but he was clearly not amused. "Let's have a look."

"It was attached to the teapot and towel. A rather graphic display of the Hun's treachery. Not for the faint of heart." Lady Bromley held the card to her chest, staring pointedly at Enid, who cleared her throat and declared herself recovered.

Like the unfolding of a bad dream, Simon watched his grandfather take the card, hold it at arm's length, and slowly lower it. With his back to Simon, he said, "Where did this come from?" He waited until Simon said softly, "It's mine, sir."

"No reason to get after the boy, Duncan," Lady Bromley said, adjusting her shawl. "It may violate decency, but if it promotes enlistment, then we have to say it is perfectly legitimate." Young Fred was twisting his head upside down to see the card. Hettie pulled him into her lap.

"Perfectly legitimate—this slathering ape?"

"A depiction of the *enemy*, Duncan."

"Prussians," Simon blurted out. "Not all Germans, just Prussians." His grandfather slowly turned to him. "Mr. Heist. He said it's not Germans," Simon stammered. "Not Bavarians, anyway—it's the Prussians started it. He said so. Not all of Germany. So the ape must be . . . Prussian."

"You got this from *Avon Heist*?" Duncan's eyes went wide.

"No! No sir. From Hennigar's. Mr. Heist was just saying in class that it was the Prussians. They're against freedom. They—"

"Mr. Heist!" Lady Bromley threw her shoulders back. "What's he on about, splitting hairs over who is and is not the enemy? At present we're at war with all of Germany, I believe, and Herr Heist would do well to remember that!"

Staring right at her, Duncan ripped the card down the middle, and ripped it again.

"Don't you look at me that way, Duncan. What do we know about him anyway, out there on the Point all alone? What's he doing tricking our students? Parceling up Germany into Bavarians and Prussians and who knows what. It's ridiculous. Unpatriotic, and just what one might expect from—"

"From . . . ?" Duncan sprinkled the shreds into the fire where flames licked them to curling ash—the beast, the breast and all. He turned to the women and in an even tone said, "I've got Rooster hitched up and can take you ladies home. The snow will be getting worse before it gets better."

In equally measured words Lady Bromley said, "Thank you, Duncan. A most generous offer. We can meet at my house next Thursday. We have our boys overseas to think of. There's a war on." She collected her papers and put her spectacles in their case.

As the women gathered their things, Duncan clamped his hand on Simon's shoulder without looking at him and said, "I'm ashamed of you and for you."

When he was gone, Simon marched to the kitchen and threw on his father's heavy wool shirt. He slammed the door and didn't care. Ashamed, was he? His father wouldn't be ashamed of an enlistment card.

In the unyielding cold of the woodshed, everything was still. Next to the wood pile, the door to his father's art shed stood open a crack. The padlock hung at an angle from the latch. Just like that. Who'd have done it? Who had the key? His mother? His grandfather? Ida? They had no right.

He poked the door with two fingers. It swung open in silent invitation. He ducked under the old beam and went down the two steps into the room and breathed in his father in the turpentine and linseed oil. In the gathering twilight he made out curled tubes of paint, stiff with cold, a jar of brushes, a scatter of sketches. On the broad shelf by the row of south-facing windows, the cans of turpentine, pens, an old inkwell and a pile of rags took shape. To the left of the woodstove, his father's paint-splattered stool.

Simon glanced at the sketches. A curlew in flight. A single herring gull. Two loons in charcoal. Some boats and seascapes. The kind of pictures his father sold up in Halifax and along the way on cargo runs. He lifted a piece of chalk from its case and put it back. He unscrewed the cap of a tube of oil paint and sniffed it.

He turned to go, but stopped at the sight of a sheet-shrouded canvas, three times the size of all the others, on the easel in the corner. He hesitated only a moment before pulling off the sheet. Rough splotches of color filled the lower half of the canvas. Simon had to step back for it to take shape. A dory? A rowboat? The beginning of an oar here, the man's hand on it. Another hand, a boy's hand, hovering above it. The start of torsos, the boy between the man's legs, yes, silver paint splattered everywhere around them, and then the canvas was blank. It was as if the man and the boy were rowing from the room right into the bottom of the picture, as if standing there, he was on the boat himself. Then he realized he was. Collar up, shoulders hunched, hands in his pockets, he did not move until darkness fell around him.

FIVE

February 18th, 1917
Arras Sector, France

"February 18th, 1917," Angus wrote at the top of the tablet in his lap. He ran a filthy hand through his filthy hair. The sack of censored letters slumped beside him on the frozen ground of the dugout. Some he'd censored himself, as was required of junior officers—a task he found embarrassing, and one which Publicover sailed through on the winds of duty. I get through mine in ten minutes flat, he told Angus. Just scan for anything that reveals location or tactics and for grievances against king and country, the CEF or the top brass. No need to get bogged down with memories of apple blossoms or hopes for Aunt Bertie's recovery.

In the process Angus had learned a few things about his men—that some, like Boudrey, could barely write; that Katz, McNeil and Wertz could turn a phrase with ease; and that some wrote no letters at all. Many were homesick, some heartsick, but they generally refrained from self-pity. Survival demanded that someone, somewhere, had it worse.

There was about an hour of daylight left, Angus figured, maybe twenty minutes of it to himself. By midnight, he'd be gone. His men, too. Off the Front Line trenches and back to the camps a few miles behind the line to drill and train, and then sent up again in the regular rotation. Two weeks done. Still alive.

He stared at the page and flexed his hand. "Dear Family" he began, then wrote with abandon,

As I write this, I'm still alive, though God knows why because, despite the unrelenting boredom, the possibility of death is in every corner, every timber, every moldering bag of sand, in the very air we breathe and the filth we lie in. It is in the faces of the men and in my every dream. As we wait and wait some more, spirits are kept up with fresh news of the enemy's treachery which we in turn inflict. It is a grim madness in which grand purpose is lost and men die regardless. As for Ebbin, I am no closer to the truth than I was before I left.

He flipped the page over. Get a grip. At the very least he had to respond to Hettie's letter telling him that her parents had gotten word—Ebbin had been officially declared missing in action. "At least not 'known dead.' Missing suggests hope," she'd written. Christ.

He blew on his hands and picked up the pen. The pen had curves in mind. That was the problem. The rounded head and upturned throat of a speckled lark, the V of its beak opened in song. Sketching would settle him. Write! he told himself.

He stared down at the mail sack. Half the letters in it were Field Service Postcards. This was the choice of Boudrey, who dutifully filled one out every day. Angus helped him memorize the boxes you could check: "I am quite well" or "I have been admitted to hospital." After the word "hospital," you could pick "sick" or "wounded," followed by either "and am getting on well" or "hope to be discharged soon." There were no options for "my arm's been blown off" or "been blinded by gas" or "the doctors don't think I'll recover." If there had been, they would have been followed by "but otherwise in the pink."

Thus, the ranks could send word home without actually sending words.

Which seemed an excellent idea. Words were too paltry and powerful, both. To write home was to evoke home. And to evoke home was to risk images of home that, like whirring shrapnel, could slice through the simplest of tasks and render him impotent.

Should he write about his first patrol and the mortar attack that left him uncertain which way was up and left the sergeant, Ricketts, not ten feet away, with his throat sliced open? Keegan was elevated to sergeant the next day. Whizbangs, Angus had learned, gave a warning whiz on release, but were so fast to explode it didn't much matter. Like so much else at the Front, mortar attacks seemed disconnected from human motives, launched by a shadowy menace across the void who every now and then showed a helmet, fired a gun, raised a sausage.

Which again made him think of the bird. And the German.

He'd seen them both that morning. Wertz, Hanson and Boudrey were crouched near a pot of water, waiting for tea. Boudrey, the mouth-breather, was so young and gullible, he'd taken on the status of a mascot. The men figured if he made it through, they would, too. Just as the water began to steam, the heady smell of cooked sausages wafted over the sandbags. It filled the nostrils and made the mouth water.

McNeil grabbed the periscope. At that moment, what looked like a bunch of sausages, fixed to a bayonet, rose high above the German parapet.

"Fritzie's showing us his sausages," McNeil said, still at the periscope.

"Yeah, you can drop the periscope. We all see them, smart boy," Kearns said.

"Sausages? Fucking Kraut bastards! Let's show him what Canadians have for breakfast!" Keegan, thick-set and agile, lunged into a funk hole and came up with a German helmet. This he balanced on the tip of his rifle, rattling it above the sandbags at the parapet. "How'd you like that, eh, Fritz?" He grinned back at the others, a toothpick between his teeth. The men sniggered.

Angus yanked his arm down. "Want them to send you a couple of whizbangs for breakfast? Set an example here, Sergeant." Keegan's mouth fell open. The helmet bounced on the hardened mud.

Angus took the periscope from McNeil and had a quick look for other signs from the enemy. The sausages waved about. No other movement in the German trench, but his eye caught something that he couldn't quite make out further east where No Man's Land widened out. A German appeared to be hanging on the barbed wire. Angus looked again. No, just a gray tunic, the German no longer in it. A hanging scarecrow. And something else. A bird flitted about its crumpled arms. It fluttered straight up, then darted down, and hopped gamely to the empty neck of the coat. There it tipped its head back and opened up in song. The song filled the air and the men were quiet. The sausages went down.

"I believe there's a bird nesting out there on a Kraut jacket," Angus said.

"Yes sir. Been there a week," Wertz replied.

"The tunic or the bird?"

"Both."

This set off an argument between McNeil and Katz as to whether they had been there a week or a week and a half.

"And the owner of the uniform?" Angus broke in impatiently.

"Below, sir."

"That's where I got my helmet," Keegan offered.

Angus risked another look with the periscope and saw the slumped form below the coat. Trousers, suspenders. His first German soldier. Saw the bloating. Imagined Ebbin left hanging askew on the wire, his features swollen beyond recognition. Wondered if anyone had found Wickham, pulled him out. "Is that a lark?"

"Appears so to us, sir. Sounds like it, too. Now, it could be a different species of lark or . . ." Wertz answered.

"Don't larks nest on the ground?" Angus demanded, as if the habits of larks had taken on military significance.

"Exactly. How could it be a lark?" McNeil asked with a trace of triumph.

"You can see the problem, sir. No grass," Wertz replied, calmly lighting his pipe.

IT WAS THIS bird his pen wanted to re-create for the very reasons the soldiers looked for it daily. A grace note. He'd have liked to include the incident in a letter, but it would hardly translate—not without inflicting the unspeakable upon the innocent.

Angus jerked open the dugout door. To his left, Hanson and Tanner sat solemnly popping lice eggs off their uniforms with lit matches. Two others beyond them were hunched over, staring dumbly at the ground in a waking sleep. Everyone was short on sleep. A medical officer told Angus it was the source of delusions and hallucinations that afflicted men and officers alike in the trenches.

The slice of sky above was dull gray, but welcome. At night, that same sky pulsed with mortar fire and blinding flares—star shells and Verey lights—as sentries were posted, snipers took aim, engineers laid wire, sappers dug saps, tick-tick-ticking their picks against the chalk earth while ammunition, sacks of tea, jam, bread, bully beef and beans, bags of mail, more sandbags to be filled, more duckboards, tarpaulins, and wire were brought up by men with white eyes in dark faces.

The pounding seas, the flat calms, the rise and fall of swells. These were the rhythm of his being—not this man-made underworld. Men said that life in the trench was like being buried alive. More like an open grave, Angus decided, where, panting and immobilized, you waited for that first shovel of dirt.

Far down the line from his section of trench and across No Man's Land, the seven-mile length of Vimy Ridge loomed, honeycombed with three rows of German bunkers and trenches. With 150,000 French and British troops lost trying to take it for two years, Angus had been prepared for a towering presence. But no. Even from a ground-eye view, it was a gradual grade, maybe a mile to the top—a hulking rogue wave that could suck you into its undertow, bury you beneath its fathoms, and move on.

In heaving seas and flying foam, Angus had somehow always managed to find the slot—the physical slot between wind and water that kept the boat afloat and the mental slot between anger at God and the hope He would save you—the point at which outward displays of courage transformed to courage itself. He knew that slot, but didn't know if he could find it here.

"What's *our* quarrel with Germany? Empire be damned!" his father had said when Angus told him he'd joined up. "Men on both sides turned to cannon fodder. Without them, the high and mighty would find another way to settle differences." To which Angus had countered, "You call a bald-faced grab for Europe, for England, a matter of *differences*?"

His father's white sleeves had glowed against the dark wool vest in the fading light. His white hair, too. His short, muscular frame barely contained his fury. He'd leaned over his desk, and said, "You can't be serious about this. You're my *son*. We're pacifists, for Chrissake!" And Angus had shot back, "*You're* the pacifist!" He'd refused to repeat that he'd be behind the lines. His father's response had triggered a foolish desire to be in the thick of it.

And now he was.

Besides dodging whizbangs, his role at the Front had been limited to keeping morale up and his head down, with a lot of supervisory tasks in between. He'd gotten to know his men, not just by their letters, but by their feet as he inspected them for oozing blisters and applied cold whale oil to them. His silent ministrations gave him the chance to check for the dreaded trench foot, which could turn feet to necrotic, misshapen blobs from the damp, from constriction and cold. Afterwards, as needed, he'd hand out clean wool socks sent over by women's groups at home. The men took them without making eye contact, probably figuring that Angus, like the other lieutenants, would be dead and gone long before the battle took place. Except for Boudrey, who always stuck his feet straight out and said, "Thank you, sir."

The battle for Vimy was months away. Everyone knew it, including the Germans. In the endless stagnation, the demoralizing term "war of attrition" had been bandied about. "Attrition?" Publicover said. "Heck, I don't even know what that word *means*. Don't care if I do. All I know is we're getting ready for the big show, and when it comes, oh mother, oh brother, *then* there'll be action! Plenty of it!" And so they waited. And across No Man's Land, soldiers just like them blew on their hands in the cold.

Angus drew a breath, put pen to the page, and in minutes produced a remarkably detailed sketch of the lark, five-inch barbs to either side of it, mouth opened in song. He placed it in his case just as Publicover bounded in. "I just passed Hiller. Pathetic," he said, and started packing his kit.

"He's a worry," Angus agreed. He'd found Hiller that morning, hands in his armpits, crouched in a funk hole. Angus had to shake him to get his attention, and when he stood, the tremors started up again.

"Hiller *should* worry you. A coward pushing for sick leave is what he is."

"What makes you so sure?"

"Because I know one when I see one. He wants out."

"A reasonable response."

"Exactly. Faking it. Either way, he's a danger. Believe me, when one of your own is a coward, you'll wish him dead when the bullets fly."

"I'm sending him to a camp doctor when we're back of the line." Angus reached for the photo envelope lying next to his writing tablet and ran his hand over the soft leather cover of it. On one side, Hettie Ellen—her high cheekbones, a slight upward turn of her chin, her lips softly parted as if distracted by something offstage. On the other side, Young Fred in short pants looked sternly at the camera. Simon Peter, arm around him, struck a happy-go-lucky pose. "Don't go," Young Fred said solemnly to Angus at the station in Chester the day he left. Angus had taken Simon aside, away from old Athol McLaren, who was strolling the platform, wheezing out send-off tunes on the pipes as best he could. Angus had put his hands on Simon's shoulders and looked him in the eye, intending to say something profound. But all he could manage was, "You're the best boy in the whole wide world. Not one boy better. You know that, don't you?" Then he pulled him in tight as the train pulled into the station. Through the clouds of steam he saw Hettie. Her hat blew up in the breeze.

What Angus remembered since was not their words so much as the spaces between them, the unspoken certainty of their decision that he should go and the heart-stopping reality that he was. What he remembered, too, was the feel of his hands around her slim frame, the slight arch of her back as she handed Young Fred off to Ida. He knew that arch, the vulnerable small of her back, her head thrown back. Even there on the platform, it seemed a long-ago dream.

As Angus stepped onto the train, she clutched his arm. Don't, he thought. Don't have doubts now.

"Promise you'll be safe," she said.

"You know I will. It's London! I'll be completely safe," he'd said as the wheels started to roll and her hand slipped away. "I'll find him," he said. "You're the man of the house now, Simon Peter!" he called out to the boy, whose face was crumpling. "Proud of you already."

"Must miss her terribly, eh?" Publicover opened the tin of

matches. "She's a peach from that picture you carry. Lucky for me I left no sweetheart behind. Maybe find one in Paris when the war's over. Course by then I'll be too old for romance." He flashed a grin and sat down. He had a beautiful smile, full of grace and happy expectation, as if the world had nothing but good things to offer. He struck a match on his thumbnail, watched it burn out, then struck another.

"You intending to use up all those matches?"

"That's my plan . . ."

Angus screwed the cap on his pen and held out his hand. Publicover reluctantly handed over the jar of matches. It was not the first time they'd been through this. Angus put them on the shelf, then glanced at the picture of Hettie once more before putting the envelope in his breast pocket. She was a beauty, alright. Spitting image of her mother, it was said—the wild and beautiful Ellen Langston, from Alberta. Buried out there when Ebbin and Hettie were barely out of the cradle. Angus had seen Amos Hant, with a few drinks in him, shake uncontrollably at the sight of Hettie entering a room. Trying to comfort him only made it worse, Hettie said.

Publicover leaned back on his bunk, arms behind his head. "Here's my plan, when we're off the line. Hot bath, first off, then a long, uninterrupted sleep. The Princess Pats can't get here soon enough for my money. I know a couple of those boys. Good lot, mostly, but I'll be happy to say, 'see ya boys,' as we pass in the night. Or wait, did I say the Pats? It's not them. It's some McBride's Kilties taking our places. Anyway, hot bath. Down pillow. Mother, mother, mother, pin a rose on me. How about you?"

"Me? Billets aboveground will do—a place that you don't burn down. Then, sleep without rats and your snoring. Then see if I can find out more on Ebbin."

"So, 'missing in action' isn't good enough . . ."

"No. Plus a friend at home thought he saw him around Courcelette."

"Yeah. Wouldn't be enough for me either, if he was my brother or pal or whatever he was—is, I mean."

"Brother-in-law. You have a brother?"

"Nope. Tons of sisters. I told you before. Back home baking pies."

"Pies?"

"Apple pies. Apple butter. Apple jack. Don't you listen? The apple orchard in the Annapolis Valley—a place called Paradise?"

"Ah yes, Paradise."

"Born and raised there."

"Lucky you."

"Lucky me—long as I end up there." Publicover swung his legs onto the floor and leaned forward with his head down. "Not everyone is, you know. Lucky. Can't always find the tags. It's not always bodies, it's bits. Hate to say it, but you know it's the truth. The 12th went through it. We all did." He looked up slowly.

Angus held his gaze and without warning found himself flung across the dugout. A few feet away, Publicover hunched on the shuddering ground. In the thunderous boom of the explosions and stuttering confusion, a crate rattled toward Angus. The shriek of a shell filled the air, and then another. Angus gasped for a breath, just one breath to get his lungs going. Breath came when he saw a timber falling. He lunged for Publicover and yanked him out from under just in time.

"Hit the line!" Publicover coughed out as he got to his feet. "Something blew. Underground maybe. A mine or—"

THE SHELLS HADN'T hit the line. They hit part of the communication trench just behind the line, wiping out eleven of the Kilties and wounding three of their officers. As for the explosion, Publicover was right. Mills bombs, stored in a tunnel, had gone off. God only knew how many dead there, Conlon said. He told them he and some hand-picked officers would stay on an extra night to settle the Kilties while their own boys marched back. Publicover and Grafton, a lieutenant Angus had met only in passing, were to accompany them. Angus was to stay on the line with Conlon and help sort things out.

The Kilties straggled up. Shadowy forms on the way out cursed forms on the way up as rifles struck packs and picks struck helmets and men tripped over cables and missed their step on the duckboards. Eventually, their own boys formed up, Publicover in the lead, fol-lowed by Angus's platoon—Hiller, in a trance, then Wertz, older than the rest, helping Boudrey get his footing, then Eisner and Bremner, both burly Lunenburgers, the ever-steady Hanson, and then Zwicker, a thick-set man with a high-pitched laugh. Then came McNeil and Katz, the scribbler. Ostler, shadowy and brooding, shoved Tanner onward. Then came the baby-faced LaPointe and the quick-tempered Kearns, a good man to have when the line was the Front and the Krauts the ones crossing it. Oxner must have been up ahead. Sergeant Keegan, a fast-moving troglodyte, brought up the rear. Ghost figures all of them. Then they were gone.

The Kilties were given a ration of rum. Mules coming up had been scattered to the winds when the shells hit, and with them went small-arms ammunition, adding to the light show behind the line. It was pretty clear the Germans knew the exact location of the communica-tion trench.

As if in confirmation, another mortar sailed overhead directly toward it. A 5.9 by the roils of black smoke. Publicover. His men. Angus gripped the timbered wall for support. A white-faced Conlon pointed to two privates and told Angus to take them out to Vicar's Crater. His hand was shaking, but his voice never wavered—routine patrol, he said, just like every other night at Vicar's.

Vicar's was a crater into which a padre was rumored to have vanished, a myth no stranger than any other in the trenches—the Angels of Mons, hovering ghost soldiers in the sky, witnessed by hundreds up and down the line in 1915; the Crucified Canadian, a soldier said to have been spread-eagled by the Germans on a tree with bayonets for nails. The Front was as rife with omens and visions as long voyages at sea. And who knew? Maybe in this bleak world of extremes, a padre could vanish and the dead could return. Angus felt himself nearly vanishing. He steadied himself as the privates stuffed extra flares, flare guns, and Mills bombs into their packs. There was a grenade launcher at the site. Conlon narrowed his eyes at Angus. "Focus on the Hun across that crater. Any movement, any sound, take the bastards out," he said.

Angus took a deep breath and eased himself over the parapet. The privates followed. Archer was an "original"—in the war from the start, that much Angus knew. Another, Andrew Dickey, a fresh recruit who looked about twelve with eyes round as saucers, had stammered out that his sergeant was wounded in the explosion as they came up. That he was screaming and couldn't move. Was he still out there? he asked Angus. Angus had considered replacing him, but with whom? He didn't know the Kilties. Besides, there wasn't time.

Now they were inching on their elbows along the shallow ditch that would take them up a slope to the crater rim, too wide in the darkness to make out the German patrol that was surely on the other side. The going was slow as they cleared debris out of their way, desperate to keep from making a sound. Finally, near the edge of the crater, they slid into a low ditch next to the grenade launcher. Angus ordered Archer to take up the left post and Dickey to take up the right. A curtain of silence hung in the air.

Dickey crept into position, but kept looking back at Angus. An hour went by. Suddenly, a Verey light shot up and blossomed into arcing stars. Under its thumping silver-white light, everything below stuttered like a flickering film. Angus saw Dickey, head down on his arms. Tiny points of red light darted about. Rat eyes. The light died out, and sparks showered down like fading fireworks at a county fair.

Then things were still again. Except for a low moaning that turned into a wail and kept up and kept up, faded, and started up again. Dickey looked back anxiously at Angus. Angus shook his head. The boy turned around, but kept craning his neck toward the source of the cries so Angus elbowed over and stretched out beside him. He could feel Dickey shudder down the length of his body. Dickey lifted a finger from his rifle in the direction of the cries, then dropped his rifle and covered his ears. Angus carefully removed the rifle. "Might be one of ours on patrol," Dickey whispered. "Why doesn't anyone help him?"

Angus clamped a hand over the boy's mouth, the lips continuing to move against his palm, the eyes pleading. Angus wanted to strangle him. He could not risk explaining that the cries were probably fake, a way of luring them over, or that, even if it was one of theirs, a separate party would have to go out. He shook his head no, no, no. He'd have to get the kid back to the ditch.

Another flare turned the ground red. Dickey arched up and pointed to the German tunic, still hanging on the wire. No! Angus lunged for him, grabbed him, but not fast enough. Dickey rolled out and ran toward the German tunic, a zigzagging figure under yet another Verey light, until he reached the coat and fell to the ground beneath it as machine-gun fire kept at him, twisting him this way and that and making him jump and jump some more. Then the air was alive with bullets screaming past Angus, bouncing off the hardened mud. He covered his head with his arms and somehow made it back to the ditch where Archer was already training the grenade launcher toward the machine-gun nest. "Bastards! Bastards!" he was shouting. Beyond them, Dickey kept jumping as bullets sliced him up. Archer got a bullet in the leg. Angus shoved him aside and slipped the grenade in the launcher and fired it off. They heard the explosion and saw a helmet fly up. The gun across No Man's Land was silenced, and the air filled with the sound of men screaming. Angus loaded the grenade launcher again and fired off another shot, and another, until the screaming stopped.

"We're okayed to go back. Get your gear and meet me back here," Conlon said to Angus when he made his report that morning. "Good job with that MG nest. Another body under that tunic. Christ. I'll find one of the officers with the 35th. They can send someone out to get him—Dickey, was it?—and have them take that blasted tunic down."

Angus grabbed his pack and stuffed the leather drawing portfolio in it. Clouds roiled overhead, and the wind picked up. The temperature was dropping fast, as Publicover said it would. Publicover . . . he hardly knew him and had known him all his life.

He lifted a shred of paper stuck to his boot—just the head and open beak of the bird on the wire remained. He crumpled it, then lit a cigarette with shaking hands and fixed his eye on the ridge—its slopes no longer a rising wave, but a menacing man-made monster—its teeth, three parallel lines of twisting trenches lined with rifles and bayonets; its intestines, the concrete bunkers, pillboxes and tunnels from which its spike-helmeted minions rose up and trained their mortar and machine guns on the Allied armies below. And on one poor boy Angus should have been able to save. He imagined the Germans biding their time, occasionally mowing down an advancing army. He imagined them lolling on their guns, eating sausages and smiling.

He spat on the ground. *Fucking Kraut bastards.*

Snow began to fall on his shoulders. He barely noticed. Conlon shadowed up beside him. They said not a word and headed out together.

⸙

CONLON TOOK AN offshoot that led to the labyrinthine Grange Tunnel, the underworld engine of war. Electric wires snaked along narrow-gauge tracks, illuminated by a series of bulbs encased in wire cages. Their light was yellow; the air, dank and close. A signpost greeted them, its arrows, like so many arms, pointed toward connect-ing subways that led to kitchens, an infirmary, storage areas, reserve stations, munitions dumps, officers' quarters. Their path took them past a giant water cistern, purification pumps plunging, pipes and valves sweating. A ghoulish line of soldiers tramped by, and the sweet notes of "Annie Laurie" floated out from a cave that could easily have held a hundred men but now had only four—two playing cards, one sleeping against his pack, one blowing gently into a mouth organ, eyes closed. "And for bonnie Annie Laurie, I'd lay me down and dee." Another column of men squeezed by before Conlon finally turned up a set of stairs and out.

They emerged to the relief of an open sky and a sweep of snow-dusted fields. Angus almost fell to his knees. In the distance, perched precariously on the only visible hilltop, was the ruined village of Mont-Saint-Eloi, the sun just catching the jagged-finger remains of its abbey spires. The fanning rays held the new day suspended until seconds later, a blushed dawn broke. Angus breathed in deeply and turned full circle, arms out.

"Not much for tunnels, eh?" Conlon said.

They fell in behind a column of soldiers and mules. In the next vil-lage, Conlon cut into an ancient cemetery and wound his way through the headstones, some tilted, some sunk into the ground. "Shortcut," he said, but then he stopped and took out his canteen. Angus lit a cig-arette and looked down at a stone slab. Leprosy-like fingers of lichen had eaten into the name and date. Conlon, canteen in hand, leaned against the pockmarked stone base of a winged angel with a missing nose and chipped cheek. Angus followed the outward sweep of the wing.

"What's the point?" Conlon sighed.

"The point?" Angus repeated dully.

"Of this." Conlon waved his canteen toward the graves. "Headstones, markers. Trying to wrest permanence out of fleeting existence. Crumbling to nothing, eh? Can't even read the names." He pulled out a cigarette and said, "Don't bury me under a stone. Please. Burn my remains and take them back to the old country, then scatter them to the four winds."

"Where exactly in the old country?"

"County Armagh, where right now McCuskers and Conlons are no doubt plotting against the Brits over their pints. And here I am fighting for them. Come to think of it, you might have to scatter my remains in secret."

Angus gave a fleeting smile, but said nothing. Dickey, jumping forever like a puppet on a string, Wickham's boots forever slipping into a sink hole—he wanted them lowered slowly, placed gently. Wanted that pause when the universe sensed their leaving.

"We'll bury ours out here after the big show," Conlon said. "The Empire already has an agreement with France for the land. We'll have our cemeteries. Do already, for some battles."

"You don't find that comforting?"

Conlon looked up at the gray angel. "The poets, they're the ones who remember what we can't speak of."

"Ah yes, the glory that was Troy. But it's heroes and heroic events that the poets write about. What about the common foot soldier? They need to be remembered. Have a grave, a marker."

"The living need the marker."

"Fair enough."

"And you're wrong. Each man is there in the poem. Communal remembering of communal actions. That's the point. Otherwise what *is* the point?" Conlon held the canteen near his mouth. "So, tell me, are you a believer?" He took a long swallow. "From Publicover's telling, you had the men wondering if you were an officer or a man of the cloth. Said the men call you 'Padre.'"

"*Padre?* Because of Orland? It was nothing. Just a piece of the burial service to send him on—to help his brother accept it." Angus turned to go.

Conlon didn't move. "You just happen to know the burial service by heart." He capped the canteen and crossed his arms. "Been to your fair share of funerals, have you?"

"Two years of Anglican seminary," Angus sighed. "Never graduated. That bit remains in my head. Maybe I was meant to bury people."

"Seminary," Conlon repeated.

"My father's idea." Angus crushed out his cigarette. "Padre. I don't like it."

"Well," Conlon sighed, "they called the last lieutenant, name of Benniton, 'Bunny.' As I heard it, 'soft on the men *and* soft in the head,' so you're one up there."

"What do they call Publicover?"

"Fearless."

"Of course. Cocky enough to make that fit."

"Trust me, it does. So what happened in seminary, Padre? Lose the faith?"

Angus winced. "I wouldn't say that. Lost interest in professing it. Or professing it in other people's terms."

"How about here? Faith holding up?" Conlon smiled, then squinted up again at the angel, patted her once more and said, "We can joke, but faith is about all you've got here. So you'd better hold on to it—whether in God or the cause or the dream that you'll come home in one piece. We didn't know that boy."

"Dickey?" Angus steeled himself for the dressing down he deserved. It was high time Conlon acknowledged what they both knew—he wasn't cut out to be a soldier, let alone an officer.

"That's right. I know what you're thinking," Conlon said. "Who knew he'd fall apart? Who knows when anyone will? No one's to blame, not even Dickey. Shoulder responsibility, fine, but don't let guilt cripple you."

"Yes sir."

"Drop the sir. We're having a conversation here. I'm the one picked him. You followed orders." Conlon put his hands on his hips, head down. "You had a crew under you on that boat, made choices, some good, some bad, I'd guess. Risked men's lives. Whatever it took to move on then, call on it now."

Angus took a deep breath and looked beyond the graves. "They kept at it, you know, long after he was gone. Kept him dancing, strafing him with bullets. Death should be . . ." Sacred, holy, he wanted to say.

"Dickey was gone with the first bullet. Gone before that, apparently. And I'm not saying *forget* Dickey. I'm saying *remember* him. Don't let his death be a waste. Dickey doesn't need a stone marker. He needs you." He leaned back against the angel with his cigarette between his thumb and forefinger, squinting at the curl of smoke. "So do I. You're a good man, MacGrath. You lost Dickey and took out a slew of Germans. That many less to kill our boys." With that he flicked his cigarette away and shoved off.

Angus picked up his gear and followed. In all his focus on Dickey, he'd forgotten the Germans, their silenced screams. He'd moved beyond them just as any "good" soldier would.

"How close do you think that 5.9 was to the men last night?" he asked when he caught up to Conlon.

"I'm doing my best not to think about it," Conlon answered.

"I hope to God Publicover is as lucky as he says he is."

"We can hope. Speaking of which, this brother-in-law of yours . . . what's his name?" Conlon turned down an alley between the church and a row of brick houses.

"Hant, Ebbin Hant." The sound of Ebbin's name reverberated against the abandoned houses, empty barns and granaries. "Got word from home that he's been officially declared missing."

"Progress . . . might make some more when we get to Arras. Check the records, now that it's official."

"Pretty idiotic to think I'd find him here," Angus said, to counter hope.

"Not necessarily." Conlon glanced up at the sky. "But you're maybe better off not searching too hard, if he's what's keeping you going."

A rooster clucked under a limber as they came out of the alley. A sergeant behind a group of privates barked orders and insults. The rooster strutted through the line and back again. From the loft of an abandoned stone house with startlingly blue shutters, a large wardrobe tipped forward and disgorged a banner of fabric in the exact same blue, fluttering up and away against the pale sky. French blue, Angus decided. He lusted after it, the purity of that blue.

He fell into step with Conlon, who said they'd better hurry if they were to make the briefing he'd failed to mention to Angus. But he just kept on at his same steady pace. They made it, just barely, as officers filed in and took their seats in the great hall of the château that was HQ. Angus and Conlon searched the crowd for Publicover.

"Sir!" a voice behind them said. Publicover saluted and clicked his heels with exaggerated formality and gave a short bow. Conlon gripped his shoulder. Angus slapped him on the back.

"Yessiree, I made it. And all the boys, too. Even Boudrey. I had them moving along so smartly that the 5.9 fell behind us. Been off the line for sixteen hours now, and no one's got killed. Not by mortar, not by their own hand. Amazing, eh?" He kept right on talking as they found their seats. "Me and Grafton spent the night in a barn with the men. They'll be in tents today. Supposed to be more Nissen huts erected. My guess? They'll be ready when the war's over. Got some cozy little digs for us 'til our quarters are ready, MacGrath. Good from the outside anyway. Haven't been inside yet. Met the proprietor—proprietess, I should say. Skinny woman, sour, too, from what I saw. So," he looked at them both, "whatchya been up to without me?"

"MacGrath here went on patrol. To Vicar's Crater," Conlon said. "Took out a machine-gun nest."

"One of ours?" Publicover grinned.

The room fell quiet and the men snapped to attention as high-ranking officers and their aides strode in from a side door. "Major Rushford, there, the spindly one, and that's Colonel Stokes, brigade commander," Publicover whispered to Angus. "This is it," Publicover whispered. "The whole brigade. They got something to say."

"Doubtful," Conlon replied.

A silver-haired spitfire of a man, Stokes hopped nimbly up on the raised platform. Career army, not to be trifled with, Conlon had said earlier. Behind him, Rushford stood a head taller. Rushford's polished leather belt cinched a narrow waist. His tapered nose twitched above a neatly trimmed reddish mustache. He was prim, almost prissy. It was his adjunct who'd sent Angus up with Wickham that first night.

Stokes clasped his hands behind his back and scanned the officers for a long minute. There were a few errant coughs and then silence. "At ease!" he barked. "Take your seats." Behind him hung a map of the entire Artois Sector. He thwacked his crop against the town of Arras. "I'm here to speak about the Battle of Arras. About a month ago, General Byng got word that the Canadians are to take this Ridge. Vimy. You know that."

"Told you," Conlon whispered. "This is all show."

Angus fixated on the map. The world had come down to a ten-mile stretch of land from the Souchez River in the north to the remains of Arras in the south.

"For us the Battle of Arras will *be* the Battle of Vimy Ridge," Stokes said. "Now . . ." On cue, his aide flipped the map back, revealing a detailed view of the Vimy Sector. Stokes slowly drew his crop from top to bottom. "This, *right here*, is our chance to prove ourselves— we've been in this war from the start, but now, for the first time, the Canadian Expeditionary Force is gathered into one great army, all four divisions lined up—the *only* force in the Empire, outside of the Imperials themselves, to stand as an army unto itself. For what it's worth, we have Sam Hughes, former minister of militia, to thank for that."

Officers near Angus rolled their eyes. They had Sam Hughes to thank for a great many things—the inferior, Canadian-made Ross rifle, entrenching tools that broke off in the hand, boots that fell apart . . . he'd created a superb army from untested volunteers, but he'd so often raged like a madman over imagined offenses, promoted the incompetent and taken kickbacks, that he'd finally been replaced. Still, it was his hubris and contempt for the Brits that now had the Canadians, flying high with national pride, the only Dominion force held together as one, not bled into Imperial forces. The rage of a mad- man had its advantages.

"And our day of reckoning will be this ridge," Stokes was saying as he lashed the map. When he turned around, his eyes bore through the men. Angus sat back, as if watching a set piece—the fiery leader, the exhortation, the rousing cheer to come—as if by refusing to play his part, he could stave off the inevitable, leave the theater and toss his program. Beside him Publicover cracked his knuckles.

"Here," Stokes said. " 'Veemy,' the French call it. But we call it 'Vimmy.' And we'll still call it 'Vimmy' after we take it. Seven miles long, four hundred and seventy feet high at its highest point. Two years of fighting, 150,000 casualties later, those slopes remain in

German hands. And behind them? The industry and mining of Lille and the Plain of Douai. I need not explain their importance. The French were so desperate to take back this ridge, they opened fire on their own for refusing to try hard enough. The British took their place and got no further. Now," he thwacked the map to the north, "the Brits will have one division, and here," he thwacked it again to the far south, "a second division. And our four divisions will be here in the middle sector. Facing us? Crack Prussian troops and Bavarians, according to our intelligence. All the better. I'll enjoy taking out their best men. When's the battle? Months away."

Publicover let out an audible sigh of irritation.

"Unless the Hun forces our hand." Stokes faked a smile. "Which they won't. Why should they? They've beaten back everything that's come their way just by hunkering down and staying put." He strode back and forth to let that settle in. Then said, "We've learned a few things—at Ypres, Mont Sorrel, and especially the Somme—Beaumont-Hamel, Courcelette, Thiepval . . ." The names of the battles rolled out with their own resonance, as Stokes knew they would. Pounding the table with two fingers, he said, "The CEF does not intend to repeat previous errors." He paused. "We've gathered the best military and scientific minds to ensure it. New methods of range-spotting—we know where their big guns are. And new tactics. I'm going to let Major Rushford fill you in on those."

Rushford and Stokes exchanged places. Rushford cleared his throat and closed his eyes as if searching for the right words. The right words turned out to be, "Preparation. Preparation. Preparation," delivered in a reed-like voice. He consulted a card in his hand and coughed.

"Jesus. Put that man behind a desk," Publicover whispered.

"What does this mean?" Rushford asked the far wall. "Precise timing between the artillery barrage and its attendant smokescreen and forward movement of the men on the ground. The barrage will be down to the split second so we blow up the enemy, not our own—not to imply that we've ever blown up our own men. Not often, that is." He sniffed several times and smoothed his mustache. His voice had a sort of trumpeting effect as it gained and lost volume, so it was difficult to follow his explanation of how they'd train the men to proper pacing on practice ground and how colored tapes would mark each division's objective—red lines, black lines, blue and brown.

When Rushford finally finished, Stokes strode to the center of the stage. "And here's another change. We all know frontal assaults are our only recourse in trench warfare. And what stands in the way? That's right—the wire."

Barbed wire. Every man and officer carried wire cutters. Wave upon wave of forward-rushing soldiers at the Somme had been mowed down by machine-gun fire as they waited for the belts of barbed wire to be cut. Heavy artillery had failed to destroy it. When those cutting the wire fell, the next ones tried and toppled over them so that those eventually funneling through were forced to crawl over stacks of corpses that clogged the narrow opening. Rarely had the term "shooting fish in a barrel" been so appropriate. Fifty-seven thousand Allied casualties that first day alone.

"Up to now we've had to rely on ordnance that explodes only on impact. Of course, the wire's too insubstantial to set it off. Well, gentlemen, we now have the 106 fuse—so finely sprung it doesn't need impact to explode. It'll go off when it so much as brushes the wire. The 106, our new wire cutter!"

Murmured disbelief rippled through the room.

"That's right. Now, something else. We Canadians may be an unruly lot, as our British friends like to say. And, thank God for it, because the high command of *this* army has figured out something that has eluded our good allies. We're going to trust the intelligence of our men. Think of that. Going to make sure if the officer's dead, a sergeant can take over. If he's out of the action, a corporal can lead on, right on down to private. Maps and objectives will be in the hands of every single section leader."

You could have heard a pin drop.

"That's right," Stokes nodded. "We won't have men stranded with their officers dead around them. We're going to trust the lowest of the ranks because we're smart enough to know that we depend on them as much as they depend on us. We're bound together, ranks and officers, and not one of you matters more than one of them. That's the army you're in.

"Never forget, not for a moment, that you are part of the best fighting force ever assembled on God's green earth. The CEF. The force that's going to take that ridge. *This* is the watershed moment for our young country, by God! Have no doubt that when you fight, you fight for king and country. You fight for the Empire. For God's great purpose. But you also fight for *Canada*! What do you say?"

Cheers pounded out through the room. With a surge of adrenaline Angus cheered almost as loudly as Publicover, then sat back, amazed. He was part of it. And proud of it. He wondered how long the feeling would last. Maybe until he blew the whistle to send his men over the top.

"Dis-missed!" the colonel shouted.

"Who designed it? The fuse. Us? Did he say? Us, I bet. Was it?" Publicover asked eagerly as they filed out with the others.

"The Frogs is what I've heard," a captain said.

"The *Frogs*?" Publicover said. "That's ridiculous."

Conlon patted Publicover's shoulder. "Not every innovation is Canadian, Sam. Let the French have their due, eh?"

"Think it'll work?" Angus asked.

Conlon shrugged.

"This idea of men knowing the battle plan," a lieutenant named Crick said with mock surprise, "awfully generous. Have the generals lost their minds?"

"No. Just their officers," Conlon replied. Everyone laughed.

"Publicover!" someone behind them shouted. "I'll be damned!" It was Andy Loftus, a second lieutenant. "Publicover of the twenty kills!" he said, shaking his head. "And MacGrath, right? We met just before you headed up. Good to see you boys. May I suggest a reunion?"

Angus shook hands, but was anxious to get to his men. He turned to Publicover as he left. "Twenty kills?"

Publicover just shrugged.

HIS MEN WERE still in the barn. "Thank God you made it," he said. "Yes sir," they responded formally, though he thought he saw relief in a few faces. He looked for Hiller. Wertz pointed with his pipe to the far end of the barn. Katz explained Hiller had refused food and water, just huddled there all night. And there he was, hunched in the shadows, bits of straw clinging to his hair. One side of his mouth was clamped in a grimace that loosened only when Angus told him he was taking him to the field hospital. Angus saw that his tunic was rippling as if alive. Because the man seemed incapable, Angus avoided giving him a direct order and began to unbutton the jacket himself. Hiller sank to his knees. Three yellow chicks fell out of his tunic. Angus pulled him to his feet as Boudrey tried to scoop up the chicks. A hen darted about in wing-flapping fury.

Hiller said nothing all the way to the field hospital, and Angus left him there with a report on his behavior. Let the doctor figure out if it was a charade. Angus prayed it was not. Hiller's trembling and facial grimacing set the men's teeth on edge. Publicover was right. Faking it or not, he'd be a liability on the line.

On the road back to the town, Angus checked his trench watch. Nearly noon. A few minutes later, passing a low rise, the sharp report of massed rifle fire cut the air. And then it was quiet. Target practice? At the top of the slope, he saw what looked like sails. It was a chaplain, surplice billowing. Angus angled up to him. Below them, soldiers with rifles were being marched away toward a brick building. By a tree, a man on a block, hands tied behind him, a hood over his head, fell forward. Two others steadied the body and pulled off the hood.

Angus whipped around. The chaplain was crawling off. His knee caught on his surplice, and he fell forward and retched. Angus picked up a silver box from the ground and walked over to him. Blocking the sun, Angus lowered his canteen. The chaplain took it, rinsed his mouth and rolled to a sitting position. "So sorry," he whispered. He wiped his mouth on the edge of his surplice, streaked with vomit.

Angus tried to hand him a cigarette, but the chaplain just stared out beyond the road. Angus sat down next to him. They were silent for a long time. Finally, the chaplain told Angus he'd been called in the night before, right after evening service, to visit with the prisoner. He'd never met the man, but spent the long hours of the long night with him. "He'd been in a lot of rough patches before he joined up. That much I got from him. He had regrets. Asked to be baptized. I tried to get the sentence commuted this morning. Asked if I could see the general, but the colonel would have none of it."

"Stokes?"

The chaplain nodded.

"Was he innocent? The prisoner?"

"Who is innocent in war?" the chaplain sighed. "His name is Ewan Ellsworth, a private. They found him in uniform a month ago, living with a family a good twenty miles back. A deserter. I thought maybe there were commutable circumstances. Why still in uniform living with that family? Why not try to blend in?"

"Did he say?"

"No. Never did, though I asked him. It was part of some elaborate plan, I suppose. Or maybe spur-of-the-moment. Who knows? I was told that my job was to see to his soul, get him to die bravely. The matter had been reviewed by every proper channel."

"What made you think he might be innocent?"

"Not a single thing," the chaplain shook his head. "Still, brought into it like that, I saw the man—saw remorse, the terror in his eyes. I wasn't trying to free him, just save him from . . ."

The firing squad had formed up again and were marching past on the road below. "I had his life in my hands," the chaplain said, his hands limp in his lap. "I didn't, of course, and yet by our very communion, I did. I was one with him all of last night. And am still."

Angus passed him the silver box. The chaplain opened it. A breeze lifted communion wafers from it, and they chased away down the slope like a stream of confetti.

Six

February 20th, 1917
Arras Sector, France

The woman, who had a brittle aspect to her, pierced Publicover's kilt and tunic with a forked stick. "No!" He lunged after them. She swung the stick away. He stumbled, and the boy laughed. All of about ten, with one milky eye and a stiff shock of white through his hair, the boy stirred a steaming cauldron on a grate over an open fire.

"No! *Non!*" Publicover shouted. "Would you get over here?" he said to Angus. "This witch and her apprentice are about to ruin our uniforms."

Angus threw his underwear over the sheet on the line where she'd had him undress and, wrapped in the threadbare quilt she'd provided, hobbled out, bare feet burning with the cold. Publicover, in a similar quilt, grabbed up what clothing he could from the ground. She scowled at him. "Wool," he said, shaking his kilt at her. His quilt slipped. He held a corner of it with his teeth to cover himself, clutching the uniforms to his chest. "Ull. Ull no good in 'oilin 'ater," he said.

She forked his tunic on her stick and swept it over the pot. "Lice!" she hissed. In English.

"We know. *Je comprends*, but—" Angus sighed.

Publicover dispensed with his quilt and waved his arms in an exaggerated X. "Wait!" he said loudly. "I have the so-lu-tion!" He ran back to his pack, stark naked except for his boots, shouting, "Tell her to wait!"

"*Attendez, attendez, s'il vous plaît,*" Angus said, and touched her arm. She squinted at Publicover, who rifled through his pack and held up a jar. "Bertie's Cream! Kills lice!" he shouted with the enthusiasm of a traveling salesman. He leapt back across the yard, and recovered his quilt. The woman scowled, then took the jar and held it at arm's length. "Better than boiling!" he said to her. "French?" he said to Angus. "Have the words?"

"For 'better than boiling'?"

"My sister Lizzie just sent it over. It's a hair tonic, see? But seems it's great for killing lice. This fellow Lizzie knows swears by it. We just rub it in our hair, and all over ourselves. Why not? And our uniforms. Seam squirrels march out—in formation! Guaranteed."

The woman looked at them, shrugged and dipped her hand in the cream and threw a blob of it into the water.

"No . . ." Publicover moaned.

"*S'il vous plaît, Madame,*" Angus said. He held out his hand for the jar. The boy ran off. Reluctantly, she handed the jar over and then in one swift move forked up the tunic again.

"Damn it. *Damn it!*" Publicover grabbed the stick and then there was a click. He and Angus whipped around. The boy had a revolver in his hands. Publicover's eyes went wide. "Whoa!" he said. "That's mine! Give it here, pal." The boy marched over and held the gun straight at Publicover. "Bang!" he said, as Angus grabbed his wrist and took the gun.

"Hey!" The boy glowered. The woman came to and started scolding and jabbing at him. "A joke! *Je le taquine!* I tease him!" the boy cried.

Angus removed the bullets one by one and shook his head at Publicover. "Should have put this away."

"This is *my* fault? It was with my stuff. Where's *your* gun? The boy's a goddamn lunatic. They both are."

Angus turned the boy around, ignoring his defiant expression. The woman fell quiet.

"A joke! Piece of crap," the boy snarled.

"No, not a joke. A loaded revolver." Angus opened his hands and showed him the bullets. "You could have killed him. Might not have meant to, but you could have."

The boy crossed his arms. "Lice," he said.

"No excuse," Angus said. "Dead. *Mort.* He's a soldier. *Un ami.* Understand?"

The boy rolled his eyes. "*Oui.*" He shifted his gaze to his mother and back at Angus. "My *papa* was a soldier. *Il est mort.*"

"I'm sorry—" Angus said.

"I am a soldier also."

"Sure, sure you are." Angus knelt down. "Protecting the home front. Good job. But never, ever point a gun unless you intend to use it. What if this had gone off? You need to apologize."

The boy scuffed his feet. "Do it," Angus said. He was shaking with the cold now.

Finally, the boy turned to Publicover and sighed in a sing-song, "*Désolé.*" After a beat, he added, "*Votre revolver, c'est merdeux. Je peux vous obtenir un meilleur . . . pour un prix.*"

The woman and Angus exchanged a look. They almost laughed.

"What? What'd he say?" Publicover demanded.

"Well, he apologized, and then said that your gun is shit and he could get you a better one. For a price. I think that's what he said anyway."

Publicover stiffened, but said, "Yeah? Tell him to be my guest. Name his price. Never much liked that revolver anyway."

The boy grinned and his mother quickly dipped the clothes in and out again. The smell of lye came on strong. Shivering, Angus and

Publicover decided there might be advantages to boiling water after all. It was too damn cold to figure out. The woman pulled her shawl tight and tapped the boy on the shoulder. *"Allons-y!"* she said, and he ran ahead of her to the house. Angus asked Publicover her name.

"Raffarin. Madame Raffarin," she said without glancing back. *"Et Paul, mon fils."*

"Ah, you speak English!" Publicover called after her.

"No, she just spoke French," Angus said.

"Aren't you the bloody riot? Where've you been anyway?"

"Witnessing the army taking care of its own," Angus replied. "After which I spent the night with my men in the barn. And you? Didn't you get my message? Where were you? Not here, obviously."

"Obviously. Got here around midnight, and she had the door locked, so I—"

Before Publicover could finish, the boy sloshed a bucket of water at them. Angus jumped out of the quilt just in time to receive the splash against his legs. Warm water, thankfully. Mud streaked off. The boy and his mother were clearly professionals at housing soldiers. The boy, Paul, cocked his head toward the house, and they followed him up the steps and into the kitchen.

A tub of water, partially hidden by a folding screen, steamed by the far wall. Shivering badly now, Angus reached in his haversack for a coin, flipped it up, and barely caught it. "Heads!" Publicover said. It was tails.

The woman lit a lamp on the table and one on the cupboard. A parchment yellow glow filled in against the gloom, and Angus saw the woman was neither brittle nor skittish, but worn and tired, and that there was dignity in her bearing. And in her lean frame, her dark hair and eyes, her solemn expression, something that reminded him of himself. She gestured at the tub. Angus shuffled over. She took his quilt without looking at him. He tested the water, steaming hot, and slowly crouched in.

Paul shoved past his mother. A photograph on the cupboard had her holding a baby in a beribboned dress. A short, sturdy man, very proud, had his arm around her waist. Paul moved the picture, pulled back a cutwork curtain from the cupboard and took out a narrow box. On the cover, a jaunty scarecrow; inside a set of jackstraws. He cocked his head at Publicover, who inspected the box.

"Jackstraws! Why not, eh, while I wait my turn," Publicover said.

Paul took out the pointed sticks and held them up. "How much?"

"How much? Are you kidding? You selling the sticks, or are we playing a game?"

"Play! How much?"

"Alright," Publicover sighed. "A penny a stick. God only knows how many revolvers you've got stashed away from your winnings."

The woman stood over Angus with a thick bar of soap and a sponge.

"You're not thinking of washing him? Not necessary," Publicover said brightly. "He can wash himself." To Angus, he said, "How's the water?"

Angus didn't answer.

"Might I add that I didn't get a bath yesterday? Had to stand under a trickle of water from a rusted pipe in the barn with the men? Cold water," he continued, following Paul to the table. "No handmaiden to wash me. But certainly, you go right ahead."

Engulfed in steam, Angus lifted the water to his face. Hot water. Clean, clear water. He cupped it in his hands, let it slip through his fingers as if witness to a miracle. He lifted it to his face again and again. A shudder went through him. And another.

He could sense the woman watching him. He put his face in his hands and fought a welling-up.

"*La guerre,*" she whispered, kneeling next to him.

He shook his head, but could not look up. The shuddering grew violent. She waited.

"*Un jour, vous serez lavé propre de lui,*" she whispered as the shaking subsided. "*Un jour . . .*"

Someday. Washed clean of it—if only. Finally, he was able to glance up. *La guerre*. It was there in the shadows beneath her eyes, in her unflinching gaze. She knew.

She lowered her eyes and dipped the fat sponge into the water, then stood behind him and squeezed it over his head. Her movements were slow and sure. She lathered his hair. He tried to stop her, but let himself fall into the slow, circular rhythm of her hands against his temples, over the crown of his head, along the back of his neck. Vague words, English and French—Publicover and the boy at their game—circled through the steam and evaporated. She reached for a pitcher and poured a stream of water over his head that cascaded down his back, over him and through him. "*Un jour.* Someday," she said.

"You're an optimist," he whispered.

"Died and gone to heaven, have you?" Publicover broke in. "Some of us wouldn't mind a bit of washing-up ourselves. Hot water, that sort of thing. What! You moved that stick. I saw it!"

"*Non!*" Paul protested as Publicover stood up, his quilt catching a jackstraw and trailing a clatter of sticks to the floor. "Arrrgh!" Paul growled. He grabbed the white patch of his hair and crouched around in mock temper.

"*Merci, Madame Raffarin,*" Angus whispered. He took the soap and sponge from her.

"Juliette," she said, and placed a towel on the chair next to the tub.

"Um, are you quite done?" Publicover stood over him. Angus finished washing quickly. They exchanged places. Juliette set a bowl of water, a razor, shaving brush and cup of soap on the table beneath a mirror. The light so dim, his hands so heavy, Angus could barely lather up, barely scrape the razor against his cheek. When he was done, he wiped his face with the towel and stared at the mirror. The hollows of his cheeks seemed deeper, as did the lines that framed the corners of his mouth—two thin lines that deepened when he smiled, and that, when he was serious, made him seem all the more so. So he'd been told. By whom? He couldn't remember. Publicover, splashing in the tub, said, "Think I might get some help here? Sponge? Or, no. I see, you have to shave."

Angus tossed him the sponge, then in a near trance climbed the narrow stairs to the bedroom, where he fell into the bed and slipped like silk between the sheet and down coverlet.

SEVERAL HOURS LATER, the smell of eggs and frying potatoes wound through his sleep. Publicover, mouth open, sprawled an arm and a leg onto Angus's side of the bed, then clutched his wrist and jerked it hard, bringing Angus back to the high-ceilinged room in Astile, at the edge of Arras. Lace curtains draped to puddles on the floor. He would find a long swath of French lace for Hettie Ellen and let it cascade around her shoulders and would twirl her around and watch the lace trail out and circle back around them both.

He swung his feet to the floor. What the hell time was it? Where were his clothes? He pressed his face into his hands and breathed in soap and lavender, and crept down to the kitchen. A pot of coffee. Scrambled eggs and potatoes piled on a platter. Their clothes were hanging on chairs and draped over a wooden frame by the stove. Must have passed the lice muster. Their freshly ironed shirts were folded on a chair.

Juliette poured cream over the eggs. Angus stared at her hands, at her long fingers, the three thin silver rings. "*Mangez, mangez*," she said, with a quick gesture and turned back to the stove, but not before giving him a fleeting smile.

Angus pulled out a chair. Publicover stumbled down and took up a fork. "Eggs. The order of the day over here. Eggs and spuds, eh? Oh my God, the smell of it! But maybe we should head to the mess tent. Kidding! Good billets, eh? Told you. *Merci*," he said to Juliette.

"Publicover, you're a wonder."

"That I am, but I didn't rate a private hair wash now did I?" Publicover pointed his fork at Angus. "What have you got that I haven't, eh? That's what I want to know. I'm the one who needs a girl."

"She's not a girl, Sam."

"True enough." He stuffed in more eggs. "Did get something from her, though." He reached behind to the cupboard and lifted up a stout bottle of amber liquid. Popped the cork off and waved it under Angus's nose. "Have a whiff."

"Scotch?"

"Yep. The boy told me, from what I could gather from his English—which is pretty good, actually—that it was left by the chap who left the jackstraws. Dead too now, apparently. My guess? The kid won it off him."

"Hmm. You pay her for it? Or him?"

"Of course. She didn't want it. Scrinched her nose up at it. Took the money, though."

"I'll pay half as long as we share it with the captain. Bring it tonight."

"Will do. Fond of his whisky, eh? Tonight we'll find out what's what in this town. Hear there's quite the brothel for officers. Not that I plan to find out."

"No?"

"Course not! Keeping myself clean. I'm waiting for a girl who'll be a sweetheart to me alone, not the entire corps. Oh!" He put the scotch away, forked in another mouthful, and said, "Speaking of our fearless leader, guess who popped over while I was bathing? Told me he heard they'd finished most of the burial duty around Courcelette—four months since, but never mind. Tough duty. Anyway," he took a deep breath. "Um, I guess the lists are in. More up-to-date. He said he'd go to HQ with you to check on your Ebbin Hant. If you want to. *Plus,* he ran into a friend of his who was near the 12th at Courcelette."

Angus went completely still.

✦

AGAINST THE NIGHT sky the narrow Flemish buildings around the town square were an uneven rupture of confusion, most of the upper stories shelled and gone. The pillared archway that covered the sidewalk, there since Roman times, remained. At the *estaminet* on the square, officers stood shoulder-to-shoulder at the bar. Publicover staked out a table by the far wall and paced menacingly until it was free. Angus grabbed extra chairs. Conlon brought over shots of whisky. When they'd thrown them back, Publicover opened his greatcoat and withdrew the scotch. "For you," he said. "For us." He poured it into the empty glasses. Conlon smiled and took a long swallow.

They were on their second round when Conlon's friend, Chris Code, a second lieutenant with the 91st, made his way to them through the crowd. Introductions were made. Code raised his eyebrows at Angus and said, "I hear you're looking for someone in the 12th D Company. It's a strange story, not one I really want to tell, but I can't refuse Jim Conlon . . . and I can be bought." He downed the scotch Conlon slid toward him. The sheen on the bones of his face and his sunken eyes gave him a skeletal appearance. No one spoke. He poured himself another. Then he began. "Got there end of August. Courcelette. Not the village, but Mouquet Farm, our side of the village." He spun his glass, eyes down, voice weary and without inflection.

Conlon hunched over his scotch, waiting. Angus fixed his eyes on Code, who continued: "The Aussies had been holding it for God knows how long. Bodies everywhere. Some naked. No idea why. Just one officer and ten or twelve men left. Communications had been cut. They'd sent a runner. Runner ran the wrong way. Can you believe it?"

"Absolutely," Publicover said.

"Right. Exactly. So, he never makes it back, and so no reinforcements. Aussies left to die, or be killed, which they'd gone ahead and done." He sighed heavily and took another swallow. "We set up in a place called Sausage Valley. You remember that, Jim," he said to Conlon. "In the old Kraut trenches. Back before the September push."

"We went up Munster Alley," Publicover added.

"Yeah. Our group went up Peg Trench. Hand-to-hand, mostly. None of it worth talking about. Give me one of those, would you?" Angus pushed his tin of Players toward Code and offered a light. His hand shook. He regretted the third scotch. Everything seemed simultaneously heightened and fogged.

"Damn, these are good," Code said, blowing out a stream of smoke and almost stopping there. "Scotch. Smokes. Got a woman handy? Okay, okay, so up Candy Trench and Taffy Trench and—"

"Dandy Trench?" Angus asked.

"Yeah. No. *Candy* Trench. German position south of the Sugar Factory."

"Sweet, eh?" Publicover couldn't help but add.

"Heaps of rubble by the time we got there. Sugar factory or refinery or whatever. Used to process beets, I know that," Code went on. "The Krauts had been using it to pump water. So, that's where I met up with Conlon and Publicover, here, of the twenty kills." Code nodded appreciatively at Publicover.

"Didn't have but five prior to that. Got another eleven there," Publicover said.

"All at once?" Angus asked.

"No," Publicover said evenly. "One by one. Too easy, really, so I don't count them. See, we'd taken a lot of prisoners in Candy Trench. Lined them up. Then one threw a stick bomb. Killed the major while he was taking their surrender. We searched the others. Almost to a man, they were hiding bombs. Orders went out after that. Any others you find, shoot to kill. And then there was the matter of the Aussies."

"The Aussies? They weren't there," Code said.

"No, I know. But that bunch found—lined up and shot in the head.

Executed. Not exactly given prisoner's rights, were they?" Publicover narrowed his eyes.

"That was later, Sam," Conlon corrected him. "We didn't find that out 'til *later.*"

"Well, yeah, but it happened *before,* even if we heard about it later."

"We didn't know it at the time so it doesn't figure in." Conlon rolled his eyes and nodded at Code. "Go on."

Code gestured at Publicover with his cigarette. "So, shoot to kill. Publicover only too happy to oblige. Didn't kill the prisoners, but got over to the back of the trench, marched along the parados, and shot every German coming up from a dugout."

"Not just me. Kehoe was on the parapet, doing his bit. And, like I said, I don't count those as kills."

"Anyway, D Company of the 12th was behind us that day. Just telling you this part to bring you up to speed." Code glanced at Angus. "So . . ." He cleared his throat. "Some days later, around the middle of September, we're lined up to the right of the Princess Pats, moving on Fabeck Graben and into Courcelette itself."

"Okay, yeah," Angus said. "A fella back home says he saw my brother-in-law with D Company, *after* Courcelette, and now I'm thinking he meant after the town was taken, not the end of the battle."

"Maybe so. No guarantees because I didn't know the man personally. But we mopped up the town with the Pats. And the Van Doos doing more than their part, going house to house. They were magnificent. Anyway, Krauts opened fire about six hundred yards beyond the village. Carnage. But some of us made it through and on to Zollern Graben and Regina Trench . . . and Thiepval."

Here he stopped. He looked beyond Angus. Minutes seemed to pass. Conlon had his head in his hands.

Publicover jumped in. "So, D Company? The 12th. Courcelette."

"Right." Code poured another drink. "This was days after the town had been taken. We were moving in on Regina Trench. There were so many shell holes that the boys to the east of us were connecting them for a temporary trench. My boys got pinned down behind a burned shed. A couple of platoons from the 12th were up ahead, flanking west. There was a slight ridge and then a ravine beyond it. No action there, and a platoon from the 12th was told to go for it. I saw about ten, maybe fifteen go over the ridge, led by their officer. It was quiet. Two minutes later, all hell breaks loose. Shells everywhere. We took a hit from a 3.9. Things went blank. Crawled out from under the debris. Medics came running. We redirected toward some advancing Germans to the right of us. That's the last I saw of them. The last anyone saw of them. They simply disappeared over that low ridge into the ravine."

"What the hell? How does an entire platoon disappear?" Angus said.

"We couldn't get back to that sector to find out what happened. We were told to move on," Code said.

"What are the chances they were taken prisoner?" Angus asked.

"Doubtful, but anything's possible," Code replied.

"Strange things happen," Publicover added in an unusually thoughtful tone.

"Men appear as well as disappear."

"How do you mean?" Angus asked.

"In Ypres we'd pick up some soldier who'd lost his group. Maybe they were dead. Or he was sent on some mission with another couple of men and left hanging and joined up with us. In the heat of it, men turn up with a group they weren't attached to and tend to stay."

Code nodded in agreement. Then he closed his eyes and took a deep breath. "Gotta go, gentlemen." He stood, thin and spectral. "Hope you find him," he said to Angus. Angus stood and shook his hand as he thanked him. Code disappeared in the crowd.

Angus was desperate for air. Conlon pulled at his arm. "Si'down, MacGrath," he said. "Sort it out tomorrow. Let's find ourselves another topic." But Angus was too agitated, too on-the-brink. He wiped the back of his hand across his mouth. "You boys carry on," he said.

"See you at 700 hours." Conlon stood and put an arm around Angus. "Answers tomorrow. I'm off, too." He swayed slightly. "Sam?"

"On that note? Not hardly. I see Tommy and Reese. And there's Andy!" Publicover waved them over. "Catch you up later. Keep the bed warm, MacGrath. Revolver under your pillow. Couple more nights and we'll be in huts with our boys."

FORTIFIED WITH STRONG coffee and more eggs, Angus was on the steps of Conlon's billet at 6:45 the next morning. Conlon, unshaven and buttoning his tunic, opened the door before Angus knocked. Thirty minutes later, they were in front of a fat little corporal who pouted over the lists in his hands. More lists. This one, a list of the dead.

"H-A-N-T," Angus spelled the name out again and was just short of grabbing the papers from his stubby fingers.

"Yes sir," said the corporal, stifling a yawn. "These just came in. They're by battalion and company and platoon, but not all in alphabetical order yet. Some are, but these . . . wait. Here it is. Found it. Hant, Ebbin—"

Found it? Angus tore the list from his hand because Ebbin's name could not be on it. "Hant, Ebbin, Pvt. First Class, 12th Battalion" stared up at him. In all those lists—lists of the injured, those taken prisoner, the dead—Ebbin's name had never shown up. And now, here it was, in black print on yellow paper.

"So *that's* what happened," Conlon said. "Code was right. Look at the numbers. Must have been shelled. Code didn't see it because his group was shelled at the same time."

"Sir? I have his disc—discs, actually. Both of them." The corporal dangled the final proof of Ebbin's death from his thumb and forefinger. The cord swung back and forth. "Oh, and this." He held up a brightly polished gold cross on a chain of its own. Angus grabbed them.

"Why both tags?" he demanded. "This one's supposed to be left in the mouth for later ID. *Why two tags?*" He shook the tags, towering over the corporal, who arched back, round eyes bugging from tight corners of pink flesh.

The corporal stepped away and said, "No bodies to speak of. Mass grave. There'll be a proper grave site later."

"Right. Thank you, Corporal," Conlon said. "Now, look over your papers and see if there is anything else you can tell us."

"I . . . yes. I see, here." The corporal shot a nervous glance at Conlon, avoided Angus. "A note at the bottom says the tags for Private Hant were found by themselves. Quite some distance from the others."

"How far away? *How far from the others?* Does it say?" Angus closed his fist over the tags.

"Yes sir. Approximately twenty yards south of the ridge."

"Twenty yards? South? What's that mean?"

The corporal looked pleadingly at Conlon. Conlon snapped the papers away from him and read aloud, "Private Ebbin Hant's tags found approximately twenty yards south of the ridge. Body not found." He set the paper down. "The explosion must have flung him back. Or . . . what was left of him."

"Or he didn't go over," the corporal said.

Angus snapped the leather cord taut.

"Thank you, Corporal. That'll be all," Conlon said.

"Sir, I need those back to send to his family, and the cross," the corporal said.

Angus opened his hand and looked at the tags. These had been around Ebbin's neck. Had he been *decapitated*? But the cord was perfectly pliable, not stiff with blood. Cleaned up. Of course. But could blood be so thoroughly washed away? And since when had Ebbin owned a cross? *Didn't go over* . . . He couldn't get the words out of his head.

Angus returned the tags, but kept the cross. "I'll sign for it," he said.

"Regulations," the corporal sputtered.

Conlon cut him off. "He'll keep it. He's family. Anything else?"

"No sir . . . I guess not." The corporal deflated like a leaking balloon.

"You guessed right," Conlon snapped. To Angus he said, "C'mon. We're done here." He steered him roughly toward the door. Outside, he shook his head and muttered a word of sympathy.

"What I want to know," Angus said, "is why he was so far from the others? Was he blown back . . . or did he stay back? Refuse to go forward? And this cross." Angus turned it over. The initials *ELH* were inscribed on it. "Never knew him to wear one. Something doesn't feel right."

"You know what they say—found God at the bottom of a trench. Happens all the time," Conlon sighed. "The tags—strange, I'll grant you, but you've seen what shelling can do. He did his part, and I'd trust that report. Dead, every man jack of them." When Angus didn't reply, he clamped a hand on his shoulder and said, "Look, take an hour or two. Collect yourself. I'll get someone to cover your duties."

Angus stood on the street, staring dumbly after Conlon, then, dodging lorries and carts and limbers rumbling over the cobblestones, he began walking. A team of mules plodded toward him, straining against a bulky, tarp-covered load. One of the mules jerked his head up and stared at Angus. Tails hung down from the tarp—mules carting their dead away. The mule lowered his head after he passed Angus, and the cart moved on.

Eventually, Angus found himself seated at a table, staring into a small cup of something he didn't feel like drinking and didn't remember ordering. He unbuttoned his coat. The scarf Hettie had knit fell away. Ebbin's dead, he said to himself. Ebbin's dead. Ebbinsdead. Ebbinsdead. The words refused to register.

He dropped a coin on the table, and half an hour later the strains of "Praise, My Soul, the King of Heaven" pulled him like the tightening loop of a bow line knot into the YMCA hut where a hymn sing was in progress. Inside, soldiers and nurses, their voices a robust chorus, nearly drowned out the piano. "Alleluia! Alleluia! Praise the everlasting King!" The echo of home in their every note.

The chaplain he'd met on the hill faced the crowd and sang out the lyrics by heart. An old sergeant sidled over to share his hymnal with Angus. Angus shook his head, but could not turn away from the purity of that gesture. He took up his half of the hymnbook as the third verse began:

"Father-like he tends and spares us,
Well our feeble frame he knows."

How he had failed Ebbin, failed Hettie. Failed himself.

"In his hand he gently bears us,
Rescues us from all our foes.
Alleluia! Alleluia!
Widely yet his mercy flows."

Where was God's rescue, God's mercy? Or was death the rescue—and the mercy? He'd never know, and not knowing was as unbearable as knowing. Angus folded his side of the hymnal into the old soldier's hand as gently as he could. Then he was out in the cold air again where he could walk and not stop.

On the furthest reaches of Astile, on a road he did not recognize, he stopped. There, a shallow stream, filmed by ice, met a frozen pond. Sparrows flitted through the leafless thicket. He turned up his collar. Above him the sky was bled white, as drained of color as his mother's lips and the white of her startled eyes before Dr. Woodruff gently closed them forever. He could see his father leaning his head against the wall as Ida cradled the dead baby with a blanket over its face, as if to protect it from the pain its birth had unleashed. Still and pale, white and lifeless, his mother was lowered into the soft spring earth, and with her, his father's joy and ease of being. He remembered his father coming back from the Banks months later with a stunned look in his eye, a rigid determination to reverse his fortunes, and the arrogance to believe he could.

What hubris, what lunacy had led Angus to think he could find Ebbin, to rescue him? He tried to imagine Ebbin's last moments, but could not. What came to him was the image of Hettie getting the news. He had to get word to her before the War Department did. On his knees, rocking back and forth, he composed and recomposed the telegram until it, too, meant nothing

LATE THAT NIGHT, long after he'd sent the telegram and checked on his men, long after he'd taught his classes with the fervor and precision of someone desperate to keep from thinking, he staggered back to the house, where he was met by Juliette. She caught her breath at the sight of him. "*Ton frère?*"

"Frère-in-law. *Le frère de ma femme,*" he corrected her, as if it mattered. "*Il est mort?*"

Angus told her the body had not been found. Only the tags. Ebbin was now officially declared dead. She leaned over slightly, arms around her waist. He took her elbows, then her hands, dry as paper, and lifted her upright and into his arms, rocking her in his embrace, staring over her head down the dark hallway. "*Mort?* I don't know," he whispered.

She pulled away and searched his eyes.

"Wishful thinking. Idiotic." He let her go and rubbed his face and paced about in agitation, hands on his hips. "It's just with no body, I keep thinking, which is the problem, I know, but I keep thinking he just walked away somehow. Left his tags. Maybe he's a deserter, though it doesn't figure. And how the hell would he have slipped away in the middle of a battle? Or maybe that's the perfect time. But where would he go? And why didn't he write for all those months before Courcelette?" He stopped when he caught her expression. "You must think I'm crazy," he said. "You're probably right."

She shook her head no, but in her eyes there was something—pity maybe, or no—compassion.

THAT NIGHT, ON top of the too soft, too clean bed, fully clothed except for his boots, with Publicover curled like a baby against him and moonlight spilling a filigree of light and shadow through the lace, Angus thought back to Mitchell Finch, whose wife fell off a boat in Shelburne. Her body was never recovered, and for years afterwards, Mitch would say, "Jenny's down to her folks in Shelburne. Back any day now."

Angus swung off the bed, walked soundlessly to the window and dug in the pocket of his jacket for the cross. *ELH*. Ebbin Langston Hant. After all those years of indifference, Ebbin had gone out and bought a cross. Had it inscribed. An expression of faith, or a hope that faith would follow? He put the chain around his neck and let the cross slip down his chest. The Ebbin he'd known nearly all his life had gone down a rabbit hole and vanished. Dead, yes, he was dead by all accounts. But his fate remained unknown.

SEVEN

February 21st, 1917
Snag Harbor, Nova Scotia

Simon heard the creak of the wheels before he saw George. George was pushing his wheelchair hard, back and forth, appearing and disappearing in the doorway to the kitchen. Simon felt a wave of nausea—maybe from the smell of cabbage boiling on the stove—but even from the hall, he could sense the menace in George's wheeled pacing. George was raw-boned and broad-shouldered. People said he'd turned mean since he came back from the Front. Simon wished George's mother would hurry up with the mufflers he was there to collect. Suddenly, George whipped around and faced him.

"That Peg o' My Heart you came on?" he rasped. Simon nodded nervously. As if in answer, Peg whinnied softly outside.

"Heart-broke. Horses worked to shivering death."

"What?" Simon asked reflexively. He looked anxiously down the hall.

"Flog them, lash them. Orders! Eyes bulging—pull our guns and shells through the mud 'til they're too done-in to eat the oats we give them. Broke their hearts, is what." George wheeled past Simon to gaze at Peg tied to the fence post. "Peg o' My Heart," he whispered, then stiffened and sat bolt upright. "Shoot them when they get like that. Wet flanks crying in the rain. None buried. No time for that. Flog more into action." He clenched his fist and kept his eyes on Peg.

"That you, Simon? I'm coming!" George's mother came in with a stack of mufflers. "Or, George, was that you?" To Simon she said, "Goodness. He don't talk for a week or two and then just starts in straight out of the blue. And then we have a right good conversation, don't we, George?" She put the mufflers down and shook out an afghan. George shoved her away when she tried to put it over his knees. Simon caught her hand to steady her. "Don't talk much, but he's strong. Eats like a horse," she said, flushed and flustered. "George? This is Simon Peter MacGrath. Remember him?"

George gave her a murderous glance and grabbed his crutches. He pulled himself to a stand and thumped back to the kitchen. At the door, he twisted around. "I've got fourteen coins in fourteen boxes for boys just like you," he said.

Mrs. Mather stood still as a statue, then shoved the mufflers at Simon. "Twenty-five years old and not a friend to his name," she said. "You ask Lady Bromley what good are neck warmers when a decent boy comes back like that?" Simon backed out the door. "Ask her!" The words rang in his ears as he leapt over the steps and set Peg to a fast clip back along Owl's Head Road.

DUNCAN SNAPPED HIS napkin and then folded it with the care he'd apply to furling a foresail. "What news of Angus?" he asked, as he always did, as if inquiring about the fate of colonists in a foreign land.

Hettie stared out the kitchen window. "Letters take two weeks," she sighed.

Simon stared at his plate and imagined horses too worn out to eat. He quietly scraped his cabbage into the napkin on his lap where it collected into a wet lump and drained onto his trousers. Duncan tapped his mouth with his fingers. Then he slapped his thigh and opened his arms. Young Fred slipped from his seat and hopped into Duncan's lap. Simon dumped his sodden cabbage in the compost pail.

"That's my boy, Young Fred. Now, what do you have to say for yourself?"

"Simon made me a sword to stab sea monsters. Plus, I don't like slush."

"Lately hasn't wanted to get his boots dirty," Hettie said with a wink at Young Fred.

"Ah. Well now, we'll have to get you some good fishing boots to deal with that slush, eh?" Duncan pulled out his pocket watch and looked at Hettie. "And what do we hear of Turley?" Young Fred clicked the latch. The watch sprung open.

"Hmmm?" Hettie said, straightening up. "What?"

"Turley! Damn it, I'm asking you about Turley. Your cousin. Fred's father. Have you *heard* from him?"

Hettie swept up her plate and scraped the remains into a bowl at the sink. "No. Don't expect to. He's up in Labrador."

"Labrador? What's he doing up there? Still no interest in what happens to the boy?"

"For heaven sake, Duncan!"

"What, you think the boy hasn't wondered? My God, Hettie. His father's a failure. You want him to grow up to be one, too? You need to be honest. Let him know what it takes to get along in the world. Backbone. Straight living, eh, now, Fred?"

"He's four, Duncan."

"Nearly five!" Young Fred piped up.

"You just turned four last month," Simon said.

"See?" Hettie frowned at Duncan.

Duncan sighed. "Doesn't matter how old he is. At least he's thinking along the right lines. Right, Fred?"

"My pencil people need a new Dad," Young Fred said, hopping down.

Hettie patted his head and lifted him into her lap. "You have a father," she said. "He's just away right now."

Young Fred buried his face against her. "Not me. My pencil people." He sat up and glanced longingly at the three pencils lined up next to his plate, then wriggled down and took them under the table.

"Well, now," Duncan said, leaning down at him. "Suppose you enlist your stick people to help with the dishes, eh? Hard work, that's what stick people need. Gets their mind off things." He grunted as he rose from the table. "I'll take my pipe in the parlor and a mug of this coffee, if we can call it that." He winked at Hettie. "C'mon, Simon Peter."

"Pencil people," came a voice from under the table. "Not sticks."

Simon hesitated. "Go on. It's fine." His mother dismissed him with a vague wave. Glad for the release, he followed his grandfather and slumped down in his father's chair staring at the hearth. Horses flickered through the dancing flames. His grandfather zipped the letter opener through a stack of mail he'd brought with him—letters from Ottawa, from England, from the States. People he was in touch with about the war. "Profiteering," he growled. "Makes my blood boil."

"Privateering?" Simon asked without real interest.

"*Profit*eering. War profiteering. I've told you about that—weapons, food, clothing and all the rest of it—making a fast buck off the suffering of others. Not all that different from privateering, come to think of it. Sending men off to war with shoddy equipment. The greed of man knows no bounds, Simon. And what's got you so sullen? You look sick." His grandfather peered at him over his glasses as he sliced through the next envelope. "Understand you were at Hennigar's so-called recruitment office again. Don't look so surprised. Got my ear to the ground, boy."

Again, the enlistment card. "I was just hanging around with Zenus. Talking with Zeb."

"Um-hmm. Have you thought about what Mr. Heist would say about that ape?"

"Mr. Heist would know it wasn't him."

"Oh? How's that, now?"

"Because he's *here*. He's one of us. Besides, it's the Prussians who are to blame. And he's not Prussian. He said so."

Duncan removed his glasses. "I ask myself how a boy as bright as you can be so dull-witted. Why do you suppose Mr. Heist is so keen to make that distinction? The longer this war goes on, the more dangerous it is for him." He picked up his letters again.

"What do you mean? Everyone knows him."

"You have a few more boys coming back like George Mather, and I wouldn't be surprised at anything that happens."

Simon sat up. "George—he's crazy, right?"

"He's broken. That's what war does. Breaks people. He may be dangerous. Probably best to stay clear of him until he gets set right again." His grandfather shook a letter out and stared at the fire.

"He says crazy things." Simon went to the window and looked for his little friend, the fox, but darkness engulfed the field and the fox was nowhere to be seen. Just before supper it had raced halfway across the snowy yard. Third day in a row. It had lifted one black paw and jerked its head toward Simon—the white of its chest against the red fur shoulders, its pointed snout, the black eyes looking right at him.

But there *was* something. A black shape coming up the road, almost to the house. Even in the dark, Simon could make out his labored walk. "Zeb Morash!" he said. "Coming up the hill!"

"What? This time of night?" Duncan strode to the window. "I'll be damned," he said softly.

Zeb stared at the house, shook his head, and then continued, slow as molasses, as if the snow were knee-deep and the path wasn't clear.

"Zeb? Zebulon!" Duncan called out, opening the door to a cold rush of air.

"It's me," came the response.

And then Simon knew. The telegraph office at the back of Hennigar's. Never had a man walked so slow.

"Come on, come on. Come in!" Duncan dragged him over the doorstep and slammed the door hard. Zeb coughed and wheezed and stamped like an old horse. He pulled off his gloves and clapped them together. Then he reached in the inside pocket of his jacket and said, "Duncan. Glad you're here, boy. Right glad of that." He withdrew a thin envelope.

Duncan looked at it, but did not take it. Color drained from his face, but he stood ramrod straight. Stood like iron.

"Telegram from Angus. For Hettie."

Hettie stood at the kitchen entryway. Young Fred ducked around her and raced up to Zeb.

"*From* Angus, you say? *From* Angus?" Duncan laid a hand on Zeb's shoulder.

"That's right. From him. Sent by him."

"Thank God." Duncan took the envelope and ushered Hettie into the parlor, saying, "We don't know, now. We don't know anything." But Simon knew. One look at Zeb's face and anyone would. His mother knew. His grandfather, too.

"Here, Hettie. Sit down. Shall I open this?" Duncan said gently. She did not sit. She stared unblinking at the envelope. Simon's mouth went dry. Zeb pulled off his hat and clutched it as if in prayer, his face red with the cold, as sad a face as Simon had ever seen.

Duncan turned the envelope over and withdrew the telegram. He fumbled with his spectacles, dropped them, picked them up.

Zeb coughed and looked panicked. "Best be getting on. Wanted to bring it up myself. I'm right sorry. *Right* sorry." He pulled on his cap and nodded at them.

"Not a bit of it, Zeb," Duncan said without looking up. "You get a mug up before you trek back to town. Some rum. I'd take you back myself, but . . ." He almost tucked the telegram in his pocket.

"Maybe it's good news! He, he found him! Right?" Simon said. The words, once out, rang with lunacy, but it didn't matter because now his grandfather had finished reading and was holding the slip of paper to his chest and looking just like Zeb.

"Ebbin," his mother whispered. "Not . . . ?"

The log Simon had laid fell in and set off a flurry of sparks. No one spoke.

"Read it," she said.

His grandfather again hooked the gold frames of his spectacles over his ears, looked at her for confirmation and read:

"EBBIN'S IDENTIFICATION TAGS FOUND AT COURCELETTE WITH REMAINS OF HIS PLATOON.
APPARENTLY SHELLED. ALL DEAD. EBBIN'S BODY NOT FOUND.
SORROW REIGNS.
I LONG TO BE WITH YOU. ANGUS"

His mother slowly began to shake her head no, holding her hand out and backing away. Simon grabbed the telegram. Under the lamplight the typed words gathered into phrases. *All dead. Apparently shelled. Body not found.* "Grandpa? What does it mean? Grandpa?"

"Sorrow reigns," his grandfather whispered hoarsely. "That's what it means."

EIGHT

February 24th, 1917
Arras Sector, France

t was late. The *estaminet* was quiet. Most of the men were at a YMCA production aptly titled, "In Harm's Way." Behind Conlon, the thin-haired proprietor slowly pushed a mop back and forth across the floor. Angus folded the telegram from Duncan and considered what it must have taken for him to write it.

Conlon placed an order and sat down. "News?" he asked.

"Telegram from my father. Said Ebbin's family got the official word and my wife is with her parents. Memorial service next week." He imagined Hettie, ashen-faced, in his father's arms. It was the only picture of the scene he could conjure up. He should have been the one holding her. "First time I've heard from him since I left. He wasn't too happy about my joining up."

"Tell me it wasn't just to find Ebbin Hant." When Angus gave no reply, Conlon added, "Men join up for all kinds of reasons—to be with their pals, find adventure, avoid prison, run from something. Not to find someone."

"Must have been mad."

"Must have been some kind of pal."

"More like a brother. Met him when I was a boy, not long after my mother died. He brought me out of it, you might say."

"And so you married his sister. She the one talked you into coming over?"

Angus almost tried to explain before he realized Conlon was joking. What wife would want her husband to join up? And yet. He remembered her flannel nightgown, folded on the bed, a single sleeve askew, the night he told her he was joining up to be a cartographer, behind the lines where he could search for Ebbin. When he finished, her silhouette against the window had straightened, like a plucked string. She'd pulled the curtain back ever so slightly. And in that silent gesture, agreement. For all her protestations afterwards and all his reassurances that he'd be out of harm's way, the truth lay in that moment. And he'd understood.

How utterly unhinged it seemed now.

"Neither of us had any idea what this war was like. Never thought I'd be in combat. And there were her parents, her father. He was good to me as a boy. Guess I wanted . . . well, doesn't much matter now, does it?" He slipped the telegram into his pocket.

Conlon gave him a long hard look. "Maybe it does. Your old man— he against war in general or just this war, or just you in it? A pacifist or—"

"Yeah. He is. Maybe not with a capital *P*." Angus shifted uncomfortably. "He's not your idea of a pacifist anyway. He's a tough son of a bitch. He was captain of a Banks fishing schooner for years, and he's never gotten over it. One of his stronger opinions is that the British Empire can fuck itself. He has a way of making his points."

"So you were running after all."

Angus downed the last of his drink, irritated at Conlon for so handily making him see things in a way he hadn't before. "Maybe so," he said to Conlon. "But still, I loved him. Ebbin, that is. Never knew how much until he went missing." Angus leaned forward and cupped his glass with both hands. "When someone's gone, gone for good, a piece of yourself goes missing—who you were with that person and maybe who you thought you once might be." His throat tightened. He sat back and looked away.

Conlon sighed. "The lost dreams of youth. Find him and you might get them back, eh?"

Angus turned back with a sardonic smile. "I think those were well shut down by the time he enlisted." But had resurfaced, he didn't add.

"Life isn't much without dreams."

"Ebbin used to say it wasn't much without risk."

"Same thing really."

"I suppose. So how about you? Why did you join up? Searching for youth? Avoiding prison?"

Conlon raised his brows and lit a cigarette. "Might say that. I was going to be a journalist. Run a paper someday. And did. Ran a small paper in Wolfville until it nearly folded. Might have ended up in prison for murder if I hadn't left."

"Why? What happened?"

"Turns out, I don't have much of a head for the business end of things. And . . ." He hesitated briefly. "Had a run-in with the owner. Over a woman. He didn't love her, but I did. A standard story, but when it's your own, it seems original."

"Did you marry her?"

"Would have, but there was a problem."

"She was his wife?"

"Exactly. The other problem is I never stop thinking about her. Or him. I've killed him many times over for having her, for the way he treats her. I thought she loved me. But I guess not enough to leave him. You, on the other hand, married the girl of your dreams. You're a lucky man."

"A good man" is what Hettie had told him he was on their wedding day. But whether Hettie meant Angus was a good man for marrying her or despite having let his passion get the better of him, or whether she meant he simply was a good man, he'd been afraid to ask. As trammeled with guilt as he'd been over the indiscretion that led to their marriage, Angus never forgot the elation and expansion that moment had held.

He thought of the thousands of times he'd imagined finding Ebbin. Throwing their arms around each other. Good Christ, what took you so long? Ebbin would say. "Doesn't seem real, to tell the truth—Ebbin's death," he said. "Something about not finding the body, I guess."

"Sure. Like I said before, hold on to that dream if you need it. Just don't forget you've got real flesh-and-blood men under your command. You're going to lose some of them. Don't let them lose you first."

"Yes sir," Angus said.

"I'm speaking as a friend."

"I know," Angus said. He did know, but there was rank between them still and things he couldn't express like the image that had just come to him of Ebbin hiding out in a pair of baggy trousers and a red bandana somewhere south of the Front. Desertion had maybe crossed Conlon's mind as well. But no, not Ebbin. It would be counter to all Angus knew of him. Angus crushed out his cigarette. There were voices outside. A rowdy crowd was gathering. "Think I'll push off," Angus said. "That performance is over. Not sure I'm up to the aftermath."

As if summoned, a bunch of privates and junior officers burst in, the music and laughter of the performance clinging to them. Played to perfection, they shouted. Stuck it to the brass! Hilarious!

There was a great deal of scraping of chairs and pulling tables together. Talk about how good Hitch looked in a dress (nice legs!) quickly shifted to the relative merits of the five known whores in town.

"Five?! Bugger! There's twenty if there's two, and I've known them all!" Roddy Gordon roared out. He flipped a chair around and took a long swallow of someone's beer. "They said to me, 'What's under those skirts of yours?' 'Come see,' I said. 'If you dare!'" He clapped a huge hand on Angus's shoulder and reared back, cheeks flushed, eyes to the heavens. "They dared, alright! Oh, they dared! And nearly fainted away! Angus MacGrath, as I live and breathe! How the hell are you?"

"Roddy Gordon! How's it possible?" Angus hadn't seen him since they'd trained together in England.

"By God, yes! We meet again. Here am I, and thank God for it, eh? I expect to bring this war to a quick end. I'm a corporal now, you'll notice." He cocked his head at his badge, sat down and slapped his huge knees. "What have you to say for yourself?"

"How's everyone and where are they?"

"Sad story, actually." Roddy started eating Angus's potatoes with his fingers. "Where's that waitress? I'm sure to get a free supper. Likes my pipes, I can tell you! Played her more than a few tunes. Okay, so a lot of the lads are down with influenza and the rest being bled into the ranks. The great 183rd broken up and scattered to the winds. Now I'm one of your lot, ready to take the Hun and drag him over his parapet. So, how've you been keeping? Met a friend of yours tonight at the play, by the way. Sam Publicover."

"Publicover, Jesus!" Prescott said. "You should have seen him! That boy is a natural born fighter."

"Killer, more like," Cheverly Heck put in. "Had to keep him from beating a Kootenay to death after the play. The Kootenay has Roddy here to thank for his life."

"Hmm," Roddy agreed, munching thoughtfully. "Good-natured fun 'til the Kootenay resorted to name-calling of a more personal nature—'skinny-boned herring choker' was one. Things turned ugly when he called Publicover a pretty boy."

"Well, he's no herring choker. But he *is* pretty, you'll have to admit," Angus said, warming to the talk, happy to be with Roddy again.

"Indeed yes! That he is. All sunny innocence up to that point, but then he turns a murderous eye on the Kootenay, comes after him, steady on, mind, lifts him by the collar, and all hell breaks loose. Lucky the MPs were otherwise engaged. But to his credit, your man backed off when he saw it was no contest. We didn't actually have to pull him off." He shot a look at Cheverly.

"True enough." Cheverly shrugged. "I grew up with him. He's got five older sisters that dote on him. Don't know what he's so angry about."

"Maybe that," Angus smiled.

Conlon twirled his glass and said, "It's always cold calculation with Sam. He chooses his fights unless it's the Krauts. Even then, he rarely loses and never talks about it afterwards." He sighed loudly. "Suppose I'll have to dress him down for behavior unbecoming an officer."

"Well, I'll tell you one other thing about him," Roddy said soberly. "He is *one hell* of a pretty boy! And, speak of the devil!"

Publicover, grinning broadly, blue eyes innocent, not a scratch on him, swung through the crowd and grabbed a seat. "Been missing me?"

Sweat, damp wool and liquor suffused the air as talk turned to the wonder of nurses, spotted that morning in their blue capes, managing to look wholesome, healthy and entirely unapproachable. Having stayed far longer than he'd intended, Angus headed for the latrine. Jostled in line, he thought back to the upper room in London—a sanctuary of measures, grids, coordinates and intersecting lines of longitude and latitude—where the cartographers he'd hoped to join bent over their stereoscopes, transforming aerial photographs into maps. There was something elemental and pristine about it, the careful, dispassionate execution, that called up the calming effect of drawing his birds—a tamping down of emotions too deeply felt. Sorry as he'd been not to join them, he was glad now not to have been part of their remote, sterile world. Line-by-line exactitude—his talent and his defeat. Maybe it was the liquor, or Roddy's presence, or the laughter and camaraderie, but he felt grateful to be in the messy reality of the Front—the fleeting moments of joy etched all the more sharply by the horrors—all of it authentic, unspoken and understood by every man there.

When he returned to the table to take his leave, Roddy stood up. "Meant to ask. Ever find anything out about that brother-in-law of yours?"

"Declared dead. They found his tags and what was left of his platoon. Blasted away. That's the official story," Angus said. "Never recovered his body."

"Aye. Sorry." Roddy looked down at the glass he was holding between two thick fingers and his thumb. "You doubt it?"

"No, no," Angus lied. "How could I doubt it?"

"So journey over, eh?" Roddy said. "Except whoops, you're still here."

"Exactly," Angus said. "Here is where I am."

"Think we're on a suicide mission?" Roddy was serious.

"Conlon there, who apparently comes from a long line of Irish fatalists, doesn't seem to think so. Preparation, Roddy."

"Ah yes, drills and more drills, specialty training, put through our paces to keep doubt at bay. We're up against it, I'm afraid."

"Afraid so," Angus said.

"Give my best to the ever-lovely Juliette and her charming son!" Publicover called out after him.

PAUL WAS UP when he got back, his mother asleep. "I wait for you," he said. He pulled Angus down the corridor to the kitchen, where a few cans of peaches stood on the table. Ever resourceful, the kid had a friend in nearly every soldier he met. Something of his pale but wiry energy engendered both pity for his situation and admiration for his pluck. Juliette was remarkably loose with him, letting him roam about and fraternize. "He finds his own way through this *cauchemar*. It is best for him," she'd shrugged.

"So, you've found some peaches," Angus said, yawning.

"*Non*. Some other thing," said Paul. He jabbed a dirty finger at the picture of Ebbin on the table.

"What's this doing here?" Angus demanded. He swept the photo up.

"It is by your bed," Paul said. "I have see *cet homme*." He leaned in against Angus and pointed again at the picture of Ebbin. "This day, I have see him," he whispered.

Angus snapped the picture. "This man? This man?"

Paul bounced on tiptoe. "*Oui. Cet homme!*"

"Where? Where did you see him?"

"With Brigitte. With soldiers and Brigitte."

"Brigitte? Who's Brigitte?"

"You know her. Soldiers know her. *Une amie*, a friend. Shhh. Don't tell *Maman*."

Brigitte—Roddy or one of the others, or a bunch of the others, had mentioned that name. She worked in a place off-limits. Naturally, Paul knew her. "No." Angus shook his head at Paul. "You didn't see him. Couldn't have." He pointed at Ebbin's image. "This man is dead. *Il est mort*, Paul," he said, measuring his words out against his racing pulse.

Paul didn't flinch. "I see him. You are not happy?"

He's making this up, Angus thought. But Paul was hardly the sort to give false cheer. What was he up to? A genuine mistake, perhaps. "You saw someone who *looks* like him, eh? It's okay. I am okay." Angus rubbed Paul's head lightly, the white patch stiff and bristly under his palm.

Paul removed Angus's hand from his head and held it in his. "*Vous avez peur?*" he whispered.

"Afraid? Of what? Of finding him? Like he was a ghost? No, no." Angus smiled as best he could and put the picture in his pocket.

"I take you." Paul grabbed Angus's sleeve. He was insistent and so believable that Angus almost let him drag him along. Angus checked the time—11:32. "Stop," he said. "I can't let you go roaming the streets at this hour. No. You can—" Take me to him tomorrow, he was going to say. But if it really was Ebbin, he could be gone tomorrow. He could be dead tomorrow.

Paul looked at the ceiling, waiting for him to reach the obvious conclusion.

"Okay, look," Angus said. "I'll go. You stay here. Tell me where."

"*Une maison à côté du fleuve.*"

"House by the river? Where by the river?" Angus said.

"It is dark. To find it—*très difficile,*" Paul said with import. "I take you. *Maman* sleeps." He dismissed her with a wave of his hand.

Angus looked at the clock and again at Paul. God, he was convincing—his thin face, drawn and nearly white, his good eye glittering. Angus pulled out a pencil and a small pad. All Angus could think to write was, "Paul is with me (*avec moi*). He thought he saw Ebbin and is taking me to him." It seemed so crazy he almost scratched it out, but it occurred to him that she probably couldn't read English, and he couldn't write French very well, so it was all pretty futile. He could have had Paul write it, but he wanted it to be from him. Besides, they'd be back before she woke up. He centered the note on the kitchen table and stared at it.

"*Allons-y!*" Paul said.

"Okay. Done." Angus wrapped his scarf around Paul's neck and followed him out the door.

AT THE EDGE of Astile, Paul scurried down this lane and the next, cutting through the skeletons of roofless buildings. The surroundings grew increasingly unfamiliar. A flicker of hope was growing. *Hurry*, Angus wanted to say. *Hurry. Hurry.*

Tents stretched away to the east, white against the black night, the odd brazier burning here and there. The wind picked up and, with it, the flap of a tent lifted from its stakes and luffed like a loose sail. A single-story brick building with rounded walls loomed up. A horse whinnied. The stables on the outskirts of town. Paul took a sharp right down a dirt lane bordered by hedges as tall as a trench wall. A quarter of a mile later, the road dipped, and Paul turned into a cobblestone courtyard flanked by stone buildings, some very large trees, and what might have been an old granary.

Like a couple of spies, they crept across the courtyard to the corner window of a narrow structure with a wide-planked door. They planted themselves in the mushy detritus of dead weeds, feet sinking into the thin coat of snow. Angus leaned in from the side. Paul crouched so his nose was just above the sill. The light was dim, the voices loud. Smoke hung in the air. Bursts of laughter rang out over the plaintive notes of a violin. The tempo suddenly picked up.

If it was a brothel, and it clearly was, it was off-limits—neither a red lamp for ranks nor blue for officers. Angus was about to head in for a look when Paul's pointy elbow jabbed him in the ribs. Unblinking, Paul pointed at a group of soldiers playing cards. A weasel of a man facing them was in British khaki. The Canadian with his back to them had a woman on his lap, her pink-and-black-fringed shawl draped over his shoulder, her plump arm casually around his neck, caressing his hair. Paul, squinting his good eye, pointed directly at him. The glass was none too clear, but Angus scanned the others. Lots of Brits, a number of unruly Canadians at another table. The fiddler was a young woman in a black tuxedo. Another woman, clad in a thin chemise, kissed her on the mouth.

The Canadian near the window leaned back, talking, gesturing, as the others laughed. Then he pushed the woman off his lap and stroked her backside as she stood. She licked her lips at him. Angus covered Paul's eyes. Paul pulled Angus's hand down and pointed again.

"Yeah, I know. You think it's him," Angus whispered. "It's not, though." Couldn't be. Not this man, this man who threw his head back, who brushed his hair from his forehead in an all-too-familiar gesture.

Angus staggered back. "Sweet, sweet Jesus," he heard himself say. He whipped his cap off, raked his hair. "Sweet, sweet Jesus." No wonder Paul had been so sure. The Canadian stood up suddenly and was out through the crowd and gone before Angus could take it in. A side door banged open. The noise of the crowd spilled out. "Not so fast, Havers!" someone shouted. "We've a little business to settle." Footsteps on the cobblestone. Running. A thud. A low moan. "Got him!" someone else grunted.

Angus raced around to the alley. Dark and narrow, it ran between the brothel and a high garden wall. There was a stack of crates, rotting vegetables strewn about, and a couple of bicycles; just beyond them, three figures. One held the Canadian. The other faced him. "Pay up, Havers, you miserable liar," Angus heard him say.

Havers?

The heavyset soldier put his hands on his hips, then clipped the Canadian in the face, grabbed his hair, and gave him two hard jabs under the ribs. Angus clamped a hand on Paul's shoulder. "Stay put," he said, and strode toward them, revolver in the air.

"Drop him, Private," he commanded. "You! Stand back," he said to the other soldier.

The short soldier cold-cocked the Canadian as the burly one rushed Angus and brought him to the ground. The Canadian fell to the cobblestones like a sack. The revolver fell from Angus's hand, but the soldier didn't notice. "Who the hell are you?" he demanded, his breath a humid fog of alcohol on Angus's face. "And what the fuck do you want with Havers?" His hand went around Angus's neck.

"*Arrêtez!* Let him go!" came a small voice.

The soldier stared uncomprehendingly over Angus's shoulder. He loosened his grip and a sloppy grin spread across his face. "What we got here, now? A little officer?" Angus pushed him off and rolled to his feet. Paul leveled the gun with two hands. Before he could cock it, the other soldier grabbed him up from behind. Paul kicked and struggled, his striped socks dangling around his ankles. The revolver fell to the ground. The fat soldier grabbed it, held it, and looked over at Angus, his dull eyes registering something.

"That's right. I'd be the officer," Angus said. "Drop the kid, and hand over my revolver."

The soldier's mouth fell open. "I . . . thought you were in for Havers here. Sir, I thought . . ."

Angus grabbed the gun and glanced at the slumped form of the Canadian who could not possibly be Ebbin and most certainly was. "I don't give a *damn* what you thought. Get out of here or so help me God, I'll kill you both."

Turning once to look back at Angus, they stumbled down the alley, melting into the darkness at the far end. Angus holstered the revolver and quickly felt along the boy's limbs, lifted his chin. "You okay?"

Paul bobbed his head up and down. "Am all okay, Lieutenant," he said.

The side door burst open. Angus pulled Paul behind it. They flattened themselves against the wall as two corporals staggered out, sniggering and laughing. The corporals swung around and faced the wall, fumbling with their trousers, then urinated loudly. Angus looked over at the Canadian, curled on his side, still as stone. If Havers was Ebbin, the only way to protect him now was to leave him lying there unnoticed.

"Hurrah, hurrah, the general's going to be shot!" sang one soldier.

"Hurrah, hurrah, the dirty drunken sot!" sang the other.

Then in unison, "For he was very mean to me when . . ." There they stopped. One scratched his head, then buttoned up his fly. "Got it!" he said, and in a deep baritone sang, "For he was very mean to me when I was with his lot!" And they finished with a high-pitched flourish, "Hurrah boys, they're going to shoot the gennnn-eral!"

They stumbled back inside. Angus dashed to the Canadian. Violin music zigzagged through the racket. A general brawl had broken out. There was the sound of gravel flying and an auto engine idling. A revolver went off. Military police were breaking it up. Angus rolled the Canadian over, and he and Paul dragged him behind the barrels. Eyes on the door, Angus put a hand under the soldier's neck and raised his head. The soldier moaned. Angus clamped a hand over his mouth and looked down. There, looking up at him, was Ebbin. The light brown eyes rolled back. The lids shut. He was out cold.

Paul said, *"Allons-y!"*

"Where?" Angus panted.

"Là!" Paul pointed down the high stone wall across the alley.

"Through the wall? A gate?"

"Oui." Paul was already lifting Ebbin's legs.

"Let me drag him," Angus whispered. "It'll be faster."

Paul crouched through a thicket of brambles and shoved hard against a hidden plank gate. Angus hauled Ebbin through. Across a short black stretch of yard stood a shed or barn. Paul pointed. Angus nodded. They shut the gate just as long shafts of light from electric torches swept through the alley. Crouching next to Ebbin on their side of the wall, Angus heard footsteps and an "All clear," followed by "Round those men up." A whistle sounded again, and they were alone. Angus blew on his hands against the cold; Paul did the same.

Angus dragged Ebbin to the barn, mentally shuffling through all that he should be doing—filing reports on the two soldiers whose names he'd failed to get, taking Paul home, getting Ebbin to his unit or the field hospital . . . Ebbin! Jesus Christ. He had him. His mouth went dry. He wasn't about to let him go.

Angus checked again to be sure they were alone. Chickens clucked briefly, pigeons cooed in the rafters, and just beyond the open door—a garden, bedded down for the winter. An isolated patch of home and hearth standing its ground.

Paul folded the scarf under Ebbin's head and found a lantern. Angus lit it, and they held their hands out as if it were a campfire. Angus lit a cigarette and his eye caught the hint of a cord on Ebbin's neck beneath the unbuttoned tunic. He slowly lifted it out and held up the lantern. *E. Lawrence Havers, Lance Corporal, 45th BN, C.E.F.* He dropped the tags and sat back. Paul swallowed and cast a hungry look toward the cigarette. Angus passed it over.

"It is him," Paul whispered through a stream of smoke that ended in three perfect smoke rings, suspended over Ebbin's head. Angus spit on a rag and wiped blood from Ebbin's slackened mouth. He daubed at the swelling and the ragged cut on his cheek, and knew he had no compass for the territory he was about to enter.

NINE

February 24th, 1917
Deep Cove
Mahone Bay, Nova Scotia

he air was crisp and dry enough to sharpen all the senses. Fresh snow had fallen, a powdered topping over the crust beneath. All the way over to Deep Cove, with the warmth of the sun on their faces, rug over their knees, and Rooster plodding on, Simon and his grandfather had hardly spoken. It suited them both.

For everything had changed. The Hants had received a telegram of their own from the War Department the day after his father's had arrived. After that, his mother shivered with her own truth. There was no body. He has *not* been found. Which left Simon torn between protecting her from the truth and wanting to make her see it. But how? He even entertained the idea that she might be right. He was only too relieved to see her two young half-brothers come up the road and fetch her back to Chester, where her family would take care of her, but still felt ashamed of his own inadequacy.

A memorial was being planned, the brothers said. She's temporarily unmoored, Simon's grandfather whispered to the brothers, a fact they accepted. High-strung, one of them said, his face drawn, throwing a blanket over the dray. She'll come round, said the other. It's the shock of it, Duncan agreed.

"Sight for sore eyes, eh?" his grandfather said as they reached the top of the ridge. Below them, the blue-black water of the long, glacier-cut cove offered up its mystery. It was so silent at the top of the ridge that they could hear the ripples under the beard of ice along the shore.

"You own this cove, right, Grandpa?" Simon asked.

"No, no, just this piece of the ridge we're standing on," his grandfather said. "Can't buy the sea, lad."

"Right," Simon agreed, and after a moment, added, "I might buy some islands, myself. Rafuse, because it has the best beach. I'd always let people picnic on it like they do now. And Oak Island, one day."

"After treasure, are you?"

"Maybe. Me and Zenus might take our dory over to Oak this summer. See how the digging's going."

"That old dory? Can't point worth a damn. Her sail is stiff as a board. Take you a week to get there." His grandfather chuckled at the thought of it.

"She can't point," Simon conceded, "but she moves along on a reach." He and Zenus had found her, an abandoned Lunenburg dory, or what had looked like one. It was longer than a dory, but outfitted the same and still had a bobber and line in it. It had washed up on the rocky beach by Oxner's boathouse. No one claimed it, a mystery that added to its appeal. In exchange for some work, quite a bit of work, Philip Mader had helped them replace her rotting planks, outfitted her with a centerboard, tiller, rudder and a new mast that they could slip into a hole in the forward seat. Wider than a Shelburne dory, she could be rowboat or sailboat, depending. Not very fast, not very responsive, but she was theirs.

"Got a name for her?"

"Not yet. We've been discussing it." They'd been arguing about it for two years. In the beginning, when they weren't arguing over her

THE CARTOGRAPHER OF NO MAN'S LAND • 137

name, they used to force the mop to walk the plank, then turn the dory around to rescue it, a drowning maiden, her thick rope hair all sodden. And they'd talk about ways to defy the sand-slipping underground caverns of Oak Island, where it was a known fact that Captain Kidd had buried his treasure. Periscopes is what they'd be searching for this year when they were out on the bay. "If I owned Oak, people could come and picnic or dig for the treasure, if they've a mind to. Pay me for the right to dig. Picnic for free. Might get them interested that way."

"Simon Peter, fisher of men, I think you have the makings of an entrepreneur!"

"A what?"

"A businessman. Speaking of your future, Philip says you've got a feel for boatbuilding. Something I wouldn't mind getting into one day. MacGrath and MacGrath. Eh? How's that? You liked working with Philip on your unnamed dory."

"Yes sir."

"Knew it. How about I send you over to Tancook for a time this summer? See if one of the Stevens boys would take you on or old Gaundy Langille—well, he's too old. Retired now. Or Reuben Heisler. Fine craftsman. He's got that forty-two-tonner going over there. *Silver Oak,* she's called."

"What about Philip?"

"Philip's small-time. Repairs, mostly. Built the *Lauralee,* but her design is way out of date. He hasn't built a new boat in years and wouldn't be much good at it anyhow. My plan is, you learn it from the ground up."

His grandfather always had a plan. Simon wasn't about to be shipped off to Tancook Island for a summer, living on fish and sauerkraut with the four or five families who lived there, and no friends. He knew exactly what he was going to do. As soon as he could get to Lunenburg, he'd ask Captain Knickle about a place on his salt banker. "What if I don't want to learn?"

"Eh? No. You need to know a business from stem to stern. You know, when we built the *Lauralee,* I took your father over to Martin's River and we searched out the straightest, strongest spruce we could find for her masts."

Simon remembered his father saying that when he put his hand on the *Lauralee's* main mast, it was the tree come to second life. He squinted at the black water below and switched the subject. "Deep Cove is so deep it could have held the *Titanic,* right? That's what Dad said."

His grandfather frowned, but allowed that Deep Cove, a glacier gut, could manage the *Titanic.*

"Deep enough for subs then. There's talk they're out there," Simon said.

"Subs in Mahone Bay, eh? In Deep Cove, no less. Where do you get such ideas?"

"Around town. And the *Herald.*"

"You quote that warmongering rag to me?"

"You quote it to me!"

"Course I do. But not because I trust every word in it. I've told you that. If we were to believe the *Herald,* every man in Lunenburg should be rounded up as a spy for their German names alone. As for the *Titanic,* that product of man's hubris rests in another ocean crevasse, never to be found. And now the *Britannic,* her sister ship—torpedoed and sunk. Both of them monuments to man's self-glorification . . . God has his ways."

The rows of caskets, some of them tiny, stacked behind the protective cover of a tent on the Halifax docks came to Simon, and all those left captive in the *Titanic's* hull, bumping against staterooms and stairways, drifting silently past portholes in the currents. "The *Britannic* was a hospital ship," he said. "She's not a monument to— whatever you said. Self-gratification."

"Exactly," his grandfather answered. "*Dragged* into the war. What you might want to think about while folks over here spread false rumors about submarines is all the boys on the other side of this war that are missing uncles and fathers. Eh?"

Simon now regretted the trip altogether.

"Your own father . . . gone on a fool's errand and now—"

"*A fool's errand?*" Simon burst out. "Who cares if he found Uncle Ebbin or not! He's out there defending us, and you—you don't even write to him!"

His grandfather didn't flinch. Didn't look at him. Just said, "Watch yourself," with that low-voiced menace that sent a shiver down the spine. Point made, he switched to a brighter note. "Well, sir," he said, "fresh snow or not, I haven't seen a thing here that indicates a camp-fire or trespasser. We'll circle round through those firs and get back to Rooster. These old bones of mine are feeling the cold. His, too, no doubt." He patted a gloved hand on Simon's wool hat and started back down the hill. "See if we can get a mug up at Toby's," he called out without looking back.

Simon seethed as his grandfather marched off with utter confidence that Simon would follow. He glanced at the smoke curling up from Toby's chimney. Toby'd be by the wood stove, mending his nets, the old pin in his gnarled hands weaving in and out. No sir. Simon would not be working for Langille or Reuben Heisler or any of them this summer. He'd be off to the Banks himself. He'd come back with money in his pocket. His mother could lean on him then. He'd tell her of his adventures and make her laugh just like Uncle Ebbin used to.

He shuffed through the snow after his grandfather, who wove handily through the spruce and stumpy pine and skinny poplars, dodging boulders and underbrush, and then at the foot of the ridge dropped heavily to the ground. And then Simon was running in great awkward leaps through snow, his scarf trailing, his limbs flailing. His grandfather slumped forward. Simon slid the last few steps and thumped against him in a blur and saw the fox at his grandfather's knees—stiff and matted, black eyes open wide, gums pulled back in death's grimace.

"*Trapping!*" his grandfather spat out.

Simon thrashed back on his elbows. His grandfather looked at him with round eyes as if Simon could explain it to him, with eyes near tears. Dumbly, he shifted his gaze from Simon to the fox. "The utter cruelty of it. Gone and gnawed his foot off to get free," he said. Blood spattered the snow. He held the little paw against his knee and rocked back and forth. Then he tore the trap from the ground and flung it off over his head. It clanged off a boulder and buried itself in the snow. He tramped after it and yanked it up and threw it again.

Simon crawled to the fox and put a tentative mitten on the fur. His own tears were falling. "We can bury it. Can't we?"

Trap in hand, his grandfather searched for others. "Please," Simon pleaded. His grandfather looked up at the sky for a long time. "Please," Simon whispered.

"We'll leave it for the crows," his grandfather said. "They need to live as well. We won't sentimentalize nature so as to call ourselves civilized."

Simon set the little paw by the fox's leg. The solitary hunter lay stiff and exposed. Simon mounded snow over the body. He took off his mittens and cut the cord that held his knife to his belt and used the string to fashion two twigs into a cross and set them into the snow. Overhead, three crows flew fast, wings flapping.

SIMON THOUGHT ABOUT the crows a week later as he left the memorial service. Their raucous rasps, their ragged wings. Gulls lifted high above his head, high over St. Stephen's square belfry, with wings that held the currents in their gliding. Crows knew nothing of the wind—how to find it, how to ride it, where it had been, where it was going.

Like so many black crows collected in a tree, the mourners had gathered now at the Hants—silence broken by little bursts of talk that grew louder as they piled slices of Finnan haddie, biscuits and boiled potatoes onto their plates and forked up slices of cold lamb. Standing by the window, light falling on her cream cutwork blouse, his mother smiled softly as friends offered their condolences—smiled in an indulgent way as she had during the service, as if sorry for their confusion in thinking Ebbin dead, but willing to accept sympathy for their sake. Balancing a slippery boiled egg on a plate, Simon found a place behind a stuffed chair next to his grandfather Hant's bulky accordion. The accordion would not be played that day. Nor the silver harmonica on top of the piano, nor the piano.

For Simon, the service had been a blur of black crepe and Union Jacks and Red Ensigns and regimental colors and ancient old Athol McLaren squeezing out "The Flowers of the Forest" and "Amazing Grace" on the pipes and speeches before the service and clutched handkerchiefs and clutched hands during. It was his mother's slow turn as she held out a gloved hand for Young Fred and Simon to join her in the pew. It was a funeral without a casket and people crowding the church from nearby villages. It was Grandma Hant, heavy and lumbering, supported by two sons, followed by the massive form of Amos Hant, like a slow-paced engine going down a track.

All the Hants were massive, except for Simon's mother and Uncle Ebbin, who were blond and fine-featured, as if they'd arrived together in a basket left on the doorstep. Which they had, in fact—a story Ida told again to Simon the day after they heard Ebbin was dead—how Amos Hant had parked the babies, just thirteen months apart, on Elma Mitchell's doorstep when he came back home to Mahone Bay from the failed farm after burying his wife in her family's plot on the Alberta plains. Each night after a day's work at the forge that he'd wanted to escape and would later come to own, he'd pick the babies up. A few months into it, he decided it might be easier to skip the dropping off and picking up by marrying Elma Mitchell, who went on to give him four sturdy, dark-haired sons.

And there standing guard over her as she sat, twisting a handkerchief around her thick fingers, was Lady Bromley with talk of God's great purpose—"fallen hero," "noble sacrifice," "angels of victory"—each word increasing Simon's dread that every man in France would end up unfound and unburied. His tears during the service had been a pouring out of that fear.

Out back, men had gathered around a fire pit. Putnam Pugsley, Vor Moody, Wallace, Zeb, Herman Weagle, Wilson Bethune, Frank Stevens and one of his boys and some others Simon didn't know. Probably talking about the war from the grim look on their faces. Simon wanted to hear what they were saying, but it was cigars and hard cider and no shadows to hide in.

A hand thrust a hot cherry square on a napkin at him. He took it and ducked through the crowd to the kitchen, where his mother was head-to-head, whispering with Margaret McInnis. Maggie or Mags, his mother called her, an old school friend who'd come down from Halifax and had hardly left her side all weekend, draped in black as she had been since her brothers were blown to smithereens at Sanctuary Wood two years before. Sorry as he felt for her, Simon decided he didn't like her much, nor her whispered secrets to his mother. He went out the back door, and decided to find himself a spot on the porch with its view of Front Harbor.

"Hant heart, faint heart, bold heart."

Simon jumped. George stood on his crutches next to a rain barrel where the path curved around the house. His pale eyes reflected nothing. His knuckles were raw and bleeding. His hair was slicked straight back, his forehead wide and pale. He'd been at the service and had several times stood up as if in protest. His mother had had to settle him. People steered clear of him afterwards.

"A medal for his heart box is what he should have. Thiepval.

Weepval. Regina trench. Nearly passed me by with the badge of the 45th, but turned back."

Simon felt compelled to set George straight because Simon knew all the names of all the battles. "My uncle?" he said. "He wasn't with the 45th. And he wasn't at Thiepval. He died before that at Courcelette." He let that sink in. Said the word "died," and meant it suddenly.

"Hant heart, bold heart," George repeated, shaking his head. "Came back running. Pal of my heart, bone out my calf, heart in his chest box, beating to the drum." He began to shiver. Spittle formed at his mouth.

"Where's your mum? You're getting cold," Simon said. But George's eyes were fixed on the cherry square in Simon's hand. Simon offered it up. "Here. Take it. Take all of it." George lunged forward, hands on his crutches, and bit into it. Crumbs and cherry filling clung to his cracked lips. The rest of it fell to the ground. Simon's mouth fell open. He backed away.

"I have five silver coins in five silver—"

"No! You don't!" Simon shouted.

Snowmelt crashed off the eaves and tipped over the rain barrel with a massive thud. George arched back, flung his crutches and dove for the ground. Hands over his head he elbowed into a hole in the lattice work at the foundation of the porch. There he jerked like a string puppet. Simon was rooted to the spot, horrified. Then the leg went still, and he thought George was dead.

He looked up to see Mr. Heist setting the rain barrel upright. A strangled choking came from under the house. "It's George!" Simon cried out. "That thing tipped over, and he dove under the porch. I'm going to get my grandfather!"

"*Ach*. Wait now, Simon. Wait," Mr. Heist insisted, coming toward him in rapid little steps. "Let's not have everyone out here, seeing him this way. Let's just give him a little time."

"Time for what? What's he doing? Why's he under there? He's having a fit. He needs—the doctor maybe." Simon looked anxiously up at the house.

But Mr. Heist was on his knees by the bushes, talking to George, very softly. "Just a rain barrel. That's all, George. It's over." He stretched out and pushed against the latticework and got himself in far enough to put an arm around George. "Listen," he said. "Silence. See? It's safe now." Simon could hear George's muffled sobs. They stayed like that for minutes. Simon knelt down, stood up, looked around.

After a time, Mr. Heist eased himself back. His suit was wet and muddy. His collar and glasses, too. "We may be here a bit longer, Simon," he said.

"It's my fault. He was trying to tell me something and I wouldn't let him. I tried to stop him from saying—"

"No. It is not your fault. The barrel went over. It was too loud for George, too sudden. I've seen this before." He took off his glasses and shook out his handkerchief to wipe his face. "We need to hope no one comes out. You see what you can do."

"*Me?*"

"Why not? He was talking with you. He doesn't talk often." Simon hung his head. Mr. Heist wiped the back of his neck and polished his glasses.

"George?" Simon said, finally, crouching down, keeping his distance. He could see the heaving of George's breath, could smell his sour sweat, and the odor of urine made his own stomach heave. He swallowed hard and held his breath, then whispered, "Peg's here." George lifted his head. Simon looked back at Mr. Heist, who nodded encouragingly. "She's wondering where you are," Simon said.

George inched out a bit and finally backed all the way out and hunched over like a baby, head in his hands. Simon looked away.

Voices above. Footsteps crossing the porch. The thumping of a cane. Simon wanted to shove George back under the porch. At the bottom of the steps, Lady Bromley nearly tripped over one of

George's crutches. She and Lord Bromley took in the scene. "George fell," Simon said quickly. "By mistake."

"We're just helping him up," Mr. Heist added.

"Look at you! Covered in mud! Have you been rolling around on the ground with him?" Lady Bromley shoved at the crutch with her cane. "Of all the bother! Why ever did he come? He should be kept at home."

"Kept at *home*?" Mr. Heist said, whipping off his spectacles, one hand on George.

"For his own protection, of course!" Lady Bromley huffed. "What would *you* know about what's best for him? Go inside, Simon, and get some help, for heaven's sake. Get Duncan."

"We have it in hand," Mr. Heist said.

"Apparently, you do not," she replied, and tromped back up the stairs herself, attacking each step with the cane. "Duncan! Mr. Hant!" they heard her call out at the door.

"*Ach*, wore him like a medal pinned to her chest when he came back," Mr. Heist muttered. "But now . . ."

George rolled over and sat up, slack and confused. Lord Bromley handed him his crutches and the three of them pulled him to his feet and brushed him off as best they could. A crow swooped down and plucked at the cherry square, then lifted away with it to the roof. Simon stared at the remains of red filling congealed in the dirty snow. "Thiepval, weepval," George whispered.

TEN

February 24th, 1917
Arras Sector, France

In the shed, with Paul standing sentry, Angus hovered over Ebbin. He was surprised to see the badge of the 45th on Ebbin's sleeve. Had he switched units? Ebbin coughed, coughed again, and rolled over. "Ebbin!" Angus whispered. Ebbin spit out blood, cupped his jaw and got up on all fours. Pale as a ghost, dripping blood, he slowly raised his head. Angus froze at the blank stare he got and then remembered how long it could take Ebbin to come to from a faint. Ebbin glanced at Paul and back to Angus. "Thanks," he mumbled. He sat back on his haunches, pressing the rag against the bleeding cut, eyes closed. Then, staring into middle space, he attempted a salute. "Lance Corporal . . . Lawrence Havers . . . sir," he said without a flicker of recognition.

Angus shot a glance at Paul, who nodded as if they were consulting physicians.

"Ebbin," Angus said, gripping his shoulder. "Ebbin. It's me, Angus. I've been searching for you."

Heartbreak ticked against heartbreak in the seconds that passed without response. Ebbin in his grasp and just out of reach.

Ebbin swayed and fell forward. Angus steadied him, pressed his handkerchief gently against the wound. Ebbin jerked back, and fending him off, tried to stand. "Dizzy," he said. His breath was shallow. He was clearly in pain.

How much easier it was then to enter in. To help the soldier up, tell him he was taking him to a field hospital, that everything would be sorted out, to break the frail moment through which the past might enter in and break his heart. He helped Ebbin up. "Steady, soldier," he said.

Paul shut the lantern down. Leaning on Angus, Ebbin stumbled forward. At the shed door, Paul pointed to his eyes, then flipped his hand up for them to wait. A cat darted at them and wound through Paul's legs. He didn't flinch. Then he motioned them forward.

When they reached the alley, a woman slipped out the side door of the brothel as if she, too, had been watching and waiting. A diaphanous shape in a loose-sleeved robe, her blond hair was wound with white cotton rags tied into knots. She ran up, barefoot, carrying Ebbin's coat. "Lurrhrey? Lurrhrey!" she said. Her face sallow in the dim light, her lips pale, she clutched Ebbin's face in her hands. The coat fell from her arms. *"Mon Dieu, mon chéri!* But what has happened?"

Ebbin stood helpless. Angus removed her plump hands from his face. "I've got him," he said firmly. "I'm taking him to the field hospital. Go back inside." He gestured toward the door impatiently. Nearly shoved her. Picked up the coat, draped it over Ebbin. There was no need to ask how she came to have it.

Paul, hopping from one foot to the other, spoke to her in French. In angry whispers, she made clear her contempt and suspicion. Paul nodded vigorously at Angus, and she reluctantly turned away. Angus and Ebbin moved on. "Come on, Paul," Angus said.

"Brigitte," Paul panted, when he caught up to them. "I tell her, go back. *Retournez! C'est* okay." He rewound the scarf Angus had given him around his neck and offered a supporting arm on Ebbin's other side. They stumbled on.

"Loohrey?" Angus looked at Ebbin.

"Laurie," Ebbin corrected him. "For Lawrence." He stopped and doubled over. He was having trouble speaking or breathing, but he wanted to clarify. "She just . . . says it funny . . . in that French way."

"Ah," said Angus. "Of course." Why not? Laurie, Lawrence . . . They said no more until they reached the field hospital. I've got him. Found him at last, Angus kept thinking, but felt his own reality slipping away as he led Ebbin on.

"ANOTHER ONE?" THE doctor said, adjusting the light, when Angus and Paul brought Ebbin into an examining area.

"Another one?" Angus repeated.

"Yes. Yes, yes, *yes*! Another one. That's what I said." The doctor, an older man, observed Ebbin from under bushy black and gray eyebrows as he rocked back and forth. He tapped a pen against his thick, pock-marked nose and took a sharp breath. "Had four other fellows in here. Dislocated jaws and broken ribs. Quite a brawl. He was in it, was he? We don't need more injuries, but there you are. Restless, pent-up. Fight Jerry, I tell them, not each other."

"Ah," Angus said.

"Pleasant, actually," the doctor continued. "Nice change from wounds, self-inflicted, and the rest. Very nice." He smiled at each of them and rocked back on his heels, as if their business were concluded.

Angus tightened his hold on Ebbin, trying not to squeeze his chest, amazed at how familiar the form, yet how light, how nearly hollow it seemed. "Shall I?" Angus nodded at the examining table.

"What? Of course, be my guest." They got Ebbin up on the table. A nurse thrust a thermometer in his mouth and opened his tunic. She gently cleaned the blood from his cheek. The doctor inspected the wound, felt his chest. Told him to breathe, listened with his stethoscope. His eyebrows shot up and down. He whipped the thermometer out. "No temperature. No influenza. No sepsis. No shrap in the abdomen. No gangrene. Wonderful." He continued his examination of Ebbin's torso and shook his head. "So messy, shrapnel in the belly. Eh? No phosgene. Just had six of those. Gas set off accidentally. Didn't get Jerry, did it? Course not. Got our boys, instead. Lungs frothy mush by the time they got here. Unwrap those puttees, would you? Get his boots off." He nodded at Angus, who pulled off the boots and began to unwrap the bindings. Ebbin stared ahead with glassy eyes. The doctor glanced at Angus. "You're glad of those long socks under that skirt of yours, I'll wager. Or should be. I have a theory about trench foot. Puttees compress when they get wet. Cut off circulation. So. It's not just about manhood, eh now? The entire force would be in kilts, instead of just a few regiments, if I had my say."

Angus moved back around the table. The doctor continued his probing. "And look!" he said, holding Ebbin's chin in his hand. "He has a whole face! Swollen, badly cut, but whole. Think of it, Nurse!" He smiled at her. "I'm imagining a brain in there, too." He tapped Ebbin lightly on the head with a spoon he produced from his pocket while he held a hand out for the narrow flashlight and tongue depressor. "Eh? Have we got a brain? Tongue to go with it? Open wide. Grand. Hmmm . . . Nurse will stitch that cheek up and send you on your way. Name and rank, soldier. Ah, wait. Swelling here on the back of the skull."

With that, Ebbin fell back across the table. "Well, sir!" said the doctor, grunting as he swung Ebbin onto the table.

"I think he was hit pretty hard or fell back on the stones. He's an easy fainter, and it's always hard to bring him round," Angus said.

"Easy fainter, eh? You must know him well."

Angus realized his mistake.

The doctor frowned as he lifted Ebbin's lids and demanded to know if he'd been unconscious and for how long.

"Few minutes. Five at the most, maybe ten," Angus said. It had all been so dream-like he had no real idea.

"*Ten?* Why didn't you say so? Did his breathing stop?"

"More like five. Maybe. I don't know. He never stopped breathing, no."

"Good, because he's barely breathing now." He bent over his patient. "Legs *up!*" he shouted. The nurse raised Ebbin's legs. "Come on, Nurse. Higher! Straight up! Yes, you help her. Get that blood back into the head." Even Paul pushed against the thighs and helped hold them in the air.

"Hello," the doctor said, listening with his stethoscope. "Here with us? C'mon. Let's get that pulse back. Good lord, where is it? He's stopped breathing."

He had. Then his eyes flew open and his breath returned in a rapid tattoo of deep grunts. Angus pushed his legs higher. He'd seen this look on Ebbin before—the fixed, unseeing stare. Had heard the death rattle as he came to. Ebbin always said that coming out of a faint was like returning from death's embrace. It was a struggle. Death isn't so bad, he used to joke. His breath began to gain its natural rhythm, and his eyes began to focus.

"You with us?" The doctor's tone was urgent. Ebbin moaned. "Hold on. We're just going to keep you like this," the doctor said, a hand on Ebbin's shoulder. "You can lower his legs. Slowly now. Keep them bent at the knee. You see," he said to the nurse. "We've just witnessed the kind of shock that can overtake the entire system from what for some people is a simple loss of consciousness, for others, is life-threatening. If only we knew why." He leaned over Ebbin. "Are you with us, man?"

Ebbin grunted, "Yeah, I'm here."

"Where is here?"

Ebbin stared at the light above him. "Hospital? Did I pass out? Am I wounded?"

Angus looked up with a stab of hope.

The doctor said, "Not wounded in the traditional sense. But yes. And you did faint, dead away, as we say. And you are in a field hospital. Right. Right indeed. Your friend here can fill you in." He rapped Ebbin lightly on the shoulder. "Name and rank, soldier."

"Ernest Lawrence Havers, Lance Corporal with the, the 45th."

"Right—good enough. Don't need your whole biography. My advice? Stay out of *estaminets*, away from drink. There's a good fellow. Stick to the trenches and you'll be fine, eh? Little joke. There you go. Right as rain. Now," the doctor turned to Angus, "we have a bit of other work to do, Nurse and I . . ." His eyes slid over Paul and back to Angus as if Paul's presence was not only unaccounted for but never could be. "Work to do," he continued briskly. "You can imagine. It's a hospital. So your job, after Nurse cleans that wound, stitches him up, two or three should do it, applies a compress to his head, is to keep this man *awake!* We don't want him falling asleep on us. Might not wake up if he does. Got that? You're right, he's a fainter. And maybe has a concussion. No way of knowing. Keep him talking. Or keep him listening. If you've got a story or two to tell, tell it now—to him, not me. In two hours, if he's not passed out again, he'll be able to leave. Got it? Someone will be around to check." The doctor tapped his nose with his pocket spoon and cocked his head at Angus.

"Got it, yes," Angus said.

"Good. Stay awake!" he commanded Ebbin, who was trying to prop himself up on his elbows. With that, the doctor left. The nurse took out dressings and tape. Angus took Paul outside. He needed to get him home. A corporal he knew with the Red Cross, just off-duty, happened by and agreed to take him. Paul wanted to stay, but Angus would have none of it.

"I had the truth," Paul said before he left.

Angus whispered in his ear, "You did. I'm proud of you. Listen, I'm counting on you to keep it a secret. For now. Can you do that?"

Paul nodded. "Havers," he said.

"Right. Good. Go home, Paul, and thanks." Angus saluted. "Well done, soldier."

Beaming, Paul saluted back.

Angus grabbed the door frame as Paul and the corporal left, grateful to be alone. Above his upturned face, not a single star penetrated the cloud cover. The night air, cold and damp, pressed against him. A fragile moon appeared. For just one more moment he wanted to close his eyes and savor the part of the dream in which Ebbin was found— before he considered how lost he truly was. But he could not sustain it. He stamped out his cigarette and went back to the ward.

The lamp was low in the long room with the lined-up cots, all but two occupied. The sharp smell of disinfectant pierced the fetid stench of wounds. It was a surgical ward, the only place they had beds that night. Ebbin, awake next to the wall at the far end, was propped against two pillows. A nurse was just leaving him. He shut his eyes as Angus approached. "You're the one brought him in?" the nurse asked. "Good. Keep him awake. Don't dare let him slip into sleep. You can talk softly. There's a chair over there. I'll be back."

Angus brought the chair over and gripped the back of it, nearly overcome by the familiar rounded forehead, prominent cheekbones, the light brows, the small black mole beneath the earlobe. A gauze dressing was taped across Ebbin's cheek, split and swollen now, and dark red with bruising. His hair, Angus noted, was parted on the opposite side. He was in blue pajamas. He did not open his eyes when Angus sat down.

His uniform, neatly folded, was at the foot of the bed. Angus stared at the badge. How had he switched regiments? He looked down at the deep blues and greens of his kilt, at the yellow line rippling through the pleats, and remembered Hettie Ellen in a plaid skirt, its greens and yellows blending into the dappled greens of the woods behind his father's house where, back against a tree trunk, he'd been sketching afternoon sunlight through the trees. Bending through the branches, light flecked her blouse, caught her swept-up hair, the silver buckle of her school pin. Your father told me I might find you here, she said. I'm home on holiday. Half a term left and I'll be done. Brought you something. She held out two thin sable brushes and took a step toward him, a willow in sunlight. A twig snapped beneath her feet. Hettie. Home from school. Alone with him.

He turned back to Ebbin. *Laurie, short for Lawrence.* What terrible thing had happened that he took another man's name, another man's uniform and rank? Angus found the situation so preposterous that he began to believe the answer would be easy to grasp as soon as Ebbin regained himself.

"Ebbin," he whispered. "Open your eyes. It's me, Angus." Surely Ebbin could not resist his voice, surely not his name. Not this time. But he did.

Angus tried his other tack. "Soldier, I'm talking to you."

Ebbin's eyes snapped open.

Angus sat back hard. "Name and rank," he said.

"Ernest Lawrence Havers, Lance Corporal, 45th Battalion, D Company, 14 Platoon," was the rote reply. Ebbin kept his eyes forward.

"I'm looking for a soldier named Ebbin Hant. Know him? He was with the 12th."

Ebbin shifted with agitation.

He was in there, alright. Angus was sure of it, but how much better if he weren't. How much better that would be. Angus would tell the doctor, who would see that this man was clearly in no shape to carry on. That he didn't have any idea who he was or how he'd jumped rank, nor who Havers was. He'd be sent off to recuperate— in a place where lush lawns stretched out to trimmed hedges, where tiered gardens led to a dripping fountain on which a stone angel might be perched, arms open. *Come to me, ye that are heavy-laden, and I will refresh you.* A safe haven away from court-martial and God only knew what punishment. Away from enemy fire and firing squads. Safe from himself until the war was over, when Angus would take him home.

Angus said, "This Ebbin Hant. I think he's in trouble. I think you can help him."

Ebbin shook his head sadly. "No. He's not." An excruciating pause followed during which Ebbin opened and closed his mouth several times. Finally, he said, "Ebbin Hant is dead."

"Dead?"

"Died at Courcelette."

"I don't think so—"

"Yeah? Were you there?"

"No," Angus admitted.

"So you don't know."

"Know what?"

"Anything." Ebbin slid his eyes, cold and empty, toward Angus.

Angus felt the muscles of his jaw tense. "Like what? What don't I know?"

"Like what it's like to hear men screaming after they're dead," Ebbin whispered.

"Is that what Hant heard?" Ebbin did not respond. Angus gripped his shoulder and shook it. "Tell me," he said with an insistence he instantly regretted. Tread lightly, he told himself. Get a grip. But his breath was irregular, and he felt the slow burn of anger rising. The man in the next bed moaned and kept moaning. The nurse materialized with a lamp.

"I said keep *him* awake, not everyone on the ward!" she hissed. She felt the other soldier's forehead, checked his dressing, gave Angus a sharp look, and was off to help lift a new patient into an empty bed at the far end of the ward; you could hear the man struggling to breathe. Angus tried to shut it out, but it was impossible. "Ebbin Hant saved my life," he whispered. "I'd like to save his . . ." His hand hovered above Ebbin's. Ebbin snatched it away. "Couldn't have. No one could. He was a lousy soldier. Froze up. More than once. Better off dead. There's plenty like him, more a hindrance than help. They're all better off dead."

"That's not the Ebbin Hant I know. Who is Lance Corporal Havers?"

"Me. I am. Lance Corporal Lawrence Havers. I told you."

"No, you're *not*." Angus leaned in close and went for broke. "You're impersonating him," he hissed. "That's a crime. You've jumped rank. A worse crime. I'm asking you one more time, who is or was Lance Corporal Havers?"

"I am," Ebbin replied without flinching.

"Sweet, sweet Jesus, Ebbin. What the hell is going on?" Angus stood up and raked his hand through his hair. "I come over here to find—"

"Hant? Wasted your time, you poor bastard," Ebbin said flatly.

It was all Angus could do not to slap him. A poisonous humiliation flared through him. He wanted to punch the wall, fling the chair across the room. He gripped the iron bar at the head of the bed and with utmost effort at control, leaned in close, and said into Ebbin's ear, "Wasted my time? Listen to me, you ungrateful son of a bitch. The best you can hope for is being court-martialed and maybe shot, unless you lay this out for me. Who the hell do you think you are?" He paused. "Forgive me. I think I know the answer to that one. What about Hettie, eh? And your parents? What about *them*? They think you're *dead*. Is that what you want? *Is it?*"

He backed away, but Ebbin grabbed his collar and pulled him down. "Yes," he whispered into his ear. "Because that's the truth." Angus jerked, but Ebbin held him fast. "Listen to me. *Listen*. We're all going to die over here. The only question is how. Ebbin Hant died early on. But not Havers. Havers lives on." He released his hold. His arm dropped to his side.

Angus sat back, incensed at his own confusion. "Who the *fuck* is Havers?"

Ebbin turned to face him and in an urgent whisper said, "Your man

Hant shot a soldier in Ypres, a pal of his. No one knew because one minute they were filling sandbags, and the next the Krauts opened up. Hant got Willie through the neck." Tears pooled above his puffed cheek and leaked into the bandage.

Angus let this sink in. Thought of Orland. Said with all the pity he could muster, "It was a mistake. It happens. I've seen it myself. Gun misfires—besides, it was probably a German got your pal. How could you possibly know?"

Ebbin shook his head. "He wasn't *my* pal. And it *was* Hant's bullet. He wasn't much good before that. He was nothing but a wreck after."

"What about Havers? Was he there?" *Had Ebbin killed Havers, too?*

"No, no. Of course not. I got the story from Hant before he died."

There was a great stir at the other end of the ward. Nurses came running with the doctor who had treated Ebbin. Lights came on by the bed. Clotted, choking sounds filled the room. Angus half-stood.

"Gas. Phosgene, chlorine, doesn't matter," Ebbin whispered flatly. "He won't make it."

The nurses had the patient leaning forward. A last, desperate, gurgling gasp for air, and then a heaving, and then silence. They laid him back down. Men on the ward, some propped on an elbow, some sitting upright, watched and listened in silence. The doctor checked his watch and noted the time of death. A nurse pulled a sheet over the soldier and he was lifted onto a stretcher and wheeled away. The wheels creaked down the corridor. Death hovered a moment over the empty bed and then slid along the floor.

"Poor bugger," the soldier in the next bed sighed.

Angus reached for the chain around his neck and withdrew the cross. He slipped it off, held it tightly for a moment and then showed it to Ebbin. "Recognize this?"

Ebbin grabbed it. "The cross! Where'd you find it?" He closed his fist over it.

"Yours, huh? You even had it inscribed." At last they were getting somewhere. "ELH."

"Yes, it's mine. First name Ernest. Middle name Lawrence, Laurie."

Angus raked his hand through his hair in desperation. "Christ," he hissed.

Ebbin sat up and rocked back and forth, arms around his ribs. "Get away from me. Leave me alone. Please."

"I can't," Angus said. "We'll figure this out together, okay? Trust me."

Ebbin stopped rocking and looked at the cross and said softly, "Ebbin Hant died but Havers survives. He'll keep on living when this body I'm walking around in is gone." With that he sank back on the pillows, exhausted. He asked for water. Asked Angus to read to him. Angus could see he needed a break. Hell, *he* needed a break. He found some water, but there wasn't enough light to read, and he didn't have a book. "Give us a poem, then," Ebbin pleaded.

There was such familiarity in that request that it gave Angus hope. He began the first poem that came to mind, one he and Ebbin used to trade line for line. It might break Havers and bring back Ebbin. Who exactly Havers was, he didn't much care. He'd need to care later but not now, not now. He began:

"I want free life and I want fresh air;
And I sigh for the canter after the cattle,
The crack of the whips like shots in a battle,
The medley of horns and hoofs and heads
That wars and wrangles and scatters and spreads;
The green beneath and the blue above,
And dash and danger, and life and love.

"And Lasca!"

Without opening his eyes, the soldier in the next bed said, "Go on then."

"I'll take some of that," another soldier struggled to say. "Some of that fresh air and free life. Yes sir. I'll take Lasca, too."

"Shhhh!" the nurse said, standing.

"Please, let us have a poem, Nurse," a soldier cried out, and others agreed. Perhaps because the soldier who died had the men astir, she nodded her assent.

Angus carried on.

> *"Lasca used to ride on a mouse-gray mustang close by my side,*
> *With blue serape and bright-belled spur;*
> *I laughed with joy as I looked at her!*
> *Little knew she of books or of creeds;*
> *An Ave Maria sufficed her needs;*
> *Little she cared, save to be by my side,*
> *To ride with me, and ever to ride,*
> *From San Saba's shore to LaVaca's tide."*

Many lines later, he came near the end.

> *"The air was heavy, and the night was hot,*
> *I sat by her side, and forgot—forgot;*
> *Forgot the herd that were taking their rest,*
> *Forgot that the air was close opprest,*
> *That the Texas Norther comes sudden and soon,*
> *In the dead of night or the blaze of noon;*
> *That, once let the herd at its breath take fright,*
> *Nothing on earth can stop the flight;*
> *And woe to the rider, and woe to the steed,*
> *Who falls in front of their mad stampede!"*

Further on, when Lasca, stretched across her lover to protect him, is dead, Angus drew a long breath and continued,

> *"I gouged out a grave a few feet deep*
> *And there in Earth's arms I laid her to sleep;*
> *And there she is lying, and no one knows,*
> *And the summer shines and the winter snows;*

His voice broke on the last lines, *"'And I wonder why I do not care for the things that are like the things that were . . .'"*

"'Does half my heart lie buried there,'" the soldier next to Ebbin said softly, and in unison they finished it, *" 'In Texas, down by the Rio Grande,'"* Ebbin joining in.

Everything went quiet. "How about one about a girl back home?" a voice across the way called out. "Not so sad this time." There was a chorus of agreement. Angus peered across the aisle. The soldier, leg up in traction, gave a little wave. In the dim light, all Angus could make out was the white of his bandages and the white of his teeth in the flash of a smile.

Another nurse entered and came swiftly down the aisle. "Hush! You're keeping the men up. Really! Now, who have we here?" She lifted the clipboard from the end of the bed and looked at Ebbin, who grinned and said, "Lance Corporal E. Lawrence Havers, 45th Battalion, D Company. Awake and raring to take my leave."

EBBIN WAS DISCHARGED from the ward, to the sorrow of those nearby. "Good luck, fella!" one called out. Another said to Angus, "Come back and give us a show, you and your pal." Ebbin and Angus were shown to an office where Ebbin could get fully dressed. He checked the tape around his ribs, then, with his uniform in his lap, slipped the cross around his neck.

"Since when have you had a cross?" Angus asked.

"As long as I can remember," Ebbin said. "Believe in angels?" Ebbin lit the cigarette Angus offered and waited for Angus's response.

Angels at the Front were not to be trifled with when the spirit cries out for reprieve from suffering too great to contain. Was he immune? "Maybe I do," Angus said. "You?"

Ebbin cranked the window open and leaned on the ledge. He blew a stream of smoke into the night air. "All I know is this. There was a soldier in a ditch who couldn't get his legs to work when the whistle blew. A blast came, raining dirt, and shook him down. A piece of shrap cut his leg. He heard screaming, but he was alone. Then a lance corporal leaps in, whips out his knife, cleans the wound, disinfects it like a surgeon in a field hospital, wraps it up, points out that his tunic is torn from stem to stern. Ribbons is all. This lance corporal had been around the day before, dancing through bullets, dragging men to safety, killing every Kraut in his path. A lance corporal—medic, avenger, angel, all in one. The kind of soldier you hoped you'd be before you had any idea of what being a soldier was."

Angus was afraid to speak.

Ebbin went on, staring out at the stars. "The company sergeant hadn't a clue who he was and didn't care. All he knew was his name was Havers. He'd come from nowhere and wasn't listed on the books, but he knew how to hold his own. But then, just as he's leaping up out of that hole to help someone else, he's shot in the back. Stray bullet. Maybe from our own. Don't die, the soldier begs him. But he's going to. He's dying."

Ebbin took a couple of deep breaths. "'God, I wish I had your courage,' the soldier says. 'You can. You do,' Havers tells him. Tells him to take his tags, his tunic, his kit, his gun and ammo, and his cross. The soldier figures he wants them sent home and appreciates the offer of the tunic. But no, he says, '*keep* them, wear them.' Says the tags and cross aren't his anyway. He got 'em from another fella two months before, and *he* got them from someone back at Ypres who maybe got 'em from someone as far back as '14. Says it's been a good run for him, but his time's up. 'We're all going to die over here, and Lawrence Havers has the courage to do it well,' he says, 'and then *lives on*. Done my bit. Proud of it. Now it's your turn.' He puts the tags in the soldier's hand. 'Wear them,' he says. 'You'll find out who Havers is.' Then he goes ahead and dies, smile on his face. The soldier sits there frozen, Havers in his arms. A stream of men pass by. Boots and legs running. And he looks down at Havers and sees how sweet death looks. But he can't move. He fingers the discs in his palm until finally he does what Havers says and takes off his own tags and puts on Havers's and puts on his uniform, too. He tosses his tags as far as he can. And then a miracle. He can stand up. Can move! And is out of that shell hole and in the thick of it."

"And you—you became Havers? Like in some fairy tale?"

"I've just told you a story," Ebbin said steadily, his back still to Angus. "Hoping that somehow you'd understand it. Whether you do is up to you. Like I said, we're all going to die over here. The only thing that matters is how."

"You really believe we're all going to die. How do you keep going, if that's what you believe?"

"Havers, that's how. Havers is in *here*," he turned around and put his fist against his chest, "a saving grace. Doesn't matter if you believe it or not, there's nothing you can do can change it. Ask around, you'll find out what Havers has done."

"Do you have any idea who I am? I'm Ebbin Hant's brother-in-law, his friend."

"Ah. Sorry about that, brother." He put a hand on Angus's shoulder and then picked up his uniform.

They were silent as Ebbin got dressed. It was Angus's turn to go to the window, to look out at the stars. But the only story he had to tell was one of loss, a severing of self from self. A lifetime of memories and all the ways he'd defined himself in relation to Ebbin had been a long, winding trail that took him finally to this place where he was utterly alone. And alone he would remain. *And I wonder why I do not care for the things that are like the things that were . . .*

Ebbin was buttoning up his jacket, adjusting his puttees. Their time was short. There was no point turning him in. Hiller had come back with a diagnosis of "nervous but fit enough"—a good *imitation* of shellshock, it was said, but the line had to be drawn. As for Ebbin, they'd break him and he'd be sent to prison, not a hospital, for impersonating an officer. Rational or not, Angus kept seeing him marched to a stump, a bag on his head. And who knew who Havers really was or what had happened to him? Or what any of the facts really were. Ebbin could have been AWOL for all those months and then—rejoined? Anything was possible. What was certain was that Ebbin was broken, but *believed* he was whole and had survived as Havers. *For by grace you have been saved through faith.* Alright, then. So be it.

Ebbin was fully dressed now. He straightened his shoulders, whipped out a comb and smoothed his hair in the reflection in the window.

Havers had as good a chance of making it as Ebbin Hant. Maybe better.

NOT LONG AFTERWARDS, they stood to the side of the road as a stream of general service wagons passed by. A lorry rumbled up, then stalled, the whine of its engine piercing the air, mud flying, tires whirring. Angus stood there dumbly, clots of mud splattering his legs.

He heard someone say, "Havers! Hi ya! Where ya been? Better check in with the Sarge toot sweet."

Then Ebbin was gone.

✧

A HALF HOUR later, drained and exhausted, Angus leaned against a stone wall, watching a lone cow meandering in the distance. Paul materialized, mug of hot milk coffee in hand. He offered it up to Angus and said that two years before, the Germans had killed all the cows in that field when they left in retreat. He swiped his hand across his neck to demonstrate. Then, like Angus, he leaned back against the wall and crossed his legs. They kept their eyes on the cow, plodding uselessly on.

"How old are you, Paul? *Quel âge?*" Angus asked as he handed the mug back.

"*Onze ans,*" Paul replied immediately.

"Eleven. So, you've spent nearly a third of your life in this war." Cottony wisps of his own life before the war drifted by. He could not grasp them and he did not try. He was trying to overcome a strange lifting feeling, as if the top of his head might come off and his body float up after it. Paul started speaking again. Angus heard the words before they took hold. Paul told him how he'd been at his great-uncle's farm when the Germans began to slaughter the cows. He'd hidden in the cellar. They'd burned the barn and killed the cows and run a knife through his great-uncle for trying to stop them. And when Paul came out of the cellar, his hair . . . He rubbed his hand over the white patch.

The words fell into place.

Paul narrowed his eyes. "One day I will be a soldier. A Canadian soldier. They found me. In the cellar. But first, a German soldier, a private. He see me. 'Shhh . . . ' he say."

"A German? Saved you?"

"*Oui.* He was my pal. You are also?"

Angus nodded. "I am that. And you're as brave as any soldier I know."

Paul gave a faint smile and blew on the milky coffee. "What happened to your . . . ?" He rephrased. "How is . . . Lance Corporal Havers?"

Angus shrugged. "Fine, I'd guess. Back with his unit now. Here, give me another swig of that."

Paul handed him the cup. "He is . . . Lance Corporal Havers?"

"Yup," Angus sighed, "he is."

"It is okay?"

"I think so. Havers is . . . his pal. Someone he made up. Havers makes him feel strong. Brave like you. Can you understand that? Pretending, no, *believing* he's Lance Corporal Havers helps him stay alive."

Paul nodded gravely.

"But it has to be our secret. Understand? We can't tell anyone. If we do, it will be very bad for him. And he won't be brave."

"Shhhh. It is done." Paul crossed his arms, one after the other, over his chest, and cocked his head up at Angus. "You are okay? You are . . . you are thinking?"

"Yes. I am thinking," Angus said, folding his arms, eyes on the horizon. "I'm thinking how things are not black and white, only gray. Like your pal, the German private, and my pal, Havers, and this whole bloody war."

Paul whistled a long falling note. He took a big swallow of coffee and said, "You are thinking many things. You will draw them? With your only chalks—*noir et blanc? Gris?*"

"That's right." Was there nothing this boy did not understand? "The only ones left—black and white. Mix them together and you've got gray. Where the heck did you come from, anyway?"

Paul smiled shyly into the mug. "Finish?" he said, lifting the cup.

"You have the rest."

"Smoke?"

Angus shook his head again. "Later. You've got chores to do and

God knows what scavenging, and I have a class to teach." Paul took a last swallow and tossed the rest away. A meadowlark swooped past a stand of splintered trees and landed on a rusted wire sticking up out of an old fence post where she broke into song, varied and lyrical. Paul, who had turned to go, stopped. "*Là!* She makes herself happy. You, too?"

"Me, too—she makes me happy. So do you," Angus answered. As if in response, the lark puffed her chest out, tipped her head back and trilled out a varied flutter of rippling notes. Across the field, the cow stopped and lifted her head.

THE NAMELESS AND the named, Angus thought as he and Paul walked back. He wasn't about to tell Hettie about Ebbin nor about Havers. That much he'd already decided. It was impossible to explain and far too risky. Even if he could find some coded way to share the news, how could she in the remotest stretch of imagination, reading a letter over a cup of tea, understand Havers? Besides, to tell her was to expose Ebbin, and open himself up as well, to her renewed hopes, her insistence that something be done when the only thing to do was to do nothing. She'd lost Ebbin once. Could she bear it again? Could he?

But he did tell Juliette. Not surprisingly, Paul had kept his vow of silence. And, not surprisingly, she, like Paul, accepted the story. She understood escape. She understood survival. He told her he was going to stay out of Ebbin's way. She agreed it was best. She understood love.

ELEVEN

March 27th, 1917
Arras Sector, France

The month of March had broken without a hint of spring in the air nor a blade of grass pushing through the iron-clad earth. Angus didn't search for Ebbin again, though there were times he thought he saw him—elusive sightings—loading ground sheets onto a truck, horsing around with his mates at the YMCA canteen, and once riding bareback in the ring by the stables.

The spring offensive was drawing near, and throughout the camps and villages of Pas-de-Calais and Picardy, everything and everyone was gearing up for the Battle of Arras, and what would be, for the CEF, the battle for Vimy Ridge—all four Canadian divisions, 100,000 men, with an additional allocation from the British 1st Army on either flank, not to mention mules and 50,000 horses. Rural roads were clogged with streams of lorries, automobiles, mule trains, general service wagons, motorcycles, bicycles, Red Cross carts, anything with wheels. The home-front factories had finally produced enough shells to bomb the world to kingdom come, which Publicover said was fine with him as long as Jerry went first. Heavy artillery was moving up to assigned destinations, cannons pulled by teams of sixteen draught horses, heads down, eyes bulging. Angus had seen their knees buckle.

Below ground, engineers dug through the old French and German trenches, shoving corpses aside as they laid their cable. Medical corps dugouts were under construction, some said to be sixty feet deep, able to accommodate up to three hundred men, with a windlass to raise and lower the wounded. Tottenham, Cavalier, International and Vincent tunnels were nearing completion, extending beyond the forward trenches and butting right up to the German line. Preparations worthy of Caesar's army, it was said by everyone. Conlon preferred allusions to Troy—victory a long time coming, but coming nonetheless. Patience, diligence, duty, he reminded them.

Diligence, duty. These were the watchwords by which Angus carried out his daily rounds. He was up the line with his men three times. Back of the line, he and Publicover were housed with their men. Paul was such a ubiquitous presence in the camp, running errands, making trades, that Angus was surprised he wasn't in uniform. Whenever he could, which wasn't often, Angus went back with him to visit Juliette.

Angus immersed himself in teaching soldiers who could barely write, let alone draw, how to duplicate the physical world in distance, depth, line and perspective. Terrain mapping, "an invaluable asset," Stokes called it when, to the astonishment of that day's class, he'd poked his head inside one afternoon. Hands clasped behind his back, eyeing the drawings, he circled the room and reminded Angus of Mr. Heist. Finally, he came to a stop, faced the men, and cleared his throat. "Listen here," he said. "Once we're over that ridge, we'll be in uncharted ground, and it'll be days before we'll be able to bring our heavy guns to firing range, during which time Jerry will reorganize, build new defenses. Our observation balloons are just slow-moving targets, and Jerry's crackerjack at shooting down our planes. So we're going to need sketches of those defenses just like the ones you're making—quickly drawn, copied and handed back to command. So pay attention and keep up the good work."

"Good" work, Angus reminded himself. He was a cog in the machine of war, it was true, but the great war machine had narrowed down to his men and he would not degrade the sacrifice to come nor jeopardize their safety with inner struggles about morality, though struggle he did. The month had begun with an event that nearly broke his resolve—a massive raid and a weapon that the CEF had thus far rejected—gas. White Star, it was called, a mixture of chlorine and phosgene. One thousand canisters of it had been transported to the front lines.

Not surprisingly, everything about the raid went terribly wrong. The minute the gas was released, the Germans put on their gas masks and laid down a barrage that decimated the first wave of Canadian troops. When the wind shifted, the second round of gas was canceled. But the order failed to reach all the gas specialists on the Canadian line. Clouds of poison drifted back onto the Canadians who, gagging and choking, were forced to run toward German gunfire to escape it. Others were killed by their own artillery. When dawn broke, more than six hundred Canadian infantrymen lay sprawled across No Man's Land, many of them piled in shell holes, suffocating to death from the after-effects of White Star.

His father's words about God's retribution rang in his ears when Angus heard what happened. But there was more. God had not yet finished raising the moral stakes. Angus and the other officers learned that the following morning, a German Reserve commander had crept through a low-hanging fog and under the barbed wire, risking gunfire, with an interpreter and a white flag. Ten minutes later, he and a Canadian major exchanged silent salutes in the center of No Man's Land. The German gestured toward the bodies. He suggested a cease-fire until 2:00 that afternoon to recover the dead and wounded. Though rare, it wasn't as if cease-fires hadn't been negotiated for such a purpose before. But this time almost all the casualties were Canadian, and on top of it the German commander indicated that his own soldiers would help. For hours, using trench ladders and whatever else was at hand, they carried the Canadians from the German side of the line to the midpoint of No Man's Land. When 2:00 came and the field had been cleared, the German commander then suggested that the cease-fire continue until 6:00 that evening to ensure that the wounded were safely removed to the rear of the Canadian line. The Canadian and German officers shook hands. At 6:00 hostilities resumed.

Andy Loftus, who had survived the raid, told Conlon that the German commander had offered cigarettes to each of the Canadian officers as they stood together in No Man's Land and that when the Canadian major had pocketed his as a souvenir, the German had offered him another one to smoke. Recounting the story for Angus, Conlon put his hands on his hips and stared at the ground. Behind him a stockpile of brass-colored shells nosed out from their camouflage netting like so many giant pencil tips. "A German general forgiving a gas attack—how do we deal with such appalling humanity?" He looked up with a sardonic smile, but Angus knew his question was in earnest. It was the same question that burned through him, sapping not his courage, but his will.

"I figure it this way," Conlon continued, as they began to walk together. "We can reject it as an aberration . . . or accept it as a sign of normalcy. The latter view should assure us there's still something among us mortals worth fighting for."

"One day the lamb will lie down with the lion . . ."

"Well, I was thinking of Germans and Allies sharing some beer," Conlon answered. "Wouldn't mind if it was with that German commander," he added. "But let's face it, short of every man on both sides laying down their arms, the best way to end the madness is to win the war. That or surrender. I'll take winning."

"Here's another way to think of it," Angus said. "God set the stage for just such an act—to remind us that in the darkest night, light shines."

"Ha. I knew your seminary training would pay off at some point," Conlon said. "Apparently, God doesn't mind six hundred dead to make a point."

"Right. Can't expect small acts from God," Angus replied. "Show me the dark and I'll show you the light."

"It's insights like that that make this war worth it, eh?"

"Exactly," Angus smiled. "Where would we be without irony?"

"Continuously drunk, I'm afraid."

As they walked on, Angus found himself so at ease in Conlon's company that he almost told him about Ebbin. But to unburden himself was to put Ebbin in jeopardy, not to mention himself. And Conlon would choose duty over all else—anything less would go against all Angus knew of him.

In Angus's pocket was a letter he'd gotten from Hettie that morning. She'd devoted a few of her spare lines to the memorial for Ebbin. Her words "everyone was very kind," "there were quite a few tears shed," "it was hard on them," sounded remote, even for her. She didn't come out and say it, but he had the feeling she wasn't one of the mourners. As if in her denial, she knew the truth.

THAT NIGHT, he found himself standing under the darkened windows of Juliette's abandoned house. He could see her in his mind, across from him, her dark hair loosely tied in a ribbon, her three silver rings catching the firelight. Her English was far better than he'd thought. His French made her and Paul laugh out loud. The three of them, with their shared knowledge of Ebbin, never mentioned his name.

On his last visit, Angus gave Paul a drawing he'd done for him of pigeons holding a chimney-top meeting, and Juliette, a detailed charcoal of the house. She studied it for a long time and said that she had a sister, Sabine, on the coast, who'd married a man from Alsace, now dead. Paul interjected that Sabine had some very perfect pigeons and so would also like a pigeon drawing if he could manage it. Juliette said she'd heard that if the Allies didn't break through the line this time, the Germans would make an end run around it to the coast and on to Paris, and there would be no safe place left. But there was no money to be made staying in Astile alone with no boarders. Her husband's pension was too shabby to manage. She would go to Sabine's. "It is coming, no? The battle?"

"Yes," Angus said, meeting her eyes. "Soon." To get away from the moment and all it portended, Angus suggested one more lesson in terrain-mapping and took Paul down the street to a clearing across a tattered yard. The night was sharp and bright. On the way, Angus explained how fog could make half-hidden objects seem farther away; how in clear air, a straight-on sighting down a narrow path, or over water or snow, could make things seem nearer. As he'd done long ago with Simon Peter, he pointed to the moon hanging low and huge, and explained how objects are interpreted in relation to one another and how deceiving it can be. Paul stubbornly argued that the moon was smaller when it was high up in the sky because it was farther away. Angus nearly gave up until Paul said doubtfully, "So, it is not what we think we see?"

"Exactly," Angus answered. "Nothing is. We both know that."

"Nothing is," Angus repeated now, staring up at the blank windows. The day Juliette and Paul left, Angus had raced up the steps to empty rooms, calling her name, then heard his own. There she was at the foot of the stairs, out of breath, looking up. He descended slowly, each step taking him closer to her and farther away.

"I wanted to say to Paul, to you—I wanted a chance to . . ." He sank down on the steps, then searched his pack for the thin oval board he'd sanded to smooth perfection and on which he'd penned a lark in black ink, head back, throat up, beak open in song. "I wanted to give Paul something more. A lark—he'll understand."

She knelt on the step below him and he pulled her in and kissed her hair. "This will end," he whispered. "We'll be over that ridge, and you'll be on the coast. Safe. No more guns. No more soldiers." He held her for a moment more, then swung his pack up. At the end of the hall, he gripped the door frame and hesitated, but he could not look back.

Looking up now at the house, Angus thought of the last drawing he'd made—tended graves in a field, row upon row. Through the silence he could hear the wind moan across a future landscape, sharing Earth's sorrow, unable to bind up her wounds.

When he got back to camp, Hiller, every man's fear come to fruition, was cowering on his bed, eyes wide in the dark. "Get some sleep, Hiller," Angus whispered to him and lightly touched his head. Hiller hunkered under the covers but did not close his eyes.

Only when their orders came and he was marching out of town with his men did Angus realize he still had the drawing of the lark in his pack.

TWELVE

March 27th, 1917
Snag Harbor, Nova Scotia

arly morning sun filled the kitchen. Hettie lifted the hot iron off the stove and pressed it against the dampened, wrinkled sleeve of the shirt on the board. Simon, looking up from his drawing, sighed audibly. The shirt was Ebbin's. She was humming.

Ida was just outside the window forking up sheets from the copper pot on the fire into the rinse tub. Her face was red with the effort, and strands of her faded red hair were plastered to her neck.

The humming persisted. Simon left the kitchen and went out to the yard. Ida wiped her forehead with her apron and told him there was nothing, not one thing better, than a fresh clean sheet after a long hard winter. He asked her why she'd washed one of Ebbin's shirts.

"Well," she said, "now I do that every week for your mother."

"But why?"

"She's been goin' about fairy-led, han't she? Drowsing here and there like one soft in the head. Picking up a fork or spool of thread like she never seen one before. And now you see how she's in there, upright."

"But she's ironing his shirt as if he's coming back."

"She'll get that shirt ironed every week and then one day she'll see it's all smoothed out, nary a wrinkle to it, and best laid up to rest."

"You think so?"

"Either that or he'll come walking up that hill and thank her for it."

"So, you think he's alive, too?"

"Well, if he is, he's fooled the Army. God, too, maybe. Wouldn't put it past him. But you let your mother be. Some things take time. Peas in a pod, her and Ebbin. Or more like, *her* thinking that way. Here," Ida bent down and yanked up a sheet in the rinse water. "Hold this end and I'll twist. Gotta get these on the line. C'mon now."

Simon did as he was told. "What do you mean, *her* thinking that way? Didn't Uncle Ebbin feel the same?"

"Oh my yes, as youngsters. But he's hardly been around since he grew up, has he? When he does choose to light here for a day or two, he charms the socks right off you." She pinned the sheet on the line. "I think once Elma Hant produced them four other boys one right after another, and was all caught up in them, Ebbin and Hettie, well, they stood apart and held on to each other. Your grandpa Hant couldn't make enough of Ebbin, but Hettie just brought him back to the wife he'd lost. So she took her shine from Ebbin. And there's your father, as strong and patient as they come, holding her hand whenever Ebbin lets her down. And now gone off to find him and . . ." She caught up the corner of her apron and wiped her eyes.

Amazed at these revelations, Simon realized that he'd somehow always known that Ida didn't approve of Ebbin. Still, it was a shock to hear it voiced, and also exhilarating. He decided to reveal a confidence of his own. "What if I told you that George Mather is sure he saw Uncle Ebbin alive after he was supposedly dead? And that he helped him on the field when George was wounded."

Ida moved back to the rinse tub. "I'd say that you should keep clear of George. He's not right in the head. Set them fires down at Mather's beach, didn't he? All lined up in a row. He was a sharpshooter in the war and a good one. Lord knows what he'll do next. And I wouldn't tell your mother what I told you. People have their own truth and sometimes that works out best. Whether Ebbin's alive or not, what I see is she's keeping the books again. And a right good thing. Didn't she and Duncan go to it last week—her claiming he'd lost an account from pure neglect. His Highness warning her to keep out of his affairs and just mind the books, and her saying right back there'd soon be no affairs to stay out of nor books to keep." Ida shook the forking stick at him. "Don't stand there with your mouth agape. Are you a help or a hindrance? Fork over that next sheet or move out of my way."

"Wait. Are we in trouble?"

"Not now, we aren't. You seen all them letters she's writing. Folks about might just say your grandfather has a new partner, and they might just be right one day. Signs each one 'H. E. MacGrath.'"

"Yeah?"

"Those initials is the opposite of her brother's, if you'll notice."

"What's *that* mean?"

Ida paused, hand on hip, and looked up at the sky. "I don't rightly know. Just came to me is all. Now, I want you to take some of my cinnamon muffins over to Mr. Heist. He's doing right poorly. A spring cold's my guess."

WAITING FOR IDA to get the muffins out of the oven, Simon sifted through the letters on his mother's desk. Ida was right, H. E. Mac-Grath was writing to customers about delinquent accounts, several to a Mr. Pethrick Cameron about lumber for a sawmill in Gold River. Numerous letters to and from Mr. Balfour. The Silver Fox, Ida called him. At the bottom of the pile was one to her from Maggie McInnis. Simon scanned it and came up short at the last paragraph.

Once I'd broken through the veil, I felt a peace such as I didn't think possible, knowing Harold and Tom are alright, as they told me through Mrs. Nicodemus. I learned how they died, and they assured me they were right here with me as I move on in this weighed-down mortal life. Yes, it's true, women have been cast into asylums, and even prison, but it's hardly a pagan practice, nor witchcraft, as has been claimed. It is but a means of confirming our Christian belief in life everlasting. I urge you to try it.

She'd been talking to ghosts and inviting his mother to do the same. But asylums? Prison? Was communing with the dead witchcraft? Was it against the law? Mr. Heist would know. He shoved the letter back into the pile.

In the kitchen Ida knotted a towel over the muffins and put them in a sack with a little critch of butter onto which she'd pressed a thistle stamp. He joked that she must be sweet on Mr. Heist. "No," she said. "I've had but one sweetheart my whole life, and I'll never tell who, so don't even ask. Just be sure you're back by supper. And see that he warms these muffins up before he eats them. Tell him we're hoping he feels better."

JUST BEFORE THE turnoff for Mr. Heist's, Simon and Peg passed the Mather property. George hobbled over from the field and stood there, shirt open to a bare chest, his hair swept around his ears. He balanced on one crutch. Peg slowed to a stop. Simon gave her a kick, but she just nudged George and whinnied softly. Simon felt a nervous flutter in his stomach and said, "She's come a-ways now—needs water. I gotta get going." George limped away. He mentioned neither coins nor boxes nor Ebbin Hant, and his retreating form made Simon sorry he hadn't shared one of Ida's muffins.

At Mr. Heist's blue cottage, all was quiet. Simon set the muffins down on the steps, and eventually found him down at his long and narrow wharf stringing some lanterns between two poles for a purpose that Simon was by then too distracted to ask about. As they climbed the steep steps set into the bank, Mr. Heist paused to cough and mop his face. Simon told him he'd seen George by the road, but that George hadn't said a word. Mr. Heist said he'd stopped in at the Mathers', and George had been quiet then, too.

Simon said, "When he does talk, it's crazy talk. Riddles is all. Right?"

"It may seem that way," Mr. Heist said as he pushed on his knee to climb the last steps. "To us, perhaps, but not to George." Simon asked what that meant. "He's doing his best to make a connection, but something holds him back."

"What? What holds him back? You mean the war? The war doesn't just make people . . . crazy like that."

"What I mean is that to communicate with others, one must first be able to communicate with oneself. There, I think, lies George's problem. He isn't connected to his own experience, maybe never will be. And maybe never should be."

"What about those fires?" Simon said.

"Ah yes, a row of campfires, maybe to bring something back to himself. The fires were well contained, well tended."

Nothing about George bothered Mr. Heist.

"That day in Chester, before you came out, he said he saw Uncle Ebbin at Thiepval. At least I think that's what he was saying."

"Ah. We can't know what George means there, can we? Did he see your uncle or his ghost, or wish he had? Perhaps he did. Perhaps he wants to make you feel better."

"Well, he doesn't make me feel better. And he's wrong. Uncle Ebbin was dead by then."

They'd reached the garden, patched with snow. They took the path, neatly lined with beach stones, to the back porch, where Simon was surprised to see a beehive-shaped lens bound by highly polished brass. A lens for a lighthouse. A tarp lay on the floor next to it. The concentric prisms above and below the center glass glittered in the late afternoon sun.

Mr. Heist rocked on his short feet, clearly pleased. "Yes," he said, "A fourth-order Fresnel lens. Recently acquired. Delicate-looking, is it not? But thick and sturdy all the same. The prisms of the Fresnel capture and magnify almost all of the light emitted from the lamp. A work of art and a practical boon to sailors. This one's just two and a half feet tall and two feet in diameter, but I believe it could signal at least fifteen or more miles out to sea, maybe as far as twenty."

Simon bent down to examine it. "But why? Are you building a lighthouse?" he joked.

"Heavens no. I was just lucky to acquire it. Perhaps I'll put it in the vegetable garden to keep the crows away." Mr. Heist chuckled. Simon helped him secure the tarp over it and tie it to the porch railing. Then Mr. Heist looked out toward the edge of the point and the patch of view through some felled trees. "I was glad when those trees blew down. I'm thinking of building a lookout tower," he said.

"A tower? Why?"

"To get a better view, of course. Over there so it would be above those evergreens going down the bluff. Not too close. I'm thinking of a little roof over it where I could take my tea and watch the boats come and go with my binoculars. You should see the sights from up here when the fleet comes in. All those schooners, schooning . . ."

"Schooning? Is that a word?"

"Hmm? It is and it isn't. Some say 'schoon' without the *h* came from 'scone,' a Scottish word for 'skip along the water.' But surely the Dutch added that *h*, and with those double *o*'s, I like to think of it as 'schooning'—which I like to think means 'glide,' even if it is not so. A little etymologic whimsy of mine. But come along now. Let's go in so you can tell me what's on your mind."

In the cottage he retrieved a kettle sitting atop a stack of books. He set it to boil and stoked the fire. Four thin black socks hung in a lonely row on a rack near the stove. Mr. Heist, without his starched collar and tie, without his vest, shambled about in loose blue trousers and an old blue sweater. He'd cast a fussy look at Simon's boots as he changed into his own leather slippers when they entered the cottage. Simon pulled his boots off.

He looked around as Mr. Heist unwrapped the muffins and told him to extend his thanks to Ida, wonderful woman. The house was unlike any house Simon had ever seen. Aside from the bedroom, it was basically just one great room, with exposed beams and a bank of windows facing the porch with a view of the bay. Mr. Heist said he'd had the wall between the parlor and the kitchen taken down, leaving two posts for the support beam so he could see out on three sides no matter where he stood. Shelves from floor to ceiling were jam-packed with books with titles in Latin and Greek, German and English. Here and there a potted plant dangled tendrils. A music stand was in the center of the room, and Mr. Heist's violin case. Ink drawings of buildings—from Europe, Simon supposed—hung between the book-shelves. One of a boys' choir coming out of a cathedral door caught Simon's eye. Newspapers, manuscripts, articles and stacks of letters, many in German, littered every flat surface.

Mr. Heist indicated a chair at the kitchen table. At one end of its glossy red surface, a typewriter sat squarely on a mat, a stack of clean paper on one side and typed pages, facedown, on the other. In the center lay an oversized, bound volume entitled *Lepidoptera of North and South America,* open to a colored plate depicting an exotic blue butterfly. "Plate 42: *Morpho didius,*" the caption read.

"Is this real? This butterfly?" Simon asked as Mr. Heist set out two mugs.

"Real? Why, of course. The *Morpho didius* is as real as any other butterfly. We'll never see it, which is the pity. Not unless we travel to South American and claw our way up to the very canopy of the rainforest."

"I might get there someday," Simon mused. He was thoroughly immersed in the struggles of the young hero of *First Voyage*, who had been chased deeper and deeper into the screeching reaches of the Venezuelan jungles.

"*Ach*, I'd like to accompany you, but I'm afraid I am too old and frail. Thankful, actually, that I am. Even at a younger age, I didn't have the constitution for such adventure, nor the spirit. I'd have never made a good naturalist," he sighed, "and I will never see this butterfly. But we must be content with what we have and who we are. Here, I will show you one I've seen many times. Drab compared to the *Morpho*, but I suspect you'll like the name of it." He flipped through the pages with ink-stained fingers. "It's among the Skippers. Ah. Here it is. Not much to look at, but you see the name, *Erynnis icelus*—Dreamy Duskywing."

Simon agreed. Perfection of a name. "Do you collect butterflies?"

"Pin them to a wall? Never! I simply note my sightings here in my butterfly notebook, and my bird sightings here—no, now where on earth is that notebook?" He shuffled through some books on the counter. "Well, in any case, you would not pin a bird to a corkboard, would you? Of course not! It is the same with butterflies. It is enough to see them and know that I have. You must come out in the summer. I've set my garden out to attract certain species of moths and butterflies and catalogue them. I've obtained gayfeather and columbine seeds, and sweet-pea seed pods from Dora MacDonald's garden. She's too good to me."

"How come you do that, write them down like that?"

"Why, so I can remember what I observe and how often. It is a way of being in this world. Understand?"

"Not . . . exactly."

"Of being part of it, Simon. Engaged." Mr. Heist gave up searching through his books and faced Simon. "Your father once said something that I have kept in here." He patted his chest. "He said that when he was on long voyages, he was no longer a stranger on the water; he was part of it. He and the boat were not *on* the water, but *of* the water. Together they *became* the roll of the swells, the lap of the waves, the rod through which the wind met the deep. Not in quite those words, but you see? No? Not sure?"

Simon shook his head. He wanted more.

Mr. Heist complied. "It was his way *of being alive*. He said it was that dimension that he wanted to get down on his canvas. So he could stay alive. In his landscapes and shore birds, he never felt he had. He wanted to paint something more. Oh yes," he said to counter Simon's surprise. "We talked of his painting. Several times. He told me he was working on something before he left. Came to him all at once. I had a feeling it was of the sea. Of course, I wouldn't know about being part of the sea, myself. I'm not a sailor." He chuckled. "But you know that, don't you! Don't have the stomach for it for one thing. Nor the courage."

Simon did know. He could still see Mr. Heist in suit and vest, clutching the rail awkwardly when they took him for a picnic on the *Lauralee*, eyes bugging out behind salt-sprayed spectacles every time the boat heeled over. He never got the hang of how to switch sides when they came about, never got his footing. Up to that point, Simon hadn't known that getting your footing on a boat was something some people had to learn. He and Zenus had laughed their heads off afterwards when Simon did an imitation. He felt pretty bad about that now.

"But you do have a little rowboat down there," Simon said.

"I do. I take it out when it's calm. Even then, I keep it tied by a long line to the wharf. And," he patted his chest with both hands, "I wear my life vest."

Simon laughed gently with Mr. Heist.

"I like to see the bottom at some depth, and especially at night with my lanterns. The starfish and sea urchins lurking in their own universe. And what is better than the green gleam of phosphorus disturbed on a night sea?"

"Nothing. But you can't see phosphorous with a light," Simon said.

"No, of course. I turn my lamps off on those nights and throw stones in the water and watch the green tail follow them all the way down."

"Me, too!"

"We have that in common, then, Simon." He poured out the tea. "Sailing is not for me, but when I hear the call of gulls or the curlew, or see the tiny beating wings of the Acadian Hairstreak on an oak leaf, or watch a starfish stretch out a single arm on the wharf pilings, I feel more alive than I did the minute before."

Simon hadn't considered birds or butterflies, and especially not starfish, as something to make you feel more alive. He turned the page back to the iridescent blue *Morpho*.

Mr. Heist took the muffins from the oven. "You like that one," he said as he arranged them on a platter. "He's a very clever fellow. His wings are blue on top but mottled brown underneath, so he cannot be seen from below. Note the name, the *Morpho*. Do you make the connection? *Metamorphosis*. Changing. Like all moths and butterflies, he's not beautiful to start, and in his case, only beautiful from above. He is ugly and attractive both. But think of it—from caterpillar to chrysalis to the bursting out of the butterfly, so light on its wing— that is pure beauty. Would it be so if it had never been a caterpillar? Think of it! Crawling on the ground, then locked in darkness, and suddenly *airborne*! But does the butterfly remember he once was not?"

"I, I don't know," Simon said.

"I was fortunate enough once to watch a black swallowtail do just that, break out of its cocoon. It was a good five minutes before it took off. And all the while, it opened and closed its wings, so slowly, as if considering the magnitude of transformation. Can I really use these wings to lift above the world, he seemed to ask. How I envied the moment when he trusted that he could."

Simon put his chin on his hand. He could listen to Mr. Heist all day.

Mr. Heist cleared his throat and took a sip of tea. "But now, you didn't come here to discuss butterflies. Ever the professor, I'm afraid. You mentioned a question, a concern."

Simon sat up and without mentioning the letter, asked if Mr. Heist knew what "breaking through the veil" meant and if it was connected to witchcraft.

Mr. Heist stirred his tea a moment, and insisted on context. Simon looked down and shook his head.

"You want to contact your uncle? Is that it?"

"No! Not me. Ma—" Simon stopped himself and sat back. "Maybe. I don't know."

"*Ach.* Of course. I myself have had three cousins killed in the war. Two at the Somme . . . Death diminishes the living, if they let it. But your poor mother. I've been teaching here for seventeen years, and I can still remember the first time I saw Ebbin Hant and Angus Mac-Grath. A pair of scoundrels, those two. Hard to believe Ebbin is gone. So tragic. Of course she wants to contact him. Perfectly natural."

"It is? But do they throw people in prison for that? Or asylums?"

"What?" It was Mr. Heist's turn to be alarmed. "For trying to contact the dead?"

Simon revealed the contents of the letter, and from there Mr. Heist launched into a treatise on what he called the Spiritualism movement, sweeping the British Isles with so many lost to the war and even so great a mind as William James investigating it to find the "demarcation between science and magic." It might once have been considered witchcraft, perhaps, or the mark of the insane. President Lincoln's wife for example, poor woman, and yes, there were tricksters and hucksters, perhaps even this Mrs. Nicodemus, whom Simon Peter now conjured in the garb of a gypsy with a crystal ball. But, Mr. Heist added, holding up his finger, one had to weigh the comfort of those left behind against indeterminate scientific proof.

This talk, peppered with words like "occult," "séances" and "mediums," was a little hard to follow. "Do you believe it? That people can get messages from the dead?" Simon asked when Mr. Heist paused for breath.

Mr. Heist considered this. " 'Belief' is the word, isn't it, Simon? We believe in many things that are unseen and for which we have no evidence. I have no experience on which to base belief. Or disbelief, for that matter. What is our evidence for life after death or for the Resurrection itself except the belief of others in whom we place our faith? Or perhaps the faith of others in whom we place our belief. Very different things."

Mr. Heist caught Simon's eye and said, "I think of it this way. Suppose you had a collection of metal filings on a piece of paper. Under it, a magnet. What would happen to the filings?"

"They'd all collect to where the magnet was, I guess."

"Just so. I believe while we are here, our spirits collect, like the filings, into the shape of our beings. When death comes, the magnet is removed and the spirit scatters back out. Just like the filings—the shape is gone, our individual beings, but the filings remain—part of the greater whole."

Simon jumped when Mr. Heist leaned forward and patted his arm. "You've asked a question, and I've given you a lecture. The truth is, I cannot tell you if these things are real, but I can give you this advice regarding your mother—consider the limits of your responsibility. Hmm?" He squeezed Simon's arm and sat back, a kindly look in his eyes.

"What?"

"Consider it. That's all I'm saying. And, Simon? Be kind to George."

"Thanks," Simon said uncertainly. "I'd better be going." He carried his mug to the sink, where another mug hung on a hook and two plates were neatly washed and stacked. Before leaving, he glanced again at the brilliant *Morpho didius*.

AS HE PASSED by the Mather cottage, Simon saw George in the field, a silhouette against a violet sky. He sped Peg on faster and faster. "*Morpho didius!*" he shouted. He thought about the unfurling leaves and the spring offensive everyone said was coming. He thought about riding Peg right out of Snag Harbor and on beyond Chester and galloping up to the top of Haddon Hill on the other side of the bay where he could look out over the tips of the fir trees to the great beyond and send a message to his father just by letting his spirit fly to the wind. "It doesn't matter whether you saved Uncle Ebbin. Save yourself! Come back! We'll fix up the *Lauralee* and take her out beyond Ironbound to the edge of the earth! Just hold the line and don't die." He had Peg at a fast clip by then. *Don't die. Don't die.* It wasn't until he was nearly home that Simon realized those cousins of Mr. Heist must have died on the other side of the line.

THIRTEEN

April 1st, 1917
Snag Harbor, Nova Scotia

"You don't mind, do you, Cottnam?" Lady Bromley asked as she positioned herself and a Miss Plante beside Reverend Dimmock, forming a kind of receiving line under the arched door of St. Andrew's after the service. The reverend followed her gaze to the freshly repaired steeple and said, "Not at all," and continued to greet his parishioners filing out. As Lady Bromley introduced her as Lord Bromley's great-niece, Miss Plante extended a plump hand, gloved tight as a sausage in its skin, to one and all. She was surprisingly cheerful, Simon thought, for one who had lost her mother at an early age and whose father was too ill to care for her. A man who had been rejected by the army, it was said. "No doubt a n'er-do-well," Duncan noted as they'd walked up the hill to St. Andrew's that morning. "A drinker's my guess," Ida had added.

"Goodness," Miss Plante said, shaking Simon's hand. "Call me Charlotte. I only just turned sixteen." Her gray eyes, so light as to seem transparent, were set in a round face with dimples on both cheeks that grew pronounced when she smiled. She made him feel strangely happy.

His attention was diverted by the brief hesitation of his mother's laced shoe above the step. She was nearly devoid of color, but elegant in her black hat and cape. Underneath the outer mourning, she was wearing a dress of robin's-egg blue. Taking his hand, she barely acknowledged Lady Bromley, who explained to Charlotte that Mrs. MacGrath hadn't intended to be rude, but had recently lost her brother to the war. "Not," Lady Bromley said pointedly, "that that should be any of *your* concern."

Simon wandered over to Maisie and Zenus under the pin oak. Not far from them, Lord Bromley was poking at gravestones with his stick. "Lawrence Mader Putnam, 1823!" he shouted. "John Blakely Jollymore, 1877! What have you got to say for yourselves?"

"My mum says that Miss Plante was talking to the dead, and *that's* why she was sent over here. For her own good," Maisie was saying to Zenus.

"Talking to the *dead*? Are you sure? Is she a medium?" Simon asked.

"I'd say she's a large," Zenus responded, as solemnly as Maisie.

Maisie giggled. "Zenus, you're horrid. She has lovely eyes."

"Lovely eyes." Zenus fluttered his lids. "That's what they say when a girl is as fat as a barrel."

Maisie turned to Simon and said, "Anyway, she gets *messages* . . . from dead soldiers."

"Bunk! Nuts-o-nuts!" Zenus said.

Simon looked back at Charlotte. True, she was a bit of a barrel, but with the gay little feather on her soft gray hat, she was no sideshow gypsy. She was a breath of fresh air. Or maybe, he thought, a soft mourning dove. Maisie must have got it wrong. But what if she hadn't? Had God brought Charlotte to Snag Harbor to give his mother peace?

"Simon Peter! Let's weigh anchor!" Duncan shouted out across the churchyard.

"I have to go. You sure about this stuff . . . ?" Simon narrowed his eyes at Maisie.

"The whole town knows. Ask your grandfather," was her response.

"So nice to see you out and about again, Hettie," Lady Bromley said as she passed by. "We won't keep you, not in this raw weather. And poor Charlotte, still tired from her long journey. Good day to you all." She collected Charlotte and marched on. Lord Bromley straightened, momentarily energized. "Suppose I should catch up to that lot. That girl might get my dinner!" He touched his cap and was off, swiping at the air at his feet with his stick.

Duncan held out a hand for Young Fred. Simon walked beside his mother, a plan hatching. "Do you think she really gets messages from the dead?"

"Who knows? It's a whole movement. Mags is part of it. I don't know if it's legitimate or . . ."

"If what's legitimate?" Duncan turned to say. "Whatever it is, I'm sure it's not." He lit his pipe with raised eyebrows, amused at himself.

"Spiritualism," Hettie answered, chin up.

Duncan looked up sharply. "Spiritualism! That girl was sent over here to get away from that cockamamie cult. No one contacts the dead. They're in God's hands."

"How can you be so sure, Duncan?" Hettie replied. "Maybe people like Miss Plante can break through the mystery, hear things, see things the rest of us can't."

"*Mystery*. That's the point, Hettie. Not for us mortals to understand," Duncan said sternly. "The resurrection of the dead is about *faith*. And as Cottnam so rightly put it for once, faith is the maintenance of hope in the face of the unknown. The *unknown*. If the mystery were known to us, we wouldn't have much use for God, now would we?"

"Perhaps *you* miss the point, Duncan—the maintenance of *hope*?"

"Good God, woman. Hope for the world, for mankind, not for—

never mind. You leave that girl in peace." He walked a few more paces and stopped abruptly. He pulled at his ear. His tone softened. "Perhaps I do miss the point," he said. "Are you thinking of contacting Ebbin?"

"Certainly not. We have no idea where Ebbin is," she said lightly, removing her hat and shaking her hair.

He frowned at this disappointing answer. "You don't give up easily, I'll give you that." Hettie glided by and caught up with Ida. Young Fred skipped down the hill after them, Simon and his grandfather following behind. At the bridge over the causeway on the Shore Road, Ida took her leave. She was off to care for her sister, Franny, suffering from that spring cold they hoped didn't turn into the pneumonia. She reminded Hettie to take the roast lamb out of the oven.

Thin clouds swept the sky and a steady southwest wind rippled a carpet of waves toward them—one after another, rushing in, breaking in short bursts on the rocky beach. Young Fred was throwing stones at a submerged log. *Ploosh!* he shrieked each time. Ploosh! A fat grandfather gull on a boulder gave him a withering look. Hettie leaned out on the bridge railing.

"C'mon, girl. I hate it when you sulk. Let's see to that lamb, eh?" Duncan said, linking his arm in Hettie's.

A message, Simon thought. A message would settle things.

Vor Moody told Simon that Charlotte fetched the Bromleys' mail every day at 3:45. "Got your eye on her, eh?" he said, shooting envelopes into people's boxes. "She'd be enough of a girl for any young feller."

Simon rolled his eyes.

"See this?" Vor said, holding up a thin envelope. "Another Kraut letter for Avon Heist. Come once a week."

"A *Kraut* letter? Let's see it."

"Can't," Vor said, shaking his head. "Against the law. Postmarked England, but this same feller," he stabbed at the letter with a crooked forefinger, "used to write to him from Berlin. I know the handwriting." He leaned across the counter. His skin shone through thin strands of red hair combed across his scalp. "Sending messages," he whispered.

"Messages? It's just a *letter*. From England."

"Exactly. Whoops. Here comes your girl. Don't worry, I won't spill the beans."

Simon rolled his eyes again. Then, sure enough, Charlotte trundled into the post office. Her smile made Simon forget to tell Vor she wasn't his girl and gave him the courage to ask if he could walk a ways with her. She happily agreed; she was planning a walk anyway. They took the Shore Road toward Mader's Cove. Along the way, he pointed out houses—Chandlers, Zincks, Fredas, Reddens, Clothiers and Hilchies—all the while trying to frame what he wanted to say. He wished he was taller than her instead of the other way around, but after a while he didn't really care, so easy was their conversation. She wanted to know about each family and about the tides and the islands. As they rounded the road into Mader's Cove, she dug into a little purse dangling from a crocheted string around her wrist and offered him a peppermint.

He took it and asked what London was like. Dirty, crowded and cold, she told him. What she wanted was to go back to her father, but her mother's people disapproved of him. He'd moved to Clonakilty, in the south of Ireland, where there were palm trees, he told her, and where he'd be better appreciated. He'd had an unlucky life, she said, and she missed him.

Simon told her he missed his father, too. They walked awhile in the silence of that bond, sucking on their mints. The air was heavy with the threat of rain. Fat drops plopped on the glassy harbor as they reached Philip's boatyard. Simon pointed to the boat sheds, big as barns, and suggested they wait it out. It was the time of day when Philip usually said, "Have a pint or two, don't mind if I do," and headed for the tavern. They went down the steps to the wharf and ducked in a side door of the first shed.

From there they watched rain splash the wharf. The smell of creosote and oily rags, damp sawdust and salt-crusted coils of hemp rope mingled with the tang of salt air and fresh spring rain blowing in, and the sweet rose scent of her beside him. She had a little shiver, and he found an oil lamp among the coffee-stained papers and pencil stubs on Philip's desk. He lit it for warmth and set it on a roughhewn bench next to them. Rain bounced harder and then great sheets of it swept through the cove and across the deck of the *Elsie* at her mooring.

In the dark reaches of the connecting shed loomed the great black hull of the *Lauralee*, up on a cradle, her rudder straight, her heavy keel exposed, her timbers thick and spongy with fatigue. "Her time's about up," Philip had said when they'd had her hauled. "Well past her prime. Wallace wants to put an engine into her, but she won't do with it. Sits heavy in the water as it is. She's had near enough, Simon Peter." Philip took long, thoughtful draws on his pipe. "I can hold off for a while, but come spring, she'll have to go or go back in the water or be taken down to her ribs. I need this cradle."

"Good thing these old sheds were nearby," Charlotte said, turning around for the first time. "Is that a boat down there?"

"Yep, our boat. The *Lauralee*. My dad's her skipper." He led Charlotte through to the next shed and rolled the sliding door at the far end back a foot or two to let in some light. Charlotte tipped her head back, taking her in. He did as well and saw the boat anew through Charlotte's eyes. Her lines weren't quite as graceful up on the cradle as he'd thought. Her stern was maybe a little too squared off and her beam a little too broad for the sharp clipper bow. He considered explaining that the long counterstern hadn't been around when she was built. Instead, he said, "She's good in a heavy sea," which was true.

Charlotte pulled off a glove and rested her hand on the thick rudder. It was a gesture Simon appreciated. "She's grand," she said.

"Named *Lauralee* for my grandmother. She died before I was born." He didn't want to break the moment, but death had conveniently entered in, and it was now or never. "Say, um, speaking of the dead, I was wondering . . . you know how you—those messages you get?"

She dropped her hand. "What?"

"I was just wondering what it's like is all." He feigned nonchalance, shoving his hands in his pockets.

"No you *weren't*. It's your uncle, isn't it? Oh, I should have known."

"No!" Simon protested. "I, I wasn't after a message!"

She raced to the shed door, then whirled around to face him. "I don't get messages!" she cried. "People think I do, but I *don't!*"

He saw that her jaw was trembling and her pale gray eyes were full. "Don't," he said, coming toward her. "Don't cry." But she did cry, shoulders shuddering, nose dripping. "Get away from me. I'm wretched. I was sent over here because my aunt in London didn't want me around, never did."

"No," he said softly. "No." He reached up because he couldn't help it, and her wet cheek filled his palm with its soft warmth. She slapped his hand away.

"Don't! People think I have a gift. I tried not to, but they begged me and I, I . . . and more people came, banging on the door, everyone wanting a message. But I don't have a gift!"

"But why'd they come after you like that?"

"Because it happened *once*! One time! And word got out. But after that . . . I lied. To make people feel better, but I lied all the same. There," she said with a choking sigh, "now you know." And she was out the door.

He stood stupefied, then raced after her. Rain pelted his face. "*I* lied!" he shouted. "I did want a message!" She stopped and turned around. "I wanted a message because my mother thinks he's still alive. You only lied to help people. *I* lied to get something."

Her expression was lost to him in the rain, but she stood where she was. "Please," he said, "come back."

He led her back to the shed and into Philip's office. Something about the way she stood there, dumbly staring at her shoes and shivering with her hands at her sides, sent a calm through him. He wiped his hands on a rag and shoved some coal into the little stove and checked the kettle for water. He found a mug on a shelf and another on its hook and the tea in the battered tea tin. He shook out her cape and draped Philip's old sweater over her shoulders. His every action was deliberate. It was as if the explosion of emotion had cleared the air and now things could begin again in a real way. He pointed to a chair, and she sat down and held her hands toward the fire that was coming up now, spreading warmth. He made the tea, and she wrapped her hands around the mug. Not a word passed between them.

He stood by the grimy window. The wind and the incoming tide kicked up waves that slapped against each other and flung spray against the wharf. The squall had the *Elsie* swinging at her mooring. In this weather Philip wouldn't be coming back from the tavern any time soon. He could hear Charlotte's breath settle from ragged gulps into a steady rhythm. After a bit he said, "I'm really sorry. Guess I'm not a very good liar. I just wanted . . ."

"Don't be," she said, staring dully into the fire. "It's not easy being a good liar or not good being easy at it. Or I don't know what I mean."

"I don't either, but that's okay." He turned to face her. "Start over?"

"I'd like that," she murmured, staring at her tea. A hint of dimples appeared. She set her mug down and pulled the sweater tighter. "Aunt says I'm too clever for my own good."

"No you're not. She says stuff like that about everyone." He sat down in Philip's chair. "She says my grandfather is a pacifist and that's just not true. He's just against this war is all."

"Yes, she did say that last night at supper. She also said your uncle and your mother were like twins."

"Well, yeah. That is true." Simon asked what else she'd said about him.

Charlotte thought for a moment. "That he was handsome, and, um, easy, and a bit of a vagabond, but everyone loved him."

"His body was never found, you know. That's why my mother thinks he's alive."

"Maybe he is," Charlotte said. A burst of rain pelted the window.

Simon took a good long look at her, but then just shook his head and swiveled his chair around. "Wish I was out in this. It'd be fun."

"On a boat?"

"Well, yeah. You get away from everything on a boat. Plus you're just in it, the weather, I mean. I'm headed out to the Banks this summer, I think. If I can."

"To the what? The bank? You're going to—"

"The *Banks*. I forgot you just got here." He explained that the Banks were ocean plateaus where the water was shallow. "Well, not shallow exactly, like two hundred feet deep, but shallow compared to the rest of the ocean. That's where the cod are and that's why schooners that fish there are called salt bankers. Salt cod, you know . . ."

"Oh, salt cod, money in the bank," she said with a smile.

"What? Oh, I get it."

"A silly joke. Will you go out there on the *Lauralee*?"

"No, no. She's not outfitted for fishing. She's a coastal trader. My grandfather was the captain of a salt banker, but he gave it up to take care of my father after his mother died. My grandfather wouldn't let my father go out there either after that, not to the Banks. Not fishing."

"Why?"

"Because he . . . I don't know. Because he likes to have his say over everything. Doesn't matter because I'm going."

"Won't he stop you?"

"He can try," Simon said, "but I'll be fourteen in June."

The sun was squeaking through the heavy clouds by then and the rain had stopped. Charlotte said she'd better be going. He asked if she'd like to go sailing sometime. He'd find a boat. She was game, she said. Anytime.

Outside, the damp air was laden with a heavy smell of low tide. She took a long, deep breath. "I can tell you about that one time, if you like."

"Now?"

"Yes." And without further hesitation she told him about the Yardley-Ransoms, neighbors in London, and how their son Jack was killed at the Somme, and Mrs. Yardley-Ransom was shut up in her room for weeks. And how one day Charlotte heard some words clear as a bell in Jack's voice. It happened three times in a row. She told Mr. Yardley-Ransom, and he told his wife, and after that she came downstairs for the first time. "She kissed me and hugged me," Charlotte said in wistful conclusion, "as I had never been hugged before or since."

Everything about the story struck Simon as true and terribly sad. After a moment he asked, "What'd he say, this Jack?"

"He said, 'I'm lucky.'"

"Lucky," Simon repeated, incredulous. "That was it? *Lucky*?"

"Yes," Charlotte replied, as if lucky was a perfectly reasonable thing for a dead man to say. "Lucky to be out of the war, maybe."

"But he was *dead*."

"I know." She walked a ways down the wharf and looked down at the float. Philip's rowboat was glistening with raindrops and half full of water. Simon pointed to a starfish clinging to a piling above it. "Will it survive without water?" Charlotte asked. He assured her it would. The starfish could climb down to the water if need be, but the tide would come in again. Charlotte bent down to look more closely at the starfish, now slowly stretching one foot out and hunching another in to move down the wet piling. "They had another son, Edmund," she sighed, "with this contraption holding his face together. That's how he came back in 1915. People looked away. He and I used to sit together in their garden . . . I'd sometimes talk for him when we were together and he'd nod yes or no for his end of the conversation." She lowered her eyes and could not go on.

"That was good for him, I bet," Simon said. "Bet he was lonely."

She gave a few quick nods of her head. "It was when I was sitting with him on the stone bench in their garden that I heard Jack's voice." Her lip quivered.

"I believe you," Simon said. He took her hand. "I do."

She nodded and turned to go. Simon walked her to the steps leading up to the road and said good-by, then walked back along the wharf past the piled-up lobster traps and on down the ramp to the float. He tipped the tender up and rocked it enough to spill out most of the water, then checked the starfish's progress. He turned around at the sound of footsteps, expecting Philip, and saw Zenus instead, sauntering down the wharf. He stood looking down at Simon, arms folded.

"Never guess who I just saw—Miss Charlotte Victoria Plante. Said she was down here with you."

"No she didn't," Simon said, without glancing up.

Zenus took out a rolled cigarette, lit it and came down the ramp. He passed it to Simon. Simon took a long drag and let the world go off-kilter and come back again.

"She didn't need to," Zenus said, leaning against the wet rowboat in his oilskins. "So what were you up to with her, eh? Seeing if the wharf would stand her weight?"

"What are *you* doing here?"

"Fetching Dad from the tavern, what else? Don't tell Ma."

"You're always fetching him. You don't tell her?"

"Are you kidding? If I told her every time I had to fetch Dad out of the tavern, she'd have killed me by now for letting him go in."

"I'm serious. You lie to her, every time?"

"Simon, my boy, you're always serious. Lately, anyway. Thinking of lying to your ma about being with Charlotte?"

"No."

"Liar," Zenus said.

"Yeah, I was with her. Give me another puff, there."

"Take it. I gotta get Dad anyway afore he ties one on with Philip."

WHEN SIMON GOT back to the house, his mother was on her bed, taking a pale spell, just as Young Fred had said. Simon sat down at the foot of the bed. "I saw Charlotte and she had a message." How easy it was to lie when the lie was in service of the truth. "She only gets one per customer. Swear you'll never breathe a word. Or she'll get in trouble."

Astonished, as he knew she would be, his mother sat up. "What are you talking about? What message?"

"He said, 'I'm lucky.'"

"*Lucky?*"

"That's what he said. Maybe . . . maybe better off—you know, in heaven, which is where he is and where he sent the message from." He took her hand in his. "I'm sorry, Ma."

"Did she say he was *dead*?" his mother asked. "No, she didn't. I can see right through you, Simon. You didn't get a message, and she didn't say he was dead."

Simon flung himself back across the bed and put his arm over his eyes. His mother lay back beside him.

They stayed like that, listening to Ida banging pots around the kitchen and the steady murmur of voices below until the voices grew faint and the sky began to lose its color. A languid contentment spread over them as they lay side by side, neither of them stirring, neither trying to convince the other of anything, as if they were drifting on a raft, lifting gently over the currents. He wasn't even sure what he believed. And was there any harm, really, in her thinking Ebbin was alive? There was no body. And no message either . . .

"Remember that picture your father painted of the phalarope? Just the belly and feet, one foot clinging to Lynch bell buoy?" his mother said in a dreamy voice.

"Sure, I do." This, too, this unexpected reference to his father, to his painting, seemed a fragile floating-up of something. The painting had the phalarope in close-up atop Lynch bell during a storm. There was something immensely sad about that one foot clinging, or immensely hopeful. When he finished it, his father had swept Simon up on his shoulders, marched out of the shed and up the slope and around the well, grabbing Simon's small hands in his and stretching his arms out. He and his father filled the yard, the sky above, and the ocean beyond. They were the only ones who liked the phalarope.

"He loved that painting. Whatever happened to it, I wonder . . ."

"I don't know. Did you like it?"

"I didn't understand it. What was the point of bird feet on a bell buoy? But now, I think I know."

"What?"

"Phalaropes—whale-birds, sailors call them—travel in huge flocks out at sea. And here was just this one. Feathers ruffled in a cross wind. One foot up . . . as if deciding if it was safe there on the buoy or better off flying on."

"Which do you figure?"

"Hard to say, but either way, very much alone."

FOURTEEN

April 6th, 1917
Arras Sector, France

eegan, spewing dirt, was filling one sandbag after another like the short-armed troll that he was. "You should get a medal for trench repair," Angus whispered to him. Maybe Keegan had been a gravedigger in another life. Then again, maybe he was one now. The gravedigger of Happy Holly Trench. One more night, Angus kept saying to himself. One more night. So far, not a man wounded. Not one killed. It was all he cared about. That and getting the trench deep enough for men to stand in, which it just about was. His platoon had been digging four nights straight, returning to camp before dawn and heading back at sundown. To the southeast the sharp report of field guns and the boom of artillery shuddered through the night, rolled down, and started up again. The massive preliminary bombardment had been stepped up, a daily allotment of 2,500 tons of shells, most of them fired at night. The men dug all the faster—the thundering roar spurring them on.

A few men down from Keegan, Hiller was fumbling with a burlap bag, seemingly unsure of how to fill it. "Just do it," Angus snapped.

Happy Holly, an abandoned trench now to be used as a jumping-off point, was so filled in and shallow that first night that it had left them all exposed, silhouettes with shovels at the edge of No Man's Land. "Suicide," Katz muttered. "Get to work," Angus had commanded, a cold sweat breaking out on his face.

Their camp was behind the Lorette Spur. Beyond it a valley led up to Gouy-Servins. In the valley lay 80,000 bodies, exactly where they'd fallen two years before—still aboveground. Some said the two opposing sides had been through too much to collect them. Some said there was too much hatred on both sides to allow the standard recovery and burial. Some said they were left there to remind them all of their own fate.

The 17th had been meant to camp in an abandoned town, but shells had upended the village graveyard, and splintered coffins had sluiced down the hill in the rain where the public well received their rotting contents, contaminating the water. The march to Fouquet Wood took them well within range of the Kraut guns. Eight shells exploded as their pipe and drum corps piped them on. The dead and wounded were hauled away on stretchers. Amid the broken drums and a crumpled trumpet, Roddy Gordon squatted down and turned a set of ruined bagpipes over in his hands. A young private named Brady asked Wertz if it might not have been better to suffer typhoid or haul in water to the last camp than to have his best friend die with his legs blown off in this one. Wertz replied that it would be best to refrain from making friends altogether. Katz noted they might do better without the band.

The date of the attack, "Z-day," was not yet known, but the orders showed the 17th would be attached in reserve to the 45th to make up for losses and to be "in support." Conlon explained that their brigade would be relegated to "tasks under," which meant hauling in supplies and ammunition, and clearing out German trenches, supporting the first wave if needed. The 45th was Ebbin's battalion. It was this stunning news that Angus carried with him on that last night of digging.

But he also carried something else. Ambrose, a gunnery captain from the 45th, bragging about their exploits back in camp, mentioned a fellow named Havers who'd joined them sometime around Courcelette. A secret weapon, he called him.

"You *know* him?" Angus half-stood, and quickly sat down. "Why, do *you*?" Ambrose asked, arching an eyebrow. "No, no," Angus heard himself saying. "Heard of him is all. Just wondering if what they say is true."

"Yeah," Publicover broke in. "What's he done, this secret weapon of yours, that's so impressive?"

Ambrose replied that Havers had been in it from the beginning and hadn't a scratch on him. Bullets didn't touch him. Single-handedly took out nine Bosche, armed only with his bayonet, at Thiepval. Might be up for a DSO.

Rosenbek, a laconic lieutenant attached to the Ottawa Rifles and en route to HQ, stretched out his long legs and said he'd heard of Havers, too—a lance corporal, right? But thought he was with another unit. He heard it was a Mills bomb that took out those Krauts. Havers had made a name for himself long before Thiepval, as early as Ypres, Rosenbek said, but there was no one left who could remember how.

The conversation turned to the big push, and Angus staggered out into the sleeting rain. Roddy followed. "You alright, mate?" he asked. When Angus didn't reply, he flung an arm around him. "I'm thinking we should maybe capture this Havers from the 45th and make him one of our own."

Angus fumbled for a match. Dropped his cigarette. Roddy leaned back, hand still on Angus's shoulder, and squinted at him.

Angus stared at the disintegrating cigarette. "Stuff of myth, don't you think?" he finally got out.

"Aye," Roddy said with a grin. "That's why we need him."

IN THE DAYS that followed, the strange and fantastic crouched beside Angus in the ditch where their digging continued under the watchful eye of the enemy, who had not fired a shot. It made no sense, yet it was so. Beyond Keegan's squat form, Hiller stood, his shovel rattling against his pick in the hardened dirt. Keegan shoved him roughly. Told him to get to work. Hiller paid no attention, but the others did. Angus pushed past and grabbed Hiller's shoulder. Maybe he was nuts, maybe not, but there was nothing for it now except to get the digging done and get out. He wasn't about to let Hiller jeopardize that. He yanked him close and said in his ear, "See these men? As scared as you. Except they're doing their job. I'm ordering you. Pick up that shovel and dig. Don't make me press the point, goddamn it." He pulled back his greatcoat, hand on his revolver.

Hiller's nose twitched. He squinted at Angus, then bent double, stood up, and entered into a loose-limbed, jaw-smacking dance, holding his shovel across his chest then stretching it up over his head. Angus lunged for him as the shovel, tossed high in the air, glinted against the flare of a Verey light.

The bullet-riddled shovel sailed over the trench as the sandbags above them exploded with a thousand bullets. Tanner, up on the trench ladder, thudded to the ground, both eyes shot out. Hiller's jaw was severed from his face. The rest of them flattened in the ditch. Angus refused to look at Hiller's profusely bleeding corpse. Hating one of his own; it had come to that.

Lying next to Hiller, arms over his head as the bullets screamed through the air and pelted the ground above, Angus saw the 80,000 rise up from the valley—their rotting corpses not yet turned to dust. Exposed, unsheltered, they continued their hollow-eyed march— neither of this world nor the next. They pressed against Angus to make things right, to keep the stench of meaningless waste at bay. To make every act a footprint that said, I was here; this was worth it—this ditch I'm digging, this traverse I'm building, this cable I'm laying, this mule team I'm leading, this gun I'm oiling, this water I'm hauling, this ammunition I'm packing, this bayonet I'm sharpening.

Worth it, worth it, worth it. If not, they all may as well throw their shovels in the air, run out naked into No Man's Land, yapping and stammering and declaring the Hillers of the world visionaries. And by so doing relegate those 80,000 souls and Brady's limbless friend, and Wickam and Dickey, Orland and now Tanner, all of them, to a permanent, unhallowed place, where they'd be forever stuck to the living in unholy communion.

He rose up, grabbed Hiller's rifle, and risked flying bullets to shove it between the jumping sandbags, and began to fire. He hadn't a hope in hell of silencing the machine gun, but he wasn't about to die face-down in the dirt. Three shots later, a velvet silence fell around them like a curtain.

Under the blinking stars above, the men slowly lifted their heads and got to their knees. They looked at each other, and then at Angus, with the wonder reserved for a god.

"Keep digging," Angus said. "Dig like mad."

BACK AT CAMP, they were told the date for the battle had been set for two days hence, April 8th, Easter morning. "I am the Resurrection and the Life," Chaplain Mercer intoned at the open-air service that Saturday evening. Angus had prayed for Tanner and Hiller and for himself because his prayer for Hiller was without a shred of sincerity. Whether it was proper to thank God for silencing the gun that last night in the trench, he did not know. Miracles were not something he was accustomed to.

Angus found Conlon later, reading his little green book. "Nothing like the resurrection to bring one comfort, but I have a feeling the men will need more than that," Conlon said.

When he gathered C Company for the last time before the battle, that evening, Conlon reminded them why they were there. Who they were up against. Reminded them of the 150,000 who had tried to take the ridge before them and failed, and of those who had given their lives in the effort. He reminded them of the bloodshed and carnage each man had witnessed at the hand of the enemy. Of how the war could turn on their efforts. He opened his little green book, but instead of reading from it, looked slowly up at them. "Rage!" he said. "The rage of Achilles, that doomed warrior, smoldered and flamed and roiled across Troy's wave-swept shores, and flung the souls of mighty fighters, great chiefs, to the dark depths below, untimely slain, lying unburied, torn and stripped by devouring dogs, moving the will of Jove toward its end."

Conlon looked at the astonished faces around him. "I ask you now, toward *what* end? You are here to vindicate every man who has gone down before you and any man who may fall beside you. You are here to restore what is rightful and just. Put on rage as your armor and honor as your shield. Unsheathe your sword of valor. Do your part, whether in support or in the thick of it, and make Canada proud. For my part, I'm proud of you already and honored to serve with you." He paused. "Now, let's astound the gods and turn this war around, and bring it to its *rightful* end."

WEATHER OR WHIM changed the orders at the last minute, and it was not until six in the evening that they marched out of Fouquet Wood, up Music Hall Line and into position in Happy Holly, under a cloak of utter silence, waiting for the dawn of Easter Monday, for zero hour, set for 5:30 A.M.

FIFTEEN

April 9th, 1917
Vimy Ridge
Arras Sector, France

Five-twenty came and five twenty-one, -two and -three . . . so quiet that Angus could hear the men's every breath up and down the line—faces white in the dark, expressions blank. Snowflakes drifted down from a steel-gray sky, then swirled and lifted in the puff of a breeze. The silence was so raw, so unfamiliar, that it stripped him down and left him naked.

Then earth and sky shattered. The mines blew beneath the German trenches. Towering fountains of earth shot skyward. The Allied guns opened up—a thousand shells every twenty seconds. The steady concussion fused into an iron wall of sound. Its thundering vibration likely trembled a cup of tea in the faint dawn of a London kitchen; made old men in suspenders, reaching for collar and tie, pause and look up through curtained windows. In trench and dugout it compressed all thought—of home, of laughter, of sorrows, of chances missed and chances taken—into a whispered prayer.

There was a catch in the shell fire as the guns angled up, then the signal and the hurtling rush forward. All thought fled. Through choking smoke and contagion, Angus could see men run—upright at first, then hunched under their heavy loads, scuttling and scrambling over the shuddering earth, desperate to keep pace with the covering barrage. They were instantly lost from view in the thick-swirling smoke and snow. And if they let loose a battle cry as they climbed over the parapet, as they ran, blood pumping, hearts pounding, it was ripped from their lungs, packed down, and trampled to death.

Behind this chaos, shivering in the snow, the 17th stamped their feet on the hardened mud of Happy Holly and hunkered down against the cold—waiting their turn with rising impatience and growing fear. When it finally came, many hours later, their hands and feet were nearly numb. A runner, dodging shell holes, slid into the trench with word that D Company of the 45th had made it to the red line, but had been pinned down near the heights at the northern end of the ridge. The runner's eyes were wild. His helmet had come off. He heaved, hands on his knees, before managing to choke out that they were all but decimated by machine-gun fire and trench mortar. Unrelenting, sir, he said, sliced the men up something awful. Most of the company officers were dead and their own machine guns clogged with hardened mud. Conlon sent another runner to carry the news to brigade headquarters.

"The 45th!" Angus shouted at Conlon. "Jesus. We got to get up there!"

Conlon blew on his hands and raised an eyebrow. "Anxious to get into it, are you?"

Twenty-five minutes later, word came back that the 17th was to send in support. Most of the ridge was in Canadian hands by that time, but there were remaining pockets of defenders. In places beyond the ridge, the Germans had regrouped. They continued to hold the high point, Hill 145, and had started a counterattack at Givenchy. A and B Companies from the 17th were to proceed southeast up to the second German line, clear out remaining defenders and hold the line.

C and D Companies were to leapfrog over them, find the 45th and help them meet their objective if they hadn't already.

They got into position. The signal came. And then they were running and dodging through a tangled jungle of protruding wire and hidden shell holes. His platoon made it past a blur of abandoned weapons, mangled bodies and blood-soaked snow up to the second German trench. B Company dove in and spread down its length to check for the enemy. Conlon led C Company on. Machine-gun fire opened up and Angus kept on running as men up ahead and beside him fell. He rolled into a shallow ditch. Two men ran toward him, then turned and ran the other way and were gone. Another stumbled toward Angus, but tripped and fell on a wounded man whose bayonet pierced him through front to back, pinning him there. It was Zwicker, Angus was sure of it. Kearns tried to pull him off.

A trench mortar shrieked past. When they could, Angus and Kearns elbowed to the next shell hole. Up the slope, Angus made out three Germans in a huddled circle in front of what looked like a pile of hay, their helmets and greatcoats dusted with snow. Angus aimed his revolver as Kearns, right beside him, pulled out a Mills bomb. Before he could throw it, a huge shape, with wings like a prehistoric bird, hurtled by—legs wide apart, kilt flying. Roddy Gordon! Without missing a beat, he charged them, stabbing the first one in the waist with his bayonet. The three tipped over as one. Roddy stepped back. A grenade clinked out of the open hand of one of the soldiers and rolled toward him. He grabbed it, pulled the pin and shouted, "Here's one for the live ones!" and hurled it up the ridge. He was instantly spun around by a bullet to the chest and crashed facedown atop the dead Germans. The hay burst into flames. Angus crawled out and heaved him over. With words surely lost to Roddy's ears, he assured him, "You got 'em. You did." Roddy's head lolled to the side, eyes open, frothing blood onto Angus's knees.

They left him and headed on, and in what seemed like mere minutes, fell, gasping, into another section of ruined enemy trench. Angus slid down over loose rubble to the bottom. His leg was bleeding, but he felt no pain. Men jumped in after him. They'd lost sight of Conlon and of Publicover's platoon. Above the trench wall a stream of prisoners, carrying the wounded on stretchers, passed by, ghosts in the falling snow, dipping here and there under their awkward loads as if in a parallel universe.

Angus led his men farther up the ridge, only it wasn't really up—it was more across and over and sometimes down. The pock-filled ridge was a featureless slope to nowhere, littered with bodies, water-filled holes, and the ground churned in places to slippery muck. A bullet got Eisner through the neck. Two Germans popped up, one after the other, with rifles, and Angus shot them, one after the other, with barely a pause between and waved the men on until his bleeding leg gave out and he rolled into a crater. Above him, the sun attempted to break through the heavy clouds. In the yellow haze, the falling snow took on an iridescence, and he thought of shimmering water and of oars dipping and falling. It took some minutes before he could grasp that his wound had widened and he was losing a lot of blood. One of the men was on it, peeling away the bloodied kilt from the gash in his thigh. It was Wertz. He bound up the wound without a word. Angus sat up. Men raced past in all directions. Keegan asked if they should get him to an aid station. Angus waved him off and asked for a count. "Eight of us here, counting myself," Keegan said. "Four missing or dead." He ticked off the names—Zwicker, Eisner, Bremner, Oxner.

"Zwicker's dead. Bremner, too," Angus said. "Died together. Eisner shot in the neck."

Katz said that Oxner was definitely dead, shot in the stomach. LaPointe was missing. McNeil swore he'd been wounded and carried off the field. As he said it, LaPointe appeared.

"Alright—nine. We'll head out." Angus winced and pulled a map of their side of the ridge and his compass from his tunic pocket. The glass was shattered. He stared at it and up at Keegan. "Dead reckoning is what we'll rely on."

"Dead reckoning, yes sir," Keegan said. "Where to?"

DEAD RECKONING TOOK them on a stuttering, twisted path up and across the broad slope to where the land rose sharply and to a final reckoning. Shells fired somewhere in the distance. The snow around them was blackened with gunpowder and bright with blood. It might have been hours, it might have been minutes, since they'd left Happy Holly. Time's linear march had ceased. Angus looked at his watch. 5:07 P.M. A corpse lay at his feet, hands clasping a rifle, eyes wide with surprise, mustache crusted white with snow. Above them, a shadow loomed through the mist and took the shape of a concrete pillbox.

They had entered the world of the dead. Before them and all around, arrayed in grotesque angles of disfigurement, among blackened stumps of trees, lay bodies. Angus peered again through the frosty mist at the pillbox, hulking above them, then cautiously brushed the snow off the man at his feet and saw the badge of the 45th, and on the next man and the next. Every one from the 45th.

The men fanned out and checked for survivors. Not one was found. Angus stumbled from corpse to corpse, yanking them up to see their faces, until somewhere through his fevered search he saw boots and heard Keegan's voice. "Sir?" he said. "I believe the battle's moved on. Should we . . . carry on over the ridge?"

Angus, holding a private by the collar, realized the man he held was sliced in half. Keegan was staring at the blood dripping steadily on the snow at Angus's feet. "You may want to rewrap that, sir," he said. "Should we move on to—"

Damn it! They couldn't move on. Did Keegan not understand that?

There were more bodies to check. "We'll check these bodies," Angus said. He felt himself weaving.

"For what exactly, sir?"

"For—never mind! I'll do the checking."

"Yes sir. We can help check if you tell me what we're—"

Again, Keegan looked at the blood, dripping.

Dropping the corpse, Angus left Keegan dumbfounded and tramped off through filthy slush, through shot-off arms and legs, jerking men up and letting them drop. Every face that was not Ebbin's filled him with relief. And horror. It was appalling what he was doing, but he kept on in a frenzy until, at the body of a man with no face left, he dropped to his knees.

He grunted to a stand and they trudged up the icy hill to the concrete bunker where they were greeted by smashed equipment and dead Germans sprawled about. Angus leaned against a wall while Hanson and Ostler stripped a German corpse of his badge and revolver. Souvenirs. *Se souvenir.* To remember. Angus prayed he'd forget. Kearns kicked one of the corpses. Angus peeled the bandage off his leg and looked at the wound for the first time—a gash about four inches long, still bleeding, but shallow and beginning to close. He rewrapped it, then got the men going. Some talked about how they'd do the Krauts in, retreat or no, they'd make them pay. But when they reached the eastern slope, all talking ceased. Mouths fell open. What lay before them was too fantastical, too unreal to be true.

Spread out below, all the way to Lille, was the Douai Plain. Tiny towns and church spires dotted the landscape. Straight roads and railways intersected a neatly laid-out patchwork of flat fields. There was a hint of green on grass and in the still-standing woods. It may as well have been the Garden of Eden. Here was not a trace of the withered, ruined, rat-infested hell they'd lived in for months, for years, for all time. Here was a place unscathed by battle—a place of German occupation, yes, but one of railroads and prospering farms, of standing barns and church steeples, and buildings with rooftops. A world of color and shape and form. It took their breath away.

Only Hanson spoke. "I'll be damned," he said.

For a long moment, no one moved. Then Angus pulled out his binoculars and scanned the plain for the Lens-Arras Road and the villages of Vimy and Petit Vimy to the southeast, La Chaudière to the east, noting their positions. He drew a quick sketch and stuffed it in his pocket.

"Get the men. We're moving out. We've got to find the rest of the 17th," he said to Keegan.

The men slowly gathered their gear. Angus, limping along in the lead, felt their eyes on him and heard their muttered complaints. They joined the streams of soldiers and prisoners, the lost, the wounded, and those who, with heads down, were just doing their jobs. Angus realized unless he got his wound tended, he would not be able to do his.

He got directions from some stretcher-bearers to the nearest aid post. He ordered his men to help support the walking wounded. When they reached it, weakened by loss of blood and the sight of faces contorted in pain at the entry, Angus thudded onto a crate with a red cross painted on its side. His leg out stiff, he peeled back his kilt and began to unwrap the bloodied bandage again.

"Here, you! We need those!" a medic said, pointing to the crate. When he saw Angus's wound, he bent down. Angus waved him off. The medic pulled out scissors and began to cut the bandage. Angus put his head back and saw only lavender sky and desultory snow-flakes spinning, each one unique. See, Simon? Cut the edges, fold again, make more cuts. Not too much, now, or you'll have nothing left. Unfold it, now. See? Simon's snowflakes filled the sky. "Don't cut too much," he said aloud.

"No sir. Just pressing it now. Cleaning it out."

The medic splashed an orange liquid over the wound. Angus sat bolt upright at the flash of pain.

"Iodine. There. That breathed some life into you. Wound's not too deep. Just a few stitches, sir, and then I'll need that crate of bandages." He disappeared into the timbered entry from which screams sliced the air, and returned with a needle and black thread.

"This'll do the trick." He pinched the wound with thick fingers and made hasty stitches on the ragged flesh, then wrapped it once again.

"Now, sir, those bandages you're sitting on, if you will." He stepped back. Angus stood and tried to open the crate. He slumped against the wall, dizzy, breathless. How was a simple wound doing him in?

"Lost some blood there," the medic said. He pulled out a small vial of smelling salts. "Here, sit down. Keep these. Might come in handy. I'll see to that crate."

Angus managed to thank him. The salts jerked him awake. He was parched, and somehow his canteen was missing. A man next to him was gulping water. Where'd he get it? It was all Angus could do not to grab it from him. "Water?" the man said, and passed his canteen over. Angus took a long swallow and held up the canteen—his own. A glance at the man's cracked lips, his round eye filling with blood beneath a bandage, and Angus passed it back.

Katz and LaPointe materialized, and with Angus they stepped around the line of wounded men. The pungent smell of blood gave rise to another wave of nausea. Angus ordered Keegan to round up the rest of the men—they'd head over the ridge, he told them. Their progress was slow, for dusk had fallen. Angus had to forge a path through the debris every few yards, then come back and lead the men. He had to concentrate, concentrate. Then he had to wait, wait until every man passed. Count them, each one. And still the men fell into holes and tripped over wire and ordnance and the dead and wounded. They bumped into other soldiers coming and going, many of them lost and without officers. At some point, Angus wasn't sure when, they were told by a gunnery captain that the 17th had indeed moved on to the other side of the ridge with the 45th.

Darkness had fallen by the time they reached the crest. They came upon a concrete dugout. The back wall had been blown away so that, like a cave, it was level with the ground. Angus flicked on his torch and flashed it over an overturned desk, four chairs and two empty crates.

"Cleaned the place out, eh? Bastards," Kearns said.

"Or maybe our own took what was worth taking," Hanson replied.

Not quite. In the corner the torch lit up the black metal shaft and pearl handle of a Luger pistol, and next to it, a dead German captain, a bullet through his head. Angus put the pistol in a pocket of his greatcoat and handed Keegan the light as he searched the soldier's pockets. The first thing Angus found was another Luger, still in its holster. He pulled it out. In the man's jacket he found a packet of letters, which he thumbed through roughly and replaced. He wanted no reminders of the life the man had led. There seemed no point in moving the body, but Angus closed the eyes and rolled it over so it faced away from them. There was no coat to cover the face, which looked neither startled nor stunned, but simply dead. If there had been, they'd have used it for warmth. He herded the men into the dugout. "No point going further in the dark. Too dangerous with all the debris," he told them, and they slumped down and huddled together against the cold damp wall.

He instructed those with water in their canteens to share it. "Got something we can eat? Anyone?" he asked. Boudrey's eyes lit up and he withdrew a chocolate bar from his tunic pocket like the treasure it was. "Got it in a comfort box." He carefully peeled back the stiff waxed-paper wrapper and broke the bar into its twelve grooved squares, taking so much time that Ostler grabbed it and the chocolate fell to the ground. He lunged for it. Angus stayed his hand and the men waited as Boudrey slowly picked up every piece. There was something reassuring in his deliberate movements. "Don't close your fist over it, Boudrey! For the love of God, you'll melt it," Ostler bleated. Breathing loudly, undisturbed, Boudrey collected every square in his filthy palm, then with a loopy grin dropped them one by one to open hands.

"Did yourselves proud today, boys," Angus said. "A moment of silence for Zwicker, Eisner, Oxner, and Bremner. God rest their souls." He paused and then told them they'd stay there until first light. But the men kept their heads bowed. "Men?" he said. Without looking up, Hanson said, "What about the rest of it, sir? Like you did for Orland?" Angus nodded.

"I am the resurrection and the life," Angus said softly. "He that believeth in me, though he were dead, yet shall he live. In the midst of life we are in death. Amen." The men sat back, satisfied. "Now, loosen your boots. In fact, take them off and rub your feet before you put them back on. Get some sleep." He started rubbing Boudrey's feet. If he'd had whale oil, he'd have rubbed it on. If he'd had a blanket, he'd have tucked them in.

Keegan and Kearns offered to serve as lookouts, and Angus joined them. The pain in his leg flared briefly and then dulled. He felt a wave of nausea, but it passed. Looking out over the ruins of the parados in the gloom, he wondered if a parados became a parapet when the trench changed hands and the Front moved on. A rhythmic ticking started up, like a halyard tapping a mast. The source—a rope, fixed at the top of the trench, stretching the length of a timber to the ground—was tapping in the wind. Angus leaned his hand against it and hung his head and let the rise of the swells take him beyond the sound of distant shells exploding, the light of flares, beyond hunger and fatigue, far beyond and back, until he was awake again, on deck, on watch.

WHEN FIRST LIGHT came, the wind turned sharp. There was no snow falling, just a gray haze. Angus took out his binoculars and scanned the plain below. Canadian troops were on the move and he hoped the Germans were in retreat. He bent his leg a couple of times—stiff, but much less painful. He thanked God for the medic. He still had the limp, but felt no fever.

It was then he sensed a presence. Pistol drawn, he inched around a pile of the rubble. A German officer fell to his knees and threw up his hands. It was light enough to see his eyes, but Angus couldn't read them.

"Canada," the man said. Angus had been prepared for "*Kamerad*," not "Canada." The officer said it again, and, in his accent, Angus pictured it as "*Kanada*," which helped him keep his distance when the officer clutched his side and moaned. Hands up again quickly, he again said, "Canada." Then added, "Gooood." He tried to smile, then collapsed on all fours. He pulled back his greatcoat. His holster was empty.

Angus took a step closer and the man lunged for him. Angus fired. The officer fell over, a knife in his hand. The Luger fell from Angus's pocket as he leaned over the man. The German looked at it sadly. "Yours?" Angus said. The man nodded. Angus kicked the gun away. "You could have surrendered, damn it. I'd have taken you in." The officer managed a smirk at this impossibility, his cheeks now pale. A line of blood, bright against the colorless lips, formed and filled and trickled down the side of his mouth.

"Royal Vic," the man said in an almost inaudible whisper.

"What?" Angus balled up the man's coat and pressed on the wound. The officer whispered, "Royal Vic." He looked at Angus intently until life faded from his eyes. Angus forced himself to go through his pockets and found a map, which he held in his shaking hand. And a picture postcard of the Royal Victoria Hospital in Montreal with German words on the other side. The sheath for the Bowie was snapped to the officer's belt. He must have had the knife up his sleeve. Angus pocketed the map and the pistol and stood.

Keegan and Kearns rounded the traverse. "Here's the owner of the pearl-handled Luger," Angus told them. "And this." He unfolded the map.

The blade of the knife glinted up at him. A Bowie, known as the German's favorite weapon for slicing throats of the wounded left in No Man's Land. Soundless death. He picked up the knife. "Sheffield" was imprinted on the outsized blade. It could have sliced a throat, alright. And gone through his groin like butter. He looked down at the dead officer, sorrow turning bitter in his mouth. "You could have surrendered," he said again as he unfastened the sheath and slid the knife into it. The postcard fluttered away.

WITHIN THE HOUR, they'd angled partway down the steeper eastern side of the ridge and caught up to the troops Angus had seen through his binoculars, but who, it turned out, were a remnant of B Company from the 91st. Angus reported to the officer in charge, a bandy-legged captain with a curling mustache, who said he thought the 17th had joined the 45th somewhere toward La Chaudière.

Angus looked at the map. "You sure they're headed toward La Chaudière?" he asked.

"Look, Lieutenant," the captain snapped. "I'm not sure of any-thing. It's one day after the battle. You can't find your own company. I think our rations party is lost. We've passed any number of lost bands of men roaming about. We were supposed to hold the line. Then I get word the line is moving by the hour as the Germans retreat. We need to pursue. Fine. All for it. Then I hear from a run-ner that we're supposed to halt. Then, no, that's wrong. I've got this map here . . ."

They compared maps, but the captain refused to take corrections from Angus. "I'll trust my Allied map over your Kraut one," he said. "And anyway, what good is that map if you don't know where you're headed. I'm going to stop at that abandoned breastworks up ahead and send scouts back to find that blasted rations party. You're welcome to hook up with us temporarily."

Angus declined.

"Should we maybe stick with them, sir, for now? You know, strength in numbers?" Keegan eyed the open terrain.

"They're not headed for the 17th. We'll find our way. Trust me," Angus said. "I know where I'm going." He tucked the map in his pocket and felt the knife hitched now to his belt. He'd shot that German before he'd even seen it. But the man did have a knife. And had faked a wound. "Royal Vic." Maybe he'd been a doctor there once. Or a patient. Left Montreal and went back to the homeland. Forced into the war . . . or had volunteered. What did it matter? Angus flung the Luger as far as he could and moved on.

Sleet dulled sound and obliterated the landscape, except for the shadow of the ridge behind them. The ground was slick and, oddly, they were moving through tall grass. Angus had it in mind to find a point beyond the Lens–Arras Road that lined up between La Chaudière and La Coulotte. From there he'd find the 17th on their way or already encamped. He was certain of it. His platoon struggled on behind him.

As they drew near the point where Angus planned to site their position, they came across a silver-haired man leading a small party. Colonel Stokes! Thank God. Or maybe not. There was a vacant look in his eye. He didn't salute. He was disheveled and alone, save for a corporal and two privates. His uniform was blackened.

Angus asked him about the camp. Stokes looked to the east, to the west, and behind to the south. "Have you seen my horse?"

"No sir," Angus replied.

"Right then. Form your men up," Stokes said.

"Form up?"

"Can't afford to have discipline break down. Lead on."

"Sir, do you know where the camp is? Your staff . . . ?"

"Had to see to these boys here from the 102nd."

"101st," the corporal whispered.

Angus pulled the corporal aside and asked him what was going on. "We got separated from our company, when we . . . came upon the colonel." The corporal glanced back nervously.

"Alone? Was he alone?"

"Yes sir. Sitting in the grass."

Angus left it at that. How Stokes had become detached from his staff and possibly from reality was something Angus had no time to find out.

The Lens–Arras Road was hidden from view by mist or by a rise in the landscape, he couldn't tell. The slope was almost imperceptible, but yes—a gentle swell, and another just beyond it. The camp was probably in the hollow between the two. There were enough trees left of the "*wald*" on the German map to indicate a wood. Where else could the 17th be? It was the only possible place if the officer from the 91st had been right, and if the German map in his hand was accurate, and if they were where he thought they were.

They moved on. Stokes stood to the side and watched the group file by as if on his stallion reviewing the troops. Angus sent Keegan back to fetch him, to no avail. To get him moving, Angus asked for orders, which he supplied with military demeanor and dignity of rank. All he was missing was context.

AN HOUR LATER they were threading their way through a group of men shoveling in bully beef at the edge of the camp. Biscuits, too. Angus nearly grabbed one off a soldier's plate. He saw a private weeping on the ground in the arms of his pal. His breath quickened at the sight of the men from the 45th. But he kept on, Stokes stumbling beside him. A few of the men registered astonishment at the sight of Stokes, his ribbons dangling at an angle, cap missing. Angus told Keegan to see that the men got fed, and turned to lead Stokes on to

Rushford, when he stopped dead in his tracks. Not ten yards away, crouched on the ground, tin plate in hand, was Ebbin. Not dead. Not wounded. Not missing.

"Know him, sir?" he heard Keegan say. Angus ignored him but couldn't move. Keegan squinted suspiciously at Ebbin and back again at Angus. Angus kept his eyes on Ebbin, who set his plate down and looked up. They stared at each other, and time stretched out between them to the innocence of boyhood and back again to the blackened corpses on the hill. There was in that moment a thread of connection to home and each other. But in that raised chin and sober face, Angus saw Havers as well. Havers who had taken Ebbin Hant through Thiepval and now through Vimy without a scratch on him. It was with a prayer thanking God that Angus left him there as Lance Corporal Havers.

WHEN HE USHERED Stokes in, Rushford saluted and said, "Sir! Thank God," but whatever relief Rushford may have felt vanished as Stokes saluted absently and lowered himself into a camp chair, where he sat fingering a button on his tunic, unresponsive to Rushford's questions. Aghast, Rushford pulled Angus aside. Angus told him how he'd found the colonel. Stokes had been given up for dead, Rushford whispered. His party had unaccountably gotten caught in the actual battle, and the colonel's horse had charged off. An explosion. Perhaps the horse threw him, Rushford said. Miraculous he was still alive, all the more that he'd been found. His immediate aides had not been so lucky. He told Angus to make a full report but cautioned him against mentioning the colonel's condition. "Amazing you found the camp," he said. "Good instincts. Well done." Angus handed him the German map. Rushford took it gratefully, then sniffed several times. "Fritz is out there, you know," he said, running his knuckles under his mustache. "Bringing in fresh recruits, preparing a counterattack. We're sitting ducks until we can build a road and get our heavy artillery over that ridge."

✧

"Look who's come in from the cold," Conlon said when Angus found him. The shoulder of his tunic was in tatters. He got up off the crate he was sitting on and smiled that slow smile of his, and they exchanged a rough embrace.

"You look like hell," Conlon said.

"As do you. Hell and back. Were you wounded?"

Conlon shrugged. "Nope. Lucky break. Bullet through the sleeve."

Publicover rounded the tent. A dirty field dressing dangled from his earlobe; a thin row of stitches held the top of his ear together. He clapped a hand on Angus's shoulder and said not a word. In the silence of their circle, Angus felt the fragments of the past twenty-four hours begin to gather and fall into place.

"Any accounting of the battalion?" he asked.

"Not yet. The numbers are coming in." Conlon paused, then added, "Stokes is missing."

"Was lost and now he's found," Angus said.

"Really. And you the one who found him?" Conlon asked.

"Now, that's a story I want to hear." Publicover ripped the bandage off his ear.

"All in good time. Got something for you." Angus was about to hand him the horn-handled Bowie, but remembered the old wives tale that handing someone a knife cuts the friendship. He placed it on the crate. "Might come in handy for your future kills," he said with a smile.

"A Bowie." Publicover whistled as he slid the knife from its sheath and slowly turned it over. He looked up from under a shock of matted blond hair. "Let me guess, found it on some dead Imperial. Or took it off a Kraut officer you killed with your bare hands."

"You figure it out," Angus said.

Publicover gave a short laugh and said, "Welcome home, MacGrath."

Sixteen

April 14th, 1917
Vimy Ridge
Arras Sector, France

"Damn it!" Publicover said four days later on hearing Conlon's news. He stomped around in a tight circle, shoving at the dirt with his boot. "Goddamn it. We had our fucking orders. March back to Château de Villers. Today."

Orders had changed, Conlon said, and now they wouldn't be replaced for another day. He had other news. Early numbers were coming in for the 17th. Some 51 killed, 280 wounded. No telling how many of them survived. But their losses were much lighter than other regiments, some of which had a 70 percent casualty rate. A road was being built and small-gauge track laid. Supplies had begun to arrive. A new front was being established all along the eastern side of the ridge. Their sector had been quiet, but a working party, sent out to put barbed wire forward of the line, had not returned. Worse, it was rumored there was a howitzer hiding in the brush near where the party had fallen, ready for the Allied advance. Rushford had ordered Conlon to take a patrol out and bring back information.

"What information?" Angus asked.

"Find the heavy gun that HQ thinks is out there and, if possible, take out the machine gun that's worrying our working parties. Seems you did such a good job of finding the colonel that Rushford wants you onboard. 'Get that Lieutenant MacGrath. Good with maps. Uncanny sense of direction' were his exact words." Conlon gave Angus a nod and said, "Strangely, he wants me in it as well. Maybe wants to get rid of me, but that's another story. Our dapper Rushford seems to be managing field command without Stokes. Our major problem is further up the chain of command—no plan for pursuit. It's as if no one thought we'd actually take that ridge." He shrugged. "Ah well. So the plan is we go out, gather what information we can on artillery. Find our way back and report in. And they'll send out a larger patrol based on our intelligence. You in, Sam?"

Publicover spat on the ground. "Yeah. I'm in. Course I'm in."

"Right. Now, help me scratch up a few men. Four will do." He glanced at Angus's leg wound.

"I'm fine," Angus said. "I'm in."

LATE THAT NIGHT at the edge of the camp, Angus felt the exhilaration and exhaustion of surviving a gale at sea. He thought about Ebbin and "the grand sweep of history." He was part of it. They both were. He was one with the company of men who had survived—the sheer luck of it. The blessing. The burden. He whispered a prayer for the men he'd lost, and for Roddy. He could hear Roddy's booming laugh, felt the strength of his presence beside him. The grasses glittered with a thin coat of ice in the moonlight across the long unbroken plain before him. Just short days ago, the ridge behind him had been the point of existence, the alpha and the omega. Soon it would be but a memory. For time had not ceased. The war had not ended. Like the icy plain before him, the war stretched out to a never-ending, unknown end. This he also considered, before heading back to his men.

⬦

AT NINE O'CLOCK the following evening, under a brilliant night sky, Angus and Keegan waited for the others at the rendezvous point on the edge of the camp. Conlon appeared from the shadows with Publicover and two others, introduced as Corporal Burwell, who spoke German, and Private Voles, a sniper. Behind them came another.

"Lance Corporal Havers," Conlon said.

"*Havers?*" Angus stammered.

"Yes, *Havers.* The secret weapon. Remember? What's the problem?" Publicover shot a look at Havers, who joined them and glanced at Angus with cool detachment and looked away.

"Surprised is all," Angus whispered.

Publicover, agitated to start with, was even more so now. "Yeah, right. What's going on here?" He looked from Angus to Havers.

Keegan knit his brows and did the same. "Sir, is this the—"

Angus flashed a look that silenced him.

Conlon pulled Angus out of earshot of the others. "You know something I don't? You look like you've seen a ghost."

"No. It's just . . . is he up to it?"

"What do you mean, is he up to it? This is *Havers*, the guy with no fear in him. Invincible. Survived Ypres, Courcelette, the massacre on that ridge three days ago. That's why I took him."

"Yeah, but maybe he's got something to prove."

"How's that?"

"He's got that reputation to live up to or a death wish or . . ."

"What the hell are you talking about?"

"Nothing. Never mind."

"What's going on, MacGrath?" Conlon's words came out slowly. He put his head down, hands on his hips. "You see something I don't?"

"No. It's just— He makes me nervous. I mean, can we trust all that's been said about him?"

"I have no reason not to trust it." Conlon looked up. "Do I?"

"No sir." Angus strapped on his helmet. There was no alternative except the truth, and it was far too late for that. He glanced back at Ebbin, standing erect, patiently waiting. He'd have to trust it was Havers they had with them. And trust that he himself would be able to believe it well enough to function.

"Do I?" Conlon repeated.

Angus shook his head.

"No reason. None that you know of . . ."

"No, damn it. None that I know of."

"Okay then." Conlon signaled the men, and they moved silently out into the still night beyond the camp.

LOW TO THE GROUND, they crept through the tall grasses, sometimes on their stomachs, and froze every time a flare shot up, waiting for it to fade so they could breathe again and inch forward. After a while there were no more flares, which could mean the enemy had their own patrols out. Out where? was the question.

Angus brought up the rear, Ebbin right ahead of him. Ebbin or Havers, and he prayed it was the invincible Havers. He welcomed the fear that sliced thought to ribbons and forced him to focus on the ground—this stub of a tree to the left, this hillock to the right—each landmark catalogued in relation to the others in this, the new No Man's Land. He prayed he would remember.

An hour and forty-five minutes later, they stole up to a rise, topped by a tangled thicket and a few spare trees and one thick-trunked oak that gave them fairly good cover. To the right in a gully below lay what appeared to be the dead Canadians from the working party, two leaning up against each other, one folded over at the waist, one staring up at the sky, his gloved hand on a tightly wound bolt of barbed wire.

In the field beyond the gully was a barn with a high stone foundation. Another massive oak stood guard beside it. In the quiet moonlight, everything was sharply defined in black and white. They could see the loft, doors open, facing them. The great barn doors below it were bolted shut. There was a low stone wall about four feet high some ten yards to the left, running parallel. Woods beside it wrapped around the open field behind the barn.

Angus took out his pad. In the light of the moon, he sketched the ground, made notes and put them away.

A German soldier came around from the back of the barn, looked up at the sky, arched his back and went back behind the barn. Far to the southeast, they could hear machine guns chattering. Then they heard voices.

Behind them.

Two enemy soldiers were coming up the very rise they were on. It was clear from their easy movement that they were unafraid, knew protection was nearby. Obviously in the barn, though maybe also in the woods. Conlon nodded at Publicover, who silently withdrew the Bowie. As if on cue, the moon slid behind a cloud. In seconds Publicover was on them, slitting the throat of the first and walking the other back up the rise with the knife to his neck. He forced the man down on his knees behind the thicket.

The soldier's eyes were wide with horror, as were Burwell's. Keegan took the man's helmet off.

"*Kamerad*," the terrified man whispered. Conlon told him to shut up, and told Burwell to tell the man he could save himself by telling them where the machine gun was, how many men were in the barn, the location of the howitzer—and, by the way, they were not his comrades. Burwell, panicky and breathing hard, smoothed his black mustache and glanced at Publicover. Publicover arched an eyebrow. Burwell knelt before the prisoner and did as he was told, whispering in halting German. The prisoner, a tall man, was shaking violently, the features of his long face gripped with fear. Publicover pulled the knife closer and straightened him up. The prisoner began to blurt something out.

"What's he saying?" Conlon demanded.

"Uh. Wife, baby. He has a wife and baby, a new baby," Burwell said. He turned to the soldier. His whispers took on a coaxing intimacy. He pointed up at Publicover and shook his head. The prisoner nodded vigorously and stuttered out answers. Six in the barn, manning the gun, but the gun was broken. They were trying to fix it.

"And the howitzer?"

"He doesn't know anything about a howitzer."

"Artillery of any kind?"

The prisoner shook his head wildly. Conlon came face-to-face with him. "Tell him he's never going to see that wife and baby again if he doesn't talk," he said with quiet determination. "Tell him we're going to leave him here with a guard. If he isn't telling us the truth now, it'll be over for him. He saw what happened to his pal. He'll go down with us if he's lying."

Burwell pleaded with the soldier and sat back. "No sir. He says there isn't any howitzer or anything else this part of the line. He says there are Prussian Guards about a mile off to the north and east, he *thinks*, but here, just the MG. In the loft. And it's dead, broken."

"He's lying," Publicover said.

"Yeah?" Conlon looked over at Publicover.

"Yeah. First off, why would they put a machine gun in the loft? It's forty feet aboveground. They'd want it waist-high for the shots to be effective, not flying out over the men's heads."

"Maybe it's aimed at this slope we're on," Angus said.

"Good point," Conlon said.

The prisoner began speaking rapidly. Burwell translated. "He says he's only a private. He doesn't have more intelligence. No more information. The gun is broken."

The prisoner's eyes were bulging. Conlon yanked his head up by the hair. "Six, eh? Six soldiers? Broken gun?"

"We'll see," Publicover said.

"We'll risk one man going in there," Conlon said. They stripped the German of his coat. Ebbin immediately volunteered. Just as quickly Angus countered that he'd go. Conlon told him they needed him to guide them back. Keegan already had the German helmet on, a tight fit. When he put on the coat, it came nearly to his ankles. He looked like a dwarf in a sorcerer's robe. "Take off the damn coat," Conlon said. He nodded at Ebbin, who pulled it on. A perfect fit. The Gothic helmet nearly hid his face. Lawrence Havers, German private.

Angus and Conlon scanned the farm again with glasses. Voles stuck a piece of chewing gum in his mouth and lay flat, rifle ready, squinting through the scope. Out of the blue, a musical note floated over the field. And another and another, plaintive and slow, from a harmonica, and "There's a Long, Long Trail A-Winding" wafted out over the ravine. Tendrils of remembered lyrics unfurled silently in the night.

"There's a long, long trail a-winding
Into the land of my dreams,
Where the nightingales are singing
And a white moon beams.
There's a long, long night of waiting
Until my dreams all come true;
Till the day when I'll be going down
That long, long trail with you."

Voles looked back at Conlon. Burwell was looking up at the stars. Havers was staring straight ahead. No one spoke.

"What the . . . ?" Keegan said. "That's ours. They can't do that. They can't take our song!"

"Can and have. The question is why?" Conlon said.

"Toying with us. They know we're out here." Angus narrowed his eyes at the barn.

"Maybe," Conlon said, sitting up. "What I do know is that they're going to miss that patrol. I'm not going to risk going in 'til we know what we're up against. And I don't trust our Fritz here anymore than Publicover does. You ready, Havers?"

"Yes sir," he said smartly. "Should I lob a grenade into the loft if there aren't too many of them? I can take cover behind that stone wall."

"We're not here to take them down. We're here to bring back intelligence. There won't be any if we don't make it out alive. Just go down there and get a look—*in* the barn, if you can. We'll cover you, and Voles here will have his scope. If you see the howitzer, shift your rifle to the other shoulder. If you think we can take them with our little band, shift it back. Then get to that stone wall and roll into the woods. Even if that MG is working, there's no way it can get you from the loft at that angle, once you're down there. Of course, there could be more in the woods. If we have to go in, we will, but our mission is intelligence. Got that? No heroics. Just scout things out."

Ebbin nodded vigorously but didn't move. "Havers?" Angus whispered. He found Angus's eyes and slowly rose. In another minute he was down to the dead Canadians and up the crest of the gully—a silhouette in a German greatcoat and heavy helmet. Then, without faltering, he went all the way in.

He sidled around the barn and a moment later reappeared and shifted his rifle to his other shoulder before turning smartly and walking swiftly back along the side of the barn. He'd seen the howitzer. He shifted his rifle back again. He thought they could take them out.

WHAT ANGUS WOULD remember with utmost clarity was Havers at the front of the barn, firing a grenade up into the loft. Except Havers wouldn't have stood there frozen when it failed to explode. He'd have tossed up another or run for cover. And so it was perhaps Ebbin, after all, who dropped from a single bullet from a single rifle.

It wasn't clear at first if he was dead or alive because the fully functioning machine gun in the loft was strafing the slope, churning up the ground in front of the hedge, splintering the trees to sawdust. Burwell's mustache drooped over his open mouth as he repeated the prisoner's cry that they must have fixed it, fixed the gun! "He didn't know!" But Publicover had dropped the soldier with a quick thrust of his knife and was running down the slope. It was Angus, charging down after him, dodging bullets, who raced up to the barn and tossed in the Mills bomb that blew out the loft.

It was a blur of smoke after that and flying timber and roof tiles and bodies, the oak tree a crackling inferno, and bullets snapping as he and Publicover, Conlon and the rest ran toward what was left of the barn and took cover behind the stone wall. Angus remembered firing and reloading Publicover's Lee Enfield, remembered shouts and screams of agony and choking black smoke and men's legs running. And Voles picking off Germans one by one. Then it was quiet.

He remembered Conlon's silhouette bending over someone on the ground—Burwell, he thought. He remembered leaping over bodies to get to Ebbin, hoping against hope that he was still alive. Remembered ripping the German helmet off. He remembered the arch of Ebbin's throat as he lifted his head. Remembered the blood-soaked tunic. Remembered how Ebbin reached in for the cross and tags and pleaded with Angus to take them, *wear* them. Remembered refusing, telling Ebbin that Havers was on the books now, that no one could do Havers better, nor make Havers more proud. "Don't let him die, Angus," Ebbin begged through shuddering breaths. Said his name. Called him *Angus*. "I won't. He'll live on, through you. Stay alive. Ebbin!" he remembered saying. Remembered Ebbin's body jerking violently, hearing him choke. And then the fixed, unblinking eyes, and the unbearable realization that remembering was all he'd have left.

Then footsteps as a German, still alive, was coming at him. He remembered throwing himself over Ebbin and being wrenched back as the German started kicking Ebbin's body, swearing at him as Angus lunged forward. Then the shock of the bayonet slicing into his shoulder and snapping off as the German wrested the rifle away. The German's open mouth and then the blows from the rifle butt slamming Angus's shoulder, and a heavy thud as the German dropped from a gunshot. He remembered Publicover rounding the barn in an easy, loose run, his flash of a smile, gun in one hand, the Bowie in the other. And then the German rising up and a struggle that left Publicover curled up, clutching his stomach next to the unmoving German. Remembered scraping over to Publicover with his good arm, the bloody Bowie on the ground, and his own hand, smeared with Ebbin's blood, on Publicover's face. Remembered picking up the Bowie and stabbing the German who was maybe dead and maybe not, but was surely dead when he was done. Remembered cradling Publicover then sitting back on his heels as Keegan walked the huge barn door open to reveal the thick, hollow death tube of a massive Krupp howitzer, its long snout black and charred, the carriage off its wheels. There was more. There was more after that and before, but he could not remember.

Conlon or Keegan, one of them, pulled the bayonet out of his shoulder and staunched the wound in his useless arm. But it was Keegan who'd lifted him up each time he began to pass out as they dragged back toward camp, saying, "Which way? This way? Please, sir, remember." He remembered. He remembered looking up at the stars. He remembered begging God to help him. He remembered the sharp bite of the smelling salts, the dizzy constellations coming to order, the landmarks he'd picked out along the way materializing as if in a dream. And he remembered cursing God and all of heaven for granting him the sense of direction that brought them to the camp at last, alive, without Voles and Burwell. Without Publicover. Without Havers, and without Ebbin.

SEVENTEEN

April 15th, 1917
Snag Harbor, Nova Scotia

After some consideration of placement, Simon spread glue on the back of the headline from the April 10 *Halifax Morning Chronicle* and pressed it into his Great War scrapbook.

BRITISH SMASH ENEMY WITH THUNDERBOLT ATTACK

AND THE CANADIANS ACHIEVE A GLORIOUS VICTORY

Satisfying.

On the next pages he pressed in the other three headings from the front pages:

CANADIANS SWEPT GERMANS FROM FAMOUS RIDGE

SIX THOUSAND GERMANS CAPTURED

TITANIC BATTLE OPENS WITH FURY OF THE INFERNO

THE WHOLE WORLD SEEMED RED AS HUNDREDS OF

BRITISH GUNS FLASHED OUT WITH VOLCANIC ROAR

Excellent. The printed stories could go on the following pages. It was the headlines that he wanted future readers to see first, so they'd get the full impact. He imagined his father on the top of the ridge—ragged, worn, his men around him. Maybe cheering or planting the Union Jack. No, no, Simon decided after a moment. That wasn't right. He wouldn't be cheering with dead and wounded all around. He'd be thoughtful. Quiet like always, his eyes shadowed and dark. "Well done," he'd say to his men.

"You can be right proud of your father," Philip had told Simon. "*Right* proud. Down the tavern, talk's all about Vimy. Put Canada on the map."

Exactly. And exactly what he did not hear from his grandfather. What he heard from him was what a sad comment it was that Canada had entered the world stage as a warrior nation. Equally sad, for his grandfather, Simon thought, was that he didn't understand that the victory would have the Germans on the run and his father home soon.

After school Simon and Zenus pored over the details in the papers with Zeb and Alvin Hennigar and a few others around the potbelly stove at Hennigar's—how hell had opened up, "tragic and frightful," an "infernal splendor" when the guns "Belched Forth Their Roar of Death." How snow and rain kept airmen from covering the ground troops who swept forward, undaunted; and best of all, how one Canadian soldier, out of bullets, had ripped the spiked helmet off a German soldier and killed him with it.

"Victory when none was coming," Zenus's father said with satisfaction. He stood up in his black fisherman's boots and doffed his cap before crossing the street to the tavern with Wallace and Philip. Simon imagined arms linked, glasses raised. "I'm not even going to *try* to stop him," Zenus said. Lady Bromley rounded the corner, and Zenus's father doffed his cap to her as well.

"This is one day when I wish *women* were allowed in there!" Lady Bromley said, opening the door to Hennigar's and turning to stare through the glass at the tavern. "Children, too! Oh, don't look so surprised. We need a communal celebration. What would you two ruffians say to a Vimy Victory Social? A fund-raiser for the Blue Cross to help the horses. Good afternoon," she nodded at Alvin on his stool behind the counter. "I just need a pound of sugar and a few cans of peas." Alvin started weighing out the sugar. She turned to Simon. "You must be thrilled with your father in it. I'm sure I can count on you to help with the social." When Simon didn't respond, she wagged her chin and frowned at him. "What's the matter with you? Where's your patriotic spirit?"

Simon had not forgotten her cane-stamping treatment of George. "How's money going to help the horses when they're being worked to death?" he asked.

"Worked to death? Who told you such a thing? Mr. Heist? Wouldn't surprise me."

"It wasn't him."

"Who then? Your grandfather? Of course. That man can't see an up without a down." She pursed her lips, then her expression inexplicably softened. "Can't be easy on you. Your father over there in it. Ebbin giving up his life for it. Your grandfather dead set against it. His high-flung ideals don't do a thing for the boys over there. It must be very hard on you indeed."

"No," Simon said. "It isn't." But of course it was, and this unexpected sympathy had thrown him.

"Well, don't you believe it about the horses," Lady Bromley said briskly, taking the sack of groceries from Alvin. "He must have heard a rumor and taken it as fact. That's what people do when they let their emotions blind them."

Simon snapped to his grandfather's defense. "That's what *he* says about rumors. And it wasn't him. It was George Mather, and he was there."

"George of all people! I don't know why you'd be talking with him nor trusting a single thing he says." Behind her Alvin nodded in agreement. She paid for her purchases and left.

"Don't you know George is nuts?" Zenus asked when the door banged shut.

✧

A WEEK LATER the last vestiges of dirty snow melted away, and the air turned gentle with a hint of spring. Simon asked if Charlotte might be able to go for a short sail. Putnam Pugsley and Davy Hume were headed to Big Tancook to pick up a couple of rowboats. Lady Bromley wasn't home, thankfully. Lord Bromley raised his glass of beer. "Take the girl out!" he wheezed. "She's hardly seen the sun!" He leaned on the newel post. "Charlotte! Charlotte Plante! The Mac-Grath boy is here to carry you off to an island! Be home before supper and you'll get away with it!"

It was a wet ride over. Charlotte plunked down on the floorboards of the cockpit, clutching her hat and pulling her unwieldy cloak around her. Simon tried to get her to sit up with him on the windward rail, but she shook her head.

"Afraid, girl? H'ain't you never been onto a boat?" Putnam's pale blue eyes shifted from her to the sails and back. "Didn't bring the right clothes for it, did you?" He handed Davy the tiller and went forward to haul out a stiff old foresail, which he bundled around her. He was old and so thin that his cinched-up trousers ballooned around his hips. He looked frail enough to blow away, but his arms were sinewy and strong.

The *Glory B*, their Tancook knockabout schooner, heeled over in the wind, pounding through the waves with a steady spray off her bow. A comforting, rhythmic sound. Charlotte ducked down, head on her knees, and asked if a storm was coming. Said she didn't know how to swim.

This set Putnam and Davy to laughing. "Oooo hee, look out now, I see a blue-wind storm comin', eh Putnam!" Davy said.

Putnam squinted out off the port quarter. "You'd be sorely right, there, now Davy. Drop the main! Batten the hatches! She's a-goin' over!"

Charlotte looked wildly about, bracing herself against the thwart. Putnam and Davy laughed some more. Simon told them to quit it, and they did. "We're having our bit of fun, m'dear. Not a storm in sight," Putnam said. "And not a one of us knows how to swim, except Simon here. Why would we? T'wouldn't take long to freeze to death in this water. Only reason Simon knows how is, like his father before him, he was dragged to some pond or other by his grandfather and made to learn. Eh, Simon?"

"May not be a storm coming, but let's just hope we don't run into one of the Kaiser's subs," Davy said ominously. "Simon, you keep a look-see for that signal tower the schoolteacher's building on the other side of the Point."

"It *isn't* a signal tower," Simon said. "It's a *lookout tower.* Mr. Heist wants to get up above the trees at the edge of his place to see the bay."

"That what he told you?" Davy asked.

"Yep." Simon looked Davy in the eyes.

"Why'nt he cut them trees down, now, eh? Who builds a tower to see a view?"

"Just talk, Davy," Putnam put in. "Don't even know as he'd know how to pound a nail, let alone build a tower."

"I hear he got some boys over to Blandford to come out and build it."

Simon could hardly stand it. "Well, it *isn't* true. I know for a fact, he isn't trying to signal anyone."

"Never know who's who in this world. Them you think is one thing turn out to be another," Davy said.

"A dark view of the world, there, Davy, m'boy," Putnam noted.

"Talk is he won't be rehired. Heard it from some as has boys in his class."

THE CARTOGRAPHER OF NO MAN'S LAND · 237

"On grounds their boys won't make it out of sixth grade?" Putnam answered.

"You can make fun all you want, Putnam. *Herr Heist*, is what some calls him. Wouldn't that be right now, eh, Miss Plante?" But Charlotte didn't seem to hear him. "I'm not saying I call him that, I'm just saying he's sure to have folks over there on the other team."

"What do you mean, not rehired? He's as loyal as anyone. My grandfather said!" Simon shouted over the wind at the two of them.

"Your grandfather? What's he know about loyalty? Were it up to him, why—"

"The boy has spoken," Putnam cut in, measuring out each word with a look that shut Davy up. "Boy's father is over there, don't forget." He turned to Simon, "Any word, Simon?" Simon shook his head. "No word is a good word," Putnam said.

Simon looked resolutely toward the bow. Fire Mr. Heist? He was the best teacher they'd ever had. Everyone said so.

Charlotte remained a muffled heap under the sail, and Simon sullen, so Putnam decided it was time for a story. Eyeing the clouds banking on the horizon, he asked Charlotte if she'd ever heard how a true blue-wind storm had come in on the Banks and blown Simon's grandfather off them forever. "A finer schooner fisherman you'd never find," he said. "A hard man, ran his boy hard, ran us hard, but knew where the fish was, like he had the ear of God."

Charlotte asked what a blue-wind storm was. Simon was torn between wanting to impress her and worrying that the story might make her more afraid than she sadly appeared to be. He had so hoped she'd be good on the boat.

"There we was on the *Zebulon Keddy*. Things had been right calm," Putnam began in his storytelling voice. "Then strange things happened. The temperature shifted of a sudden. Warmed up, but with pockets of cold with dead air in them. Everyone knew what that meant." He waited until Charlotte asked "What?" to be sure he had a good audience.

"Gale coming, she's gonna blow," Putnam said with grave foreboding. "Blue-wind storm. Duncan, Simon Peter's grandfather, got his boys back in right quick and got the dories stowed. The boat was hove-to, to ride it out. Wind came up like a bat out of hell. Murder and lights she blew, like we knew she would, and churned up the seas to match." Another dramatic pause.

Charlotte obliged him. "Then what?" Her entire head was now out of the sail.

"Wind veered! That's what. Come up even stronger. Sea went black. Foam roaring off the crests and waves a-roarin' down over us. Other fellers were hove-to, but some tried to run her out. Even under bare poles, the seas were throwing green water over the bow, over the sides, over the stern! Fellers thought they might drown where they stood. When the seas calmed some and the wind lightened a bit, we could see the *Alice Miner*, a schooner from Gloucester. Them boys were running home, loaded to the gills with fish, they was. Nearly a full set flying. Greed driving their dash to get in ahead of the fleet." He looked at her darkly.

"Ohhh, a race!" Charlotte whispered, eyes bright.

"A *race*? Not hardly, unless first-place trophy was best price for the catch. We're talking Banks fishermen! Not fancy yacht racing!" He turned to Simon. "Where'd you get this girl, Simon Peter?"

"She's from England," Simon said.

"Ahhh . . . alright now. So the *Alice Miner* was overpowered, too much sail up. They were trying to haul them down when her masts snapped in two, one after the other. Her sails dragged in the seas and the seas were foaming at the mouth and pulling her sideways, then onto her side, and before they could cut the rigging, she was a goin' over." He looked from Charlotte to Simon. "But before she did,

Duncan MacGrath steered smartly up to her under just enough sail to keep headway, steady in the wind without going into irons."

"Irons! What's that mean?" Charlotte sat up straighter.

Simon said, "You lose headway, which means you lose steerage, which means you can just be rolled over by a heavy sea."

"Very nice, Simon." Putnam lifted his cap, revealing a flash of his narrow bald head. "I've come near the end. Do I go on?"

"Yes!" Charlotte said.

Simon put in that Putnam's father had been a collector in Newfoundland. Of course, then he had to explain that a collector was someone who went from village to village and was fed and put up for nights at a time, his job being to gather up stories and tell them.

"No finer teller of tales in all of Newfoundland," Putnam said, allowing the interruption.

"Putnam here, not near as good as his father," Davy put in.

Putnam noted that he didn't have time to do this one justice, being as close as they were to Big Tancook, so he was giving the short version and was just as pleased to leave it there if he should suffer further disruption. He waited for encouragement, which he got from all three of them.

"So, let's see . . . we fellers see the *Alice Miner* is foundering bad. Duncan, expert helmsman as he was, pulls us up just close enough to throw out lifelines. Men in the water by then and men sliding off the deck, and us boys get the whole crew off except one—boy about your age, Simon Peter. The boy was tangled in the lines. The *Miner* was on her side by then, and t'wouldn't be long. We make out the boy—see him carried high and dropped low in the troughs. Bobbing up and disappearing. Then finally he pops snug up next to the hull as the *Miner* starts to roll. But he couldn't free himself from the rigging, and they couldn't pull him in. Duncan couldn't rest with that. 'Unlash that dory!' he shouts. 'I'm going over to him.' A bunch of boys try to drive some reason into him, but he gives them no heed. Over the dory goes and Duncan down in it, and that's all the time it took for the *Alice Miner* to slip under the waves and drag that boy to the bottom. Fellers say on a cold, blue-wind night, when there's a frosty moan about, you can still see his hand rising up from below."

"Seen him myself of a time or two. Fellers say he's still trying to grab ahold of Duncan," Davy said. "Last time *I* heard it, Duncan was over the side and in the water swimming after the boy! Makes a much better story for my money."

"Who told it that way?" Putnam asked hotly.

"None other than Dolf Chandler."

"Well, he wan't there, was he? Nor Wallace. Dolf got that story from the bottom of a bottle, is what. Duncan had ripped off his sou'wester and was about to jump in, but I'm telling you, that boy went down afore he made it. Duncan would have been sucked in the undertow if he'd a swum over. But he sees that boy go down and come back and sailed the *Zebulon Keddy* straight for home. Never went out again."

"Never again?" Charlotte whispered.

"Never again," Putnam said grimly, looking straight over the bow. "Not to the Banks, anyway. Sold the boat, had Reuben Heisler build him the *Lauralee* for coastal trade. Named the boat for his wife, in her grave two years, and the baby by the same name. Blamed himself, is what Ida Corkum says, for his wife's death. That boy was the final straw. Never went to the Banks again."

"Afraid that boy's arm would drag him under," Davy added with a shake of his head.

"Rightly so," Putnam said. "Chased him right off the water."

"So that's why he didn't let your dad . . ." Charlotte looked over at Simon.

"No he wasn't!" Simon said. "He wasn't *afraid*!" Up to now he'd only considered the heroic part of the story—saving the crew, all but one. "He came back to take care of Dad."

"You're full of complaints," Davy said. "That boy is why he come back and why he stayed away. A story is a story. Is what it is."

Putnam nodded solemnly as they eased the sheets and headed toward the Tancook harbor. Then he looked down at Charlotte. "How you feeling now, m'dear? I see some color back onto your cheeks. I believe you can come up without getting washed overboard. Take a seat next to me. Wind's behind us, now. See? Makes a gentler ride. Help her up, Simon."

Simon clasped her hands and leaned back, surprised at the supple strength of her grasp. Davy steadied her at the waist. "You're a hefty one, you are. Good ballast, eh Putnam?" Davy winked. Charlotte sat just forward of Putnam, surprisingly reinvigorated. Putnam patted her knee and pointed. "See now? Big Tancook dead ahead."

"Why's it called Big Tancook?" she asked.

"Because it isn't Little Tancook. That's why. There's Little Tancook over to port. And there be our rowboats tied to that stake. Simon, grab that boat hook and catch that line when I come around. We'll tie them onto the stern."

Simon hooked the line and knelt to untie the boats from the stake. Davy fended them off as Simon, with a bit of a swagger, walked the line back toward the stern just before he tripped on a cleat. It was Charlotte who caught the line that fell from his hand. And Charlotte who inched her way aft, balancing with newfound ease, to hand the line to Davy, who secured it to a ring on the stern.

"Well, now, m'dear," said Putnam when the boats were lined up smartly behind them and the sails filled again, "you're to come out with us any time. Teach the boy here how to stay upright."

Simon laughed. Charlotte climbed up on the rail next to him. "I'll get her some oilskins," he said, "and some fishing boots!"

"That's right. Never know when the weather's going to turn foul," Davy said.

"Davy, you don't know a good day from a bad one. Never have," Putnam said.

For Simon, it was fair weather all the way home, with Charlotte's thigh pressing against his, strands of her hair licking his face in the wind.

LATE THAT NIGHT, he let those strands of hair brush his face again, felt the smooth skin and padded tips of her fingers, the springy feel of her hands in his, her thigh pressed against his own, imagined dimpled knees. These were not the kind of thoughts to lull him to sleep. He got up and went down to the kitchen. There he found his mother in his father's thick socks with his old plaid wool shirt over her nightgown. She had her arms stretched out along the length of the sink and was staring out the window. She didn't move when he entered. Her chin was lifted. A portrait of solitude in the moonlight.

He coughed so as not to startle her. "You okay, Ma?" he asked.

She pushed away from the sink and slowly turned to him. "I think so. I have something to tell you. It's taken me a long time . . . but I know now that Ebbin is dead. I can feel it."

Simon slowly sat down.

"Dad came up to the house this morning, my dad. Gave me this." She reached into the shirt pocket and pulled out a leather cord at the end of which dangled a round disc. "Ebbin's tag," she whispered. "They keep the other one for burial. Even if there is no body." Her hands shook as she lit the candle. Simon stared at the tag nearly glowing in the candlelight. "Go on," she said. "You can touch it." He picked it up and ran his thumb across it. Here was the visible proof he, too, had been missing. He felt his mouth go dry and thought of crows flying.

She pulled his father's shirt around her. The kettle was going. She took down two mugs and very deliberately sliced pats of butter and put them and some sugar and some kind of spice in each mug, and then added some rum and a good deal of hot water and a little cream on top. "Why not?" she said.

Simon took a sip. Apple rum pie without the apples, and a whole lot better. The tips of his fingers tingled. "Yeah," he said hoarsely. "Why not?"

His mother stared into her mug. "Ebbin and I always felt we came from somewhere else." When she didn't go further, he said, "Well you did. Alberta is someplace else." He took another sip and wiped the cream off his mouth with his sleeve.

"And . . . we were both named for our mother, Ellen Langston. I look like her, which always made my father sad, and that made me sad, growing up. He was sorry for it, but he said to look at me sometimes was to see her on her little horse, her hair flying. Maybe that's why I like riding Rooster all over. But anyway, it meant he never saw me, not really." With her elbows on the table, she slowly stroked her temples. "When he gave me the tag, you know what my father said?" She looked up abruptly. "He said, 'You're alive, Hettie Ellen. We both need to bury the dead.'"

Simon nodded, his heart on tiptoe.

"He was right. It's not right to give up life. Ebbin made his choice. I'm making mine. There are things I need to do." She glanced away. "This hideous war thinks it can take everything. I'm not going to let it."

"You're going to become a pacifist?" Simon whispered.

"What? No. I'm going to take care of things right here. Grandpa's letting things slide."

"His business, you mean."

"That's right."

"Are we going broke? Ida said . . . should I quit school? I can work. I can go . . ."

She dismissed this with a vague wave. "Settle down. Of course we're not going broke. But I'll tell you something." She picked up the jar of strawberry jam beside the sugar bowl. "Do you know why Ida calls this 'live jam'? Because it's not preserved. Because even in that simple task, I fail. I only just figured out why. Because I don't like putting up jam. Nor carrots, nor peas. I don't like serving tea, nor gossiping over it. I don't like blacking the stove—"

"Okay, okay. But you can't just . . . run things."

"Why not? Why shouldn't I? I've kept the books." She swept her hair up behind her ears and let it fall. "I've been Ellen Langston's daughter, Ebbin Hant's sister, Angus MacGrath's wife," she said. "Now I'm going to be me, Hettie Ellen MacGrath. H. E. MacGrath. That's how I've been signing the correspondence I write for your grandfather. I get good responses to my letters. And to my bills."

"You're going to work? Like a man?"

"Your grandfather loans us Ida. Lets us live in this house. Your father never seemed to care—out there on the *Lauralee*. But I did. And besides, maybe *I'd* have liked to have been out sailing on her."

"But you get *seasick*."

"That's true," she said, amused at herself. "The point is that I see what's going out and coming in, and mostly it's been going out with poor return, and I'm going to fix it."

"But how?"

"I'm not sure yet. We need a plan. That's what I've been thinking tonight. Things are changing. Branching out—investing. That sort of thing. There's more than boats and cod—"

"You mean war buccaneering," Simon said, folding his arms across his chest.

"Buccaneering?" She tilted her head. "Oh. Profiteering. No, no. I can't explain it all. I just see it."

Simon leaned toward her. "I can help. Let me go out on the Banks this summer. I'll give all the money to you. It's what I want more than anything. Let me go, *please*."

She took his hand. "Simon, Simon. I know you want to be out on the water, and maybe one day you will. I would myself if I were you. If I didn't get seasick. But right now, I need you here."

He looked at his hand in hers. "Do you?"

"I do," she said. But she wasn't really speaking to him. She was staring at Ebbin's tag. She lifted it gently and put it in her pocket, then got up and set her mug in the sink. Standing, Simon took a deep breath and blew it out slowly. Then he closed his eyes and gulped down the rest of his buttered rum.

EIGHTEEN

April 17th, 1917
No. 18 Canadian General Hospital
Saint-Junien, France

bove him the ceiling, dim and white, high and arched, seemed an overcast sky, but globes of light spread out into separate suns, attached, he saw, to an iron chandelier. Was it swaying? He closed his eyes and immediately snapped them open. He concentrated on colors—blue and white next to him. A white curtain? No, an apron—stiff, starched, and bibbed over a blue dress. And a white muslin headdress above, crisply folded below the ears, framing the face. The face was speaking.

"Welcome back, Lieutenant," it said. A clean face, startling and disturbing in its beauty. "You've come round. Good." Blue and white. Bluebirds, they called them, the Canadian military nurses. The voice and the face vanished, replaced by a row of cots to his left. Above, a gallery and banister. More cots up there, and mattresses lined up on the floor. He heard whimpering and crying out, orders given, and hushed responses. Sunlight streamed through arched windows behind the gallery down to the lower level. It dappled his blanket. What country was he in? Where were his men?

The nurse, whose name was Lydia Lovell, told him he was in a Canadian military hospital in Saint-Junien, between Calais and Étaples, just across the Channel from England. His chest wound was septic and nothing could be done about his shoulder until the infection cleared. "I'll just see to that wound now," she said.

"Where's Conlon?" he demanded.

She stuck a thermometer in his mouth and pulled back the sheet and wool blanket and unbuttoned his pajama top. His right arm was not in the sleeve. It was propped on a pillow, in padded bandages except for the fingers. His shoulder was taped up with gauze dressings. As she worked at the bandage, the nurse said: "I don't know where this Conlon of yours is. You called out his name any number of times over the last day and a half. His and others. I'll see if he's among the wounded if you give me his full name and rank."

She was an idiot. That much was clear. Beautiful, but an idiot. Conlon hadn't been wounded. He'd squatted next to the stretcher at the camp and given Angus water. Angus remembered how thick his tongue had felt, remembered asking about Publicover and Ebbin. Ebbin! Had he said Ebbin's name?

He ripped the thermometer out of his mouth. "I've got to find Conlon."

"Be still!" She thrust the thermometer in again and told him to close his mouth. He clamped his lips over it. She checked his pulse and finally withdrew the thermometer.

"How soon can I get back to the Front?" Angus asked.

"Back to the Front? I hardly think so. Let me finish this dressing now."

"No. Yes! Go ahead. But then I'll need my clothes—I'm an officer. I need to get back to my unit."

"Lieutenant, you do not outrank me, you'll notice. And as to going back to the Front, I'm afraid you wouldn't make it to the end of your bed." She dropped a putrid dressing into a metal bowl.

Pain flamed through him. He started to shake. The nurse dropped her scissors on the cart and pressed one hand on his forehead and the other under his neck. Her hands were cool and firm. She didn't move her eyes from his. "You will find him and your men when you're ready." Minutes seemed to pass. His trembling subsided and he sank into a leaden fatigue.

"There," she murmured. "You need to get well before you can do anything else. All right? I'll get another blanket."

As soon as she left, he forced himself to sit up. It was then that he realized his arm, his right arm, wasn't moving. The bayonet had gone in just below his shoulder. He couldn't feel his arm. He followed its length down to the hand, lying palm-up on the pillow by his side. He willed his fingers to curl, to straighten, but they did not. He willed his wrist to lift the hand, but it remained still. He willed his shoulder to raise the arm, but nothing happened. Worse, it seemed to belong to someone else. He ripped back the blanket—his legs. Still there, thank God. He swung them over the cot and planted both feet on the stone floor. His right arm rolled off the pillow like an anchor. He gripped the bed frame, too dizzy to stand, then bent over and heaved. Nothing came up. He fell back. He wanted to weep.

He barely heard the nurse scolding him, a different one this time, tall, her eyes hidden by the glare on her frameless spectacles. She got him under the covers and placed the arm properly on its pillow. To his right a great commotion started up. A soldier was in convulsions that would not stop, until they did, and he was dead.

Angus turned away. "Shrap in the head," the man in the next cot said. "Been doing that for over a day. Jerking like that. A goner now, poor chap. Or lucky bastard, depending. How about you? You've been yelling up a storm. Who's this Ebbin? And 'Sam, Sam,' you kept saying. Peter. Simon. Hattie. A raft of names."

Angus did not trust himself to speak, but the man persisted. "Shot through the arm, were you? Can't move it, eh?"

"No," Angus whispered. He felt he should ask the man about his wounds, but he was too busy clawing at fragments. Debris shooting out from the loft. The tree flaring up like a matchstick. Publicover rounding the barn. The bloodied Bowie next to him. Publicover. Conlon's tortured disbelief when he saw Publicover was dead.

And Ebbin. And now he remembered Conlon's words. *You were right about Havers. Must have had a death wish.* A shudder raced through him.

"Got the willies, eh? You'll get through them," the man said in a kindly tone. "This is my third time in hospital. Sent back every time. I'll have to lose my leg or my mind to get sent home. Wait. I think I did that already. Know how I can tell? I don't bloody care if they send me home or not." He tried a laugh.

Angus shut his eyes. He prayed he'd never open them. Everything was shutting down. He reached over the side of the dory and gathered up a handful of water and held ripples of sunlight in his palm. But the water slipped through his fingers, stiff and bloody, and sloshed beneath the floor boards. And he looked up empty-handed at his young son.

OVER THE NEXT days, as his fever subsided, Angus regained focus. It was clear that his immobilized arm was God's punishment for not speaking up about Ebbin, for Ebbin's death, for Publicover's and the others. The doctor assigned to his case—a tall, eager, broad-shouldered young man, "so clever and so spic and span," the nurses described him—was named Boes, pronounced "Bays." He was an American from Nebraska, now in the CEF. Angus repeated the name "Ne-bras-kah" slowly as if trying to make sense of it.

"That's right. Means 'flat water,'" Dr. Boes said in an American accent as flat as the state he described. He told Angus he'd left Nebraska for London to study with Dr. Purves-Stewart, a temporary colonel and consulting physician to His Majesty's forces. "An expert in disorders of the nervous system." When the war broke out, an older

associate had told young Dr. Boes, "There's the place for your training. There's where you'll find nerve damage."

"And he was right! Nerve injuries are rampant," Dr. Boes said, eyes
wide. So now he'd had a lot of field experience fixing up just the sort
of injury Angus had, he said. "Bullets and shrapnel can sever nerves,
bruise them with bone fragments, or create hemorrhagic pressure,
squeezing the function out of them so they're tangled—unable to send
messages to and from the brain."

A tangled web we weave, Angus thought as the words jumbled
past.

"Preventing," Boes continued, "messages that are protopathic, epi-
critic and, of course, motor." The "of course" thrown in as if Angus
were a fellow physician. But Angus encouraged this medical lesson,
and together they entered a pact of abstraction in which they could
keep the actual effects of these injuries—the withered, paralytic,
deformed limbs and cases of unremitting pain—at bay. Boes wasn't
patronizing, merely earnest—almost cheerful, a quality Angus found
refreshingly out of whack.

"There is always hope," Boes finished up, leaning down at Angus
from his dizzying height. "Nerves can be repaired, not always, but
often, with the finest of cat gut." It was his job to figure out which
nerves were impaired and if they could be rescued. But they had to
wait. The initial lesion was not the whole story. Swelling pressing
against the nerves might be the cause of the paralysis. Waiting was
the hard part. They had to wait for ten days after the sepsis cleared to
check for "electrical responses," which Boes promised he'd be only too
glad to explain at the time.

"At the time of what?" Angus asked.

"At the time you're connected to the condenser apparatus," Dr.
Boes said brightly. They were lucky to have one so close to the Front.
But now was the time for Angus to rest. Could he do that? Could he
rest and wait for the swelling to subside? Yes? Good.

Angus refrained from asking what the condenser apparatus was and refrained as well from asking whether the world would right itself, because he clung to the answer that it would—as soon as he got back to his men. He pulled at the chain around his neck, and closed his fist over the cross. He wouldn't let it end here, lying in a hospital cot. He'd get back to the Front, make up for it. Make it worth something, make it mean something.

NINETEEN

April 22nd, 1917
Snag Harbor, Nova Scotia

In the parish hall, the women were washing up the cups and plates, and some of the men and boys began folding the chairs with a steady thump, thump, thump. Simon helped Wallace take down the BLUE CROSS FUND banner and the sign with VIMY VICTORY SOCIAL painted on it. Money had been made, all the raffle tickets sold, and the prize, a hooked rug with the image of a schooner and the Union Jack on it, had gone to Tim Barkhouse.

Before the raffle, a Major Edwin McDonald from Halifax had read a letter from a colleague in the medical corps, which referenced those "invaluable members of the corps to whom we owe a debt of gratitude," the mules and horses transporting the wounded and limbers of hospital tents and supplies. Illuminating, edifying, everyone agreed. His speech was followed by a plea from Lady Bromley for funds. The social ended with a blessing from Reverend Dimmock, a call for enlistments from the major, and a round of patriotic hymn-singing at the piano with Mr. Williams. "Onward, Christian Soldiers!"

Through it all, Simon worked hard to block out horses falling to their knees in the rain. The image could choke the breath from him when he least expected it. It hadn't helped that George showed up at the end of the social. Seeing him made Simon decide he'd just ask Major McDonald outright if George was right about the horses. If he was wrong, then chances were good he'd never seen Ebbin at Thiepval either. But to ask was to have an answer. So Simon circled the edges of the major's conversations with Delsie and Ida, and his taking of tea with Enid Rafuse and Dr. Woodruff. It was not until he found Major McDonald alone in the hallway, preparing to leave, that Simon stammered out his question. The major frowned impatiently. He thrust his arms in his coat and squared his features in the mirror. "Certainly, horses are wounded and die. That's why they're heroic. They're beasts of burden, doing their job." He adjusted his cap and opened the door.

"But of *overwork*," Simon persisted, following him down the steps. "Flogged to death, or too tired to eat."

"Everyone at the Front is overworked," the major snapped. He strode past Reverend Dimmock to wait for Lady Bromley's car.

"Wonderful evening," Reverend Dimmock said, tipping his head up to the great swath of stars misting the sky. "The Milky Way. Breathe deep of this spring air, Simon Peter, and let God's majesty above be your guide, and his great purpose, inexorable and mysterious, your inspiration." The car pulled up and he dashed over to hold the door for the major. Watching them was George, who sidled up to Simon. "I've a raft of silver stars in my pocket, one for every heartbroke, mud-soaked horse on the field," he said, as the Reverend bid the major and Lady Bromley good night. "And three silver bullets."

SIX DAYS LATER, word came that Angus had been wounded. In the shock and grief that followed, Ida took Hettie upstairs. Duncan stayed at the house to get supper going. With an apron tied over his vest, he was slashing potatoes at the sink. Gluey bits of dough clung to his fingers from a raisin duff he had been making for dessert. As if they needed dessert. As if anyone wanted to eat. His white hair was plastered to his forehead and beads of sweat inched down his cheek. "We'll have a scupper supper, eh? Simon! Peel these potatoes."

"Can I help?" Young Fred dragged the stool over.

"More the merrier. Come here, young snapper!" Duncan put an arm around him. "A scupper supper is what I used to cook up on the *Lauralee*. It's been a while, but a good seaman can do for himself. You know," he tapped the knife on the sink, "this just may be good news. He's wounded, but out of harm's way. The bright side of things—let's try that on for size. Now, Young Fred, help me get this cod out of the pot so's we can chip-chop-chip it up and set it to boil."

The bright side? Which side was that, Simon wanted to ask. The one where his father came home with a useless right arm or where he got better and went back to the Front?

Young Fred dug out as much of the white flesh as he could fit in his hands, all of it dripping, some of it slipping to the floor. Duncan gathered the rest and slapped it on the table. Simon jammed raisins in the dough and slung it into a loaf pan and into the oven. He didn't know if a duff needed to rise or not, but it sure needed to cook.

"Got to pump fresh water into this pot!" Duncan boomed out at the sink. "There's a boy! Pump hard!" He jerked Fred's arm up and down, then left him, water gushing from the pump, and strode in and out of the cold room. He held up a wrapped piece of salt pork and two onions in triumph. "See here? We'll fry these up. Know what we'll do next, Master Fred?" Young Fred was rubbing his arm, about to cry.

"We're going to . . . let's see now." Duncan set the onions and pork on the table and leaned on his hands. "Flake, no, *boil* the cod, then flake it," he mumbled. "Boil the potatoes. Fry the onion and boil the potatoes." He ran a sticky hand through his hair.

"Cook the lot. Layer them in the bowl with the drippings over," Simon said.

"Right!" Duncan snapped to attention. "Now we'll need a bowl big enough."

"I can get it!" Young Fred was already hauling himself from the footstool to the ledge of the sink. As he did, two figures appeared through the window. Zenus and his father rounded the corner and were at the kitchen door. Duncan waved them in.

"Me and the boy heard you had bad news from Angus. Thought we'd see how Hettie's faring." Cap in hand, Herman Weagle shifted his eyes from Duncan's apron to the slabs of raw cod dripping on the table.

Duncan rubbed his hands. Snakes of dough shredded to the floor. "She's upstairs with Ida. She'll be alright. Letter says he took a bayonet in the shoulder. He's in a military hospital somewhere on the French coast. Under the best of care."

"Which arm? His *right*? Is he going to keep it?" Herman asked.

"Right arm. He'll keep it. Far as we know." Duncan's voice faltered. He squeezed the bridge of his nose and took in a deep breath. He blew it out slowly. "He's not among the dead. Not among the missing . . ."

"That's right," Herman said thoughtfully. "That's something." Hand on his hip, he shook his big head. "You heard about Clem and Ernest Younge on the Banks? Fine pair them two. Dory mates these last ten years."

"What? What happened?

"They was seen going down just as the fog cleared. Seas come up of sudden. Washed over the gunwales. Went down like a rock—they was that loaded with catch in the dory—is what I heard." Herman had fished the Banks and had three missing fingers to prove it.

"God rest their souls," Duncan whispered. He stood with his hand on his chest, his head down.

"Lucky for them it was quick," Herman offered. "Better than rowing for days on end, never to be found—dying of thirst and cold. Missing forever."

Duncan took a ragged breath.

Herman slapped his cap against his leg. "Well, best be going. You got plenty to do here, I can see, and the missus will wonder what's become of us. Come on, Zenus. You send Angus our best. Tell Hettie to hold on."

Simon pulled Zenus over. "Dad was in *hand-to-hand*," he whispered. Zenus's eyes went wide.

Duncan struggled to fill his pipe. Damp fibers of tobacco spilled from the pouch and clung to his fingers. Herman put a hand on his shoulder. "Angus'll be alright," he said. "If he's packed off home, well, then he made it, and did the country a good turn. He's a strong feller. He'll come through." He slapped his cap again and steered Zenus to the door.

Water bubbled over and sizzled on the stove. The smell of raw onions filled the room. Duncan looked about vacantly and said he'd take his pipe outside since they had things well in hand, and wandered off in his apron.

"Thought I heard a clatter down here!" Ida said, clumping into the kitchen. "Who's got supper going?"

"Us! Me mostly," Young Fred piped up. "But, but Grandpa ran away." He began to cry. Simon pulled him onto his lap.

"I see," Ida said, tying on an apron and bustling to the stove. "Well now, I'm going to make your mother a sleeping tonic, then we'll finish cooking this—whatever's got started here. Fetch me the brandy, Simon. I'll heat some milk. What's that smell?" She whipped open the oven and pulled out the duff. "You boil this, Simon. In a bag. You don't bake it. Can't anyone in this family cook?"

"How is she?" Simon asked.

"Worried. Upset. Like you. Like all of us. What else would she be?" Ida attacked the duff with a knife to loosen it from the pan. "She'll come round." She tipped the pan over and dumped the remains in the sink. "There, now," she said, pouring milk into a pot and uncorking the brandy. She gave it a sniff and took a sip. "That passes muster. I'll just test it again. Yes, it'll help your mother get through the night. The shock of it, you know. For her. Duncan, too." She peered out the window. "Go see to him Simon. I've got my hands full here." She lifted Fred up and stirred the milk.

Simon did as he was told and found his grandfather on the bridge over the causeway. He stood a few feet from him, knotted up with anger and sorrow at the war, at his grandfather for suddenly caring and for needing care. But his grandfather didn't seem to notice him. Apparently out of breath, he was leaning over the railing. "Maybe the war will be over soon," Simon said. "That way he'll come home and get better, both." When his grandfather just shook his head, Simon added, "People say German morale is broken."

"Oh?" His grandfather pushed away and stood straight. "And where'd you get that piece of intelligence? Lady Bromley? The world's authority on the war." He took out his tobacco pouch and filled his pipe. "Just yesterday, I heard her tell someone our troops don't use gas."

"Well, do we?"

"Good Christ, we'd use *flame throwers* if it didn't set our own on fire! How'd you like that? Being burned alive? This is war, Simon, not some Christian mission. And I'll tell you, Hespera Bromley's only mission is to outshine the ladies of Halifax in providing for the troops. Those comfort boxes, those 'little needfuls'—balls of string, chocolate and pins—*pins* for God's sake—end up in the hands of desperate men for whom the only good package is a round of bullets and a gun to shoot them. Comfort to those at home is all those boxes bring." He struck a match on his thumbnail, cupped his palm and drew the flame to his pipe in rhythmic pulses, sucking his cheeks in, eyes on Simon. "You need to get your facts straight." He waved the match out.

"Why are you always against him? You don't even care he's wounded."

"Don't you speak to me like that, boy! I told you. I'm against this fool war, not him."

I'll speak to you any damn way I please, Simon thought as he pounded back up the hill. He found a stick and swiped at the bushes. He wanted to kill the German bastard who sliced his father's arm. He wanted to slice up every word that came out of his grandfather's mouth.

HAVING ENDURED THE SUPPER that no one wanted to eat, dishes done, Ida gone to her sister's, his mother and Young Fred sound asleep, Simon stood in the kitchen trying to collect the jagged confusion of the day. The idea surfaced that his father might never make it home. He threw on a wool shirt, checked the stove, grabbed two apples and slipped out the back door. For a long time he stood with his head against his father's shed, but he could not face its abandoned brushes and paints.

He went to the barn instead, where he fed Peg and Rooster an apple each, comforted by their nuzzling. Rooster looked for more. "Don't get used to nighttime treats, now," Simon murmured. Finally, he turned to go. Leaning against the barn door, staring up at the stars, everything spilled over itself. His chest heaved with the effort of keeping tears at bay. "He'll make it. He'll make it. He has to," he whispered.

Up the hill, his grandfather's house was dark, not a light on. But there was smoke coming from the chimney. Had the old man forgotten to bank the fire?

Reluctantly, Simon walked up the rise and along the path and slowly opened the front door. The fire in the parlor was still going, just as he'd thought. No screen. And there, sitting in his wingback chair, still wearing the apron, was his grandfather, a bottle of brandy between his feet.

"Gold and diamonds," his grandfather's voice boomed out. "King and country. *Plunder* in the name of valor. That's what he died for!"

"Whoa, Grandpa. Dad's just wounded." Simon came over and

stood in front of him, shocked at the opened vest, loose collar, disheveled hair.

"My brother, Geordie, I'm talking about," Duncan growled. "Seventeen years ago today." He took a swig of the brandy from the bottle. It was then Simon saw the gun in his lap. A jolt of panic went through him.

"Went back to the old country, the so-called homestead in the Lowlands. Couldn't make a go of it. Tossed about for something to do. I said, why not the army? Just about pushed him into it. Thought it would keep him off the drink." He swirled the contents of the bottle in his hand and took another swallow. "It didn't. Joined the cavalry." He set the bottle on the floor. "Met his death in Africa."

Simon had hardly ever heard his grandfather mention his long-dead brother. He lowered himself into the opposite chair, calculating how to get the gun.

His grandfather slumped his hand on it. "Came to me in a crate, packed with straw, this did. Bequeathed, you might say. A note, unsigned, said, 'Your brother, George Gordon MacGrath, wanted you to have his pistol.'" He picked it up. "Colt .45. Ever seen one?"

"Uh, no sir. Is it . . . loaded?" Simon reached a cautious hand out for it.

"Course it's loaded!" His grandfather gripped the gun harder. "One bullet missing. Maybe Geordie put that one through his head." Turning it over in his hands, he said, "Not his medals, nor a pair of cuff links, nor a well-loved book. Just this pistol—a message as sure as there ever was one." He paused and wiped his mouth on his sleeve. "Make a man partake of the brutality of combat day after day, and he either thrives or is broken by it. Either way, it strips him down to base instincts until finally, his humanity fails him, and he's defined by this alone." He sat back, defeated. Simon kept his eye on the gun.

"Suffering comes to all of us," Duncan began again, staring into the fire. "Lost my wife and baby, and a few years later, a boy on the Banks. A boy younger than you. Watched him *slip through my fingers*." He looked up sharply. "A boy I didn't know, was known to me then."

Simon nodded, unblinking.

"Ever seen a boat sink? No? It's like watching someone die. She hovers for a moment on the edge of life, then is sucked down all at once and the seas cross over as if she'd never been. I'd have given my life for that boy . . ."

The clock ticked loudly, every swing of the pendulum measuring out the silence. Simon jumped when his grandfather started up again. "Saw my own boy slipping through my hand, all I had left in the world. Came back to him. Stayed on shore. Tried to be a good father, a good man. Paid attention to the state of my soul. Then comes Geordie. Dead on the veld. For what?" He pounded the arm of the chair and leaned forward as if about to spring at Simon. "If we can't find meaning in death, how can we find it in life? Tell me that! Was Geordie's purpose to die for the greed of other men? Is my son to do the same?"

Simon swallowed hard. Amazed at how steady his own voice was, he said, "Dad's not dead. He'll get better."

"He will, will he? And then get another chance at being killed? My God." His grandfather weighed the gun in his hands. "Thought I'd learned something about humility. About vulnerability, damn it! How vast the ocean, how small the boat. But I'll be *damned* if I know what more I'm supposed to learn through the suffering of my only son." He cast a withering look at Simon. "Eh? I *begged* him not to go." His eyes were fierce. "But it wasn't enough! He had to go. And for what? My every effort come to nothing." He stood suddenly, waving the pistol about. Simon lunged for it, and in the struggle his grandfather crumpled to his knees, then half-crawled past Simon to the stone hearth and gripped it with his hands. He leaned there, shoulders shaking.

Simon picked up the pistol, heavy and black, and backed away. The last of the embers blinked red through the ash.

"Hall chest," his grandfather said in a ragged voice. "That's where I keep it."

Simon slid the key off the top of the chest. His grandfather fumbled with the fire screen, cursing it and righting it twice before it stayed in place. Simon opened and closed the chest and turned the long shaft of the key in the lock until he heard it click. By then his grandfather was in the hall. Head down, he thumped his hand on the newel post and ascended the stairs with labored steps, swinging the bottle of brandy by the neck. "Go on home," he said, voice blurry. "Midnight ramblings of an old man."

SIMON STOPPED WHEN he reached the bridge. The boulders were slick with yellow-brown rockweed. The pungent smell of low tide hung like fog, and the shallow water lapped the stone walls of the causeway below. A light wind ruffled his hair. He reached in his pocket for the cigarette Zenus had given him and cursed the fact that he had no matches. Then he leaned out over the railing and uncurled his fist and let the key fall from his hand. A brilliant swath of green bubbles foamed around it and trailed up as it plunged to the bottom. Phosphorous. Of all nights. He picked up a stone and threw it over, and another and another, desperate to churn the water into green bubbling light and to feel himself plunging down through it until he disappeared into its unending iridescence.

But there was more to do. He left the bridge and headed for Mader's Cove and walked down Philip's wharf, grabbing a set of oars as he went. He took the ramp down to the float and pushed Philip's little tender off into the water. He set the oarlocks and slipped the oars in as quietly as he could, grateful for the bit of wind that damped the sound. With every stroke, phosphorous danced around the oars and in the wake. He rowed, green light trailing, past the black bow of the *Elsie,* past the *Glory B,* and out to the open water. He could have rowed forever. Finally, far beyond the boats and the cove and well into the bay, he shipped the oars and set the pistol on the forward seat and knelt down before it. A dull black menacing shape, it slid sideways as he shifted his weight. He wondered how the bullets got in and how you got them out and if there really were bullets in the chamber. But he didn't want to know. He lifted it up by the handle, feeling the weight of it in his hand, then leaned over the gunwale and held it suspended above the black water. And let it go. Soundlessly, the pistol, encased in pale green froth, plunged down. Its phosphorous trail bubbled up, then thinned to a narrow beaded column and disappeared. Simon stared until spots formed before his eyes, then crouched back to the center thwart. Looking up, he found the Big Dipper, but it brought him no comfort, and he began to shake. I am alone, I am alone, I am alone. I want my father back. Hunched over, rocking with hands in his armpits, for a long while all he could hear was his own ragged breath and his own heart pounding.

How long he stayed like that, he didn't know, but when he looked up, nothing was familiar. Then he realized the wind and current and ebbing tide had him drifting fast past Owl's Head. He was too far out. He could feel a cold wind against his face, wet with tears, and he began to shudder. He'd never make it back. The black ocean grew blacker and the wind stronger. A vision of his father rowing the boat in long even strokes helped him shove the oars out. Helped him grip the oars and pull. He tipped his head up and sighted up the handle of the Little Dipper until he found Polaris. True North. Not the brightest star, his father once told him, but the one around which the others collected and moved and found their bearings. He kept his eyes fixed on it, and arms aching, but no longer shaking, rowed the boat back to the harbor, where the wind shifted and, like the breath of God, pushed him along into the cove and back to Mader's wharf.

TWENTY

May 17th, 1917
No. 18 Canadian General Hospital
Saint-Junien, France

he garden walls were easily seven feet high and partially covered with ivy—as old as the walls themselves, with twisted trunks as thick as Angus's arm and leaves as broad as his hand. His good hand. The dirt at his feet was loamy, soft with the smell of spring rain, and clean in its very blackness—nothing like the chalk mud that had defined his world. Miniature shoots of something were poking up three rows over. A brown hare streaked out from a thicket and reconnoitered with his companions at the new shoots, their noses pulsing. In a long-ago life, he might have tried to capture their interlude in the garden, and his own, in pastels. But the sanctuary of the garden only accentuated his dislocation.

At the sound of his name, he spun around, lurched forward and sank onto his knee. The nurse—"Brimmie," she was called by the others, with her reddish-blond bangs peeking out of her headdress, the spray of freckles across her nose, her determined little mouth, brimming with orders and admonitions—gave the rabbits no heed as she approached in brisk little steps. "Lieutenant! Here you are! Time for your treatment."

She offered her hand. He waved her off and rose awkwardly on his own and followed her across the lawn to the hospital. In the weeks since Vimy, he'd come to know how important the swing of the arms was to the swing of the legs, and had made the required adjustments to his gait. Balancing on a rolling deck would be impossible.

Under the shadows of the arched west entryway, a cool dampness, captive of centuries, penetrated his cotton shirt. Brimmie waited while he removed the rubber boots. Easy to slip on and off, those boots. He neither knew nor cared whose they were. Once ambulatory, he'd been issued a fresh uniform. He could dress himself, unlike some who had to endure the ministrations of the nurses, holding a sleeve or buttoning up a fly. He'd perfected a system for the kilt that involved holding the band between his waist and the weight of his arm, then swinging it around his hips. Leaning against a wall, he could button the waist and buckle the skirt with his left hand.

By rights, he should have been invalided back to England. But Dr. Boes, hoping to prove the condenser apparatus useful for treatment, had confessed he was loath to let him go. Electrotherapy, Boes called it, stimulating the muscles and nerves with electrical impulses, keeping them alive. Angus had heard men scream with it, including two mute soldiers who had found their voices when electrodes were placed down their throats by a consulting physician who'd come from England and gone back. Stimulating the nerves was a nice term for delivering shocks that made the muscles twitch. Angus did not feel the shocks often, but his muscles did twitch. Afterwards, he was drained.

He understood it was his arm that drew Boes—their separate patient, to be treated, observed, and discussed. It was fine with Angus. The closer he was to the Front, the more likely he'd get back to it. Make it right. It was all that kept him going. And Boes insisted that he'd seen miraculous things—men who regained function suddenly and quickly.

Boes was late. Angus stared with dull eyes at the familiar cotton pads and saline solution, at the fruitwood case of the metronome that timed the delivery of shocks, the tangle of wires and electrodes dangling over the table, and the machine to which they were connected. There were voices in the hallway.

"What's his status, this MacGrath?" It was Colonel Cobb, the tall, stoop-shouldered physician-in-chief.

It was Boes who answered. "I believe he's getting better overall."

"On what do you place your belief? This is a medical practice, Boes, not a community of faith. He's had a vigorous regimen of passive movement and massage, and electrotherapy. What's your machine say?"

There was a pause. "It's the muscles innervated by the ulnar that concern me. They respond to low levels of stimulation—less than 0.5 microfarads—yet he has no voluntary movement of his wrist."

Angus looked down at his wrist and willed it to elevate his hand. Nothing. The padding would have prevented it anyway. But he *felt* nothing.

There was a rustling of papers. Cobb spoke. "Let's see here. Bayonet lodged just below the brachial plexus. *Below* it. Lucky man. Blade removed on the field. Hemorrhage . . . infection . . . cleared. Surgery . . . bone splinters and fibrous mass compressing the nerves. Compressed, but not dissected—right?"

"No, the radial—"

"Yes, I see. Radial nerve sutured."

"I'm convinced he'll recover. As the physical wounds heal—"

"You're convinced of many things, eh, Boes? Well, you listen to me—what does this add up to? Loss of sensation in the face of minimal atrophy? The lack of deformity? The failure of voluntary movement along the tracks of undamaged nerves? I suspect this is largely in his *mind*. Would you agree?"

"I'm saying that, if anything, it's mixed—psychical *and* organic. The nerves were badly concussed."

"It's been six weeks. There should be more progress. What happened to the man?"

"It's in the notes."

"What happened, Boes," Cobb sighed. "Not his injuries, their *circumstances*. A man's mates are killed, he survives, and reacts to the slightest injury as if it were paretic. Often enough, if these boys are told a furlough is in the offing if and *only* if they can demonstrate voluntary movement, you'll find they're ready to take up their duty again."

"He wants to recover," Boes protested. "He's an artist. Surely he wants to be able to use his hand again."

"An artist? Ah, a sensitive sort . . ."

"He's as anxious as the next man to get back to his unit, I swear to you."

"Anxious? No one is anxious to get back to the Front. Have you ever been to the Front?"

"No sir. But I think I've seen enough of the results to inform me of its nature."

"Do you, indeed? You make me laugh, Boes."

"But if I may?"

"Yes?"

"I believe you said that after a brief sojourn, men return 'ready to take up their duty again.'"

"Ready to take up their duty, not *anxious to return*. I wonder about you, Boes. I do. As confident and well trained as you are. In a month or so, I'm up to the Front to inspect our field hospital situation, and I'm taking you with me so you have a better feel for how men develop these hysterical symptoms."

"He's quite sane, sir," Boes insisted. "No twitching or hallucination. He's quiet, very serious. But when he does speak, there's a sincerity, an intensity. He's been very engaged in his recovery. As the organic symptoms subside, I'm sure the rest will follow suit."

"Alright. Continue your blasted nerve therapy. But my advice is pound it into his head that he does have capacity in the nerves and muscles *that are healthy*. And for God's sake find out what happened to him. Only a coward of the lowest order would refuse to get better once he faces things. If he's not better in four weeks, he's to be invalided back to England."

Angus stumbled back as Boes strode in.

"Four weeks, huh?" Angus said. "You up to it? Or shall we just assume I'm crazy or a coward or both and call it a day?"

"Steady now. That was meant to be private. I doubt you understood—it's a very mixed situation. Here, sit down."

"I understood."

Boes cleared his throat, pulled a chair over and sat facing Angus. "Look, no one is saying you're a coward. You had a lot of very real, physical damage."

Angus cradled his arm and leaned away. "Not enough, apparently. If I'm supposed to be better than I am, I want to know."

"It isn't as simple as that. Suppose you let me be the doctor."

"Suppose I let you be the honest doctor. How about you share the truth with me?"

"How about you do the same. What happened out there? If you heard what Cobb was saying, you know that's the truth you need."

Angus felt himself go cold. "You think I'm hiding something? Here's the *truth*. I need to get back to my unit. I owe them. Owe *myself*. Do you understand honor? How do you think it feels to have escaped and left my men back there, slogging through it. I belong with them."

Boes sat back. "Let's get a hold of ourselves here." Then in a softer tone said, "Tell me again the names of the men who were killed when you were injured. Let's start there."

Angus tipped his chair back against the wall. He hadn't noticed the ceiling before—narrow-planked, dark wood with a soft patina.

He closed his eyes. "First Lieutenant Sam Publicover, Corporal Richard Burwell, Private Anton Voles, and Lance Corporal Lawrence . . . Havers."

"This fellow Havers—your voice broke."

The chair came down with a thud.

Boes leaned forward. "Was Havers a good chum?"

"I didn't know Havers. He wasn't one of us."

"Alright . . . you've mentioned this Publicover a lot. You once said he looked like your son. Is that part of it? Outside of their names, you never mention your family. Perhaps a leave could be arranged if—"

"Family leave *across the Atlantic*?" Angus said. "You're grasping at straws. Junior officers in the CEF don't get family leave. You know that."

Boes gazed longingly at the condenser apparatus.

"Look, there's a good chance I'm nuts, right? I must be because if I *could* move my wrist or my arm, I *would*. And I can't. Get on with the machine," Angus sighed. "And just so we understand each other, my family is not part of this story. To bring them into it would be to render them . . ."

"Render them what?"

"Unclean," Angus said.

TWENTY-ONE

June 30th, 1917
Snag Harbor, Nova Scotia

og wrapped the gray dawn in a shroud. Simon set his mug in the sink. It would be a long sail over to Lunenburg if the fog didn't burn off. Still, the muffled world suited him. The last time he'd been to Lunenburg was with his father. They'd gone to pick up new blocks for the *Lauralee* from Dauphinee's, where rows of blocks, dripping with caramel-colored lacquer, filled every window and dangled overhead like taffy lollipops.

His father's last letter lay on the table. Up and about, but still in the hospital; unable to move his arm, but "on the mend." Simon could read between the lines. And there weren't many lines to be read in the uneven, left-handed print. His mother had wept when the letter came, saying it was all a horrible mistake and that he was *supposed* to be in London drawing maps and that she never should have agreed to it, and that to have lost his right arm was to have lost too much. A few hours later, she'd pulled herself together. He *had* to get better. He *would* get better. And if he didn't, they'd have to adjust. All of them.

Gone were the loose threads of her, the day-dreamy drift, the pressed-flower fairies, the shells strung together to clatter in the wind. Now it was deals sealed with a handshake, purposeful trips on

Rooster, and a brimmed leather hat, that his Uncle Ebbin had won off an Australian, tied under her chin. And short hair. She'd chopped it off and looked like a dandelion gone to seed. And liked it that way.

"You just quit your moping and let her work," Ida told him. "Better than thinking Ebbin's alive. She may not know a lick about house-keeping—we all have our talents—but look at her now. Workmen's boots, skirt hitched up. I've never seen the like. Tongues wagging, and she just sails right through it. She's on her own path. Knows what she's about. His Highness isn't stopping her, you'll notice. So don't you think of it."

After the night of the struggle over the gun, a bad chest and continuous cough had kept his grandfather housebound. His mother had hitched up Rooster, headed on over to Gold River and negotiated the sawmill deal herself. Got a better price than his grandfather expected and a better price on timber transport to boot. "Should have brought you on years ago," his grandfather hacked out on her return. She offered a shy smile of triumph and said that the mill owners knew her as Duncan's agent anyway through all the correspondence. Surprised H. E. MacGrath was a woman, suspicious at first, but came around when she began to negotiate. And without the slightest hesitation, she added that Duncan might want to think about the *Lauralee*. Scrap her or get her fixed up. She wasn't earning a dime up on the cradle. Duncan sank into his chair and refused to answer.

When she left, he shuffled to the window, quilt around his shoulders. He'd never again mentioned the gun. Simon found it hard to look at him without seeing the parts he'd exposed, but having faced what lurked below, he felt stronger, protective almost. People were not what they seemed. It felt odd and uncomfortable, but at the same time, he felt he'd gained a bit more of a foothold in the world.

Watching Hettie stride down the path, Duncan clapped his hand on Simon's shoulder to steady himself. "Put a pair of trousers on that woman and she's what her brother might have been. What I hoped your father would be. MacGrath and MacGrath. Maybe it'll come to pass after all."

"But scrap the *Lauralee*? She's crazy," Simon said.

"Ah, we won't let her do that, now, will we?"

"No sir." Simon knew what they both were thinking, and in that moment understood something more than he had before.

HE PULLED HIS oilskins off the peg, glad for the chance to be out on the water. At the foot of the hill, a cluster of spruce, silver-green ghosts at the water's edge, signaled the end of the visible world. When he got to the town wharf, the Masons—Frank and his grown son, Stevie—were whispered shapes in oilskins on the deck of the *Elsie*, their forty-five-foot fishing schooner. Frank lifted a hand through a patch of mist. Wallace materialized in the companionway. The creak of block and tackle, a laugh from Stevie, and Simon's own footsteps on the wharf were damped down and swallowed whole.

On another day, in another time, Simon would have stepped deftly along the "duckboards" of the wharf, "rifle-oar" in hand, piercing Germans with his bayonet, never even stopping to watch them pitch to their deaths. But he was far beyond such games now. Two days before, he'd turned fourteen.

"Simon Peter! Come aboard!" It was Frank.

"Let's try her now." Stevie crouched down in the engine cuddy. The two-cylinder "make-and-break" auxiliary shuddered to life in a nerve-jangling, earsplitting *put-put-put-put*. Puffs of greasy smoke blew out the *Elsie*'s stern and the smell of gas filled the air. Stevie popped up, rubbing a rag on his hands, grinning. "She's a-goin'!"

"Shove us off then," Frank shouted over the racket. Simon and Wallace hopped up on the wharf. Hands on the rigging, they walked the boat forward, keeping her clear of the pilings, then stepped lightly aboard the stern. Stevie shoved her into gear. The shuddering settled into a steady vibration. Whirlpools of slate-colored water, etched with gasoline rainbows, stretched out behind them. Simon swallowed hard to keep his oatmeal down, wishing engines had never been invented.

"What?" Frank held his hand to his ear.

"I say, how's she handle with the engine in her?" Wallace shouted.

"Well, she don't drive the fish away, like Putnam says," Stevie said.

"Wouldn't mind if she scared 'em *out* of the water and *into* the boat, but she don't do that, neither," Frank laughed. "Get a good five to six knots out of her. Carries us handily out beyond Tancook to Dunn's Ridge. Good fishing out there. She's a Canadian Standard. Got her over to Hawbolt and Evans in Chester. Had her installed at Hilchey's. What d'ya think, Wallace?"

"I'm thinking she'd shake the *Lauralee* to pieces," Wallace said glumly, then, eyes bulging, gave a blast on the copper fog horn. "Weather helm worse than before?"

"Bit worse, maybe. She's always had a weather helm come any bit of wind. Bluff in the bows. Keeps us drier than some of those salt bankers, weather helm or not."

"Keeps us slower, too," Stevie noted.

"Yup, that too. We're better off slow in this fog, though." He had the boat moving at a snail's pace.

"Sweet Jesus, yes," Wallace said. "Watch that stick now." A black pole, tethered to a rock below, loomed up and disappeared in the fog.

Simon hopped up on the foredeck away from the fumes. "Be our lookout there, Simon!" Frank shouted. Wallace handed him the horn and Simon wrapped himself in the blankness of the fog, leaving the conversation behind.

A short while later, the fog vanished, the wind shifted, and the motor quit. In the sudden silence, Frank cursed. They all cursed except Simon. As Stevie and Wallace fiddled with the engine, countering each other's advice, a pair of dolphins broke through the ruffled water off the starboard bow. Simon scrambled across the deck, and they promptly resurfaced to port. As he slid over, they dove under again and poked their bottle noses up from the bow, one on either side, smiling their happy grins. Simon inched up to the stubby bowsprit and hung his arms down. They ducked beneath and exchanged places again. He could see them under the water and he thought he heard them laugh when they surfaced. Lying on his stomach, he laughed back.

Frank decided that with a freshening wind coming up behind them, they'd make better time under sail. The dolphins had already figured that out and surfaced twenty feet ahead of the boat, waiting.

"Let's go with the full set, boys," Frank said. "Take the tiller, Simon."

Simon scrambled back. "Me?"

"No one else by that name, is there?" Frank abandoned the stick, leaving Simon to hold her steady as Stevie hauled up the mainsail. Wallace readied the foresails. Frank tailed the lines. Simon tried to hold the boat steady, but a sudden gust caught him off guard. Halfway up, the wooden hoops froze to the mast with the pressure of the filled sail. Frank didn't even look back. Simon sheepishly headed her up into the wind, easing the strain on the half-hauled main. Then up went the gaff boom and mainsail. Up went the foresail, the staysail, and jib. Expectation and readiness shot up through the hull and up through Simon in the thwack and shudder of the canvas, in the whirr of slack rope hauled fast through the blocks.

Wallace and Stevie secured the halyards. Frank took over the helm from Simon. To cover his disappointment, Simon helped Wallace shove the main boom over and ease the massive sail to starboard. Stevie hauled in the main sheet.

"She come up of a sudden, eh?" Wallace said, eyeing the wind and heaving himself up on the windward rail next to Simon.

"We'll make good time if she holds steady," Frank replied, unbuttoning his oilskins. "Stevie, see what you can do with that blasted make-and-break. Wind may die as fast as she come up." Stevie climbed down to the engine housing.

"I'd say 'make-and-break' is the term alright," Wallace said, huge grin on his face.

Frank tipped his head back and laughed. "I'd say you're right there."

Pounding along now, Simon looked ahead for the dolphins. He'd tell Mr. Heist about them. He'd been helping him fence in the garden, turn over the soil with fresh seaweed and plant vegetables. They'd hauled the Fresnel light to the center of the garden to keep the crows away, though it seemed to draw them in. Simon had also started leaving Peg in George's care and walking the rest of the way to Mr. Heist's cottage. George would meet him by the road. Simon would hop down, and George would put his crutch up on Peg and climb on without a word. Once, on his way back, Simon saw him, naked to the waist, long hair flowing, trotting around the field on Peg with his arms open. "How many coins today, George?" Simon asked on the way back the last time he'd been there. "Forty," George answered. "In silver boxes. Avon Heist's time is up."

"How do you mean, his time is up?"

"Heist heart, down heart," was all George would say.

As Cross Island came into view, the wind shifted. They tacked up Lunenburg Bay. Simon hooked his arm around the foremast as they passed Battery Point. Though the fleet was out and the elevated fish flakes were empty of cod, the wind bore the smell of fish, as it always did in Lunenburg. He dipped his knees as foaming water rushed past the lee rail and they swung up into the harbor, where the sun caught the reds of the shore buildings, the purples and greens and pale yellows of the gabled houses on the hills. Wallace hitched his overalls and pulled up the sleeves of his sweater to reveal the dirty cuffs of his long johns. "Them down in Gloucester think they're the cod capital of the world. And they're good, but they don't stand up to our boys. Well, some do. Course, them boys is from Lunenburg anyway," Wallace chuckled. Simon just grinned. He'd heard it all before.

"Dropping the main!" Frank shouted. The sails flapped and cracked midships, then dropped down the mast in a rush. When the sails were stowed and the lines made fast and coiled, the four of them sat back with the pleasure that comes from a long sail over. They had a mug of cold tea and cold beans, topping them off with buttered bread from Elsie Mason. Stevie brought out a wet comb and square mirror, and they made themselves presentable and hailed a ride from a couple of boys.

They threaded their way through double-decked rows of barrels, teams of oxen, and carts of salt and barrel staves at Zwicker's wharf and agreed to meet on the *Elsie* in two hours. The others went off on their various errands and Simon was on his own. A sign in Rhuland's Ice Cream Parlour—CALIFORNIA TANGERETTE! FIVE CENTS!—caught his eye, as did a boy who sat on the steps, his dirty hair cut every which way. He had on an oversized wool jacket and black, knee-high fishing boots. Inside, the clerk idly slapped at a fly. "I'll take one of those," Simon said, pointing at the sign in the window. The boy was standing now, staring through the glass. "Make it two," Simon said.

Outside, two cold bottles of brilliant orange fizz in hand, their thin white straws bobbing at an angle, he stopped in front of the boy. "Looks like you could use a drink," he said, trying for a rough edge. The boy eyed the bottle suspiciously.

Simon pursed his lips around the straw, took a tentative sip, and raised his eyebrows at the sweet mystery of it. The boy grabbed the offered bottle in his thick hand and did the same. "Aww!" he said, rubbing the end of his nose. "A trick."

"No sir," Simon assured him. "Bubbles is all." At this the boy smiled.

Simon sat beside him on the steps. The boy said his name was

Lathen Pike and he was from Reeks Cove, Newfoundland, a town of five families and no shops. And he'd been saved.

Saved? Simon immediately imagined an itinerant preacher towering over him, hands lifted, shadows leaping in the flickering torchlight, pronouncing Lathen the Lord's own. Zenus had been saved once at a tent meeting in Blandford.

"Yup. Saved," the boy repeated. By a doctor, as it turned out, not a preacher. The story came out fast. Simon struggled with the Newfoundland accent, but got the gist. Lathen had been working on a fishing schooner out on the Banks when a hook got caught in his hand. The hand got hot and red so's he couldn't bend his fingers. He was "hagrode and in a fever," so the captain dropped him off in Sheet Harbor. The doctor had him in an infirmary until the hand got better, then sent him by rail to Lunenburg to wait for his boat to come in and take him back out to the Banks.

Had been on a train? Out on the Banks? "How old are you?" Simon demanded.

"Twelve. Two more 'n I can count and that's a fact. Big for my age."

"Your parents let you go?"

"Let me? Sent out is how it was. My uncle took me on as his dory mate." Lathen shrugged. "T'weren't but a bawbeen to scoop into our bowls at home."

"So what's it like out there?" Simon asked.

"Hard," was the answer. "Plenty to eat, though, and never once got a beating."

"What was your job? Were you a catchie?"

Lathen took a long sip, then laid it out. "Nope. In a dory. Yer up and out on the dories at dark, see? Me and Uncle Albert is dory number six. You skiver your caplin onto the trawl line aforehand, then drop it to the bottom. Drop a bobber at one end of it, and row a goodly ways away. I drop the line. Uncle rows. Then start hauling her in—a fish on most every hook. Do it all again. Then when yer dory's near down to waterline with a load, you row back to the schooner. Fork the fish into her, row back and start over whilst fellers on board counts and cleans and salts 'em and stacks 'em in kenches. Don't sleep for days if there's a good catch going. Got to work fast to bait the trawl—as fast as the other feller's rowing down the line. That's how I got the hook in my hand. T'were bejesus cold. Uncle forgot my rubber nippers and mine was wool and the hook went through 'em. See?" Lathen offered his palm. He and Simon studied the stitches and the black and purple mark as if reading a message. "Swole near as big as my head. Fever so bad the doctor didn't know if I'd live or die."

Simon looked up at him. "It works now, right?" The boy nodded. "You couldn't bend your fingers, but now you can. My dad was wounded. Can't use his arm. Not yet, anyway. He's in France. A bayonet got him."

"A what?"

"Bayonet. France. You know—the *war*? Don't you even know about the war?"

Lathen sipped thoughtfully. "Know'd some as died in it."

They sat in silence for a time. "You should see them halibut," Lathen said. "They put up a fight, jumping about. You might have to club them with a stick to get them into the boat." Seeing Simon's eyes widen, Lathen stood, and with maniacal grunting, he whacked his empty bottle through the air, clubbing every which way. "There!" he said, and sat down with a grin. He set his bottle down.

Simon shuddered and thought of the dolphins.

Lathen sighed and said, "When I got here, I figure I'll have to find a barn or patch of a place to sleep in. And that's where I got saved again. There was a note pinned in my jacket which said I didn't know what. So the train man reads it and tells me when I get to town to find Mrs. Isaac Gates's Boarding House, just down there a-ways." He pointed toward Lincoln Street. "I'll tell you what she done, Mrs. Isaac Gates. She hauls the note out of its envelope—I have it here." He extracted the creased note from his pocket and handed it to Simon. "I had her read it to me a bunch of times."

Lathen leaned in toward Simon as he read aloud,

"My dear Mrs. Gates, this boy is from Newfoundland. He was injured on the schooner George S. Merton, *and has been cared for at the Halifax Infirmary for three weeks where he nearly lost his life. Would you be so kind as to put him up, at my expense, until the* Merton *returns to Lunenburg a few weeks from now?"*

Lathen, looking out at the harbor, joined in on the last line. *"'He is an upright lad, a long way from home. You can send the bill to me at the above address. Signed, John K. Whitford, M.D.'"* Lathen plucked the note from Simon's hand and stuffed it in his pocket. "Upright. That's me. Didn't know that afore, and now I do." He closed his eyes and smiled. "I been saved. Twice."

Simon looked out at the *Elsie*, thinking how life can turn on the thinnest of threads. He sucked the last of the bubbles from the bottom of his bottle, then tossed it over his shoulder into a barrel. Lathen did the same and said, "Wanna see the schooner they're building down at Smith and Rhuland's?"

"Sure," Simon agreed. Philip had said his building days were over—it was mostly repairs now—but he and Simon liked to put their feet up and talk about the ideal boat, balanced and fast, usually after Philip came back from the tavern.

They ran down the street and up to the top of the hill, where the ring of hammers, saws and axes spiked the air. Below them stretched the long red-brown sheds and empty cradles of the Smith and Rhuland yard. Simon leaned over to catch his breath, already anticipating the sweet pungent smell of pine and spruce shavings, the clutter of tools and hanks of rope spilling off shelves to the grease-and-paint-spattered floor, the carved wood molds in the sheds. When he looked up, Lathen was pointing to the water's edge. There, balanced between the tall supports of a cradle, was the most beautiful boat he'd ever seen. And the biggest. "How long is she?" he asked.

"One hundred and sixty feet," Lathen said, clearly pleased.

"Huge," Simon said. Something about her lines made him want to cry. Her bow was curved like the back of a spoon, not sharp and angled like a clipper bow. Rounded, ample. Without effort, Simon imagined the masts and crosstrees, the gaff booms, the long deck, the angled stern.

"Bowsprit?" he whispered.

"Sixteen and a half feet. Main mast, one hundred and twenty feet tall, twenty–two inches round. Douglas fir. A feller from America is having her built." Lathen was sliding down the stony grade. Simon followed. They angled around some men in dark green overalls sliding a thick plank of pine from a massive steam box and stood as near as they could to the boat. Simon tipped his head back to take her in.

"What's her name?"

"*Repulse Bay.*"

"What? Who names a boat *Repulse Bay*?"

"The man who's paying for her to be built. That New York feller. Wears a white hat and a polka-dot handkerchief. Asked me if I'd ever heard of Repulse Bay in Hong Kong. I said I never had and never would, with names like that. Hong Kong must be somewhere in New York, I figure."

"*Repulse Bay*," Simon repeated.

"Yup. Told me it was the fittingest name he could find. Said there was a story behind it not fit for telling. I asked him if he'd been saved. Told him I had."

"And?"

"Said nope, but there were stranger things had happened to him. Said he didn't know how to sail and didn't care if he ever learned, but when I was older he might take me aboard. He's hiring crew. Might go back to Repulse Bay to make things right, he said. Or just might sail her off and sell her."

"A man who can't sail, and doesn't want to, builds a boat like that." Simon spat on the ground. "I wouldn't step foot on her." But still he couldn't take his eyes off her.

A couple of men up on the cradle waved at Lathen. Simon shot him a stunned look. "Here every day after chores," Lathen grinned. "Might get work on the caulking gang or some such if the *Merton* don't come get me. But I'm not going out with that New York feller neither, no sir." He squinted up at the sun, then looked at Simon. "How about I never see the *Merton* come in, and you and me work every day on the caulking gang, and drink orange fizz after supper?" He flashed a smile, then said he had to be going. Had chores to do for Mrs. Gates. They wished each other luck. Lathen turned to go and never looked back.

Simon backed up to a nearby boulder and sat down in a trance, watching the *Repulse Bay* come to life, memorizing her every line, her dimensions, deck to waterline, beam to length, itching to get them down on paper, maybe build a model, show Philip. And thinking how he'd been saved once and for all from clubbing fish to death by a boy he met on a step.

DARK CLOUDS WERE gathering when they met back on the *Elsie.* They suited up in oilskins. There was a heavy chop and they sloshed along out of the harbor and turned away from Cross Island on a close reach. Simon was surprised when Frank asked if he'd like to take the tiller again. He and Frank traded places.

Stevie, up at the rail with a pair of binoculars, told them that the boys on the *Runabout* had spotted a U-boat on the bay side of Ironbound.

"In Mahone Bay? And you believed them," Wallace said.

"Maybe scouting things out. Wouldn't call them fellers the type to lie."

Frank squinted suspiciously at Wallace. "Sounds like Duncan's rubbed off on you. Papers say there's all kind of spies, foreign-born aliens, most of 'em, all along the coast, doing the Kaiser's dirty work."

"Talk going around says Avon Heist is building a lighthouse of his own," Stevie chimed in. "Now you tell me, why would a man do that? To signal subs for one, and Duncan still making the case for him as schoolteacher. That right, Simon?"

Simon stared at him. The mainsail luffed heavily and the boat stalled.

"Mind the wind! Lord Jesus!" Frank barked. And then they were in irons, dead in the water, slipping back, wind on both sides of the sails. "Goddamn it!" Frank shouted. "Hand over the tiller!"

Simon slammed the tiller hard to port. The *Elsie* hesitated, then turned ever so slightly and the wind just caught the forward edge of the mainsail. They slacked the sheets until she picked up headway, then hauled the lines back in as Simon slowly eased her up again. "Now, keep her on course, boy!" Frank yelled.

The *Elsie* was lumbering. "C'mon, schoon!" Simon whispered to her. The pressure of the water against the rudder came up through the tiller into his arm. She did have a weather helm! Simon eased her up gently. Tension strained through the rigging. The *Elsie* hovered like a seabird, then found her place between wind and water and surged forward, sails filled, power released. Simon had found the slot.

"Alright then. A right good skipper we've got, eh, boys?" Frank said, cleating the main sheet and ducking spray. "Might be as good as his father one day if he can keep his eye on the sails."

The clouds opened up and rain poured down in sheets, then came in sideways as the wind blew hard from the southeast. "Now we're in it!" Stevie shouted. He and Wallace went below, and it was just Frank and Simon on deck. Frank eased the main when gusts slammed against them. Simon, standing now to counter the heel of the boat, with both hands on the tiller and his right foot against the leeward seat, headed her up and fell off in near-perfect synchrony with the roaring wind and waves. His hood flew back. Green water came over the bow. Salt spray washed down his neck. Rain stung his face. He had to tell Mr. Heist—tell him to get rid of the Fresnel light. Sink it.

"When you're wore out, I'll take her," Frank yelled, ducking spray.

"Mr. Heist, he's a good man," Simon shouted, holding tight to the tiller.

Frank didn't answer.

TWENTY-TWO

July 3rd, 1917
No. 18 Canadian General Hospital
Saint-Junien, France

Destiny?
I thought I had one once, says Canada.
I made a name at Vimy
Took the hill then bled to death.
Your dear one,
Smiling Jimmy

ngus stared at the poem, if you could call it that. Written in Jimmy's hand and waiting now for the censor's. Poor Jimmy—whether he'd meant that he'd bled to death or that Canada, without a plan for pursuit after Vimy, had done so, didn't much matter. Jimmy, who had died of infection, had not bled to death. Nor had Canada. But both had bled a great deal. The numbers were mounting—Private James Perry of Winnipeg, just one more. Angus had been censoring his letter when Brimmie came with news of his death. She told him to bring the letter to her when he'd finished censoring it.

"One more death to add to the Vimy list," she sighed. Angus knew the numbers by then—4,000 Canadians killed, another 7,000 wounded—all for a four-mile dent in the German line that hadn't done much but prove the Canadians a force to be reckoned with. The French had all but given up. Not long after Vimy and the Second Battle of the Aisne, some 30,000 of them had walked out of their trenches demanding better food and more leave, demands that were eventually granted. At the end of June, hope arrived in the form of 14,000 American troops on French soil. Two nurses from a hospital in Étaples said they'd never seen men so tall. They were giants, but apparently without guns or knowledge of how to fire them. America was in the war but wouldn't be fighting it for God knew how long.

All the while, Angus remained in No. 18 Canadian General Hospital. He focused again on the letter. It was hard to tell if it was a letter because apart from the salutation, "Dear Mum and Dad," the poem was all there was. Angus put his pen down next to the bottle of black ink on the desk. He could make black lines with his left hand if the paper was anchored, which is how he ended up censoring hospital letters. Truth, the first and great casualty of war, he thought. Who better to blot it out?

Angus had received letters of his own that day. Katz, the scribbler, had written to say the boys missed him and hoped he'd join them soon. They'd been assigned a new lieutenant, who made Keegan growl more than ever. LaPointe had met up with a lone Zouave trying to find his Algerian platoon. LaPointe traded a couple of postcards and one of his harmonicas with him for a wind-up tin monkey that performed rude tricks and gave the boys a laugh. The new lieutenant wasn't amused and had ordered LaPointe to trash it. Now that's just wrong, McNeil had said. Katz said they'd come across some women bathing in a river who invited them in. Kearns and Hanson had splashed on in fully clothed. They all nearly had, except Boudrey, who'd run for his life.

Conlon had written as well. The Kilties had used the map and landmarks Angus had drawn to locate and secure the Krupp howitzer at the stone barn. They'd found Publicover and the others where they'd fallen, the bodies unmolested, and buried them there together. They'd later be located and brought back for burial at Vimy. "Sam will have his stone marker, and for what it's worth, I'm glad of it," Conlon wrote. "I must be going soft. Get back here, would you, before I go to mush."

I will, Angus said as he folded Jimmy's letter. He imagined the parents back in Winnipeg, slowly opening the parcel—his mother holding his socks to her face, breathing in a last whiff of her son. Then whispering to her husband, "Look here, Alfred, a letter. One he never got to send! Our poor Jimmy." He imagined them opening it . . . No, it wouldn't do to send it. Not to the grieving, uncomprehending parents.

He turned down the oil lamp, sat back, and let the tears fill his eyes. Help me now, he whispered. God help me keep moving forward. The grieving parents. His father's reaction to his own wound was something Angus tried not to imagine. The war will break you, he'd said. Or no, he hadn't said that at all. Angus just kept imagining him saying it. Maybe to keep himself from breaking.

And Ebbin's father. How would he face him? There'd be no marker for Ebbin Hant at Vimy. His name would be registered somewhere among the missing. A soldier without a grave. But there he'd be, forever uncelebrated beneath a marker for Lance Corporal Havers. God help me, Angus repeated. He carefully tucked the folded poem in with Jimmy's other effects. Yes, it would go back to the parents. Maybe in a hundred years, looking back, it would mean something to someone, or maybe not, but his would not be the only tears shed over it.

A WEEK LATER, Angus and a small group of ambulatory patients were led down the hill by several nurses, got up in their dress blues, to the town of Saint-Junien. The Matron had ordered Angus to go—the outing considered good therapy for convalescing patients. He'd protested, but the Matron had persisted, noting he hadn't been off the grounds since his arrival; it was therapeutic and not a choice. "Do you good," she said.

Walking down the steep hill was not easy. A smattering of red and orange poppies bobbed on the roadside, flanked by purple delphiniums. The delphiniums were lined up in a row, as if they'd escaped from a garden but, once free, had been uncertain how else to position themselves.

At the intersection of the town's cobblestone streets, the group prepared to go their separate ways. Brimmie pointed to a hairdresser's shop and explained that some of the nurses would get their hair washed there. Others would be off to buy trinkets and postcards and maybe take a cup of tea. Orderlies were to accompany the men who wished to go to a hymn sing at the YMCA.

Angus declined the hymn sing, but was uncertain of where to go. He hung near the entry to the shop as the nurses exchanged greetings with Sabine, the woman who ran the place. He pulled a cigarette from his pocket. It was then he heard her name. "*Juliette*," said Sabine, clear as day, "*ma soeur.*" He slowly lowered the cigarette. "We didn't know you had a sister!" the nurses exclaimed. And then he saw her—carrying an immense pitcher, nodding at the women. As she set it down, she lifted her eyes to the mirror above the sink, then turned toward the open door, her eyes a mirror for his own.

In a glance, she took in his sling and said that yes, she was helping her sister, but today she'd be stopping at two o'clock to meet the 2:40 out of Boulogne for some supplies. She did not break communion with Angus as she said this, and the nurses paused to exchange curious looks. The spin of the earth paused as well. Angus heard Brimmie say, "Indeed! Well, we'll be long gone by then. We're collecting our patients at two o'clock."

THEY DID MEET at the train depot as the 2:40 pulled in. But not then. Not for another month. A month in which General Currie considered whether to commit the Canadian troops to another Allied push in Ypres. Third Ypres, it was called. And it had another name—Passchendaele.

It was a month in which Cobb, having forgotten his four-week deadline, decided Angus would benefit from leave—lift the spirit and might just promote his return to health.

Juliette had not visited Angus in the hospital. She must have sensed what a violation that would be. An hour after he'd left her holding the pitcher that day at the shop, he'd gone back and stood in the shadows of the connecting alley. Pink and lavender sweet peas fluttered on a vine—their scent, light as air, filling him with a temporary amnesia for the war. Behind the vines, beyond the sheltering branches of an elm, the women rubbed their hair with thick towels and then sat in a circle in the sun, each one combing the next one's hair with wide-toothed combs. Their laughter spilled out over the dappled yard. Juliette came out the back door and through the gate and tossed a tub of wash water into the dirt lane. It raced down a gully and eddied into a sudsy pool. He backed into the shadows. She straightened, as if sensing his presence, and peered down the alley. What he saw in her face was a solace so tangible it might leave him utterly undone. He slowly turned on his heel and left her.

AND SO THEY did not meet until the 2:40 pulled into the depot a half hour late on August 10th. With a military pass in his pocket and an uncharted course, he'd stationed himself on a wooden bench, waiting—for what, he did not know. Two trains had come and gone—one *40 hommes*, as the troop trains were called; one with civilians and soldiers both. He hadn't bought a ticket for a ferry because the thought of being in London, tossed about in a sea of innocent civilians, was intolerable. And no one, not even a crazy one-armed Canadian lieutenant on leave, went to the Front for a visit, which is what he longed to do.

He stared at a collection of flattened cigarette butts at his feet. The train pulled in. Steam shot out as the great red and black wheels slowed to a hissing stop. Through the steam a pair of worn black boots beneath the hem of a dusky red skirt marched past, turned, and came back. He didn't lift his eyes. He couldn't, and so she sat down on the bench beside him. For a long time they didn't speak. Then he found voice enough to tell her that he was on a six-day pass. She said she and Paul were living in her sister's cottage on the coast, seven miles away, and could he make it that far? And he said, yes.

SHE HAD A bicycle. It wobbled and bumped on the cobblestones as he walked along, wheeling it with his good hand and somehow balancing his pack on his good shoulder. He fixed his eyes on her boots. Worn and dusty and cracked, they looked as if they'd been to the Front and back and could go again, a world away from the blue leather shoes he'd slipped onto Hettie Ellen's arched and innocent feet.

When they approached the *charcuterie*, she took over the bicycle without apology and set it against the wall, managing to make him feel neither pitied nor ashamed. She haggled over the price of chops and sausage; he sat at a table outside the *pâtisserie* next door. He ordered a coffee and looked up at Saint-Junien's multispired presence, dominating the end of the street. He had stopped there on his way to the station that morning. In the misty darkness of the vestibule, rows of candles on a stand illuminated the feet of an incredibly large and extremely sad Christ, hanging on the cross. The thick smell of wax sucked the oxygen from the air. There were religious paintings in ornate gilt frames along the walls—lurid scenes of violence and supplication.

Inside, instead of pews, scattered chairs took up lonely stations on a cold stone floor. The interior was immense, a sanctuary of suspended time and sorrow, misting up to a ceiling too high, too dark to see. Multiple arches framed a set of wide steps leading to a distant altar. Backing out, he was again confronted by the weary Christ who had likely grown more weary in the past three years, and maybe in the past three minutes, and who, from his expression, held out little hope for mankind. Among the flickering votives were unlit candles which Angus understood could be lit to illuminate a wish, a prayer, a hope. Praying for his recovery seemed a selfish act, given the injuries he'd witnessed—the ones that led to a tortured prayer for death. Praying for forgiveness was ludicrous. Instead, he prayed to find his way back, whatever road it might take.

Now, looking down the nearly empty street as he waited for Juliette, the sharply peaked roofs and flat fronts of its row of Flemish houses, their long unblinking windows bound by painted shutters of faded blues and yellows and greens, seemed a street-long façade, a stage set.

Juliette returned then, a bit flushed, and with her the rush of the here and now. With a trace of triumph, she handed him the sausage and chops, wrapped in brown paper and string, and he put them into the wicker bicycle basket. They walked with the bicycle between them as the cobblestones gave way to a hard-packed dirt road that took them on a southwesterly route toward the sea. Several miles later, they passed a thick woodland, alive with rustling leaves and the flick and twitter of birds on either side of the road. Cheerful poppies fluttered in the grassy ditch, and the sweet smell of wild raspberries filled the air. It was as if they'd walked into an illustrated children's book. Beyond the wood, the road curved down onto the lonely stretch of land that led to the dunes. The sun bore down as they left the shade behind. He grew weaker and finally stopped to take a swig from his canteen. He had to angle it between his knees to unscrew the lid. She didn't try to help. She took it when he offered it and passed it back to him to close.

The road dipped past an eclectic collection of stone and stucco cottages at the end of which she turned up a hard-packed sand path. Bound on either side by thin lengths of wire stretched between fence posts, the path ran up behind the dunes toward a bluff. Sharp sea grasses brushed his legs, but it was the barbs on the wire fencing that brought him to a stop. Fresh salt air swept down the dunes. He lifted his head. There was no sound of the sea, just the wind rushing the grasses along the tops of the great rolling dunes. No voices, no gunfire, no shells. Just wind. Salt wind. He felt himself pinwheel through space.

TENDING TO HIS pigeons in a shelter at the side of the cottage, Paul had his back to them as Angus and Juliette approached. But at the creak of the bicycle, he came out, shielding his eyes. He was in his usual short trousers, suspenders, sagging striped socks, but on his head was an army helmet. When he saw Angus, he ran full out, the helmet bouncing to the ground behind him. He put on the brakes, retrieved the helmet, and then ran again holding it on his head with one hand, the chinstrap flapping against his neck. When he got to them, he stopped short, saluted and said, "*Bienvenu, Lieutenant!*"

Angus fell to one knee and held out his arm. Paul let himself be hugged, but only for a second. He kissed his mother on both cheeks, saying, "*Maman!* You have bring him home. I knew it one day!" He clapped his hands.

Paul had, of course, known Angus was in the military hospital. "It kill me, see? I talk to Nurse Lovell. *Maman* says do not go. Now you are ready. You are here!"

Angus struggled to stand. He took the helmet off Paul's head. Paul put it right back on. It was disturbing how well it suited him. Then he and Juliette led Angus inside the cottage. With its beamed ceilings and whitewashed walls and painted furniture, it had none of the gloom of Juliette's dark, high-ceilinged house in Astile. Paul wanted to drag him everywhere, out along the headland, down to the beach, out to the shelter to visit his pigeons and the fat hens, out in the field to meet Sabine's twin goats. But Juliette, pumping water for Angus, told him to stop. There would be time later.

Handing him the cool glass, Paul stared at him with concern. He looked *trop* pale, he said. Angus gulped down the water without stopping, and followed it with another. He must have looked as debilitated as he felt because Juliette immediately said he must lie down on the bed he'd share with Paul. Paul said he'd be happy with quilts on the floor, so Angus could spread across the bed that night, and for all the nights that Angus was there.

They led him up an enclosed stairway that opened to Paul's room. Late afternoon sun through the dormer window bathed the walls and sloping ceiling with creamy light. He dropped his pack by the bed. A gentle push from Juliette, and he sat down heavily on the patterned quilt, warm from the sun. She smiled down at him. "Sleep," she said, unlacing his boots. And then she steered Paul out and down the stairs. Angus closed his eyes and fell back across the bed, drunk with the sun's warmth and the trace of a breeze against his face.

Paul shook him awake two hours later for supper. When they came down, Sabine breezed in with a painted mouth and a patterned shawl that she flung off her shoulders while Juliette cooked. She resembled Juliette, but only vaguely and in a blousy way. Her chin was rounder, her smile more forthcoming, her color lighter, and her hands more square. She sat at the table, set her foot on the rung of the chair next to her, lit a slim cigar and cast an approving glance at Angus, whom she'd already seen through the door the day he'd stopped by the shop. He bristled as she remarked on the width of his shoulders, the breadth of his knees beneath his kilt, the strong jawline, as if considering a mule she might or might not buy.

Sabine took no notice of his discomfort. She opened a bottle of Pommard she'd brought, and carried on in French and English while Juliette and Paul set plates and forks on the table. She said she was off to Paris the next day and would close the shop for the entire weekend, and maybe a day or so beyond that. She was off, she said, to check on a lead for another shop on a well-known Parisian street where she could provide a variety of beauty treatments the likes of which the stinking philistines of Saint-Junien would never appreciate. So, she winked, that would leave half the bed she shared with Juliette empty. Ah, poor, dear Juliette, she said.

Juliette ticked her tongue and set out a platter of sausages, fresh peas, mushrooms and browned onions. Sabine got a long loaf of bread from her bag. Juliette told Angus that Sabine's lead in Paris was in the form of a "friend"— "*Oui! Un ami!*" Paul chimed in enthusiastically— who would provide the shop if Sabine would marry him, or so he said.

Sabine broke in to say there was plenty of space in his rooms for Juliette and Paul. He was making money even now, and one day this criminal war would end. When it did, the women of Paris would want to celebrate in style, and she'd be there to provide it. The first thing she'd do was cut off their long, tiresome hair. And if the Germans were to enter Paris, the first thing she'd do was cut off their heads! At this they all had a laugh.

Pouring more wine into her glass, Sabine said she was capable of far more than any of them knew, and, lifting a hunk of sausage from the serving dish, said that her *ami*, if too old for the army, made up for it in other ways, one of which was to understand the need for women to feel beautiful, which Juliette, by the way, might want to investigate. She then paused for breath, a crunch of bread and several noisy gulps of wine.

Juliette leaned back from the table and reached for a candle on a dish on the cupboard behind her. If embarrassed by Sabine, it was only Angus's presence that made her so, Angus thought. As different as they were, there was no doubting their bond. Juliette placed the candle in the center of the table and leaned in as she lit the wick. The candle flamed up and her skin took on a peach glow. She sat back. Angus forced himself to keep his eyes on the flame.

Sabine pointed at his arm and asked how it happened, when would it get better? He gave them the short version, which amounted to "bayonet to the shoulder following Vimy. Hospital. Treatment . . . seems to be helping."

"Ah, Veeemy! You are a hero! A Canadian hero! *Nous aimons les Canadiens!*" Sabine said. "So manly! Find me one that wants to desert, and I'll cancel my trip to Paris and run away forever! No need for love in the bargain."

Juliette rolled her eyes.

Paul explained that before the war, Sabine had been in love with a round and sturdy man who must go unnamed. He stood and circled his arms and thumped from side to side in imitation. Sabine laughed and clapped her hands. "Perfect! *Parfait!*" Paul sat back down. He said the man was from Alsace-Lorraine, and on the eve of the war had joined the German infantry and was killed in the Argonne. Sabine was very sad but then canceled her mourning, Paul said, because by then her bastard husband had been killed also, and Paul's father, too, perhaps by Sabine's soldier. Who had killed who? No one could know.

"Nothing but loss," Sabine said, pushing her plate away and allowing Angus to light her a cigarette from his packet. Exhaling, she said, "But we make our choices, no? To be dead or alive. I am not dead yet, so I choose to be alive."

"Me, too!" Paul said.

"Hush! It is not for you! Here," Juliette said, indicating the dishes.

THE CARTOGRAPHER OF NO MAN'S LAND • 295

"*This* is for you." He whistled and raised his eyebrows, but began clearing the plates. "It is not just a choosing," Juliette said.

"Oh, *mais oui*, it is. We *choose* to be alive while we are here. Or not. Do you not agree, Lieutenant?"

Angus sat back and lit his own cigarette. "Some things can sap the life out of you . . . can make you—"

"*Pathétique!* Make you what? Do you think you have no hand in your destiny? You are a leaf on the wind?" Sabine asked impatiently.

"No—"

Sabine broke in, gesturing at Juliette. "I say to Juliette, if you have no plan, there is no future. But you must feed the present or you will have no future. 'Before' and 'after,' what are these? They are today, right now. You must find today, eat it up and swallow it." She removed a trace of tobacco from her tongue and flicked it toward the candle. "The pain is there. Of course. Who does not suffer?" She shrugged. "*La guerre*, is this new? It is always so. One war, another war."

"And I say, Sabine, you think I have no joy?" Juliette said, pulling Paul close.

"You have no *dreams*, Juliette. For yourself, for the boy."

"We hold on," Juliette countered. "It is enough."

"*Oui! Exactement!* At this you are an expert. All of France is joined, hand by hand, holding on. It is our humanity, *non*? We hold on to each other. But we must do more, we must use our heads, not scratch in the dirt like chickens. You disapprove. What can I say?" Sabine leaned over and cupped Juliette's chin in her hand, "You, *tu es ma* ... um, what is it that the English say? Ah yes, *ma boussole morale*. But I, too, must make my way—for you and for me, and the boy."

Juliette held Sabine's wrist and they linked hands. Then Sabine stood and announced that she must now retire to pack her satchel, for tomorrow she would grab their future. Juliette began the dishes and said it was a good time for Paul to show Angus his pigeons.

"What did that mean, '*ma boussole morale*'?" Angus asked as he pulled the planked door shut behind them.

"'*Boussole*'—um," Paul made a circle in the dirt and an *N*. "*Nord et sud*. You see?"

"North and south. Compass? Ah, moral compass?"

"*Oui*. Compass, *boussole*. What is moral compass?"

"Someone whose soul points to true north," Angus replied, but by then Paul was scampering to the shed. The pigeons grew animated as he approached, waddling in place, cooing and poking their beaks at the chicken-wire fronts of their crates. There were three of them. Paul explained that there had been four, but that poor Babette had died. Killed, he said, somberly. By soldiers.

"What? Shot down?"

Paul shook his head sadly. The pigeons, which were Sabine's and which she had given to him, had been taken away by the BEF, "British bastards," because they thought perhaps Sabine was a spy.

"A spy?"

"*Oui*. She had the pigeons. She had the letters from the *ami* in Alsace, in the German infantry. Maybe she sends the pigeons over, too, they say." But, he went on to explain, there was no other evidence, and so Sabine was not shot. *Très bon*. But the pigeons were forgotten at the army camp and not returned. Paul was furious. He got them back later, but by then poor Babette had died of thirst because these bastards did not give her water. Three remained—Édouard, Papete and his very favorite, Angelica, close to death herself.

Angus shook his head. "Evil," he said.

"*Oui, très mal*, but . . ." Paul looked up at Angus, hardly able to contain himself. He was, he said, helping to train carrier pigeons with none other than an Allied signals corps. He lifted Angelica out of her crate and stroked her. "I am good with pigeons. I speak to them. They speak to me."

"A member of the signal corps! Congratulations!" Angus said. "Tell me first how you got the pigeons back."

"Ah. *Très facile*," Paul said. "First, I offer the stupid sergeant some excellent *vin*. Sabine has it a very long time from her *ami* in Alsace, Rudolph. Shhhh . . . we do not say his name. The sergeant take off the cork and sniff and smile and drink. But he wants more. So, I offer packets of Players." Paul held out three fingers underneath Angelica for emphasis. "*Trois!* I get them from a corporal for a jar of honey and two postcards of women with"—here he set Angelica back down and cupped his hands at his chest—"*poitrines*."

"Women with breasts?"

"*Oui*. I find the postcards under a tent in Astile. I am sorry to let them go. *Très belles*. The sergeant is nearly all okay. He smoke his cigarette. He drink the wine. He drink some more. But he will not give me the pigeons. I see Édouard and Papete and Angelica, but Babette does not move. I want to hit him on the head with the bottle. But I give him *ma meilleure offre* . . ."

"I can't wait to hear it."

"Silk *pantalettes*. Sabine's! I hold them up. *Ooh la la!* He grabs. I stuff them in my pocket. He chases me, but he stumbles with the wine. He says okay, okay. He dance with the *pantalettes* on his face, like this." Paul turned his head up and circled with his arms out. "I take Édouard et Papete *et la première étoile*, Angelica, and he say it is fair and no one will know and no one will care. I say in French that he stinks and Babette is dead."

Angus shook his head. "What did Sabine have to say about the silk drawers?"

"She say she would give all her pantalettes for Édouard and Papete by themselves! And go naked under her skirt forever for Angelica."

As if in appreciation, the pigeons cocked their heads and cooed all the louder.

"So now you're training pigeons for the BEF signal corps?"

"*Non!* The CEF! *Maintenant, je suis Canadien, moi!* Two times a week." Even his milky eye seemed to shine. "They give me a helmet. They pay me."

"I salute you, Signal Corps Private Raffarin!" Angus stood erect and saluted with his left hand. "I'm surprised you're not with requisitions, but that will surely come."

Paul laughed and said, "I do not know this requisitions. One day you will salute with your right hand, *non?* But now you have one hand and I have one eye."

"That's right," Angus said, holding his sling. "Together we are one—"

"Soldiers! We are soldiers!"

Angus nodded and smiled. Paul introduced him to Sabine's hens clucking in the small barn next to the shed, and to some pole beans, and to the rooster, standing on the wheelbarrow, to the goats, one gnawing on a tattered fishing net, and to a row of onions growing in a box. The cottage and barn were once Sabine's husband's, a man who tried to be a fisherman, Paul explained. This husband beat her and then was killed in the war. Paul said Sabine was happy because she could feel good about the fat Alsatian, and she hoped he had killed the bastard husband. "Rudolph was the one she loved, the only one she will ever love, even if he is a German," Paul whispered. "She says she does not need to love again."

Angus looked across the wild field at the point where the bluff met the horizon and dropped to the sea, to the edge of nowhere.

He lit a cigarette and handed it to Paul for a drag. Paul followed his gaze across the headland. "You wish to go there?"

"Think we have time before it gets dark?"

"I am not afraid of the dark!" Paul ran toward the house. "*Maman! Maman!*" he shouted.

She joined them. Buoyed by Paul's enthusiasm, Angus matched

his pace, and the three of them followed the rutted trail through the grasses and scrub brush. Various paths forked off to the right and left. Not far from the point, the one they were on widened. A narrow branch angled off toward a railing and a long flight of steps leading down to the beach. They kept on toward the point. Rabbits streaked ahead, crisscrossing the path. Paul flicked on Angus's torch and tried to follow them with the beam as they jumped the brush. Juliette told him to keep the light on the trail. Twilight gave way to night as they reached the point. Angus could just make out a thin line of white surf breaking some fifty feet below. There was no moon, and it was almost too windy to hear the sea rolling in, but he could sense the swells beyond as if he were in them.

For a time they were quiet, then Paul looked up at Angus. "Lance Corporal Havers?" he said.

Angus took a deep breath. The word "dead" didn't come easily. But he didn't need to say it. Paul asked how it happened.

"He was shot. Killed at the same time I was wounded."

"He was . . . Havers when he—?" Paul asked.

"Said so with his last breath." Angus kept staring ahead, then dropped his gaze. "I never should have let him—"

Juliette put her hand firmly on his arm. "Havers. It was *his* choosing, *non*?" she said. "*C'ést ce qu'il a voulu.*"

"What he wanted," Paul repeated.

What he wanted, what he needed. But at what cost? Angus thought of those last breaths and his last words. "He called me by name at the end," he said.

The wind billowed up from below the bluff, whipping his kilt around his legs and the hair across Juliette's face. She turned away and faced the wind, but he caught her words, "You were with him. He was not alone."

The three of them, Paul in the middle, leaned into one another and let the stiff wind push against them.

✦

Sleep eluded Angus that night. When they got back to the cottage, everything seemed heightened and simultaneously diffused. The
blue of the kitchen chairs, a dusky gray-green in the lamplight, seemed
richer, more saturated in color. The lingering scent of fried sausages
and onions, pleasing before, enveloped him now in a soft embrace
cut through with a painful awareness of Juliette's every movement,
the low music of her voice, the fine hairs at the nape of her neck, her
silver rings, her every breath in and out. He claimed exhaustion. Paul
arranged a bed of blankets for himself on the floor. They opened the
window and the breeze blew in. After some chatter, Paul settled into
a gently snoring sleep, his arm around a rag of a stuffed bunny, the
helmet on the floor next to him, the stiff patch of white hair sticking
out from the quilt.

Angus sat on the bed in the dark and removed his sling. The soft
salt air touched his face with day's end, and a memory of the swing
up to the mooring, the drop in the wind, the drop of the sails, a wave
from Davy and Putnam coming in on the *Glory B,* the silhouette of
tall masts against the dying sun, its last rays catching the crust of salt
crystals on the compass, and the long afterglow filling the sky, casting
the harbor in pearl-pink luster. *There's a long, long trail a-winding into
the land of my dreams . . .* dreams of a place he might as well have made
up and that was moving on without him. When Simon had been
about six years old, leaping about the boat, playing some pirate game,
he'd stopped suddenly and lifted his head as if listening to something.
Something far off that only he could hear. His eyes had grown distant, his expression utterly calm. And in it, Angus had seen something of the man he would become.

What of the man who'd sung to this boy of all the fishes in the sea,
who'd rescued him from troubled sleep, stabbed the monsters and
mastodons lurking in the corners of his room? A man who by his own

hand had shot a wounded soldier in the chest and stabbed another, and kept on stabbing him long after he was dead?

The weight of his lifeless arm pressed against him, and he went rigid with the thought that he might never recover and might not deserve it if he did, that all that he and Boes had tried had failed for a reason. His mind raced back to Publicover rounding the barn one minute, bleeding to death the next. And to Voles and Burwell. Had Angus stopped Ebbin from going on the mission, had he not let Ebbin leave the hospital, had he told the truth . . . He jumped up, left the bed and was down the steps and out the front door. Under scudding clouds, he rushed on, but he could not outrun the pain of Ebbin Hant. Nor Wickham, Dickey, nor the German with his post-card of the Royal Vic. "Franz," it said in the salutation. Franz, whose eyes when Angus shot him registered the surprise of life, the surprise of death, and all the moments in between. They were his dead, he their unworthy living repository. *Manifold sins, miserable offenders.* He thought of the other German he'd killed, the one who'd kicked Ebbin's lifeless body and killed Publicover. Saw himself with Publicover's Bowie in his raised hand, stabbing the German over and over until he was stabbing a bloody corpse. And knew if he had the chance, he'd do it again. There was no health in him.

He blundered on across the bluff. The bending sweep of the grasses led him to the edge of the point. He staggered against the gusts. The empty beach below angled around and stretched away to the south-west, where the white surf curled in off a black sea. The tide was up. Wave after wave raced over the sandbars to lick the beach and suck out again. "Over there" was no longer the Front in France. It was the shores of home. And he belonged to neither. He was alone in an eternal limbo with the pull of the sea below and the forgotten stars above.

His knees began to buckle but as he dropped, he caught the faint green flash of a starboard running light. Someone was out there, out on the rolling, dispassionate sea, keeping watch. He could not take his eyes off the running light. But it wasn't out at sea; it was bobbing on the beach curving beyond the bluff, carried by the inky and dissolving shape of a figure standing now at the edge of the breakers. A woman.

He had to keep on the path, he knew that. Had to resist the urge to cut through the brush or he'd lose his way. He had to angle around 'til he got to where the path broke off and led to the steps. He had to take them slowly, keep his balance, hold his arm. He had to pray she was still there. And then he was at the bottom, running as best he could to where she stood in the whipping wind with the green lantern by her side.

He slowed as he approached, gathering himself in. But when she turned and faced him, when she lifted her shawl, he grabbed her wrist and pulled her in and she pulled him down so they were both on their knees, his face buried against her neck, his right arm limp at his side. All the pain and guilt, all the horror and all the longing he'd bottled up leapt and bolted through him and shattered the air around them. He was devastated and alive with release. His mouth found hers, so soft against his hunger that he drew back. She kissed his eyes and cheeks and his mouth again. And his desire to pour all he had, all that was left of him into her, overwhelmed him.

She pulled him in with a pliant strength against which he was powerless and felt more powerful than he'd ever imagined. He knew it wouldn't last, but knew, too, that nothing lasts. Nothing on earth.

SABINE LEFT THE next morning under a clear sky soon after her *ami*, in his polished black auto, pulled into the drive. An immaculate man with charcoal-gray hair and perfectly trimmed mustache, he was in far too much of a hurry for conversation. He bowed briefly, kissed Juliette's hand, and held the door. Sabine took Juliette's hands in hers.

She nodded and smiled at Angus, then secured her hat, buttoned her gloves, and blew kisses to them all.

For the next five days, Angus stayed with Juliette and Paul at the cottage on the bluff. Paul let his pigeons fly and circle home. In the late afternoons, sitting on a blanket spread out on the soft sand above the pebbled tide line, the three of them ate raspberries and crusty bread spread with goat cheese. Paul threw bits to the swooping gull scavengers and chased after flocks of sandpipers, who raced ahead on toothpick legs and lifted in unison to skim the water's edge. With the wind against his face, Angus could hear the run of the sheets through the *Lauralee*'s blocks, feel the broad swing of her bow as he took her up into the wind and she leaned into the next tack. It was all of home he allowed himself. Juliette sat under an umbrella and sometimes rolled off her stockings and waded into the wash of the sea, letting her bunched-up skirts get wet and her hair fly. Angus held her boots in his hand. He ate. He slept. He went barefoot over the hard-ridged sand flats, walking for hours. She sometimes went with him. The beach was nearly a mile wide at low tide, a vast stretch of white, with white shells tumbling in on the waves. Not a rock nor clump of seaweed to be seen. He let the surf foam around his legs and, for moments at a time, felt almost clean. In the early mornings, the sea was always the same hazy green close to shore and the same deep blue where the sandbars fell off. The surf was gentle. It did not pull him in nor under. Paul said the very best thing was that when they were not there, the sea went in and went out just the same.

Watching Paul, dripping wet in his sagging undershorts, running zigzag up the beach, cradling a sand crab in his hands, Angus saw the child Paul might have been, the child that Simon Peter was, innocent of buzzing planes, of the knowledge that birds could be enlisted in combat, that aunts could be taken for spies, that cows could have their throats slit, innocent of the shifty mutability of all that mattered. Unscathed, secure in Snag Harbor, Angus kept him there, standing on pink and gray boulder-strewn shores, watching the tides rise and fall.

One afternoon as Paul ran back to the water, Juliette stroked the puffy curled fingers of Angus's right hand. Perhaps because he could see but not feel her touch, he told her of his anguished and misbegotten attempts at capturing intersections, the binding together of the seen and the unseen, on canvas. And how cartography was the thing he was probably best at—a map of the physical world that, in its black-and-white precision, denied reality.

THEY DID NOT speak of his family, nor of her husband, whose picture stood on the bed stand at night and the kitchen sill by day. One night, lying flat on their backs on a blanket on the beach, a floating moon above them, he told her about his men and what Conlon meant to him as a leader and a friend. Then he sat up and, looking beyond the beach at the waves collapsing over themselves, told her everything that had happened at the stone barn. She sat up as well, and after a time told him it was she who had taken Paul to the uncle for safety, the very day the Germans had slit the uncle's throat in the barn and slaughtered his cows and left their corpses in the field to rot. She who had abandoned him while she ran back to attend to the demands of the German soldiers tramping into her house.

Angus lowered his head at this and the demands he imagined the Germans had made. He reached out his open palm and she slipped her hand into it, and they lay back again and watched the moon drift between the clouds. They held on to what they had just then, which was all they had and enough.

Outside on the afternoon of the fifth day, Angus stood by the door. Next to Juliette, Paul hung his head. Angus reached into his pack and drew out the smoothed oval board with the ink drawing of the lark. "Remember her when things get tough. She finds the good, like you." Paul bobbed his head up and down, unable to speak. Angus gripped the back of his neck and told him he was the best soldier and best friend anyone could have. Paul sank against him. "You will go back to the Front?" he said into Angus's shirt. Angus told him he would try. Paul stepped back and gave him a salute. Then he turned and ran to Édouard, Papete and Angelica. Angus stared after him and, without looking at her, drew Juliette in and held her with all the strength in him.

TWENTY-THREE

August 15th, 1917
Snag Harbor, Nova Scotia

r. Heist was on his knees, plucking at weeds, as Simon approached. He was relieved to see the Fresnel light back under its tarp on the porch and no sign of a lookout tower—though there was a stack of lumber by the shed that hadn't been there the week before. He had warned Mr. Heist against the tower again and again.

"Simon!" Mr. Heist said, shielding his eyes from the sun. "You're early by a day for your lessons! Did you bring *The Iliad*?" He arched his back. "*Ach*, this weeding is a trial."

"I'm not here for lessons." It seemed a long time ago that Mr. Heist had given him the book—had given him the choice, actually, between *The Iliad* and *The Odyssey*—the battle for Troy or the homecoming? Simon had chosen the battle, even though Mr. Heist had claimed the journey home was equally if not more entertaining. The truth was, Simon had lost interest in Troy after his father was wounded. Men could do a lot of things without their right arm, but not sail a boat, tie a rope, paint a picture. Hoping against hope that his father would recover, he didn't actually want to think about battles because now what Simon wanted more than anything was for his father to be safe, to stay alive, to come home. His grandfather was right. The war was unending. Yet, when he pictured his father, it was on top of Vimy Ridge, "noble in sacrifice," quiet in victory. A crippled arm would not undo him. The worse the situation, the stronger and steadier his father became. Simon remembered a time when lightning was striking the ocean all around the boat a mile or two off Peggy's Cove. Terrified, he began to hope that if the mast was struck and the boat sank, they could swim to shore. He knew the water was too cold, but he shouted out anyway, "If the boat sinks, we could swim to Peggy's, right? It's not that far! Just a mile or two. We could make it!" Dodging spray, his father kept his eyes on the sail. "Wish that were true," he said.

Mr. Heist had said that to truly appreciate either story, *The Iliad* or *The Odyssey*, Simon should read it in the original Greek. Even the best translation could not hope to capture the epic's cadence and rhythm nor the layers of meaning that made up what he called the "poet's armament—a quiver of arrows that could pierce the thickest hide and reveal shared pain and ineffable joy."

When Simon had asked what "ineffable" meant, Mr. Heist had said that if he knew the classic languages, he would not have to ask. And so it was that Simon began a study of ancient Greek twice a week with Mr. Heist, who had claimed after a month that a boy right here in Snag Harbor with such facility for languages and thirst for knowledge was itself a source of ineffable joy.

"I'm not here for lessons," Simon repeated. "I've come to warn you."

"Another warning," Mr. Heist said, ticking his tongue. "Alright then." He mopped his face, but before Simon could begin, Mr. Heist said he had something very exciting to show him and hurried toward the cottage. Once inside, he unveiled a high-powered telescope and tripod. "Excellent for the night sky and think how far it takes me during the day!"

"A telescope? Are you—?" *Nuts*, Simon wanted to say. "I told you, everyone thinks you're building a signal tower. What're they going to say about a *telescope?*"

Mr. Heist carefully scrubbed the dirt from his hands with a stiff brush at the kitchen sink. He replaced the brush and the bar of yellow soap in a dish, wiped his hands, and sat down with an almost amused expression. "And I've told you," he said, "how could it be that a wooden platform on stilts—an act so bold and a structure so obvious—would ever be construed as a means of secretly signaling anyone? And what secrets might a mere schoolteacher have access to? That blueberries are in season? That monarch butterflies passed through last May? That with my telescope I saw a whale spouting off Big Tancook?" He glanced at the instrument fondly and said, "Here, let's get it out onto the porch so you can see—"

"Don't you see, Mr. Heist? You could sight a submarine periscope from up here with that thing," Simon pleaded. "I told you, Frank Mason and other fellers say subs have been sighted here in Mahone Bay."

"To my knowledge, Simon, there has not been a single confirmed report of submarine activity in Mahone Bay," Mr. Heist sighed. "And although it is powerful, my telescope cannot see beyond the bay, over the curve of the earth."

"*Please*, Mr. Heist, you have to think how it *looks*."

"Ah yes. But one can't narrow one's existence down to how things look. One has to respect oneself above all. Besides, come September, the townfolk will see me back at my desk, teaching their children, just as I taught them in their day. They'll see me as the loyal, upstanding member of the community I've been these past twenty years—fifteen years a citizen."

"But that's just it! That's what I came to tell you. Grandpa says there was a meeting, a *secret* meeting, about whether they'll hire you back next year. There's talk they're not going to."

"What meeting?"

"I don't know! I think Lady Bromley and Vor Moody, the Bethunes, some others. Grandpa was worried."

"Well, I am not. I have already signed a contract. That is a legal and binding document."

This was a relief, but a minor one. "If you're so sure people aren't against you, why have you stayed out here all summer?"

"There is a war on. And you're right—I am sensitive to the perceptions of others. As a teacher, I wear a badge, the honor of the profession, and am a respected member of the community. In the summer, I am just a man with a German accent. So, I have kept to myself. But in the end, I trust the majority of the community to behave rationally."

He rubbed his glasses with his handkerchief. "My tower and my telescope are my connection, my way of breaching the boundaries of a narrow world."

After a few moments of awkward silence, Mr. Heist asked if Simon wanted to take his lesson now. But Simon said no, he had taken the morning off from his job with Philip and had to get back. Mr. Heist patted his arm and said he was glad Simon so enjoyed his work and to stick with it. He had a feeling it would pay off someday, far more than Greek translation. Simon had told Philip all about the *Repulse Bay*, shown him his drawings, but hadn't found the words to explain it to Mr. Heist, who didn't know a hatch from a halyard. Yet, he somehow seemed to understand.

PHILIP WASN'T AT the boatyard, but Charlotte was. She'd brought him lunch. They dangled their feet off the end of the wharf as she unwrapped the sandwiches and brought out a bottle of tea. He told her about going to see Mr. Heist. "I don't know how a man so smart can be so dumb."

"Do you think something bad might happen?" Charlotte asked.

"If he builds that tower . . ."

"Why's he building it anyway? It doesn't make sense, does it?"

"It does for him. He wants to see beyond Owl's Head Point. You'd have to know him to understand." Simon picked up his sandwich, but didn't eat it. Instead, he surprised himself by telling Charlotte about his recurring dream.

No wonder he felt bad, she said, when he'd finished describing how the sea was sucked out, and all the fish lay flopping in wilted ribbons of kelp, and how the boats lay on their sides. It was a horrible dream. After a moment she said, "Don't you think that dreams, good or bad, shape things to come?"

"You mean foretell the future?"

"No, like they color the whole next day. Cheery dreams make things a bright sunny yellow. But scary ones—everything seems smoky green afterwards."

"Yeah, exactly," Simon said. The *Glory B* rounded up into the cove, and Philip thumped down the steps to the wharf. "Charlotte, Simon, how's by you? How's by me? Not too bagatally. The *Glory B*'s coming in for her new gaff boom. Look smart and grab their line, Simon."

Simon caught the line from Davy. "Miss Charlotte!" Putnam said in his high, foggy voice, ducking under the boom. "Kindly catch our stern line, m'dear." Sure enough, she caught it, and Simon showed her how to make a couple of half-hitches over the piling. "Got your oilskins yet?" Davy asked her.

While he and Simon furled the mainsail, Philip conferred with Putnam about a few more repairs the *Glory B* needed. Then Putnam held out his hand for Charlotte, and they all stepped aboard. "I'd say you look poorly, Simon," Putnam said. "Hain't this girl got sweetness enough to cheer you?" Putnam opened a jug of coffee and passed out mugs all around. "Have some coffee, boy," he said to Simon. As Philip poured a little something from his flask into Putnam and Davy's mugs, Davy said he'd heard the *Repulse Bay* was being refitted. "Feller name of—what was it, Putnam, feller who owned her?"

"Baxter B. Weatherly," Putnam said. "From somewhere in the States. Seems he lost his every dime in an export scheme gone bad."

"That's right. She's been bought by a consortium in Halifax. Going to fit her out as a fishing schooner, so far without a name."

"I know what I'd name her," Simon said.

"What's that?" Philip asked.

"*True North.*"

"Well, there you have a name," Philip said, rolling a toothpick around his tongue.

"Fix on true north and you'll get where you want to go," Putnam said, taking a long draught from his mug.

Simon asked if they'd seen a boy named Lathen Pike when they were in Lunenburg and told the story of how Lathen had come to be there from Reeks Cove, Newfoundland.

"Believe I did. He might be working down to Smith and Rhuland's yard. Saw a boy there of about that age. Burly feller," Davy said.

"Reeks Cove!" said Putnam. "That boy must be a Tilley. Those are my people."

"He's a Pike," Simon corrected him.

"Course he is. I heard you. Pikes and Tilleys are all mixed in. Noseworthys, too." Not to be outdone by Simon's story of Lathen, Putnam said he had one from his father about old Etta Tilley, eighty-one at the time, born and bred in Reeks Cove and clearly an ancestor of the boy, Lathen. He cleared his throat. "Now as it happens, my father was visiting one of the Tilleys in Reeks Cove, don't rightly know which. After supper, everyone from all around crowded into Bascom Tilley's house to hear him tell stories when Hebron Noseworthy bust in, white as a sheet. Struck dumb, he was. T'were all he could do to point out the door. So they all ran out, and their jaws hung open, for what they saw was a harbor empty of water. Tide had sucked so far out that boats were lying on their sides. But t'weren't no ordinary tide. Happened all at once, see? And then Heb cries out that what the sea took out she'd be a-flinging back and they better run for their lives. That's when they saw a wall of water a-roarin' back in. They ran up the hill 'til they could run no more—old folk, young ones—Etta, too, but not afore she grabbed the wooden cross off the partin'.

"That wall of water came crashing in, and she took the boats, took the wharf, and the houses with. She was a-roaring up the hill, sure to swallow them up. Etta Tilley stops dead in her tracks and turns. Stood her ground on a granite rock and faced down that wall of water with her wizened face fierce and her black dress a-billowing out, and the cross held straight in her outstretched arm. And by God, as I live and breathe, the sea stopped right there and drew itself back."

"Holy smokes!" Simon said. He glanced at Charlotte, who was staring at Putnam with wide eyes.

Putnam tipped his hat.

Davy, leaning back, crossed his legs and said laconically, "You didn't say a word about the dogs and goats and such, Putnam."

"What dogs and goats? Oh yes, I see how you mean. Turns out the goats and cats and dogs all about scrambled up the ridge *before* Heb Noseworthy even saw what he saw. Seems they knew aforehand what they needed to do."

"That's better," Davy said. "That's more of a story—made her more lively, see?"

"She was lively enough in the first telling. Look at them young ones here. Looks like they seen a ghost, so I'd say she was fine enough in first telling, without your dogs and cats. And goats."

"Nope, t'weren't," Davy said. "It's them small things make a story worth the time it takes to listen."

"Who's the collector here? You or me?"

Simon broke in. "So, when—when was this?"

"Years afore you were born. Afore I was born, and I must be near a hundred now." Putnam smiled.

"But what was it? What made that happen?" Charlotte asked.

"Don't know. See, Davy? Miss Charlotte here was right taken with my telling."

Davy scratched his jaw. "Could be something come out of the sky, made a hole in the sea and sucked the ocean down into it."

"Doubt that," Philip said, foregoing the coffee and drinking straight from his flask.

"Or one of them earthquakes."

"Well," said Philip, "how could it be an earthquake if it happened out at sea?"

"Alright, a seaquake, then," Davy answered.

"Now that's just stupid," Putnam said.

THAT EVENING, HIS grandfather's response was yes, he'd heard of an undersea quake before the turn of the century that had struck the southern part of Newfoundland with what he called a tidal wave, and, of course, earthquakes could and did occur on the ocean floor because what was the ocean floor if not the earth covered by water? These answers led Simon to the conclusion that the world as he knew it, the world without end, could erupt at any moment and sweep away all that is and was.

THAT CONCLUSION WAS verified the following week as the Mounties hauled away Mr. Heist's telescope and Fresnel lens, pulled down his wharf lamps and packed them off as well, and raked through all of Mr. Heist's books, tossing them on the floor, and seizing all the ones written in German and all of his papers, and even his butterfly notebooks, as "potential evidence." It was Simon's grandfather, not Mr. Heist, who had to be physically moved from the door of Mr. Heist's cottage; his grandfather who followed the Mounties from house to garden protesting their search, imploring them to stop; his grandfather who got roughly knocked to the ground when he tried to wrest the telescope from their hands. Throughout it all, Mr. Heist, who had been informed his services at the school would no longer be required, sat slumped in shock at the red kitchen table.

It was Simon's grandfather who stood up in church the following Sunday after the Apostle's Creed and accused the congregation of turning on one of their own, claiming that God would rain down retribution upon Nova Scotia, that there would be hell to pay, before he stalked out the door. And it was Simon Peter who walked out with him.

TWENTY-FOUR

August 15th, 1917
No. 18 Canadian General Hospital
Saint-Junien, France

In the filtered sunlight of the woods on the way back to Saint-Junien, Angus stopped. He'd been walking fast, with his head down to keep from turning back to the cottage and with the thought circling round his head that the only way he'd been able to stay with Juliette and Paul was knowing he would leave them, and the only way he could leave them was to think he might see them again. In the shifting shadows, birds flicked from branch to branch, and small feet scurried through leaves on the forest floor. Nothing else broke the silence. For a moment he considered idling there and obliterating all thought, but a tingling down his arm and pinpricks in his hand brought him back to the road he was on.

Boes had said it would take three months for nerves to regenerate. It had been more than that, but all the same—his arm seemed to be tingling. His hand as well. Surely it was evidence that the paralysis was physical, not in his mind. He resolved to ask for therapy three times a day. He picked up his pace. He nearly ran. He would recover. He would recover.

Full of his own purpose, he reached the top of the hill overlooking the Saint-Junien station, but there came to a full stop. Below him convoys of wounded soldiers were being offloaded from the trains. Transport vehicles, lorries and motor ambulances were rumbling to and from the station. Angus ran down the hill into the confusion of stretcher-bearers and the walking wounded, the bleeding out, the gassed, the lame and the nearly dead. Cradling his arm, he managed to hop onto the running board of a truck headed to the hospital.

As the truck entered the courtyard, Angus jumped off and found Brimmie directing the flow of wounded men. She told him Cobb and Brown had been killed with five nurses while touring field hospitals at the Front. Boes had been spared, and had been in surgery with Spinner and Sadler nonstop for twenty hours. If he wanted to help, go to supply. There he helped a Corporal Lee load boxes onto a wheeled trolley headed for Ward D. Lee told him that Lovell and three other nursing sisters had been shipped off to London with iodoform poisoning days before. Angus looked at the boxes of the crystalline antiseptic on the trolley and imagined the nurses' hands yellow and swollen from overapplication of it. He wheeled the boxes to Ward D himself. There amid the shrieks of pain piercing the air, he was soon carrying bedpans, handing out packages of cotton wool, holding basins for dirty dressings and vomit.

From what he could gather, divisions of the CEF had been part of a force that had taken Hill 70 above the town of Lens, long held by the Germans. Taken it in twenty minutes and then, supplies dwindling, hungry and mired down, had nonetheless repulsed some twenty counterattacks that included mustard gas and flamethrowers. All while he'd been at the cottage. He had no idea who among his band had survived. More than once he was sure he saw Conlon, but was wrong every time.

Every bed was occupied and extra cots set up again in the great hall where he'd woken up so long ago to Nurse Lovell's face. In one of the cots he found Wertz struggling for breath from a chest wound.

Angus clasped his hand and leaned in close. Wertz told him Conlon was alive, and Boudrey. And LaPointe. Maybe Katz and Hanson. He didn't know who else. But who would take care of Boudrey, he asked. Angus tightened his grip. "I'll see to it, if I can," he said. When he returned late that night, Wertz was gone, his bed occupied.

At four in the morning, Angus made his way back to the ward he'd shared with the other rehab cases Boes had been working on. They'd been shipped back to England two days before, he was told. In his own bed lay a private with mustard-gas blisters bubbling across his face.

In the hallway Angus slumped down and, with his back against the wall, shut his eyes. Wertz. All his men. He wanted to suffer with them, to savor small victories, be with them at the razor's edge of life and death—not as some kind of penance, but to feel whole. As he felt now in the chaos of the hospital. His arm was alive with pins and needles. His hand was coming back. He couldn't flex it, couldn't move it; but in his exhaustion, he was sure he felt blood pulsing through it.

"MacGrath?"

It was Boes, standing across the dimly lit hallway, removing a bloody surgeon's gown. He motioned Angus into his office and col-lapsed into a chair behind his desk. The lamplight was low. Boes looked up with sunken eyes. Behind him, the tangled wires of the condenser apparatus dangled over the edge of a table. He told Angus to take a chair. For a moment neither of them spoke.

"Cobb's dead. Did you know that?" Boes said.

"I heard."

"And some of our best nurses." Boes reached for his pen. "I'm a major now, for what it's worth. I'm having you invalided home."

Angus jerked upright. *Home?* "But . . . May I speak?"

"Of course. Speak at will, but it won't change my mind." He unscrewed his pen and began filling in a form on his desk.

"But I'm getting better. I swear to you. I've felt pins and needles in my arm just like you said I would. Those are my men out there. I need to be with them, see this through."

"Your men are headed toward Flanders to join the British 2nd Army. Currie's finally committed them to Passchendaele. They'll be in it in days. How is it you're going to be with them?" Boes stopped writing and gave him a weary look. "You're an officer who can't hold a pistol and a cartographer who can't hold a pencil. I'm sending you home."

"What about a hospital in England? I can recover. I know I can."

"You've had months of therapy and it hasn't helped. More than I should have given you. Maybe I wanted to prove something." He glanced up. "I'm sorry, but they'll have nothing more to offer you."

"Well, maybe this is all in my mind. You thought that once. What about one of those, those war hospitals for whatever you call it—hystericals?"

"MacGrath," Boes countered slowly, "have you any idea? There are six civilian hospitals in Britain that can manage what they're calling 'shell shock,' and the military has set up another six for officers and some thirteen more for ranks. They're filling up with gibbering, incoherent men who can't speak or walk, who have lost all balance. That's not you."

Angus sat back and looked Boes in the eye. "You don't think I'll recover."

"I didn't say that. I said you'll manage, just not as a soldier. You'll find your way. Trust me."

Angus jumped to his feet. "Why should I? You said I'd get better. You said to trust the condenser apparatus. You can't just change your mind like that. You're a *doctor*. Why should I trust—"

Boes dropped the pen and held his head in his hands. "Because," he said softly, "I am a *good* doctor." Without another word, he filled out the rest of the form.

✧

FIVE DAYS LATER, Angus was gripping the rail of a hospital transport steaming through misty rain and choppy seas to the other side of the Channel. His hand was numb again. He could hardly find his balance, yet refused to find a seat inside. Insisted on staying on deck. Prayed he would not lose his footing. From England he'd be sent home, while Conlon and the rest of them marched to Flanders. As the French coastline disappeared from view, he felt a despair such as he had never known.

TWENTY-FIVE

September 15th, 1917
Snag Harbor, Nova Scotia

imon Peter stared for a long time at the scale drawing
he'd made of the *Lauralee*. The thought of giving it to his
father was now unbearable. He put it away in the bottom drawer and pulled out his Great War scrapbook. He adjusted the
book on his lap and opened its wide cover. Staring up at him in white
ink on the black page was THE GREAT WAR 1914– in his own hand.
Beneath the title were the gay little Union Jack and Red Ensign that
he'd cut and pasted in when he got the book and which, as he looked
at them now, seemed altogether too small next to the printed letters.

A stack of newspaper articles, weighted down by a pair of scissors, lay untouched on the floor beside his desk—stories on Vimy and
Hill 70, on Third Ypres, on U-boat sightings—uncut, unpasted, and
some of them unread. Next to the news clippings was the *Lepidoptera of Eastern North America*, which he'd rescued the day Mr. Heist
had been hauled away, along with Pope's translation of *The Iliad* and
Mr. Heist's Greek-English dictionary. Tucked away in the back of the
desk drawer was a lacquered box. In it was the key to Mr. Heist's cottage. Mr. Heist had asked him to take what books he wanted and to
care for the plants and garden, if he was able, while he was detained

in the camp. "Detained" turned out to be a nice way of saying "held prisoner"; "camp," a nice way of saying "prison."

The camp, in Amherst, up on the New Brunswick–Nova Scotia border, was a former ironworks factory, requisitioned for prisoners of war and suspicious enemy aliens. Mr. Heist was not an alien, though he hadn't been able to produce his papers. He was not an enemy combatant, obviously, nor an enemy sympathizer, which is what he was called. But there he was with the rest of them—hundreds of sailors from the *Kaiser Wilhelm der Grosse*, sunk in 1915, sailors from other ships, various untrustworthy, roughshod Canadians, and a large group of "suspicious" aliens—many of German origin and few, if any, men of letters, according to Mr. Heist. They were stacked up in bunks two deep and three high with hardly space to breathe. German officers, some of them quite gallant and gentlemanly, had their own quarters, he'd written to Simon.

Simon had hoped to have the scrapbook ready to show his father, but he had no energy for it, not anymore. And he doubted his father would either. All that mattered was that he was coming home. Like Ida said, it was a miracle. A long nightmare over. We'll get that arm of his better, she said. The hats-aloft wave on the troop ship, his father and Ebbin running down the gangway, people cheering, flags waving and a band playing—the fixed image Simon used to snap into place when needed—was long gone. Tucked away like his lead soldiers in a box. The scrapbook slipped. He lowered it to the floor and reached for the lacquered box. Next to the Heist key was a tiny framed oval of Charlotte, much younger, but with the same gray eyes and open expression. He wanted his father to meet her. They'd taken a long walk the day before the Bromleys had shipped her off to Edgehill School. They'd vowed to write. They'd agreed that his father would set things right by Mr. Heist. His father was an officer, after all. A wounded officer. A decorated officer. Comfort was in her hand in his as they parted, and there in the upturn of her generous mouth, and in the very softness of her lips when, unexpectedly, he'd pressed his mouth against hers. In the trance of it, a memory as close as the moment itself, he set the box down and touched his fingers to his lips.

H.M.S. *Regina*
September 15th, 1917

In the damp claustrophobia of the cabin he shared with an amputee named Peers, Angus watched a pencil roll from one side of the foot locker to the other, letting it drop in his hand each time it fell off the edge. Peers finished vomiting into the bucket and sank back in his bunk. Angus pressed a damp cloth against his face, lost his balance and nearly smothered the man. Peers moaned. The cabin reeked. Lurching and slamming against the walls of the airless corridor, Angus found his way to the head and emptied the bucket. There wasn't much but bile—Peers had been retching for an hour. Angus rinsed it as best he could and nearly vomited himself. When he got back, Peers was asleep, his breathing steady. He slept on and, finally, Angus went up on deck so he could breathe.

The ship sat high above the ocean, detached from wind or current. The deck shuddered as the engines clanged below. Twin screws churned up the water at the stern. The furious white-green chaos of the wake rose up and fell away to sudsy bubbles in the swells—a long, long trail winding back to all that was left behind and left undone.

To starboard, a darkened patch of rippled sea swept toward them. Just a gust. But the pressure was dropping. A storm was coming. The sky was gun-metal gray, and up ahead, angry cumulus clouds gathered. Green lightning zipped through them. They'd be in it in less than an hour, he told a crewman, who nodded in somber agreement. Black smoke belched from the stacks above and Angus considered the effects of the coming storm on the rattletrap of a converted troop ship. The captain would have to alter course to keep the seas from hitting them broadside. And if those engines failed, what then? They'd be flotsam, tossed about until the sea rolled them over and moved on. There was nothing heroic about death by drowning. But perhaps it was a fitting end.

They were south of Newfoundland when the storm hit. Winds howled. Seas raged. It was as bad as Angus predicted. But the gale's fury engendered a familiar fortitude until a wave caught them from behind, lifting the stern so that the props churned helplessly in the air and the rudder failed to catch. Then they were rushing forward and down, but not, as it turned out, to the bottom.

How many times he fell on the gangways and hallways below decks to get to Peers, he did not know, but finally, hunching along on his knees, his entire left side in pain, he found the cabin. There was Peers, jammed against the bunk board, near-catatonic. Angus had intended somehow to drag him to the upper decks near the lifeboats, but the lights went out, and drained of all caring, Angus heaved himself up on the bunk. There he lay beside Peers, his good arm across him, gripping the board to keep from slamming back in the nosedives and from crushing Peers when the ship pitched up against the next towering wave. He said nothing, for he had no voice.

At some point the lights came on and the ship turned back on course. The storm had come; the end had not. Angus made his way to the upper deck in a daze. In the main saloon, a couple of sailors swept up shattered glass. Out on deck, stars winked out from a fast-moving cloud cover. The ship steamed on. A day later they were told they were within sight of Nova Scotia and coming onto Halifax. Angus helped Peers, limp as a rag, out to the rail, where all those who could ambulate had gathered for the landfall. A cheer went up. Then another, louder, and louder still. And then the men fell silent. Home. Her jagged inlets and coves smoothed to a solid line by distance, a washed-clean purity against the broken land they'd left.

"Chezzetcook!" one of the men up forward shouted. "They say

we're just off Chezzetcook!" Those who knew the land they were passing hung on the rail and conjured up wild sea grasses, bluffs and spongy bogs, stony, boulder-strewn beaches, and the dark green firs and turning maples of the eastern shore. A blinded soldier said he could smell low tide. No one corrected him.

When they passed Sambro Light, the fog rolled in again. It held as they made the turn into the deep water passage to Halifax Harbor. The low moan of the steam foghorn on Chebucto Head could be heard. As they passed McNabs Island, an apparition in the mist, a private from New Brunswick began singing, soft and slow.

"Un Canadien errant,
Banni de ses foyers,
Parcourait en pleurant
Des pays étrangers.

"Parcourait en pleurant
Des pays étrangers
Un jour, triste et pensif,
Assis au bord des flots,
Au courant fugitif
Il adressa ces mots . . ."

"What's he singing?" Peers wanted to know.

"An old folk tune. *'Un Canadien Errant,'*" Angus replied. "'The Lost Canadian.'"

Peers shook his head.

"A man is banished from his homeland—from Acadia when the English took it, I'd guess. He travels on, weeping through foreign lands. Then he sits by a rushing river."

The song ended with the sad refrain,

"Si tu vois mon pays,
Mon pays malheureux.
Va, dire à mes amis,
Que je me souviens d'eux."

Peers looked to Angus. "He says to the river, if you see my country, my sad, sad country, go say to all my friends that I remember them," Angus translated, and added, "Our sad country . . ."

"Lies back there," the soldier next to him quietly filled in.

"That's right," another said, letting the tears fall. "Good men, every last one of them."

"We won't forget," another said.

Angus leaned out over the rail. With each familiar landmark, buoy and channel marker they passed as they were piloted up the harbor, a widening gulf opened—one he could not bridge back to himself. Yet, still his heart was beating.

WHEN ANGUS STEPPED off the train at the Chester station, Zeb was there in his truck, alone, as Angus had requested. The ship had docked a day ahead of schedule. Papers signed, discharge complete, Angus had been free to go in so short a time that he'd wandered the streets in a daze. At the North Street Station he bought a ticket, then waited in the tearoom of the King Edward, the plush comforts of which nearly suffocated him. He stared at his cup until his tea went cold.

Zeb scratched his chin and gave him the once-over. "By Christ. Look like you been in a war," he said. "Did like you said. Didn't tell the home folk, but we can put in a call at the stationmaster's, if you've a mind to. Call the store and have Alvin run up to your house with the news."

Angus shook his head and got into the truck.

Zeb held the steering wheel in both hands before shifting into gear. They bumped along in silence around the back harbor road and up to the Chester bandstand, where Zeb slowed and idled the engine. Angus stared at Lobster Point and out at the whale-shaped mound of Quaker Island, bereft of trees, cows grazing contentedly, and at Meisner's, her sparse, pointed firs, black silhouettes against the sky. Then he leaned out the window and twisted back at Little Fish, Gooseberry and the Western Shore. The blues and greens of the bay and the islands in all their bright, clean, alien beauty, and the wharfs and boats and nestled shore houses were somehow still there, patiently waiting—a flat picture postcard suspended in time.

"Some things don't change, eh?" Zeb said.

Angus leaned back and closed his eyes with the warmth of the sun on his face. Zeb turned the engine off. "Look there now." He pointed to a boat coming in, running before the wind. "One of them pleasure yachts. Feller from the States, Philadelphia, Baltimore maybe, owns her. Built a house up on the hill there just for the summers." Angus kept his eyes on the boat, her main and jib set wing and wing, like a great bird. Zeb waited a moment more, then turned the key, put the truck in gear.

They drove in silence with the occasional nod from Zeb at some point of interest—a new cottage or a familiar landmark. As they neared Snag Harbor, Zeb shifted around in his seat and began talking rapidly, as if he was nervous about something. "Plenty of changes since you've been gone," he began. "That boy of yours is growing up fast. Not much taller, but some. Has a sweetheart now name of Charlotte Plante, the Bromleys' niece, over here from England. And let's see now. Hettie's cut her hair off. She tell you? Lord Jesus, she's Ebbin all over again."

"Cut her hair?"

"Cut it right off. Has the women talking nonstop. Course you know that Duncan's 'bout turned the business over to her. And han't she taken to it. Heading off on that horse of hers, buying up land and sawmills and timber and Lord knows what." He shook his head, smiling. "Folks don't like it much, but she don't seem to notice. Not Hettie. Never did." Angus ran his hand across his mouth to cover his shock, to hide from Zeb how much he didn't know. He reminded himself of all he'd kept from Hettie.

"Then there's that Heist business," Zeb was saying. "Guess you know about that. Him being a spy." He jerked a look at Angus. "Duncan didn't write you about it? Or Hettie?"

"Heist?"

"Yep, yes sir," Zeb said. He flexed his fingers on the wheel. "Got no papers to prove he's a citizen. Hauled off to the camp up at Amherst. Mounties ransacked his house. A traitor, turns out."

"A traitor?"

"Had to get a new teacher for the upper grades. Miss Engle. Stick legs and a scrawny neck. One hundred and ten, if she's a day. But Avon Heist is gone for good."

Angus was shaking his head. "I don't believe a word of it. Heist a traitor? It doesn't make sense."

"Well, now, that'd be your choice. That'd be the choice Duncan made, but I'm telling you it's the wrong choice. Heist had letters from the other side. Vor Moody said so all along. And he was building a signal tower to contact submarines."

"C'mon, Zeb." Angus tried to picture Mr. Heist in his suit and vest up on a tower flashing Morse code to a surfaced sub. He nearly laughed.

"Yep. All them years telling us he was a citizen." Zeb shifted into a lower gear. "Dickie Bethune says Heist had family killed over there— might have tipped him over the edge. Good thing you're home, boy, wounded or no, is all I can say. With those ribbons and medals on your chest, it'll make a difference."

"What kind of a difference? What are you talking about?" By then they were jouncing down the rutted turnoff for Snag Harbor and into Mader's Cove. As they approached Mader's boatyard, Angus asked Zeb to stop the truck. Zeb shook his head. He flexed his hand on the wheel. "Don't you want to get home?" he asked. "Stop the truck," Angus repeated. That's an order, he almost added. "I just want a look at her. Let me out."

Zeb slowed the truck and narrowed his eyes at the road. "No you don't," he said softly. "You don't want to go down there. Not just yet." But Angus had the door open. Zeb put on the brake and gripped his arm. "There's some things as happened here now that are no good. No good a'tall." Angus was out of the truck and down the wharf. There, lifting in the shallows of the slipway, were the charred remains of the *Lauralee,* the imprint of her name still visible in gold scroll along her bow.

The burnt timbers receded. The cove with them, telescoping away, until all that was left was her name. "There now. Terrible. Terrible shock. Weren't meant to see this. Not yet." He heard the voice, but the ringing in his ears grew louder, a high-pitched buzzing that canceled out sound. And then he was on the move, down the ladder, up to his ankles in the water, up to his knees, reaching for the bowsprit until he got his hand around it.

Men gathered behind him on the stony beach. The buzzing subsided, and in the silence he could hear their every unuttered word. The pity of it, the sorrow, the shame. Come home to this. At his feet through the clear water, the spine of a green sea urchin spiked up at him. A pod of yellow rockweed swayed forward and back in the hush, hush, hush of the waves lapping the keel and blackened hull. God did this, he thought. Sealed his fate. Emotion slowly drained out of him and the numbing cold of the water entered in. He lifted his head, loosened his grip on the bowsprit. He had nothing left. He would ask the necessary questions, receive the proffered answers, and move on.

Philip gripped his shoulder when Angus finally waded out of the water. He stood there in his dripping kilt, looking at him with dull eyes, and waited. Philip patted his overalls and pulled out his pipe but didn't light it. "Duncan wanted her in the water of a sudden week or so ago," he began. "Maybe 'cause you were coming home. I needed that cradle. He knew that. Had me do a few repairs. Not enough to get her back in business, but we launched her, stepped the masts that afternoon. Anchored her here in the cove. I was to check her fittings. There was a storm that night. Not much rain, but lightning bouncing off the water. Must have struck her masts."

"She was ablaze and adrift, headed toward the *Elsie*," Wallace added. "T'were Frank and his boys got a line onto her and towed her out to the harbor. Rain came up and she burned to what you see there. Towed what was left back here." He took off his cap.

Zeb spoke up. "Some say the fire was set, and she was set adrift. By George Mather, maybe, or by some as wanted to give your father a warning for calling the town a bunch of traitors when Heist was arrested. Some say the old man set it himself for insurance money."

"Shut your mouth, would you, Zeb?" Philip sighed. "You saw the look on Duncan's face when she was burning. It was an act of God."

"An act of God," Angus repeated dully.

"That'd be my summation," Philip said, then he reached down for a canvas sack, out of which he pulled the *Lauralee*'s compass. "Took it off her myself. You can repair the glass. The brass was blackened, but all it needed was polish." He held it in both hands, angling it around so the needle spun. "See? Still works." Angus ran his fingers across the broken glass, then met Philip's eyes. Wallace fingered his cap and slapped it back on. The incoming tide inched slowly up over the wreckage.

Angus climbed into Zeb's truck without looking back. By the time they crossed the causeway, he was as detached from the boat as from himself. He left Zeb at the bottom of the hill and walked the rest of the way alone. He wanted to enter quietly. To take in the surroundings slowly, as if waking from the fog of dream, preparing himself for the letting go and the taking in of the tangible world. Here the old spruce trees, there the house, and there in the yard under the gnarled old tree a young boy, who was not Simon Peter, as he'd thought with a quickening heart, but Young Fred. Of course, Young Fred, who was lining up pencils—his pencil people, it came to Angus—on the swing. When Angus knelt down next to him, Young Fred gave him a shy smile as if his presence was no more fantastical than his talking pencils. Or perhaps too unreal to be true. It was a moment before he leaned toward Angus and let himself be hugged. "You're wet," he said. "You were fighting sea monsters." Angus said that was just about right. Young Fred turned back to the swing. "The ones who are naughty fall off when I push. The good ones stay on. See?" He gave the swing an almost imperceptible push. All but one of the pencils rolled off, a long red one with teeth marks up and down. Fred picked it up and thrust it toward Angus. "It's you," he said, beaming. "This good one is the Dad." It was then, with Young Fred's hand gripping the red pencil in one hand and the other resting lightly on his shoulder, that Angus wept and could not stop.

SIMON KICKED PEG'S flanks when they reached the Mathers' field, but she wouldn't budge. Simon hadn't seen George since the *Lauralee* had burned. But he'd seen the look in George's eyes when the Mounties had hauled Mr. Heist away. It was said that he broke his mother's crockery that night and ripped up her roses and buried them upside down in the yard. Even from the road, Simon could see that they were chopped down to nothing. But he didn't risk getting close enough to see if they were upside down. He may not have believed that George had burned the *Lauralee*, but the world had turned dark and dangerous. Though not to Peg. She lowered her head and began to nose the grass. He jumped down, turned her into the field, closed the gate and started walking.

The Heist cottage was set far enough off the road and behind a bank of evergreens, so if you missed the path leading up to the back of the cottage, you'd miss it altogether. The first time Simon had ventured inside on his own, the front room had been a sea of splayed-open books. He'd shaken each one out as he re-shelved them. There were gaps in the shelves where the confiscated German books might have stood. He'd checked every emptied drawer, but had found only a tin box of matches embossed with a German cross on the lid and a few flimsy envelopes, none of which held Mr. Heist's citizenship papers.

The next time, he'd cleaned up the mess the Mounties had made of the kitchen and bedroom. Both times he'd sat for a while on a rocker on the front porch facing the bay and the garden and ended his visit down on the wharf, where he made sure the rowboat was secure and pictured Mr. Heist in his life preserver, rowing out with the long line tied to the wharf. The last time, Simon had sat in the boat itself, reading and rereading Charlotte's letter—a very long letter in rounded script with stories about the girls and teachers that made him laugh. She had no idea about the *Lauralee*. He hadn't been able to find the words to describe the sight of her that night, adrift like a fire ship, flames licking up her rigging, her mast crashing into the water. Huddled on shore with everyone in town watching her burn, Zenus had whispered to Simon that she'd come back, just like the *Teazer*, to haunt the South Shore. His grandfather, eyes rimmed and red, said the next morning that with her trading days over, she didn't want to be stripped down, nor left to rot. Simon took immense comfort from this. God had acted, had a plan. But he couldn't imagine what that plan was for Mr. Heist unless it was that Simon was to help him find a way out.

When he reached the cottage, he headed around it to the bayside and into the front garden. He intended to take the path to steps down through the woods to the wharf. All he wanted was to sit there and think, to try to pull all the threads together—his father coming home, life without the *Lauralee*. He needed to be alone.

But he was not alone. He froze at the sound of glass shattering, followed by a thud and jeering laughter from the back of the house. As he turned in confusion, the air was shattered by the crack of gunshot. He raced back through the garden and crept along the side of the porch and on into the juniper and twisted rhododendron at the corner of the cottage. From there he made out Robbie McLaren, hunched over, and Tim Bethune flat on his stomach in the yard. Next to them a pile of sticks and rags, a can of gasoline and a box of matches. Tim looked around wildly, but there was nowhere to run. Because there was George, up on Peg, slowly coming down the path from the road toward them, shirt open, rifle pointing to the sky. He lowered the gun, shoved the bolt, and took aim again.

He fired off two more shots. The first made Tim's hat spin in the air. The second took out the rock at the top of the pile. Simon flattened against the wall, then sank down, his breath short and shallow. Robbie and Tim were pleading, "Don't kill us! Please don't kill us." George, gun resting easily across Peg's bare back, steered her over to them on a slow walk. He squinted at the house. Simon could hear the boys sobbing now. "Sharpshooting easy-shot," George said. "I have forty rounds in silver casings for cowards like you. Come back again, and I'll make them count."

The boys didn't move. George waited. Finally, Tim struggled to his hands and knees. George cocked his head toward their bicycles. The boys scrabbled over like crabs, choking and sobbing. Robbie couldn't make his pedals work. He grabbed the handlebars and Tim did the same, and they ran their bikes to the road.

George walked Peg directly to the rhododendron. Simon squeezed his eyes shut, quivering against the wall. A chickadee let out a two-note call.

"Simon Peter?" It was the first time George had said his name in all the time since he'd come home. He was leaning over Peg's neck and holding out his hand. Simon went rigid. "Safe harbor," George said, sitting back up. He waited, still as a statue, staring out at the bay, his long hair catching the breeze. It was a long time before Simon, still shaking, slid upright against the wall. A longer time still before he sidled out from the bushes. George turned Peg around without a word and they walked around to the yard. Simon kicked the pile of sticks and rags and picked up the matches. "They set the *Lauralee* on fire," he said.

"Nope," George answered. "Lightning down the mast."

"Lightning? You saw it?"

George nodded. "Couldn't save her. She'd broke free."

Simon stuffed a towel in the broken window, locked the door, and came down the steps, then gripped George's hand and swung up on Peg. He leaned back against George's bare chest. George put his strong, tanned arms around him and shook the reins, his shirttails fluttering in the wind. "There's my girl, Peg," George said softly.

WHEN HE MADE it home alone on Peg, Simon sensed something going on even before he walked down from the barn to the house. Zeb's truck in the yard. The Fredas' door wide open. Voices in the kitchen. And there at the kitchen table was someone who looked just like his father, staring at a slice of Ida's bread on a plate as she buttered it, staring at it as if he'd never seen such a thing.

This man looked up slowly and knocked the bread and the plate to the floor as he stood, as he lurched around the table to pull Simon against him.

ALONE AT LAST—the Fredas and Zeb long gone, his father still up at his house, Simon Peter helping Ida—Angus sat on the bed. He looked down at the rim of salt on his kilt a few inches above the knee, then went to the bureau and pulled out a pair of old trousers. He laid them on the bed and pictured himself pulling them on one-handed, the potential defeat of the buttons on the fly. Five. He counted them.

The *Lauralee*'s compass, like a severed head in a sack, was on the bed next to the trousers. He pulled it out and traced the crack in the glass. "Home is the sailor, home from the sea, and the hunter home from the hill." Those were the words his father said on welcoming Angus home—or had he said, "home from the kill?" It didn't matter. "Requiem," by Stevenson. Angus knew the verse, and knew the opening line. "Under the wide and starry sky, dig the grave and let me lie . . ."

He'd taken the compass with him, intending to give it to his father when he finally walked up to his house. How frail the old man had looked there in the study, just where he'd left him. Still in his white shirt and dark wool vest. Except this time in the wing chair, head back, mouth open, sound asleep. Angus paced quietly about and sat down behind the desk. It was strewn with news clippings and letters and old ledger books. There was a check made out to the Union of Democratic Control—the UDC. Angus had heard of it—a stop-the-war organization in Britain filled with intellectuals who had never been on the field, as far as he knew, and social agitators and labor unions. The check was for $500, about what it might cost to build a new boat or maybe a house.

Angus stood abruptly. The desk chair slammed back. His father jerked awake and blinked uncomprehendingly, then his mouth fell open again. "I'll be damned," he whispered. "Am I dreaming?" He got to his feet, hand tentatively holding the chair. "Home is the sailor . . ." he said and the rest. They stared at each other until finally Angus came around the desk and they exchanged a rough embrace.

There was no small talk. His father went directly to the cupboard and pulled out a bottle of whisky. "Single malt. From Scotland. Been keeping it for this day," he said, searching for the crystal tumblers and pouring it out. But once poured, he simply stared at Angus and sat back down. When they finally spoke, it was about the *Lauralee*. They agreed to believe it was lightning, the hand of God. Agreed it was fitting. Angus tried to give him the compass, but he wouldn't accept it. She was as much yours as mine. She wouldn't have made it under another skipper, he said, glancing at Angus's wounded arm. Wouldn't have made it anyway, Angus said, stating outright what he'd been afraid to admit for so long.

His father's eyes remained on the sling. Angus instinctively crossed his left arm over it. "The monstrous atrocities you've seen. Participated in. I can't imagine," his father said flatly.

Participated in. Angus let that sink in. Waited for more. But his father was not about to turn the conversation to Angus, not directly. To the war, yes—the insanity, the unending horror of it. His own efforts and the UDC. The necessity of a negotiated peace this instant. He grew agitated, walked over and jabbed at papers on his desk. "This man Sassoon, a Military Cross to his credit, a lieutenant like you, has refused to continue. Did you know that?"

Angus indicated he did, hoping to cut the conversation short, but his father kept right on. "His letter to his commanding officer was read aloud in the British House of Commons." He whipped a sheet of newsprint from the stack. Fumbling with his spectacles, he leaned over and ran his finger down the page. "Said, and I quote, that England is now engaged in a war not of 'defense and liberation' but of 'aggression and conquest.' Said he was acting on behalf of all soldiers." He looked up at Angus. "There's courage for you. Begged Parliament for a negotiated peace. And what was the response? Sent him off to the looney bin to shut him up." Spittle had collected in the corner of his mouth.

"They're called war hospitals," Angus said evenly. "Craiglockhart. It's a British war hospital. And Sassoon does *not* speak for me. I speak for myself."

His father ripped off his glasses. "What do you mean? Of course he does. I'm on your side. That's what I'm trying to tell you."

"And what side is that? The one where men died for nothing? Now we just stop the war and hand them France and whatever else they want?"

"Exactly! End this bloody war. Prevent this—look at you. You want more men to come back like . . ." He pressed his thumb and fingers against his eyes.

Angus had no feeling for a moment. Then it came to him just how afraid his father was. Better to stand behind the shield of righteous anger, to think of death and sacrifice as abstractions, as without purpose, than to imagine those deaths, one by one, or see the crippled son in front of him. "I have come back," Angus said firmly. He took a step backward, and, eyes on his father, leaned down, picked up the compass, and left.

IT WAS NOT long afterwards that Simon came home. "Don't speak," Angus had said. "Don't say a word. Let me just hold you." He felt the surprising muscularity of the boy's arms, felt him sink against his paralyzed arm, and held him far too long. When he did let him go, there was Publicover in the freckles and blond hair, the cheery grin. He pressed his eyes and sat back heavily in his chair. Simon stared at Angus's medal. Avoided his arm. Told him about Mr. Heist and how he was innocent. Said he'd told Mr. Heist that his father would get him out of prison. Rattled on. Thankfully, did not ask about the war. They talked about the *Lauralee*, and Angus said it must have been a horror to watch her burn. Simon grew quiet, and Angus assured him they'd get on without her and that all they'd do was think of the good times and what a brave old girl she was. Ida set out tea and more bread and some chowder. Simon shoveled it in, talked some more, filled in every empty space. Told Angus he'd worked at Mader's all summer.

Told him all about a boat once called *Repulse Bay*, now unnamed, at Smith and Rhuland's. Spoke with surprising technical detail about her lines. Grinned some more. Flicked a look at his arm again. Grew serious. Mentioned Vimy. Said, You showed 'em, Dad.

Ida pulled out some meat tarts and said it may as well be supper because Hettie would be late getting home. She was over to Gold River to check on the new foreman at the sawmill. Ridiculous her riding all over the place. Duncan had agreed to get a truck, and Zeb was going to teach Hettie to drive. Drive a *truck*, mind, she said. Right on up to Dawson lumber camp, next thing you know. She checked Angus for his reaction. Seeing none, she said, "She's your father's eyes and ears and more. But maybe she always has been, because the men she deals with don't seem to mind her being a woman, far as I can tell, as long as her money's good. Of course, it's all Duncan's."

"As long as there's money left," Angus said.

Ida nodded. She knew what he meant. "Puts his money where his mouth is, I'll give you that."

IT WAS NEARLY SUNSET, a blush of pink overhead deepening to red, by the time Hettie came up the hill on Rooster, Ebbin's old hat hanging down her back by its leather ties. Immobilized on the porch, Angus watched as if witness to a passing dream. Rooster nodding with each slow step, Hettie's heavy boots in the stirrups, the drape of her rough brown skirt, the tousled short hair, her face sunburnt and purposeful. She didn't see him as she rode up.

In the barn he said her name. She was closing the stall door. She went rigid and slowly turned to him. "Hettie. I'm sorry," he said. He walked over to her. She touched his lips with trembling fingers. They sank down on the straw with Rooster breathing over them and held each other until she pulled back and wiped her downcast eyes. He picked bits of straw from her short locks. She touched his arm, a touch he did not feel. He shook his head. They sat back against the stall door, side by side, and the enormity of all they had not written to each other hung between them.

"I found him," he said. Said it compulsively, without thinking, but glad of it. He wanted to tell her, wanted his guilt to overwhelm him, be purged from him. Wanted to make sense of it with the only person who could understand, the only other person who knew Ebbin the way he did. The great weight of knowing pressed down on him.

"Found his body?" she whispered. "The army said . . . I thought, I thought—"

"No," he said, before she could finish. "You don't understand, I found him." But she refused to hear it. Said she could not bear to hear his name. That she had buried him. And had found life without him—

He stared at her dumbly as the words "*found life without him*" registered. The tremble of her upturned chin, the anxious confusion in her eyes—all this he took in and weighed against his selfish need, his reckless words.

"No. I meant . . . I found out about him. That he was . . . heroic in the end. At the end."

"Oh," she said, and sank back against the stall.

He waited to see if she wanted more—if there was even a shred of a possibility that she'd open the door. But she kept it firmly closed. "What does it matter? The war took him, hero or not," she sighed. She stared straight ahead. "For a long time, a very long time, I couldn't accept it. But finally . . . the day my father brought this to me, I knew he was gone." She reached into the pocket of her skirt and pressed Ebbin's tag into Angus's hand. "You need to bury him, too," she said. Then she picked up Ebbin's hat and stood, holding the leather brim with both hands. "Remember this hat? Remember that story of his? How he won it off a 'mad Australian'? How he made us laugh? That's how I want to think of him. Not as a corpse, not as a soldier blown to bits, his body mangled—I don't care what he did over there, nor how he died. Please. Just let me keep him as he was so I can keep going."

Angus closed his fingers over the tag and slipped it in his pocket. He stood as well. "Hettie," he said, stretching out his hand. But she stepped back and turned her head away and closed her eyes. Angus let his hand drop.

She took a deep breath and, without looking at him, said, "There's something else. Something you need to know. Something awful. I don't know how to tell you—" She faced him. These were tears in her eyes.

"You don't have to. I saw her. The *Lauralee*. I couldn't have sailed her, not like this." He nodded at his arm. "And she was in no condition anyway. We all knew that. She's gone. Like Ebbin."

Gone but not. Vanished but present. Dead but not buried. Not really.

Rooster shook his mane and stamped. Peg sidled up to the edge of her stall and hung her head over into his. Hettie stroked Peg's nose, removed Rooster's bridle, rubbed him down quickly, and fed them both oats. Refused Angus's help. Only take a minute, she said. I'm used to it. And of course she was. Angus had barely ever ridden Rooster, let alone rubbed him down or fed him. His father and Hettie had always been in charge of the horses—just one more element of their partnership, he thought now, watching her. How deft and sure her movements were. How efficient and robust she seemed. He remembered his father telling him to give her some certainty. She had it now. She was no longer the wraith wandering the hills. The air and the smell of horses grew thick around him. He stepped outside.

She finished her tasks and joined him. He lit a cigarette and nearly offered her one. "You've had a lot on your shoulders," he said, somewhat stiffly. "I've heard you've taken over the reins of Dad's affairs. I'm proud of you. Grateful to you."

She shrugged it off. "Keeps me going," she said. He could imagine how her offhand manner might work in a negotiation, how it would disarm those who took it too literally.

"Keeps *us* going, from what I've heard."

She cocked her head. "I was thinking," she said softly. "With the *Lauralee* gone, and you—I'm not sure what you'd want to do, but we've bought up more timber. Paper mills, maybe. Is that something you'd be interested in?"

"Paper mills?" He almost laughed. And then he felt it. The cool detachment of the question.

"But what *will* you do?"

"I just got home," he snapped.

"I know, I know," she whispered in a soothing voice. "I'm sorry. I should have asked about what you've been through. But . . ." She bit her lip and looked away. "Duncan said, this pamphlet said that soldiers coming home don't want to talk about it. If you want to—I mean, your men, they sounded a fine bunch . . . from what you wrote."

He stopped her. "It's alright. My father was right. The pamphlet was right." He looked up at the purple sky, the first stars. *A fine bunch.* Conlon had warned him that stirred-up memories could overtake the physical world and pull you back. But so too could uncomprehending souls threaten that hallowed ground. "It's getting dark," he said. "Let's go in."

She hesitated, maybe waiting for him. When he didn't move, she started down the hill. "Did you think of me?" he thought he heard her ask as she brushed past. "Yes," he said. She was at the well by then and down the yard and into the house. And he knew he had imagined those words. "Did you think of me?" he whispered.

LATE THAT NIGHT with Ebbin's tag in his hand and Havers's cross around his neck, Angus went down to the beach below the house and sat on a boulder where he used to sit as a boy, waiting for his father to come in from the Banks. He stared out at the islands and thought about how his father would swing him up on his shoulders and parade him around the town wharf. He thought of his phalarope out there under the waves. The frigate bird he had seen gliding low over the trench in a hallucinatory moment came back to him—a bird he'd drawn from pictures, but never seen. And Paul's pigeons circling, and moonlight glinting off a bayonet, the glaze of ice on grass, the pounding of his heart as they crawled through it, the neatly tied laces on Wickham's upside-down boots, and Publicover's freckles, his smile, his laugh, and Conlon's voice breaking, his own as well, on the slow-paced drumbeat of "Brave Wolfe" one night in an *estaminet*, weeks before Vimy. *The cannon on each side did roar like thunder . . . And youths in all their pride were torn asunder . . .* Angus repeated the lines in a whisper. The charred timbers of the *Lauralee* merged with the blackened tree stumps at the riverbank so long ago. He searched the black water beyond the *Lauralee's* empty mooring. But there was no hint of a green running light.

STILL LATER, in the bedroom, he stood over his wife, watching her breathe. Had he thought of her over there? Not often and not enough. And when he had, it was as a schoolgirl when the world had just begun. Angled across the bed, only too used to him not being in it, she lay on her back, mouth slightly open, arm flung back. He feathered a lock of her chopped hair through his fingers. Who was he to disturb such reinvention? To soil such brave efforts? Maybe she had buried Ebbin after all, and maybe half her heart with him.

Still dressed, he sat in the rocker and undid his boots. Undid his sling. The one place he had not gone in the years and years since he'd stepped off the train and into Zeb's truck was the art shed. He pulled the faded blue and gray quilt around him and leaned back.

There'd be a stone marker on the hillside at Vimy for Lance Corporal Havers. Of that, he had no doubt. But for the rest of time, only he and two other living souls would know who was buried beneath it. And they, like Angus himself, were very far away. His arm was heavy in his lap. His shoulder ached.

TWENTY-SIX

November 28th, 1917
Snag Harbor, Nova Scotia

imon Peter pushed the shed door open. Two and a half months had come and gone since his father's return, and he hadn't bothered to lock it. Yet Simon had seen him go inside, swinging the lantern up the yard at night. He'd seen the rumpled quilt on the cot near the stove. The studio was dry and still— an empty husk, just like his father. Simon stepped in boldly. But once inside, he softened his steps. It remained sacred ground whether his father cared or not.

His father did not care about many things. Life went on around him, and he stared out at it through sad and vacant eyes. He dressed and shaved each morning, then sat with his knees pressed close together on the porch when the weather was fine, or by the fire when it was not. He used his good arm to move his bad one up and down in what he called "passive exercise." He kept a book in his lap and a pair of binoculars by his side. He kept the *Lauralee*'s compass hidden away in a cupboard. He did not care to have visitors, nor go into town. He would not go out on the water, and didn't want Simon in the dory. It wasn't safe, he said. He would not talk about the war. He barely talked at all.

When Reverend Dimmock came that first week, saying he'd like to have a ceremony after the Sunday service to welcome the war hero home as they'd done for George Mather, his father had refused. Reverend Dimmock pleaded that it would go a long way to heal the town after the Heist affair, and that it might even bring Duncan back to the fold. Simon's father had stood up, towering over the reverend, who cringed and held his tea biscuit up like a shield. He said that he was no hero and that Reverend Dimmock understood very little if he thought Duncan MacGrath would be placated by glorifying war in a house of God. Reverend Dimmock, red in the face, clamped on his hat and said that Angus might want to consider his own soul. His father shut the door and leaned his head against it for a long time.

Simon debated whether to tell his father what George had said about seeing Ebbin after Courcelette. When he finally did tell him, his father took a long time before responding and said something like "sometimes we see what we want to believe," which was saying nothing and sounded eerily like George.

Ida said to give his father time. A wise woman, our Ida, his grandfather agreed. But time was running out for Mr. Heist, as the letter in Simon's pocket proved. His father just sat in his rocker, in the shadows of the porch, refusing to help. The fact that he was a veteran and an officer wouldn't matter to those in charge of the camp at Amherst, he said. Your grandfather has done all that could be done. And maybe Mr. Heist was better off in prison, protected there until the war was over, he said. He didn't seem to understand what was happening to Mr. Heist. Worse, he didn't seem angry over the injustice of it—just defeated.

Meanwhile, in prison, Mr. Heist grew more miserable and heartbroken by the day, which is why Simon was determined to send him the blue *Morpho didius* that he'd copied in meticulous detail from the picture in *Lepidoptera of Eastern North America*. In earlier letters, Mr. Heist had told him to keep working on his Greek translation. Strangely, his father had taken a fleeting interest in his translation—

said a friend of his, a Captain Conlon, carried *The Iliad* with him at the Front, *The Odyssey*, too, and quoted from them. The poets remember, he said. Simon had waited for more, but no more came. Standing right next to him, his father had already drifted away.

In his last letter from Mr. Heist, the one in Simon's pocket, there was no reference to the suffering of Agamemnon or Troy, only to the suffering of Mr. Heist in the wretched conditions in which he found himself. He said the search for a single thing of beauty was fading and that even as he witnessed the sun's rising and setting, he felt his eyes growing dim.

So Simon needed blue paint. The watercolors were as dried-out as the brushes, but all they needed was water to come back to life. He couldn't send the book for fear of what might happen to it in prison. He didn't want to rip the page out. So a drawing would have to do. He sat on the stool by the ledge and mixed the color he wanted, then filled in the black ink outline he'd made. When the paint dried, he filled the veins and tips of the wings with more black ink, leaving little spots of white, just like the pictured *Morpho*. It was a tedious process, but it gave him pleasure.

As he leaned down to replace the watercolors, a sheaf of black papers caught his eye. He picked one up and saw that the paper wasn't black, but was nearly covered in thick rough strokes of charcoal. Had Young Fred been in the shed? Used his father's charcoals? Simon turned it over. On the back, in a primitive hand, it said, "Deliverance, 1917," and then "A. A. MacGrath." Simon rifled through the lot of them, each one signed, each one the same with the strokes leading to a point of white, perfectly round, randomly placed—about the size of a thimble in some, a jelly jar in others, a mere dot in one.

The door creaked open and in strode his grandfather, demanding to know what Simon was doing there with his father's paints. Ignoring the question, Simon handed him the charcoal papers. His grandfather shuffled through them impatiently. "What the devil are these?"

Simon turned them over, and his grandfather pressed his fingers against his eyes, leaving two black marks. "Deliverance? My God," he said hoarsely.

"What's it mean?" Simon asked.

"I have no idea. But it isn't good." He tossed the papers on the ledge and turned to face the huge canvas still covered on the easel in the corner. He ripped off the sheet and stood before the half-finished image of the man and the boy in the rowboat. "Here's what he could have done, if he hadn't—"

Simon's mouth fell open. "You've seen it?"

"Of course. Don't tell me you haven't. I know you've been in here. Looked at this many a time yourself would be my guess." He didn't look for confirmation, and of course he was right. "All these years," his grandfather said, "I thought his painting was a waste of time. Those blasted birds and seascapes . . . But this—this has imagination. Splotches of paint jabbed on the canvas is what I thought at first. Lunacy. But when I stood back, it jumped out at me. Rowboat coming out of the bottom of the canvas there as if you were on it. Sunlight in the water. To see this picture is to be in it."

Exactly, Simon thought.

"Ah. He had greatness in him and I missed it. All the same, he never did anything like this before. I know. I searched every picture in here. I imagine you have, too. And there it sits. Never to be finished. That's the utter tragedy of it. The terrible price we're all paying."

To stop his grandfather from launching into the terrible price all of Nova Scotia was paying, and to cut off the rising sympathy Simon was feeling for his father—the man who barely knew he was alive— Simon picked up the sheet to cover the picture. But his grandfather stayed his arm. "Remember that old lapstrake rowboat we had? I used to sing to him, 'Of all the Fishes in the sea—'"

" 'I like the best the bass. He climbs upon the seaweed trees and slides down on his hands and knees . . .' I know. Dad used to sing it to me when we were out in that old rowboat."

"Did he?" His voice fell to a hushed whisper, and Simon saw that his mouth was trembling.

"Wait," Simon said. "You thought the picture was—you think it's you and Dad? You're the man and Dad's the boy?" He looked again at the picture and back at his grandfather as the pain of that possibility registered.

His grandfather put his arm around him. "Well now, who it is isn't important, eh? It's every father and son, suspended there. What do you think?"

Simon jerked away and shoved the charcoal drawings back under the shelf. "He's nuts, that's what I think. Nuts."

"Hold on, boy. He's lost his compass is all. He'll find it."

"What's he need a compass for? He's not going anywhere." Simon pointed at the map of France with its colored pins. "That's the only place he cares about," he said.

THAT NIGHT, ANGUS lit the lamp in the shed as he did every night. It was cold enough for the stove, but he sat shivering. Unlike some, Angus did not shake with every sudden noise; but he shook often and his head was filled with shrieking noise, his mouth with ashes, and when it was over, he found it best to remain very still. Very still and very far away so as not to corrupt the world around him. So as not to tell the story he had to tell of a friend, brother-in-law, brother and son whose memory would be tarnished by those with ears that could not hear nor ever understand. Marooned on his island, alone with his war, he watched his family head off to their appointed rounds. He opened books and reread the same sentences over and over. Hours would pass unnoticed. He had to force himself to eat. He willed himself invisible. He sent for an enlarged map of France and Belgium, pinned it up in the art shed, and followed every scrap of war news, keeping watch with the fervor of a religious convert and the longing of a lost pilgrim. Some days, in the dark well of grief and memory, he'd get a flash of how bright, how brilliantly white, death's deliverance could shine. The white hole that hovered above the pit.

It was at night that the claustrophobia of his landlocked existence fell away—when he could look out to black water and see nothing and feel and know the nothingness of himself.

He sat down and opened Conlon's most recent letter, which carried, as had all his letters, a thread of connection—news of the men, those alive and those dead, news of the battles. Passchendaele was over. The Third Battle of Ypres had spread a sea of blood over the mud of Flanders like a flood tide, Conlon wrote with journalistic flair. That sea included the blood of the 16,000 Canadian casualties Currie had predicted months before.

Boudrey was the latest, his death leaving those still alive in a state of shock. Fell off a duckboard and drowned in the mud, Conlon had written. Hanson, Katz and Kearns had died of wounds. LaPointe, Oxner and McNeil—having stood waist-deep in water for five days straight as German shells rained down—had been taken off the field with fever. Now, Boudrey. "Survival is the surprise," Conlon wrote, "death expected."

As he tried to fathom Boudrey's death, it was Agamemnon who came to Angus. Where in all that suffering was the wisdom Zeus had promised? The grief of memory "dripping in sleep against the heart" was without end. And how he longed for an end. Things he'd barely noticed at the time loomed larger than life—a button on his shirt could bring back buttons hanging by a thread from Publicover's torn and blood-soaked jacket . . . He stood abruptly, let the letter fall from his hand, lifted the lid off the stove, struck a match and threw it in. When the flames were going, he grabbed his "Deliverance" pictures and held them to the flames, one by one. One for each man who had died. And then the rest of them, one by one, watching the curling paper turn to ash.

Something moved. He felt it more than saw it. There—behind the stove, the sheet had slipped from his easel and revealed the father and son in the boat. Why now? To taunt him in all their unfulfilled promise. He flung the canvas across the room and the easel after it, then raced his hands blindly along the high shelf, found the knife and knelt over the painting. As he raised his arm to slash it, a paper landed like a breath on the floor at his knees. A butterfly. "*Morpho didius,*" the carefully hand-printed letters at the bottom said, and beneath them, the words "Remember, this is your way of being alive."

Angus slowly got to his feet and took the butterfly to the lamp by the row of windows and studied it. When he looked up, the reflection of his crazed, ravaged face stared back at him.

The note was in Simon Peter's hand. "Your way of being alive." Angus sat back amazed. Simon, so secretive, so angry at him for failing to rescue Heist. He'd tried to tell him how useless it would be— yet another failed mission, he'd thought, but hadn't said. He'd tried to explain how much safer Heist was in prison—safe from those eager to fight the war at home and for whom Heist had already proven an easy target. Staring at him with confusion that transformed to dull-eyed detachment, Simon had dropped his spoon in his empty mug. The clatter of it reverberated through the distance between them. Angus sat there, a ruminating, broken man with nothing to offer. And now, his son had sent him a message.

THE FOLLOWING MORNING, before he left for school, Simon Peter found his father leaning on the shelf, asleep—brushes and paints splayed out next to him. He noted the canvas flung up against the flattened easel. He refused to care. Under his father's elbow lay the butterfly, still intact. That he did care about. His father stirred and sat up, blinking.

"The butterfly," Simon said. "It's mine."

"You made it? Copied it from that butterfly book?" His father rubbed his face. "The note at the bottom. *This is your way of being alive.* What did you mean by it?"

"Nothing. Just something between me and Mr. Heist."

"So it's a message . . . for him?"

"That's right," Simon said. "I made it for him. He needs it. A thing of beauty. Because that's what keeps him going. He said so once."

He picked up the butterfly and left.

TWENTY-SEVEN

April 9th, 1918
Snag Harbor, Nova Scotia

ive months later, a year to the day after Vimy, the *Morpho didius* with its iridescent blue wings and white-spotted wing tips—all its unattainable beauty—fluttered through Angus with nothing to offer but regret. It came to him on the train back from Halifax, where he had been since late December, helping to orchestrate relief work—not for war's victims overseas, but for her dead at home. Half of Halifax and half of Dartmouth had been leveled in an explosion that shook the ground in Snag Harbor, over sixty miles away.

In a navigational blunder of epic proportion and cruelest irony, the S.S. *Imo*, a Norwegian tramp steamer loaded with relief supplies for Belgium, collided with the freighter *Mont-Blanc*, loaded with the makings of weapons for the war—picric acid and TNT in her hold and thirty-five tons of benzine strapped to her decks in casks. The final and deadly irony was that the sight of the *Mont-Blanc* in the harbor brought people out to watch, as a ship on fire always did. Unaware of her lethal cargo, they stood mesmerized on the streets, at office windows and at the water's edge. Then she blew.

More than 2,000 were killed, 20,000 left homeless, hundreds

orphaned, and many more blinded by flying glass. The explosion sent boats careening through the air. It forced the harbor waters apart, then set off a tidal wave that raced in over the city—news that left a white-faced Simon unable to speak.

And then came the blizzard, one of the worst on record, coating the ruins in ice, burying them beneath snow, bringing to a halt trains with supplies and aid from all over Canada and New England. And, despite clear evidence from the inquiry that the explosion had been neither an act of war nor the work of spies, but rather the result of human error, those of German descent, some of whom had relatives in Snag Harbor, were attacked on the streets, and many placed under temporary arrest. Duncan had stood up at a town meeting organized by Lady Bromley to step up relief efforts. Stood up without being invited and spoke about the desperation the tragedy had wrought, not just in physical suffering, but in spirit. And he spoke of hearts blackened by revenge. "Let not the death toll include the *souls* of men still living," he said. There was no doubt whose souls he was talking about, and this time his words were met with silent approval.

Ida told Angus it was his finest moment. She held her apron to her face, her knuckles red and raw. "When the explosion happened, he wondered if it was God's retribution for us being in the war. He always said Nova Scotia would pay. He didn't say it to other folks, mind. Just to me. But when it come out how bad it was, he left that notion behind."

"You love him, don't you, Ida?" Angus said, sitting at the kitchen table with her.

"I do, warts and all," she said, and met his eyes.

With Hettie's blessing and stated relief that he wanted to be of use, Angus had packed his things for Halifax, and there discovered that despite his arm, he was of great use in helping the relief effort. His military service was not without benefit. He was lifted from the ranks of helpers to a temporary position of some authority. He knew how to navigate human suffering.

When his work was done, he returned to spring leaves unfurling and ice in retreat in Snag Harbor. He had written to Simon, but had received only the most cursory letters back. Hettie wrote more regularly—her usual five-line notes that let him know all was well, and he assumed better, without him there. How could it not be? While in Halifax, he'd felt a welcome sense of military demeanor and welcome stabs of pain in his shoulder and hand. He operated with calm detachment, organizing the distribution of supplies, checking their deployment to shelters, whispering reassurances, listening to stories of loss. He could move his arm at the shoulder, but the pain and movement disappeared upon his return. It was as if the nerves had tried but failed. Darkness again settled over him. He became convinced that his own life was meant to be played out only in the most savage of circumstances. Beauty was neither his to behold nor create. God had hamstrung his arm for the hubris of once thinking it possible. But he thought, too, of hands passing out food and blankets and of the toddler he'd found wandering the snow-filled street who fell asleep on his shoulder, whose tiny breaths warmed his neck as he carried her to shelter.

IN THE MIDDLE of June, one year and two months after Ebbin's death, Angus learned in a letter from Keegan that Conlon, always on the edge of grace, steady, steadfast, recently elevated to major with a Distinguished Service Order medal pinned to his uniform, had died.

Conlon, Angus's confessor in absentia, to whom he whispered his transgressions without giving them voice, from whom he'd never asked for absolution, had written to Angus in May, saying that had it not been for Havers, they would not have discovered the howitzer at the stone barn. And had it not been for Angus, barely alive, the three of them, he and Angus and Keegan, would never have found their way back to tell Rushford where it was.

In that strange letter, recounting their times together, he'd asked Angus to go back and put a wreath on the graves of their comrades at Vimy and Passchendaele when the war was over. He predicted it wouldn't go on forever, but it might very well end in defeat. "Promise you'll honor our graves, in victory or defeat," Conlon had written in an uncharacteristic plea.

In his response, painstakingly composed with his left hand as all his letters were, Angus reminded Conlon of the abbey cemetery—how Conlon had scoffed that stones crumble and names fade away and no one remembers, "except the poets who help the rest of us remember what we dare not say." But Angus gave his word—he'd place a wreath on every grave when the war was over—victory or defeat. But he wanted Conlon with him when he did. Wanted him to recite what the poets knew.

Now, Conlon of the soft voice and softer smile, who, as Keegan said in his letter, had led his shredded forces at Passchendaele to feats more heroic than they had a right to, who had unfailingly kept spirits up, had found his way out. Enclosed with Keegan's letter was Conlon's copy of *The Odyssey*, which he'd asked Keegan to send to Angus should anything happen to him. The note to Angus from Conlon, tucked inside the book's worn pages, said that unlike Odysseus, and unlike Angus, he did not think he could find his way home, but he hoped that Angus could find it in his heart to cherish his memory as much as he had cherished Angus's friendship. Days later, he'd taken his own life in a hotel in London.

Angus turned *The Odyssey* over in his hand and placed it on the ledge. He opened the cover and laid Conlon's note inside. Before he closed the cover, he pressed his palm flat against the words. Then he left the shed door swinging open behind him. He walked on, spoke to no one, and headed up into the deep woods and hills, until finally, stumbling through a bog, he turned southwest toward the coast. Hours later he staggered across the boulders on the beach at

Owl's Head. There he let all the tortured whys fly out on the wind. Gusts rushed through the tops of the trees. At his feet a growing surf drenched the rocks in cascades of foam, unceasing, unending, uncaring. He'd been prepared for Conlon's death, but not by his own hand.

Angus no more understood why he'd resisted than why Conlon had succumbed. Nor why he continued to resist. There was no answer, and all that Keegan might tell him later about the circumstances, the bits and pieces of Conlon's last days, would never be explanation enough. We cannot know the whole poem from a single word, he finally found the strength to say, nor a life from a single act.

Forced up against the limits of human knowing, on bended knee to the mystery, not just the fact of Conlon's death, Angus glimpsed the greater mystery. There was more, but known only by a knowing beyond all knowing. His tethered life stretched away from him and he was in that moment unbound.

"MACGRATH!" HE HEARD someone call minutes, maybe hours, later. He spun around, nearly slipped off the rocks. There was George, crazed and undone, balancing on a boulder, his crutch in the sand. "Thiepval," he shouted. "He was there! Saved my life."

"I know," Angus said. "I believe you. I saw him, too. At Vimy, and after that." The released truth of those words carried him at a rapid pace across the slick rocks to George.

George's hair whipped across his face. He slowly pulled it back. "With the 45th?"

"That's right. Called himself Havers. But it was Ebbin. I watched him die. Watched him die a hundred times since."

They met each other's eyes. "End without ending," George said.

Angus lost his footing, grabbed George, and they fell together onto the sand and struggled up and hobbled over the stony beach to the shelter of the trees, then sank down on the steps leading up to the

Heist cottage. Angus huddled over and lit a cigarette and handed it to George.

George held it between his thumb and forefinger. "Boy cried out for his mother. Passed him one of these," he said.

Angus glanced up at George, then lit one for himself. A misty rain began to fall.

George blew out a long stream of smoke and dropped his head. "Die or go on. Either way won't bring them back. Or us. Heart-broke, head-broke."

Angus leaned back against the railing. George's hands went slack between his knees. Angus closed his eyes and remembered the scrape of a muddied kilt on bare knees. After a time, the wind began to die, and the air took on a softness. A blue jay sounded a series of hollow notes above them.

Angus said, "There was a lark nesting in a Kraut jacket on the wire in the middle of No Man's Land. Singing her heart out."

George lifted his head and listened, then reached for a twig of mountain laurel that had blown onto the steps. He broke a leaf in half, held it to his nose and inhaled deeply. He passed the other half to Angus, who did the same. The fresh scent of the wet woods—blueberry bushes and laurel, drenched pine needles, damp earth—flooded in, overtook memory, canceled time. They slowly took the steps up to the Heist cottage. There George stopped. They clasped hands and Angus left him there rocking on the porch.

AS HE WALKED BACK, alone on the hilly road, the evening sky took on a tremulous violet-blue that filled in and grew deeper until, suddenly luminescent and silvered, it faded to black. "In life," he had said to Orland, futilely staunching his dead brother's wound, "we are in death." Nothing lasts. Every moment is a moment passing and gone.

Yet, as he walked, and dusk faded to night, that violet-blue stayed with him in its essence, calling up his longing in the bottom of a trench for the whole sky. It was above him now, vast and star-filled. Every star the brighter for the depth of unending darkness.

The war was in him, part of him, but not all of him. Memory would always haunt him, as it haunted George. He knew that. But he knew, too, that the sacrifice could not be honored by memory alone, but in the purest part of self where it was understood it could not be fully known. *Now we see through a glass darkly . . . now I know only in part.*

When he reached Mader's wharf, he stopped. He took the steps down to it, and walked to the end. The shed door creaked open and a figure stepped out.

"Angus? That you?" Philip called, peering into the darkness, one hand on his pot belly, the other scratching his neck.

"It is."

"Knew it. That one-armed way you got of walking. Come down here in the middle of the night to see how I'm doing? Well, I'll tell you. Seventy-two years old and still got me powers." He winked, amused at himself, and said, "C'mere now since you're out and about. Got something I want to show you here. C'mon, c'mon," he wheezed, motioning Angus inside.

In the shed he pointed with his pipe to the beautiful little hull of a boat, a sloop, about twenty-four feet long, up on a cradle. "Honduras mahogany," he said. "Got it cheap if you can believe it, but don't believe it." He squeezed out a high-pitched chuckle.

"She's a beauty," Angus said.

"Yep. She is." Philip strutted around her through the sawdust, and got up on a stepladder and rested his gnarled hands on the gunwale. The deck was not yet finished. Just the carvel-planked hull, a soft reddish-brown, unvarnished and sanded smooth. "Your boy and me designed her. Didn't think I could build a boat again. I liked her so much, couldn't help but build her. He pushed me along. Mostly his design. Wanted that long counterstern, that spoon bow. Been helping every step of the way."

"Simon Peter?"

"None other. How many boys you got?"

Angus circled the boat, eyeing her graceful lines, the deep keel, the oval at the end of her transom. She was the most perfectly balanced, beautiful little boat he had ever seen. "He helped design her? How do you mean?"

"I mean he and I talked dimensions. He even made some *drawings*, to scale, he told me, if that don't beat all, afore we lofted her up. He don't want to paint her. Just varnish so that color stays true. I never seen anyone sand so fine. Wants me to name her *True North*, but I told him that'll be up to whoever buys her."

Dumbfounded, Angus ran his hand along her planks and then pressed his hand against the curve of her smoothed spoon bow.

"He and I figured the mast about twenty-eight foot tall," Philip said, climbing back down. "He's already picked out the tree. She'll carry a lot of sail, but she's good for it. That keel will keep her from going over in a fifty-knot gale with a couple of skinny boys on her windward rail."

Philip pulled out his flask and offered it to Angus. Angus took a long swallow and leaned back against the door frame, staring at her transom. "Philip," he said, "I'm thinking that *True North* would look pretty good on her stern."

"Well, sir, that it would. It's a right good name," Philip agreed. "Right good." He shoved his pipe back between his teeth and smiled broadly. Then he switched off the light and bade Angus good night.

Angus walked down to the end of the wharf and felt a release that filled the sky. Beauty had not abandoned him. He'd abandoned it. On the battlefield he'd risked life in the midst of death. And he had not risked it since. He closed his eyes and let the stars fall around him.

BACK IN HIS shed, he found himself warming tubes of paint in his hand and mixing the most perfect blues he could imagine—the near navy blue of Mahone Bay on a crisp October day, the deep violet-blue of twilight, the French blue of the shutters in Saint-Junien, the dusky iridescence of the *Morpho didius*, the sea-glass green-blue of the sea water beneath the bluffs at the cottage in France, the ice blue of Publicover's eyes, the gray-blue of his son's. He lifted a brush with his left hand and swirled it thick with paint. It felt awkward at first, but the strangeness of it was freeing. He righted the easel and placed a clean canvas on it and in great thick jabs began to create not a perfectly rendered reproduction, but the very truth of that blue.

What shape it took was of no interest to him, but once on the canvas, in shuttered shadows, in rounded curves of gravestones and drumlins and bird wing, it became all of those things. He worked for hours with different mixtures of color, and the more he worked, the more he felt the blood rushing, pulsing through him. Then he added a hint of green. And then he was done.

Completely spent, he slumped onto the cot in the corner and saw that the rumpled old blue and gray quilt was neatly folded at the foot, the sheet and blanket turned back, and the pillow plumped. Hettie. He ran the back of his hand gently across the pillow, and it came to him that the cot had been made up just like that, night after night.

AT SUNRISE THE next morning, he woke to Ida shaking him roughly. "You better wake up and see to your boy. Hettie's off to Bridgewater. You'd better get up."

Angus sat up and rubbed his face.

"Look here at this letter from Mr. Heist. Hettie forgot to give it to Simon yesterday, I guess. He's read it now." She thrust it at him. "That man never thanked him for that butterfly. Did you know that? Now he sends this letter. Says he's not one of us."

Angus unfolded the letter and read. In the letter Heist said he'd found new reason for hope. His new friends, Dymetro and Johann, sturdy fellows who shared potato-peeling duty with him, had rescued his spectacles when a fight broke out and mercifully taken him under their wing—a godsend, given the louts and bullies that populated the camp. They'd become followers of a Russian named Trotsky, who himself had been hauled off a ship in Halifax en route to Russia from New York and sent up to Amherst for fear that his call to overturn corrupt governments would spread. "And so it should," he wrote. Imprisoned for a month, Trotsky had held mass meetings and garnered many followers among the prisoners. Things were going to change, and that, Mr. Heist said, had given him the courage to survive. Heist said Simon Peter probably didn't realize how critical this moment in history was. "Few of your countrymen do," he said.

Angus glanced up at Ida, and read on, picturing Heist on all fours, dodging blows, trying to reach his glasses. Heist noted he'd had to smuggle the letter out of the prison. He had friends now. And there the letter ended.

"Does my father know about this?" Angus asked hoarsely.

"No. I brought it straight to you."

"Poor Heist."

"Poor *Heist*?"

"Yes, poor Heist. He's trying to survive, is all," Angus said, standing up. "It's what people do." Look around you, he wanted to say. He pulled his suspenders over his shoulders and asked where Simon was.

"He took off. Who knows where. Down to Mader's be my guess. His heart is about broke."

"Christ," Angus said. At the mercy of his own demons for so long, he stood there immobilized by all the ways he'd failed his son, all the ways he didn't know him, by all his imagined efforts at protecting him from the war when the truth was he'd given him nothing to hold on to.

OUT OF SIGHT of the house, Simon began to run, pounding Heist into the ground with every step. All these months of defending him. *Trusting* him. He'd throw his stupid books into the bay—his butterflies and Greeks. The key to his stupid cottage. As the road came into town, Simon slowed down, feeling stupid himself. Small and stupid and pitiful—as alone as he had ever felt. He would never trust anyone or anything again. He had learned his lesson. You could count only on yourself. For months and months it had been staring him in the face, but he'd been blind to it. Well, the blinders were off now. Lesson learned. He hoped his father would leave again. Go back to Halifax, to France. Wished him back in the war, the father he'd thought he'd known but who didn't know he was alive. At the fork in the road, he headed toward Mader's Cove, intent on taking off in the dory on his own—anything to get away and be alone as he was meant to be. Every step of the way he recast his knowledge of his father—a man he knew he'd never really known. Thought he had, but never had. Just like Mr. Heist.

AT MADER'S, SIMON found Zenus already in the dory untangling some line and Daryl Nauss on the float. His little brother Purdy was climbing in the boat. Simon took a deep breath and stared down at them from the wharf.

Zenus looked up and cocked his head. "You comin' out with us, or would that be breaking the MacGrath law?" He shielded his eyes. "Jesus. What's *wrong* with you?"

Simon barely rocked the boat as he stepped aboard. Daryl, heavyset, leapt in after him and the boat dipped. He punched Purdy's leg without looking up. "Start bailing," he said, and handed him the wooden spudgle.

Zenus grinned at Simon and set the oarlocks. "Thought your old man said the boat wasn't seaworthy enough for you."

"Who gives a damn what he said." Simon took up an oar. Zenus took up the other.

They rowed away from the wharf. "Whoa. Slow down, will ya?" Zenus said to him. "You got us going in circles. Are we in a race here?" Simon didn't answer, just slowed to match Zenus's pace. Once they got into the rhythm of it, the boat shot forward with each long pull. To hell with Heist. To hell with his father.

They were halfway up the cove in short order, looking for hints of fresh wind in the harbor. Purdy was leaning over the bow, his leg resting on an old trawl barrel, his arm dangling to the lapping waves. Daryl, in the stern, was hooking bait from a wooden tub onto the jig lines. "There's wind over there," he said, nodding to the northwest, "and pollock by the lee shore of Mountain Island."

"Are you nuts?" Zenus shook his head. "If there's fish to be caught, they'd better be in the harbor. We haven't got us a decent sail for this rig yet. And the wind's barely come up." He stopped rowing. "Uh-oh. Look there, Simon." He pointed back to the wharf.

"Simon!" came the shout across the water. His father was waving his arm, had run to the end of the wharf.

"Keep rowing," Simon said to Zenus. "Pretend you don't hear him."

Out in the harbor, they stepped the mast for the little sprit sail into a round hole in the forward seat. It caught the dust of a breeze that grew by the minute off the starboard quarter and they headed off on a close reach. Zenus managed the sheet. The others cleared the lines. Simon steered. After a time, the sail began to luff. Zenus flashed a look back at him. "You forget how to steer a boat?" he said. He pointed to leeward. "There's where we're headed. Remember?"

Simon nodded. He flexed his hand on the tiller, gripping it so his knuckles were white.

"Yeah. Keep us on course, would ya? Thought you were supposed to be as good as your old man," Daryl said.

Eyeing the sail, Simon said, "Yeah, well, people aren't what you think. Maybe he never was that good."

Zenus coiled the anchor line and shook his head. "No idea what that means, but I'll tell you what, boys . . ." He wiped his hands on his trousers and pulled out a leather pouch from which he withdrew a crumple of tobacco and some cigarette papers. He rolled a cigarette against his knee, licked the paper and struck it with a match. A curl of smoke rose up and dispersed to the wind. He handed it around to the others, each taking a draught in turn. "This," Zenus said, "is about as good as it gets. We should sail her across the bay this summer."

Purdy piped up. "Well, we would, but come summer, me and Daryl are going to be catchies on a salt banker."

Zenus rolled his eyes. "Doubt that to be true. Bit young, aren't you, Purdy?"

"I'm nine!" Purdy said.

Ducking beneath the boom and eyeing the water to leeward, Daryl said, "Well, *I'm* goin' to the Banks, but Purdy here can't go. He'll have to wait 'cause he's too little no matter what age he is."

"Am not!" Purdy stood up. "Lookit here what I can do." He passed the cigarette back to Zenus and in two seconds was teetering on the gunwale, holding on to the mast with one hand, none of which made any sense. The boat dipped to windward.

"Quit it, ya little bastard," Daryl said on the inhale. "All you're doing is rocking the boat."

Simon shifted his weight to leeward to compensate. "Yeah, get down, Purdy," he said. As if to show greater prowess, Purdy let go of the mast. Daryl tossed his cigarette and stood up to grab him. The dory lurched. Purdy smiled in triumph at his balancing act just before he bent at the knees, arms flailing like a windmill, and splashed into the dark blue chop.

"Purdy!" Daryl screamed. Simon lunged to windward and stretched an arm to the sinking Purdy as they passed. The boat rocked again. Simon pushed the tiller hard to starboard. "Coming round!" he shouted. "Mark the spot and keep it marked!"

Zenus hauled in the sail. The boat turned to the wind. The sail luffed, then whacked across the boat. Daryl ducked under the boom. Zenus eased the sheet, and the boat lumbered back toward the slapping, gasping Purdy, who rose for a second and slipped below again as Daryl shouted, "Over there! There he is!" Purdy's hand was the last thing they saw.

Simon already had his boots off. His cap tumbled onto the seat. "When we get there, drop the sail and use the oars," he said from under his sweater. He flung it over his head, and as the boat came close, they could see Purdy still flailing in slow motion below the clear waves. Simon, the only one who could swim, jumped in.

The shock of cold, a vise grip around his chest, took Simon's breath away. He kicked hard again, and got his wind. Two strokes and he ducked under to grab the now-sinking Purdy. Down and just out of reach. He kicked hard and, clutching the back of Purdy's sweater with two hands, hauled him up, took a breath, then dipped below and rolled him over his head, praying Purdy was alive enough to reach for the oar he knew would be there. His hand still pushing Purdy, he gave a violent kick and downward sweep of his free arm and surfaced himself. A great gasp for air. He let go of the sweater and shifted his arm up Purdy's chest until he had the little chin in his hand. Purdy's legs drifted along Simon's. With his free hand Simon pulled in a sidestroke against the dark water, looking for the boat. He stroked and kicked against Purdy's dropping body, the chin firmly in his right hand, waves washing over both of them. An oar stretched out to him—too far away. And the dory slipped by. The oar dipped in. Daryl was rowing her back. Sunshine above. Cold below, slowing him down. The dull yellow dory loomed near again. Oar in the water. Just a little farther. The knot of a line hit his head and dropped below. One hard kick and he caught it, wrapped it around his hand in a twist, then, still holding Purdy, felt himself dragged against the cold and the numbness until he was beside the hull. Daryl speared the boat hook at Purdy and caught his sweater under the armpit. Simon let go his chin clutch. Purdy rolled over. Simon found he could not reach up. Rays of sun fanned out behind the shadowed face of Zenus, who caught his wrist and put his hand on the gunwale. "We got him, we got him. Hold on, Simon," he said.

Daryl grabbed Purdy by the scruff of the neck and the seat of his pants and heaved him over the rail.

"C'mon, Simon," Zenus shouted. "We're going to haul you in. Ready? Kick!"

No blood left in his legs. He tried to kick. He couldn't get his breath for the cold. His hand slipped off and the boat nudged by. And then the boat was gone. And he felt himself sinking into a netherworld where action ceased. He felt bubbles as his breath escaped. A stream of bubbles encasing him in a world without sound. An emptiness. A peace. But there was something . . . a line slowly swaying in the water, brilliant white against the depths, a loop at its end, a white hole through which he saw his hand slip. Then the jerk as the line went taut and he was dragged forward, Zenus hauling the rope hand over hand, then the bump of the hull against his shoulder and Zenus grabbing him under the arms until Simon, who had no kicks left in him, somehow ended up in the boat. The downed sail and outstretched boom dipped in the water as the dory righted herself. Daryl was thwacking Purdy's back. Water dribbled out and then a gush. Purdy coughed and sputtered and opened his eyes.

Simon hunched on the floorboards, coiled tight and shaking. Sucking air. "He's alive!" he heard Daryl shout. "Purdy's alive!" Slowly,

Simon became aware of the motion of the boat, the sun on his back, the sound of Zenus hauling in the sail and hoisting it up the mast. Daryl was rubbing the shoulders of the blue-lipped, snuffling Purdy. "Sweet Jesus," Daryl was saying, "thought you were done for." He gave Purdy a rough shake. Purdy sniffed and nodded. Zenus gripped Simon's shoulder tight as he stepped around him to shove the tiller over and turn the boat around. "We're headed home, boys," he said.

Simon tugged the loop of the bowline knot loose and slipped it off his wrist. Kneeling now, he watched the water drip from his hair onto the center thwart, each drop splashing and separating out into rounded beads that wobbled tremulously with the yellow of the boat, the blue of the sky—each bead catching another, inching into one.

When they were near the mouth of the cove, they saw a tender coming toward them in an awkward zigzag pattern. "Who rows like that?" Daryl snorted.

Simon squinted at the rowboat. Stood up. The eastern sun had the man, his back to them, in shadow. A man with one arm could not row. But a man with one strong arm and one weak one would row just like that. A man, he could see, as they drew closer, who had tied his right hand to the handle of the oar.

When they were at right angles to the rowboat, Zenus turned the dory sharply into the wind, so the boats were stem to stern. The sun shimmered the strip of water between them. The gap widened as they began to drift apart. Angus fumbled with the rope to free his wrist, but could not take his eyes off his son. His oar angled down in the water. At the very last moment, Simon reached out and caught it.

Author's Note

This is a work of fiction set during the First World War. With the exception of public figures, boatbuilders Alfred "Gaundy" Langille and Reuben Heisler, and sailmaker Randolph Stevens, all of the characters are fictional, and any resemblance to real people, living or dead, is unintentional.

The time line of events on the Western Front, the physical details, casualty statistics, weaponry and tactics, the lead-up to and outcome of the raid on March 1, 1917, and the battle for Vimy Ridge and all references to schooner fishing are based on a wide variety of primary and secondary sources. Additional information was obtained during visits to the Halifax Citadel National Historic Site and the Cambridge Military Library in Halifax, Nova Scotia; the Fisheries Museum of the Atlantic in Lunenburg, Nova Scotia; the Vimy Ridge National Historic Site of Canada in Vimy, France; and other memorial sites on the Western Front, as well as correspondence with historians Lieutenant Colonel Phillip Robinson (retired) and Reverend Nigel Cave, who have worked closely for many years with Veterans Affairs Canada at the Vimy Memorial site.

A novel set during a major historical event must rely on current histories but also on the perceptions of those living at the time. I am especially grateful to John and Pat Noseworthy for the loan of the six-volume, limited edition *Canada in the Great War* (Various Authorities, Vols. I–VI, *Patricia Edition*, Number 942 of a set of 1,000, Toronto, United Publishers of Canada, 1919). Published a year after the war, each chapter written by an invited military or civilian official, it is an account unfiltered by time, reflecting not only the facts as they were understood then but also the language, views and sentiments of the immediate postwar period. This is true as well of official battalion histories written by eyewitnesses. Entirely different types of sources include those that help identify the intersecting dimensions of memory and myth or, as Paul Fussell writes in *The Great War and Modern Memory* (New York, Oxford University Press, 1975), the means by which the Western Front has been "remembered, conventionalized, and mythologized." While formal histories and stark battalion diaries present a view of the war or a given battle as an organized set piece, personal war memoirs such as William R. Bird's *Ghosts Have Warm Hands* (Ottawa, CEF Books, 1968), originally published in 1930, make it clear that almost anything that could happen did; and that while no single account can capture the whole, some are better able to capture the mutability of circumstances in, as Bird puts it, "that land of topsy-turvy."

The specific actions witnessed and committed by the book's characters in the war and on the home front are necessarily imagined to serve the story. The towns of Snag Harbor, Nova Scotia; Reeks Cove, Newfoundland; and Astile and Saint-Junien in France are fictional, as are the No. 18 Canadian General Hospital and Happy Holly Trench and the battalion names Royal Nova Scotia Highlanders, Ottawa Rifles and McBride's Kilties.

Of note, only certain regiments wore kilts; most wore standard uniforms. Kilted regiments, however, typically wore their kilts into battle as do the fictional Royal Nova Scotia Highlanders. With the exception of the Princess Patricia's Canadian Light Infantry (the "Princess Pats"), the "Van Doos" (the 22nd) and the Kootenay (54th), mentioned in passing, the numbered infantry battalions referred to in this work are not among those that served in France. This was a deliberate choice made out of respect for those who did serve with the Canadian Expeditionary Force in France and their descendants. A list of the battalions that were with the Canadian Corps during the First World War can be found in *Canadian Expeditionary Force, 1914–1919: Official History of the Canadian Army in the First World War* (Colonel G. W. L. Nicholson D.D., Army Historical Section, Authority of the Minister of National Defense, Ottawa, Queen's Printer, 1962).

My research took me to battlefield cemeteries in Belgium and France, many of which are tucked away in the undulating farm fields where battles were fought, barely visible from the sunken roads. In most there is no fanfare, no presence of any kind except the whispering wind. But the rows of white headstones, sometimes in the hundreds, sometimes in the thousands, are fronted by beds of lilies, roses, iris, and poppies with not a weed or brown leaf to be seen—kept immaculate by Commonwealth War Graves Commission gardeners these nearly one hundred years later.

Standing on that ground, the trajectory of the story emerged, but I was afraid to set it at Vimy Ridge—as iconic to Canadians as Gettysburg is to Americans. Then on one of my visits to Nova Scotia, I happened to sail with an "old salt," probably in his 80s. He asked me outright if I was going to write about Vimy. Oh no, I protested. He squinted out at the horizon and back at me. "You do it," he said. "These young fellers forget. People forget."

Acknowledgments

In writing this book, I have been sustained by the generosity of many people. I am grateful to all early readers of the manuscript for their valued comments and insights. It is my great good fortune to have the vision and commitment of an exceptional agent, Julie Barer, and two outstanding, experienced editors, Katie Henderson Adams at W. W. Norton and Adrienne Kerr at Penguin Canada, whose thoughtful and intelligent edits inspired me throughout. I also want to thank Dean Cooke of the Cooke Agency in Toronto for all he has done on behalf of this book in Canada. Special thanks to Ralph Getson and Cliff Zwicker at the Fisheries Museum of the Atlantic in Lunenburg, Nova Scotia, for their unfailing interest and assistance; to Mark Sadler and Susan Rahey of the World War I Interest Group in Halifax for their early support and to Laurel and Kathleen Walsh, whose comments on the manuscript and enthusiasm at a pivotal moment made all the difference. I thank also Rich Katz for advice on "story" and for the long-ago train trip to Ypres and all that came from it. I am indebted to the incomparable Barbara Toman, whose advice never failed and whose dedication to this book has been nothing short of extraordinary. To Jim Duffy, for whom time past is as real as time present and for whom the characters in these pages are as real as they are to me, my heartfelt thanks for taking this journey with me. I am blessed beyond measure by family and friends who have been there in countless ways, and above all by my husband, Joe Duffy—whose love is unceasing, whose faith never wavered—my constant reader, my first reader, always.